SECRETS OF THE
SEA LORD

LORDS OF ATLANTIS

USA TODAY BESTSELLING AUTHOR

STARLA NIGHT

Cover by Earthly Charms
Editing by Linda Edits

For inquiries:

Starla Night
starla@starlanight.com
https://starlanight.com

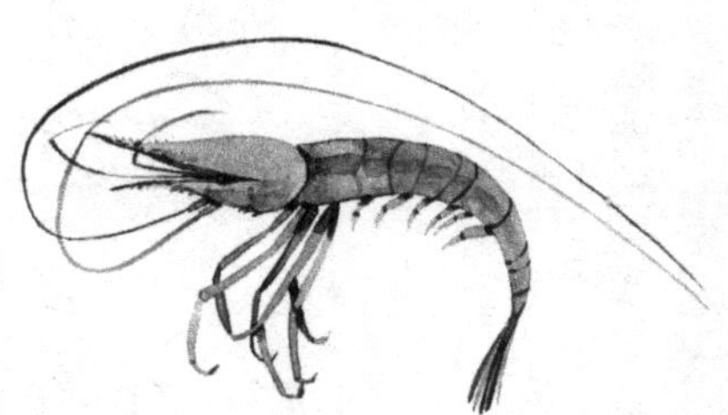

PROLOGUE

The sea was hot and rough. Blue sky extended in every direction. Choppy waves sprayed her storm-torn raft.

She'd survived.

Harmony's mouth tasted sour, and gunk crusted her eyelashes. Salt powder? It stung. She hung her head over the side of the rotted wood, cupped a handful of seawater, and washed her face. Then she stared out.

The sun baked the ocean into a watery desert. Miles and miles of gummy, bleary, Caribbean desert.

She was alone.

Dread pooled in her stomach.

Harmony pulled herself back into the raft and ducked her head against the glaring sun. Her dry throat hurt. She tried to swallow.

She was alone in the middle of the ocean. No food. No water.

No protection.

So, she was vulnerable to the monstrous Sea Lords.

She had to—

What was that?

A shadow moved on the other side of the raft.

Shadow?

Harmony rubbed her eyes again. Her vision sharpened.

A humanoid creature crouched on the far side. Dark, wet hair obscured his face. Sloping shoulders betrayed a broad back and tough, muscular limbs. Purple marks slashed his rubbery skin.

Her blood ran cold.

Monster.

He halted and rose. Towering.

A dead fish hung in one knotted hand. Bare bones reflected white.

The monster tilted his head to profile. Torn flesh dangled from his teeth.

She sucked in an endless breath.

Between the wet locks of hair, a dark eye fixed on her, stopping her heart. Strange iris. Brown with mauve threads. Like fish scales, the mauve threads gleamed, mesmerizing.

Her belly tingled with warning. The monster had hunted. And now, she was his prey.

He dropped the dead fish and turned on her.

Harmony screamed.

ONE

Twenty-five hours earlier...

"This is the spot."

Harmony pointed to the nautical chart. Rough waves plunged the yacht up and down. Her finger roved over the chart. She peered out the skinny galley window and tried to swallow back her sour throw-up.

"And today is the date. The date and the spot. Yes, this is definitely the spot."

"Then where is your sea monster?" Her ex-boyfriend, Lifet, flicked ash onto his wildly rocking metal tray. It missed and tumbled to the grimy floor. "Where is his sea pearl as big as a man's head?"

"Sea Opal." She forced the throw-up down.

"Yes. Where is it?"

"We have to wait. My great-grandmother's tribe said he'll come here."

"To these exact coordinates. Right near the Florida

islands. Where the Coast Guard likes to chase little fish. Eh?"

She swallowed hard. This wasn't about her life anymore. Her life was over. One way or another. "We have to wait."

Lifet threw his twisted stogie into his ashtray and leaned into her space. "If you are wrong, your cousin dies."

Sour acid pushed like a fist against the back of her throat. Her throat muscles worked. She must be as green right now as her little eleven-year-old cousin, Evens, had been when Lifet's lieutenants had dragged him out of class while his teachers had looked on, helpless.

In the Haitian ghetto, the local gangster was king.

"Understand me?" Lifet's hot breath sprayed her with spittle.

She nodded tightly.

Lifet's cheeks grayed to the ash color of his marijuana. The last shipment's drugs had made him angry and paranoid. He had been smoking so much recently.

She got only an instant's warning.

His dark aura changed from dangerous to deadly.

Lifet lunged out of his seat and clenched her throat. He screamed so loud, her ears rang. "Understand me?"

She squeaked.

"Understand me?"

If she opened her mouth to answer, she would projectile vomit in his face.

"Understand me? *Konprann!*"

"Lifet..." His second-in-command, Jean-Baptiste, shifted in his gold velvet seat. A Panamanian beer sweated in his diamond-adorned hands. "You told me to say something... like, you need to calm down..."

"She's not answering me!" He shook Harmony. "You

are betraying me. That's it! You are lying and betraying me. *M 'pral' touyew!"*

"I think she's seasick."

"Leading me into a trap. Eh? I'll kill your cousin. I'll rip his little head off. You want that?"

She clawed at his hand, tearing up as he squeezed. "Nnn. Pleehee. Nnn."

"She's seasick, Lifet. Seasick."

"And then I'll kill you. Throw you into the ocean where you meet this mythical, money-bearing sea-beast. You know the only reason I don't kill you right now? For running away? And lying to me?"

The room went fuzzy with her tears.

"Because of that." He jutted a stubby finger at the massive white Sea Opal locked in a velvet display box bolted to the wall. "Because your stick-wielding jungle tribe had that. In a shrine. To your mythical sea-beast."

She tried to nod her understanding.

He leaned in and whispered, "If you lie to me, I will chop you into pieces and feed you to him. You think he will eat your body? He's already planning to eat your soul."

"Nnn—"

"Don't lie!" He shoved.

The floor fell away beneath, and then the cabinet door slammed into her forehead. Her head rang like a bell. She collapsed onto the gritty wood.

Lifet moved in and out of her range of vision. He lifted the thick, metal ashtray over her stunned body. His lieutenant seized it. They wrestled out of her vision again.

Once, Lifet had been nice. Smooth. A player to end all players, and he'd made her smile with his pickup lines cribbed from American movies. He'd been a bright spot in the hell that had increasingly defined her spinning-out-of-control life.

His boss had a boat, he'd said. Maybe one day, he could smuggle her back to America, he'd said. They could eat a Sonic Burger and shop at Walmart and never run into Customs and Immigration. He'd said.

And being the girlfriend of a gangster had had benefits. An American who couldn't speak a word of French or Kreyòl in Haiti stuck out. She'd been in real, daily danger. Lifet had kept her safe.

Until the years had passed. His eyes had grown dull. His aura had turned dark. He'd risen from carefree gang member escaping his own hell to an unstable, backstabbing, deadly gang leader.

Beating her offered him more stress relief than sex.

Evens had gotten so scared for her. He'd convinced her to flee into the jungle to shelter with the mysterious great-grandmother Customs and Immigration officials had found in Haiti, the whole reason she'd been deported to there rather than to any other Caribbean island.

Her great-grandmother had been only too happy to meet her. With long flaring hair and wild eyes, shrieking like a voodoo priest, she had foretold a prophecy to curdle Harmony's blood.

You will restore our tribe to its rightful glory by sacrificing your soul to the all-powerful Sea Lord.

She'd thought that terrible prophecy was her darkest hour.

But now, Harmony was stuck between two horrors. One, that Lifet would lose to impatience and kill her and Evens.

Or two, that the monster Sea Lord would appear to

exchange his gemstone for dragging her to the bottom of the sea and consuming her soul.

Lightning streaked the dark sky, and torrential rain beat the windows. The radio growled in French. She picked out the few words she had learned. She was so wretched with languages.

...pluie...danger...orage...alarme...ouragon...

"Ouragon" sounded like "hurricane." A word she'd learned too well in Haiti when her middle-class house was made of tin plates tied to sticks.

She could die at sea. That was a third horror she hadn't considered.

So many horrors she hadn't considered.

"I will kill her!" Lifet screamed, still out of sight. "Kill her!"

"When she betrays you," Jean-Baptiste, his most reasonable lieutenant, soothed. "When she betrays you, Lifet. It won't be long. Go. Have a walk."

Lifet crossed her vision with a polished black machine gun. He pointed it at the ceiling. "I will turn back this storm! You know the most frightening monster on this ocean? Me!"

He exited. The door slammed.

Her stomach lifted and dropped and lifted. The yacht's rocking was getting worse. The lights extinguished and then flickered on. From below, she heard the frantic talk of the crew sailing the ship. Gang members struggled to keep the yacht afloat and stay out of Lifet's way.

Rat-a-tat-tat. Rat-a-tat-tat.

He was literally shooting at the storm.

Everything hurt.

Her entire body was made of stone. Her bones. Her chin. Her forehead.

How much longer could she wait for a rescue?

She closed her eyes.

Evens was counting on her.

Lifet was too insane. He'd kidnapped Evens and he would never let him go. Even if she traded her soul for a Sea Opal, her cousin would never be released to grow up and live a normal life. He'd be crushed in Lifet's gang. First they'd destroy his soft, childish body and then his curious, hopeful mind and finally his gentle, loving soul.

No. She *would* save Evens.

Harmony just had to endure a little bit longer.

Jean-Baptiste's aura impinged upon her even with her eyes closed. Some people had an acute sense of smell. Harmony had an acute sense of auras.

His shoe crunched glass.

"I know you are not sleeping. Just like I know Lifet isn't so crazy."

Maybe if she kept her eyes closed, her rescuer would appear. It had to arrive soon. One of Evens's favorite teachers had helped her come up with this final, desperate ploy to save Evens's life.

Soon, the Coast Guard would carry away the Haitian gangsters, save Evens, and apologize for their mistake deporting her a decade ago. They'd welcome her back to America with open arms. She only had to endure a little longer. Then, she'd save everyone.

"I know you are betraying him."

She squeezed her shut eyes tight.

A soft towel wiped her forehead. It lifted and touched her again, damp and tender. "Your cousin's teacher. Monsieur Joseph. He talked about you to the Americans."

Her stomach lurched. *No.* She shook her head.

"Yes. He talked to the wrong American. One we pay to

watch out for us. Our work is very dangerous, you see. And now the teacher sees too."

Her last, desperate plan crumbled to pebbles.

Please be a lie.

The Coast Guard had to be coming. Evens had to get rescued. Willowy, dignified Monsieur Joseph just had to be okay.

Jean-Baptiste chuckled. His damp cloth cleaned her cut. "You know your teacher used to run with his children during recess? He was a baseball player. And a baseball coach. But no longer. We cracked both his knees with his own baseball bat."

No. No. No.

Lifet had known about their plan to betray him? All along?

Her sacrifice here would accomplish nothing?

She finally opened her eyes and squinted at the gangster tending her face. "Wh...y...w...?"

"Oh, good. You are awake." Jean-Baptiste tapped the bloody kitchen towel on the tip of her nose. "I couldn't tell whether you would awaken. Lifet leaves so many bruises."

Yes. And they hurt.

"Up, up. Here we go." He helped her out of the cabinet and rested her upright against the marble counter.

Good thing Lifet had thrown her through the breakable wood instead of against the unyielding stone.

The machine gun noises stopped.

Her stomach rolled counter to the dangerous swinging of the wave-smashed boat. Her hands and feet froze to ice.

Lifet would throw open that door, and Jean-Baptiste would announce that she had betrayed him, and he would finish the job of killing her.

"Don't worry." Jean-Baptiste glanced over his shoulder. "I won't let him kill you."

He wouldn't?

"Once, he was an ordinary man, but now, thanks to my influence, Lifet is the perfect leader." Jean-Baptiste rested on his heels. "He's crazy. Everyone knows, so no one will cross him. But he is rational enough I guide him. It is a perfect relationship. He smokes the hashish I lace. I stand behind him and rule."

She choked on a big ball of blood, coughed, and spattered his suit.

He wiped at the spatter with cold eyes. "Yes. Well. Anyway. Do you know why you are still alive? For now."

Shaking her head made her sick. "Nnn."

"Because this 'Sea Lord' monster is real. Not a scam. I have confirmed with a very reputable organization: the Sons of Hercules. The fish monsters lost their women long ago. Now they take whores in exchange for huge treasures."

He opened his fist.

Her great-grandmother's Sea Opal dwarfed his palm. He had removed it from the locked case. Its pale light reflected the swinging lightbulbs like white magic. Or a unicorn's horn.

She reached for it on impulse.

If she touched it, all poison would be ejected from her body, and she'd fly to a fantasy land like the Mall of America food court where she'd never hurt or hunger again.

His fingers snapped shut, breaking the spell. He shook the baseball-sized gem in her face. "This is worth a hundred million US dollars. Do you know that? It is worth more than the drugs we have been smuggling. I deserve riches. I deserve riches and more."

She choked on another loogie of blood.

He pressed the stained bar towel to her mouth, absently suffocating her with damp cotton. "And the powder from this Sea Opal can cure anything. You know that? It could fix your face. All your bruises. Your teacher's cracked kneecaps."

His gaze dropped to her. His aura darkened.

Violence.

She whimpered.

"You are alive until we trap your sea monster." He removed the bloody cloth.

He eyed her as if she were a thing. Utterly inhuman. And his impersonal blankness was more frightening than a drugged, manipulated, enraged Lifet.

"We will use our harpoons and nets to drag him from the water. We will take his Sea Opals. And then we will toss both your bodies into the ocean."

The cold traveled up her arms to her elbows.

"Unless..."

She shivered.

"Unless the American you trusted plays both sides." Jean-Baptiste tugged her blood-crusted locks out of her face. "If we see the Coast Guard, we will murder you and your cousin and your dirty tribe. If your game has ended with the Coast Guard..." He ground his knuckles into her throbbing fat lip until she cried. "Lifet will hunt them like...what is your saying? Shooting fish in a barrel."

"Jean-Baptiste!" Lifet threw open the door. "There is a thing! In the water! A water thing!"

"Eh?" Jean-Baptiste tucked the Sea Opal into his suit pocket where it dragged down the fabric. "A monster?"

Lifet screamed over the thundering hurricane. Her former lover's face contorted into that of a madman.

"Hey!" Jean-Baptiste called. "A man? Or a creature?"

Lifet disappeared. The open door battered the frame.

Rain lashed the deck. The waves swelled into monstrous animals battling beyond the safe wood of their deck. When it went dark again, dread built in her stomach.

Jean-Baptiste forced her to unsteady feet and, with an iron vise grip around her shoulders, dragged her to the door. "Which do you think he saw? Good fortune? Or the lives of your family?"

He swaggered into the storm's fury.

Powerful floodlights dimly illuminated the flooded deck. The life raft was gone. Lifet hung from empty rigging. He fired into the sky.

Rat-a-tat-tat.

"Come and get me!"

Rat-a-tat-tat!

"What have you done?" Jean-Baptiste dropped her and pushed across the deck. "Lifet! Stop shooting!"

The noise stopped, but Lifet held his pose. He'd expended his ammo.

Jean-Baptiste grabbed Lifet and shook his shirt. "Where is our life raft?"

"I set it free." He flung the gun into the water. Whatever drug Jean-Baptiste had put in his weed had sent him well over the edge. Lifet was unhinged. "It is free to catch fishes. To its death!"

"Crazy—you— Where is the monster? The Sea Lord?" Jean-Baptiste released Lifet and searched the heaving water. "Where?"

"Come out, fish man!" Lifet screamed over the storm. He lofted her great-grandmother's massive Sea Opal. "Come out, come out!"

Jean-Baptiste patted his empty suit pocket and shrieked, "Lifet!"

Lifet threw it into the rising black storm. "Eat! Be merry! Aha ha ha!"

Jean-Baptiste gripped the railing as the yacht rolled hard.

She slid into the wall.

Jean-Baptiste shook as if his rage had tilted the boat. "No. No! NO!"

The boat righted itself.

He turned on her. Lifting her by the collar, he screamed, "Where is the Sea Lord?"

Bile erupted from her mouth and exploded across his soaked suit front.

His brows lifted in shock. His soul plunged to deadly black.

This was the absolute bottom. The utter end.

"I'm sorry," she wept. "I'm sorry."

He wiped his dripping face and snarled. "Is he coming? Is this the true location?"

She shook her head. Her great-grandmother had given her vague directions to an abandoned island deep in the Caribbean. Not the southern tip of the Florida Keys.

Jean-Baptiste let her collar slip through his fingers. He strolled across the wave-rolled deck, muttering, "They will all die."

"Yes! Starting with her!" Lifet pounced at Harmony's waterlogged feet. His teeth shone white. Red veins popped in his dilated eyes.

"No!" Jean-Baptiste turned and slipped. He threw out his hand. "No, we still need her!"

Lifet dragged her to the railing.

Behind him, red and white lights blinked. A crack of lightning revealed the owner. A naval gunboat bore down on them.

Rescue.

Too late.

"Eat!" Lifet scooped her up as he'd done on their first date. "And be merry!"

Instead of swooping her over a street-wide mud puddle, he threw her into the roiling black sea.

TWO

"Captain." The human male braced long tube-glasses against a beam and peered through them at the yacht. He drawled, "They threw something overboard."

"Something? Meaning what?"

"Waves blocked my...hmm."

Everyone studied their blinking screens. Or they strained without the benefit of the long glasses to see into the dangerous storm.

Faier also peered through the thick panes of ship glass. Reflections of the command deck of the Coast Guard cutter obscured his view.

"Well? What was it?" The tall, dark-haired female captain stood in the command center. "Drugs? Weapons? A second lifeboat?"

No one answered.

The captain sucked air through her teeth. She had been doing so since the storm warnings coincided with their breakthrough tip to arrest drug smugglers. "Is that idiot still shooting at the storm clouds?"

"No, sir."

"What's he doing?"

"Throwing his gun overboard."

"Has he seen us?"

The spotter licked his lips but did not answer.

The crew had been on edge since leaving the harbor into a forbidding wind.

Normally, they pursued enemies with a helicopter and small boats on calm seas. An unarmed pleasure yacht sailed by wanted drug lords? Anchored right on their normal route?

Tempting.

Already, several things had gone wrong. The smugglers' boat hadn't been anchored at the coordinates where their tip had said it would be. It hadn't been anchored at all. And brewing storm clouds cloaked their "satellite" tracking. They'd stumbled upon the yacht by luck on their way to safer seas.

Plus the yacht was clearly armed.

"What's the bearing on the storm?" the captain asked.

One of her officers answered with exact coordinates, and added, "If they continue their drift on this route, the storm will miss us."

"So we could follow them out of the storm." Her soul light burned bright in her chest for the first time in hours. "They won't outrun us. Maybe we'll have a little pleasure cruise after all."

The other officers chuckled. Their hearts lightened with relief. Instead of being forced to weigh safety against justice, they could follow and arrest these dangerous trespassers on their terms.

"Keep them in our sights," the captain ordered. "We will do this smart and safe."

Faier gazed upon the massive, storm-shrouded swells that poured over the bobbing metal deck.

He had never seen such waves until he'd surfaced two years ago. He had never—

Light flickered in a valley between waves.

He pressed his face against the glass.

Where was it? Had he been wrong? A trick of the glass, a blip reflected off a computer—

Flicker.

There. Between swells.

Flicker. Flicker.

"They threw a human," he said into the quiet room.

His announcement impacted the crew like a thunderclap.

"A human!" The captain strode to the window and stared out. "Are you sure?"

Faier pointed. "Between the swells."

"How can you see out there?"

"I see the light."

"Light! Come about."

The cutter wheeled. The bow plunged through a wall of rough water.

"You turned too far," he noted. "Come back."

"Come back." The captain addressed her spotter. "Do you see?"

"No, sir. It's black as a barrel of tar out there."

Faier traced the dip and dive of the soul. "There. Go fast. She is being sucked into the storm."

She was so strong against the crashing waves. How amazing that this fragile human struggled again and again for the surface as the ocean crushed her.

"I don't see any light." The captain squinted. "Is it a flare? Flashlight?"

"Soul." Faier touched his chest.

She leaned back and took a good hard look at the thick rubbery coating of his cold-water suit. "You see his soul?"

"Her. A woman."

The cabin dropped silent.

He felt the weight of their disbelief. He was used to that reaction. "Believe me."

"I do." She sucked air between her teeth again. "The gangster must have realized his girlfriend led him right to us. Does anybody else have eyes on?"

The crew reported in the negative.

"How can we contemplate a rescue if we can't see where she is?" she muttered to herself.

His fingers closed around the zipper of his suit. "I will."

"No, Faier. Even if we could see her, the seas are too rough."

"Not for me." Faier unzipped his suit and stepped out. He was nude underneath. A faux pas for humans, but necessary.

The captain and crew averted their eyes.

Scars bubbled across his tissues and hamstrung his muscles. They disrupted his full-body mauve tattoos, unbalancing the swirls of honors and effacing his accomplishments so only little ink spots remained. His past imprisoned his body. But he was still the best chance the drowning female had for survival.

He stepped free of the suit. When his weight rested on his right leg, the weakened joint collapsed. He staggered.

"You go into that water and we're not getting you back out." An extra-tall wave smashed into the windows, illustrating her point. "Not you or her. And trying risks our lives. It's irresponsible to even consider that course of action."

"My skill is rescuing in water."

"You're our responsibility. How would I explain to your king if anything happened to you?"

"King Kadir would understand." He forced his wrecked, protesting body straight. "I am a warrior."

The captain held his gaze for one long moment. Respect glinted in her eyes.

Then her gaze dropped to his scarred, twisted body. Doubts flitted. Her soul light dimmed. "Put your suit back on, and keep an eye on the girlfriend."

"Captain. The yacht is turning."

"They saw us." She strode to the navigation panel. "Prepare for a chase. We herd them away from the storm, not into it. Hail the yacht."

"No can do, Captain." The spotter scanned the ocean. "Their comm tower broke loose half an hour ago."

"That's right. I forgot."

The woman's soul light disappeared. Its sudden loss punched Faier. "She is now under the water."

"Under the—?" The captain swore. "This is the tenth death we can attribute to these two gangsters in American waters. We're nailing these two. We're nailing them to the wall."

Faier kept his gaze on the last place he'd seen the struggling female. She must be terrified. She must have—

There! *Light*.

"She is alive."

The captain cut off a stream of obscenities. "She surfaced?"

"No." He could see her light beneath the surface. Strange. Most humans dimmed when they drowned.

The captain grimaced. "Focus on the yacht."

Another officer drew her attention. "Should we fire a warning shot?"

"We can't board or tow in this weather. Stick with a nice, gentle pursuit."

While they discussed strategies to trap the criminals, Faier slipped out the door and hobbled across the rollicking deck.

On an ordinary day, officers preparing for a rescue readied white floating rings, orange life jackets, and rubbery suits. Their souls glowed in their chests.

Now, only Dive Officer Peters braved the storm to chase after him. "Faier! Wait!"

He gripped the railing while sideways rain and waves spackled him. He was here today because of Dive Officer Peters.

And he was grateful.

Fewer than a hundred warriors had surfaced in the two years since the secret existence of the mer had been exposed to modern humans. The undersea war between traditionalists who wished them to return to hiding and rebels who wished to forge a union with humans raged hard, preventing all but the brashest warriors from daring to surface.

A thousand years ago, the two races had coexisted in peace. But a catastrophe had driven the mer into hiding—and into human legend.

Only a few isolated "sacred" islands knew of the mer's existence up to modern times. They upheld an ancient covenant to hide the mer's secret. And after the mer's females had died out, their sacred brides had joined with mer husbands and repopulated the emptying sea floor.

But then, due to rising ocean levels and modernization, the sacred islands had emptied. The mer had dwindled once more. Rebellious voices had challenged the ancient covenant. And, two years ago, centuries of secrecy had been broken the instant an injured mer warrior had been captured by a human's "GoPro underwater camera" machine. Days later, a highly respected warlord flouted mer law and took a modern female for his bride.

The undersea world had cracked into pieces.

Faier now hailed from the rebel city Atlantis. He had surfaced to find a modern bride and defy the traditionalist All-Council still ruling the largest pieces of the fractured seas.

The surface rarity of mer warriors was both a curse and a blessing. Faier was the subject of great curiosity, but it was still possible for him to visit grocery stores, bowling alleys, and tourist attractions and be mistaken for a human with strange facial tattoos.

When he'd first met Dive Officer Peters, the Coast Guard male had clearly mistaken Faier for a human. Both had been touring the Statue of Liberty when a ferry boat had overturned. Both had dived in to rescue trapped passengers.

"Hey, buddy! You're taking too many risks, okay? Don't drown," he had shouted to Faier while they'd bobbed on the icy black waves.

The irony.

After Faier had rescued humans quickly and efficiently from dangerous areas of the submerged ferry, Peters had called Faier a hero. His shipmates had received clearance to explore a unique partnership with the mer. Since the ferry incident, whenever a special circumstance arose, the Coast Guard had contacted Faier for assistance.

Faier enjoyed assisting. It kept his mind off his failure to secure a bride quickly and return to his besieged city. He preferred not to dwell on the disappointment he must be causing to his king, Kadir.

Dive Officer Peters ran into the furious wind. A tether clipped him to the railing for safety. "Where are you going?"

"A woman is there." Faier pointed at the soft brightness in the deep black ocean.

Peters followed his gesture and took a faceful of water. He sputtered and coughed. "You can't go out there. That's a deadly storm!"

He nodded.

The man's dark brows lifted. He frowned at Faier's injuries. Doubts clouded his gaze too.

He was the same height, similar breadth. Faier had muscle. But where Peters's skin was smooth and unscarred, Faier's was unbearable wreckage.

That was why he had failed to find a bride.

Peters's soul burned pure with his mission. "We have a duty to return you to shore."

Faier clasped Peters's forearm. "You are an honorable man."

Half of Peters's mouth curved up in wry amusement. He returned the shake with reluctant respect. "Don't drown."

"I will not." Faier turned to the railing. "Because, as you know, I am immune."

Peters stepped back, and then a shout dragged his gaze back to the command center.

The captain had noticed Faier's exit and realized what he was doing. She screamed. "Faier! Stop! I won't risk your life for hers."

But I will.

Without answering her, Faier avoided Peters's surprised tackle, and he threw himself over the side.

The high seas slammed into him.

Warm, slick water gripped his body, prised into his mouth, and gushed down his throat.

Salt. Choking oil. Bitter, nasal gasoline.

These flavors disappeared from his tongue as he shifted to mer.

The stormy black ocean lit up as his eyes changed. The glowing souls of fish and creatures churned, somersaulting, beneath the boats and under the waves. Their noises bounded around in his chest cavity.

Gills perforated his lower back and squeezed heavy liquid through his transformed lungs.

His toes unfurled into long fins. His body's separate legs made the same profile as a human "scuba diver," only his natural foot-fins were much larger and more effective. Thin webbing flexed between his fingers.

An assistant had once called him a "sexy, tattooed Swamp Thing" because Faier, like all mer, had separate legs. He hadn't known how to respond. Why did human legend portray mer with no legs but a fused fish body? Such an unnatural, impractical idea, and strange.

A distant light glimmered. *Human.*

He kicked his mer legs toward her.

Humans did not survive underwater. But she had survived a long time. And her distant soul twinkled. How? She must be dying, but her soul glowed. Drifting deeper into the abyss.

He kicked hard.

His right knee, tendons severed in an ambush and never properly healed, ached. He kicked harder with his left.

She was limp. Unconscious. Thin fabric floated around her lax body like the skin of a jellyfish.

No air bubbled from her mouth.

That was bad. Humans required air. Why was her soul so bright?

He reached for her.

I must not touch her. She is not my bride. A mer must only touch his bride.

Faier shoved off those useless thoughts and hooked an arm around her midsection. *I apologize for this touch, human female.* He lifted her toward the surface.

Her soul brightened.

Strange.

When humans or mer were fearful, their souls dimmed. Death carried the lights away entirely. He had seen it in his rescues, above and beneath the waves, more often than he wished.

This female seemed asleep rather than dying.

Asleep? No. His senses must be mistaken.

Faier broke the surface.

Rain smashed the moving mountains of surf. White cracked the sky.

Faier lifted the female's mouth above the surface. She coughed, spluttered, spasmed. Her soul light flickered like a small candle.

Where were the—ah! In the distance, the Coast Guard cutter chugged after the smugglers' damaged yacht.

Between them, a mountain range of water boiled with fury.

And the surface current dragged him into the heart of the storm.

He kicked to the first valley. They had to reach the cutter.

A large wave plunged them both under. Seawater lodged in his throat.

Caught between worlds, he struggled to hold one form.

She thrashed. Again, her soul light brightened.

Stranger and stranger.

He struggled to bring her to the surface once more. His right leg screamed. Surface waves, like large palms, slapped and plunged them under once more.

He shoved her head above water and dove into the rollicking waves. His right leg trembled. It would fail.

He stopped and went limp, resting it, while the current dragged them both away from the boats and deeper into the storm.

Faier could drop under the swells and follow the cutter.

But she couldn't.

The woman needed shelter. Driftwood. A surface boat to collapse in and rest.

He tried to hold her above the deadly surf.

She shoved him off and paddled for—a miracle! A raft of salvaged materials the captain had called a cut-rate lifeboat; one of the early things the notorious gangster had thrown off his yacht. It still had survival materials lashed inside. She could live well on this shelter.

Faier pushed her onto the wood and grabbed the ledge. The waterlogged wood broke off. A dangerous hole gaped.

Curse it.

She heaved herself onto the rotted ledge. Half-in, half-out of the lifeboat, she scrabbled for a cable. Her hand hooked it. She pulled hard and thrashed, almost rescued. The cable released, dropping her lower body back into the water, and she collapsed.

The waves broke over her, dragging her farther backward.

"Female!" He tapped her. *A mer must not touch.* "Enter the boat!"

She did not respond.

"Human female!" Faier used his shoulder to roll her in.

A wave smashed the other side.

His momentum pushed their side down.

The entire life raft lifted. Important materials—flashlights, jugs of drinking water, rolls of fishing line—rolled out from under the unhooked cable and disappeared into the sea. The life raft capsized.

She followed the supplies into the depths. Her soul darkened. She'd given up in her mind, body, and soul.

No!

He dove after her and secured her to his scarred chest. Her heartbeat steadied to match his. He heard and felt it. Strange warmth filled the water. Her soul light brightened.

Strength filled his limbs.

He kicked for the surface. With one hand, he threw the life raft into the wind and current, righting it. Water had swept the inside clean. He kicked hard and launched the female into the center of the raft.

It creaked.

She spewed out the liquid in her lungs and collapsed on the floor with ragged breaths.

He had done it. Saved her.

Faier's right leg cramped.

He slipped off the raft and clenched the waterlogged edge while his body folded in half with blinding pain.

His injuries made him unfit to claim a bride. Traditional mer warriors had long ago determined his sad fate.

Only King Kadir had given him new hope and responsibilities. "*Go to New York. Find your bride and become the first warlord of Atlantis to fill your castle with young fry.*"

But Faier had not found his bride in New York. Not even with the help of the newly established mer dating website, MerMatch, dreamed up by modern brides Queen Lucy, Queen Elyssa, and Queen Aya.

The traditionalists had been right. No female, sacred bride or modern human, could bear to look on Faier's damaged body. If he could not find a bride in a surface city as large as New York, he must be the one mer whose soul had no mate.

He should have died years ago.

Why did he carry on?

Faier slogged through his joint pain and dragged himself onto the raft to check on the female. His gills expelled water and sealed to human lungs. His long fins shrank back to ordinary toes.

She curled into a fetal position. A wave crashed over the side and filled the life raft, floating her. She spasmed and moaned.

He broke the waves with his shoulders, sheltering her, as much as he could, from the wet and cold.

She clung to him and nestled into his chest.

Her trust, as she curled against him, gave him new strength even when he thought he'd reached his limit.

The storm howled. Rain pounded. Waves rolled and tilted the raft, threatening to tip them back into the surf. The boats grew distant. The Coast Guard light disappeared, plunging them into darkness.

While he rode out the storm, tensing his muscles to hold her to the raft, her trust warmed him like the sun. His heart beat faster. His body thrummed with awareness.

He had always defended his city, protected his fellow warriors, fought for his king. But protecting a female? Never.

This must be why the traditionalists ruled never to touch a female.

He never wanted to let her go.

Faier kept his rescued female safe in the raft through the long, stormy night.

In the dawn, the wind calmed and the rain abated. The swells flattened.

He shuddered, releasing his stuck muscles, and sat up.

His rescued female was asleep.

The rise and fall of her chest was so...so...human. She was a tan beige. Human skin came in many colors.

But what was this?

A darker bruise swelled her forehead. A sticky red scab marred the back of her head. Both sets of lashes creased in puffy black eyes. Her soft lips had swollen and split.

The wreckage continued.

Long purple bruises the size of a man's fingers closed around her throat. Greenish black and painful yellow splotches marked her skin beneath the edges of her dress. Small nicks and cuts abraded her knuckles, elbows, forearms. Yellow finger marks encircled her wrists.

Had the storm done this? Or was she a warrior? Humans had warriors. Like the Coast Guard captain.

He stroked a new scar. A pink line creased her damp cheek. Her skin felt so different from his. Soft and female.

She moaned and tilted her head to follow his touch.

Faier curled his hands into fists. He must not touch her. The captain had called her the girlfriend of the gangster. He must have lost his senses to throw her over the side of the boat. Had he given her this beating?

Anger stirred Faier's heart.

He turned the helpless feeling into a useful channel.

She would be hungry when she woke. Her body was malnourished.

Faier dipped his arm in the water, feeling the currents. He crouched to dive in.

She moaned. Her lashes fluttered.

He stopped.

She struggled to rise. "Lif...Lifay..."

Life?

He leaned close and spoke in English. "You have your life."

"Sorr...so sorry." She sucked in a shuddering breath, and her lashes opened to reveal stunning gray-green eyes the color of a lagoon kissed by sunlight. "Oh. You're not Lifet."

"No."

"Coast Guard?"

"They chase your drug smuggler, Lifet."

She closed her eyes and smiled. Her soul light burned sharp white with relief. She laughed. "Thank you. Thank you. Thank you."

"You are wel—"

She threw her arms around his shoulders and covered his mouth with her lips.

Kiss.

She kissed him.

Her lips were cool and thick and expressive. She sank into his embrace. Her tongue teased his seam.

He opened to her.

She tasted like freedom and abandon, sunrise and sunset and every hour in between. She tasted like new endings and old beginnings. She tasted like female.

Her tongue slipped between his shocked lips and delved into his mouth.

Heat.

His cock flooded with pounding heat.

She sucked on his tongue. Nibbled his lips. Teased his teeth.

Everywhere she touched, fiery hunger erupted.

More. He needed more.

She consumed his mouth, drinking the safety he represented just as he drank in her feminine wildness. She was every unpredictable thing, every wild current, every beautiful flicker of a distant fin.

And then she released him and collapsed on the raft, limp. Her soul light dimmed. She fell unconscious with sleep.

He gripped the edges of the raft so hard, the wood cracked and his knuckles whitened.

A hard erection stiffened his thick cock.

She was his bride. His one and only mate. *Mine.*

He would protect her with his life. Challenge monsters above and beneath the waves. Behind his shield, her bruises would heal and her skin would smooth with health. He would wrap her in his faithful protection, and she would never hurt again.

Never.

Awe mixed with his fierce protectiveness.

She had kissed him. Faier. This small female who had lured a notorious gangster to justice and survived near-drowning in a storm. She had braved Faier's appearance and...

Wait.

His stomach lurched.

Had she? Her eyes were closed. Had she braved his appearance?

Had she seen him?

Faier's heart thudded out of rhythm. A sour taste threatened his tongue.

Had this female—his mate—truly witnessed his monstrous form? His scars and slashes? His wreckage?

Had she understood who she was kissing?

Or, when she awakened, would she fear him and cry at her mistake?

THREE

Present Day...

Harmony screamed again.

The monster at the other end of Lifet's life raft shrank back. His muscles bunched like coils of wire. Even if he were the size of Evens, he could kill her with a thought.

He's the monster. The monster. She was alone on a raft in the middle of the ocean with a Sea Lord monster.

She sucked in a huge breath and screamed.

He dropped the fish and covered his ears.

Hurt. Her screams hurt him.

She didn't want to hurt anyone. Not even a monster.

Her scream died.

He kept his distance. As much as one could on a raft made of old crates salvaged from the docks, hammered together with prayers, designed for six comfortably and fourteen uncomfortably.

Monsieur Joseph had dreamed of stealing this raft from Lifet and sailing away back when he and Harmony had spent hours fantasizing how to escape the slums of Haiti together. He'd imagined teaching his brightest and most vulnerable students how to sail. She'd promised to lead them to the shores of freedom and beg for asylum.

Now Monsieur Joseph was an enemy of Lifet's gang and gravely injured. And Harmony was...Harmony was...

She struggled with control. Her dry, ragged throat hurt. "Who are you? What do you want?"

The monster flinched.

Did he not speak English? She didn't know Taino. Or Kreyòl. Or French or even Spanish.

She gulped a dry, choking swallow. "Are you...?"

The Sea Lord raised his head.

He was more human than she'd feared. His face was obscured by dripping hair but he had a nose, mouth, and jaw. His skin was lighter than most Haitians, and darker than the Panamanian sailors who delivered drugs to Lifet's harbor. Purplish gray marks colored his body. No, not marks. Intricate mauve tattoos crossed by nasty, painful-looking scars.

She sucked in a breath.

His gaze fixed on the water as though he was afraid she would scream again.

She let out her breath and focused. No sudden moves, no sudden screams.

He watched her.

She watched him.

Neither moved.

His chin lowered. "Am I?"

The sea monster spoke English. Good English. Accentless, fluent, American-movie-star English.

She didn't know how to complete her question.

He lowered his shoulders as though to approach.

Fear stabbed her in the throat. He would consume her soul.

She squished into the corner, bruised knees braced in front of her chest, trying to make herself a smaller target. "Where am I? Where's Lifet? And Jean-Baptiste?"

"The Coast Guard pursued your boyfriend. He is surely in custody."

His soft voice was filled with masculine assurance. He could command an army with a whisper. Goosebumps stood up on her arms. His timbre was strangely enticing.

She pushed the feeling away. "What about Evens?"

"His companions on the yacht are in custody."

"Evens is my cousin. Back in Haiti. Lifet's gang kidnapped him to punish me." She rubbed the old yellow bruises encircling her wrists where Lifet had grabbed and shaken her. "I was supposed to tell the Coast Guard."

"You fell overboard and were swept away."

Now she was on the raft alone. With *him*. A Lord of the Sea.

She studied him carefully. Her life depended on it.

Ropes of muscle bound his biceps and bulged in his powerful thighs. Hard forearms and broad pectorals promised his ability to carry her to safety.

The skin she'd thought rubbery was merely dotted with sea spray. As the moisture dried in the sun, he looked more and more ruggedly male and human. She wanted to slide her fingers across his skin and confirm the texture for herself.

Harmony curled her hands around her dress hem.

He raked his hair out of his face so he could fix his unnerving gaze on her more directly.

A long scar crossed his forehead and underscored his deadliness.

His jaw was hard, implacable, and yet the slash of his full lips was oddly gentle. Firm power wrapped in a velvet glove, which somehow she held the strings to unbind. He'd kidnapped her for his own purposes and yet his calm demeanor soothed, entreated her to trust him against her will. His steadiness pointed to a great deal of well-earned confidence. He silently assured her that he could move the entire world for her if only she pointed where she wanted it.

His dark hair was shorn at the back of his neck. The ends twisted into an innocent ducktail that invited her come over and curl it around her index finger. He would let her approach and touch him. Not only would he let her, but he would turn the rest of the way to face her and then trap her in a hard, pleasurable, unyielding kiss.

A tiny thrill ran up her spine.

Not of fear.

Desire.

Her heart beat hard in her chest. Pleasant heat pinched her sensitive nipples and stirred her womb. A sensation of liquid readiness opened her body to this confident stranger's mastery. She welcomed, wanted, hungered for him.

His mesmerizing gaze intensified. As if he could see her desire.

Could he?

The feminine heat in her belly suddenly struck her with terror. She tried not to feel it radiating into her veins, opening her chest, tingling in her fingertips.

Was this how he tricked her?

One foot—human, masculine foot—slid across the wobbling raft. He lowered his center of gravity, half bent, and held out the fish. "You must—"

No.

She crammed herself into the corner.

He stopped.

Then he leaned toward her. "You—"

She held her breath.

He stopped again.

How much would it hurt? Would he suck her soul out her mouth like in a horror movie? Or would it be much, much worse?

His brow wrinkled. Disappointment emanated off him in a wave. "You fear me."

She shook her head as much as she could with every muscle in her body paralyzed. She mustn't upset him. Upsetting powerful men only hurt her in the end.

He stared at the dead fish in his hands. "I want to give this to you. May I?"

Strange feelings pulled at her like warring tides.

Fear and desire. Desire and fear.

This Sea Lord didn't seem dangerous. He was gentle. Kind.

That must be how he *got* her. As soon as she relaxed. As soon as she lowered her guard. *Bam.* Lost soul.

Keeping his gaze averted, he gestured at himself. "Do not fear. I will not cause harm."

Just give in. Close your eyes. Accept the inevitable.

Because apparently, this destiny was inevitable. From the hour the old tribal priestess, her great-grandmother, had uttered the prophecy.

"You belong to the Lord of the Sea. He owns your body. Your womb. Your soul."

She'd even schemed with Monsieur Joseph—poor Monsieur Joseph!—and led Lifet to the wrong place. And yet, she begged for mercy from this Sea Lord.

"Believe me." The monster's aura darkened. He reached for her once more.

Her soul!

Harmony heaved herself over the side.

Salt water crashed across her. A welcome relief from the beating sun. Bubbles flurried around her. The yellow sun shone overhead, marking the barrier between sea and air. Water flooded her ears with cotton. Her own heartbeat filled her mind.

Lub-dub. Lub-dub. Lub-dub.

More strange desires curled around her body, encouraging her to relax, promising that everything would be fine. All she had to do was stop fighting and give in.

Gungsh.

Another body rolled into the ocean. The shadowy figure oriented on her.

The monster!

He chased her. Of course he chased her! He was a Lord of the Sea!

Her heartbeat sped.

She turned and kicked. Her legs floundered. She'd never learned how to swim.

Deep blue encased her. If she could escape into it, disappear into the dense ocean fog, hide with the blurry, darting fish—

Crunch.

A predator snapped onto her ankle.

She thrashed. Shrieked. "*Blab! Ab!*"

And sucked in water.

Her throat locked. Salt invaded her nose and made her eyes burn. She coughed. Bubbles exploded. She sucked in more water. Heavy, lifeless water.

The monster—he gripped her ankle—tugged her.

Yellow reflections danced on the air-water barrier. He broke the surface.

She turned away and strained for the blue fog deep below...

The deep blue fog cleared. She saw hundreds of feet. Thousands of feet! The vast view showed her tiny whales and pinprick schools of fish. The ocean opened around her—

Her head broke the surface.

She spluttered.

The monster hauled her onto the raft.

Tears burned her eyes. Coughs burned her throat. She collapsed on the raft floor.

He hovered over her. A malevolent shadow.

"Do not swim away from this raft," he ordered, his voice soft, despite his obvious anger, and authoritative. "You cannot survive."

He hunted her so easily.

There was no escape.

She curled into a protective ball. Tears flowed. The end was now. She'd tried to escape this fate. Her life. Her child. Her soul. But she'd never had any choice. Just like every other fate forced on her.

The Customs and Immigration office. Lifet's slum. Her great-grandmother's prophecy.

She had no choice. No choice but to endure. Endure and survive.

She sobbed.

"Do not cry," the monster said, destroying all her fantasies that he was good and trustworthy and would move the world to protect her. "I will guard you."

She cried harder.

He sat on his haunches. "You do not want my guard."

"Please," she choked between wrenching sobs. "Leave me. Please."

He straightened. "Leave?"

"I don't want to be your wife."

"Wife?" He dropped silent. Anger and bitterness darkened his aura.

Of course, the monster had an aura. Harmony had always been able to see through lies and sense true emotions. The emotions appeared as a glowing light around people's bodies. She'd honed her ability to perfection in the Haitian slums filled with dangerous people she couldn't understand.

She'd kind of assumed everyone could see these auras and never talked about them. She'd stopped talking about them after her third grade recess teacher had given her a funny look and threatened to report her to the school counselor.

The monster's voice broke. "*You* are the one who claimed *me.*"

"Please. Please."

He forced her gaze to his. His dark irises drew her in. Dark brown threaded with deeper mauve. The same color as his iridescent tattoos. Compelling.

Monstrous.

Awareness throbbed between her legs. Hunger slicked her feminine vee. He was an addiction, a drug combating her numbness, making her feel every instant of his male attention—and crave more.

This must be how he'd steal her soul.

She buried her face in her hands, breaking the connection to his mesmerizing eyes.

"You are the one who claimed me for your husband," he repeated.

She rocked her head.

"You kissed me."

"Never."

He swooped. "Yes—"

"No!" She scrabbled back, hands up in defense, and squeezed her eyes shut tight. Desperation made her shriek. "You horrify me. Get out of my sight!"

Silence.

His heat-filled aura receded.

The raft bobbed with tension.

Her heart thudded.

Splish.

His aura faded.

She opened her eyes.

He no longer hovered over her.

She rose onto her knees.

The raft was empty.

Empty?

...No. It was a trap. A trick.

...

Wasn't it?

...

She had fended him off?

No. She had done nothing. The monster had given her a reprieve. But he would be back.

She moved to the exact center of the raft and hugged her knees again, rocking and sobbing.

He would be back. He'd dragged her away. Stuck her on a raft in the middle of the ocean. She wasn't going anywhere. He had all the time in the world to woo her. Break her. Seduce her. Make her beg.

And when she least expected it, when she trusted him— out of hunger or desperation—he would strike.

FOUR

You horrify me.

He horrified his bride. Faier horrified her.

Pain sliced deep in his scarred chest.

He rubbed the half-destroyed tattoo star above his aching heart and kicked under the raft. His fins unfurled. The entire ocean opened around him as his body completed his shift into mer.

Silver fish swirled below. A wily marlin picked at the school's edges. Its long, sharp beak slashed unwary fish.

Faier rubbed his barren biceps.

Humans were uncomfortable with a warrior's knives and trident. The Coast Guard had vowed to keep him safe from any danger that might require such weapons.

His disobedience had forced them to break their vow.

A warrior without weapons had no more chance of surviving in the open ocean, alone, than a human had of breathing water.

He kept the raft in his sight overhead. Surface currents changed unexpectedly, and he could not let it get too far away or else—

Get away from me.

—he might lose it in the vast ocean. Lose her.

His bride—no, she was *not* his bride—the human female was weak and frightened. Would she see the fish he had cleaned and pulled into bite-sized pieces? Would she know it was for her?

He must provide.

Faier descended into the school.

The marlin darted close.

He should steal its spear for a weapon.

The marlin swam below him.

He twisted. Kicked.

His tendons clenched. Pain stabbed his right calf. Overexertion of the scarred tissue from protecting his bri —*the human female*—on the raft.

His fingers brushed the marlin's hard, sharp spear. It cut his rough fingertips as the marlin swerved away.

His blood salted the water.

Curse it.

A younger, healthier warrior would have succeeded.

The leg cramped.

He hunched over his agonizing cramps and stuck his cut finger in his mouth. His blood tasted metallic. The silver fish swirled away. They knew his scent. He was a predator.

And now he'd advertised his presence to other predators roaming the surface.

Injured. With no weapons. Far from allies or friends.

Surface predators were the most deadly.

Faier worked his fingers into the knotted muscles.

You horrify me.

He was supposed to be in New York now.

Faier swallowed the hard hurt. His soul throbbed with pain.

King Kadir had found his Queen Elyssa mere hours after surfacing. First Lieutenant Soren had set eyes on his Queen Aya even sooner.

Now Faier's bri—human female who had kissed him—rejected his scarred body with horror.

Mermen only desired their brides. So why did Faier react to this female with hunger? Want? Need to wrap this human female in his arms and lance her wet softness with his powerful cock?

His soul reached out to her.

But she did not reach back.

And that was devastating.

It meant he was mistaken. Had a mer ever made this mistake? Warriors had fought over brides in the past. In some stories, brides had synced souls with both males. But *never* had a warrior desired a bride who did not also desire him.

He craved her bright soul.

Her fear repelled him with black ice.

Yet he still craved her. Even floating in ice, he craved her.

He craved a female who did not crave him?

Faier must be the most tragic warrior in mer history.

And his deepest fears had come true.

He had no bride.

A lump formed in his throat.

He allowed it to exist, just another pain, while the gills in his lower back flushed water through his lungs.

You horrify me.

The pain receded, leaving him with a metallic tang on his tongue and a useless ache in his twisted leg.

He kicked into the shadow of the raft.

On his own, he would leave the surface, descend to

coral fields. Reforge his blades. Prepare for the brutal dangers of crossing the ocean alone.

But he would never abandon his...the human female.

Despite the pain shredding his heart and crushing his soul, he would never shirk his duty. He had sworn to protect her. Not only on the ocean. For always.

He would do so from the shadows.

Get away from me.

He would obey. She wished to never see him? He would hide from her sight.

She must find happiness.

He wanted her soul to light up. Fear to leave her limbs. Warmth to fill her gray-green eyes.

She must be safe. Secure. Well-fed. Happy.

He hunted a slender mackerel and pounced, breaking it before it could thrash away. The forearm-thick fish would feed her. He cradled it to his scarred ribs.

Humans could not see in the dark. He would rise before the moon and slip it over the side before she realized he was present.

Maybe she would never look at him without disgust. With enough caring, perhaps, she would someday fear him less.

That was his wish.

Then, maybe, she could glow with the soft tenderness of her first kiss.

His heart cramped.

He rubbed his scarred chest.

Maybe—

No. His feelings were wrong. Her soul did not sync with his. She did not crave him. She was not his bride.

All that mattered was the human female. Her safety. Her wellness.

Hiding his horrifying form deep beneath would make her happy.

FIVE

Harmony was very unhappy.

The sun fried her and the dead fish on the other side of the open, shelterless, dry raft.

You kissed me.

Impossible. Lies.

The monster had kissed *her* while she was unconscious. Now he tried to turn her inside out, manipulate her, make her doubt herself.

Just like the Customs and Immigration officers who'd insisted she must remember the first hours of her life and should have been able to identify her birthplace from memory. Or like Lifet, who'd always insisted his anger was her fault. Or her great-grandmother, who'd demanded her sacrifice.

Harmony rose and stretched.

Her bruised forehead ached. Her exposed cuts stung.

She rotated her yellowed wrists.

How long would the monster leave her to stew?

Spray pools dried out, leaving a white crust of salt on the barren wood.

Her head hurt. Her throat was parched. Her stomach growled.

The life raft was supposed to be stocked with gallons of fresh water, a crate of emergency food, flares, a first aid kit, fish hooks and line, and supplies for surviving at sea. But all she found of the supplies were snapped cables and frayed ropes.

The dead fish shimmered in the heat.

Did she dare...?

Harmony hugged her knees.

No. She didn't dare.

The monster was waiting for her to make a mistake. Eat his food. Believe in his lies.

You kissed me.

Something stirred deep within her. A wish. Hunger. Calling her over the side, into the deep blue.

You saw the light at the bottom of the ocean. It's cool and safe there. You'll never be thirsty again.

Just fall in and let yourself drown...

Harmony tightened her hug.

She would not be confused. She would not be tricked. She had reached her end, but she would not give in.

So...she needed food. To keep up her strength. And defy the Sea Lord.

Right.

Harmony released her knees and leaned forward.

The raw fish beckoned.

Fishy fishy fishy fishy fishy.

Was this a test? If she took a mouthful, would the monster erupt from the ocean and drag her into the sea?

Or was it his lunch? Would he be mad she ate it?

The empty ocean reflected harsh sun on her darkening skin.

In Haiti, they had called her white. Lots of Haitians were midnight black, and her skin was Indian brown with cool beige undertones. It was funny because, in Omaha, they had called her the N-word. She'd known her mom's accent wasn't African—that she was from somewhere in the Caribbean—but she'd never asked which island they came from. It hadn't been important.

Ha.

Her stomach growled.

She crept across the raft.

He'd torn the fish to pieces. Its open mouth and round eyes looked shocked. Entrails dripped in black strings from glistening white ribs.

Yum?

She picked up a chunk of white flesh. Pink tinged the dangling scales.

Empty ocean...

She put it in her mouth.

Dried, desiccated flesh tasted like salt. She chewed. Her salivary glands tingled. She swallowed dry, choked, and forced it down.

Her throat hurt. But her stomach perked up.

Food. More. HUNGRY.

The ocean was calm. If the monster watched, he waited until she finished her meal to strike.

She gobbled the rest, picked around the bones, chewed.

Her stomach protested. She had eaten nothing since jungle tribe mystery stew that had given her stomach cramps and dysentery.

More.

Harmony scraped the fish-scented wood for any little flakes. The bones were poky and hurt her mouth. She sucked on the sharp fins. In another few hours, she'd eat them anyway.

The ocean was still empty.

In another few hours, thirst would break her. Not hunger.

How long could she go without water?

Harmony resettled herself in the crook of the raft where she felt safest.

If the Sea Lord rose out of the ocean and promised to save Evens, then she'd sacrifice herself to him immediately.

She'd sacrifice herself in a hot minute.

Evens's mom, Fabiola—Fab, as she'd introduced herself to Harmony outside the Haitian church resettlement office with nothing to her name but infant Evens and a giggle—must be crazy with worry.

Over the past decade, she'd sheltered Harmony, shared her meager food and irrepressible smiles, and taught her how to survive. In exchange, Harmony had improved Fab's English enough to gain a foreign job. She'd sent money home and saved for Evens's future.

After the kidnapping, Fab probably left her nice job in the Dominican Republic. She would be begging, borrowing, or rallying to get her son returned.

If only Harmony could have spoken with the Coast Guard. Why hadn't she placated Lifet a little longer? The Coast Guard would have rescued Evens. Instead, he was still in danger and she was stuck in the ocean wasting valuable time with nothing but her thoughts and fears for company.

Hours passed.

Her throat dried out.

Her headache worsened.

She mustn't drink seawater. The salt would only make her gag and dehydrate.

Harmony hugged her scabbed knees.

The sun went down. The night grew cold. She hugged herself and shivered.

Despite this, she fell asleep and awoke the next day in the hot sun. The ocean steamed. The horizon melted sea into sky. The sun glared overhead.

She was still alone.

He would break her. Make her regret her selfish demand.

The sun rose higher.

Her tongue rasped like sandpaper.

Her head ached...

What if this wasn't a punishment?

No, it must be.

Except...gods didn't sulk. They took.

What if the Sea Lord wasn't a god? What if her words had hurt him? What if he'd swum away and left her?

What if he wasn't coming back?

Panic chased agony as her thoughts overlapped each other and fought.

She would die like the fish, baked by the relentless sun.

And what about Evens?

Harmony hunched in a ball and closed her eyes.

Splish.

She opened her eyes.

The sun was in a different position. She must have slept again. Huh.

Another fish baked on the raft's plank. Wet. Fresh.

The monster was still here!

She scrambled over and pounced on the dead fish, tearing into it with ragged fingers and teeth. Her aches receded with the delicious influx of tasty meat. She licked her fingers.

Of course she was still hungry.

She crawled to that side of the raft and searched the ocean.

Waves. Large, empty waves.

Then, where...?

Oh. Of course.

She gripped the splintered wood, sucked in a deep breath, and plunged her head into the water.

Relief flowed over her. *Finally.* The ocean cooled her as if she'd stuck her head in a soothing bucket. Her headache eased.

Slide in. The water's fine. Stay forever.

Don't worry how it feels to drown...

She shuddered.

Something was wrong with her. Her very un-Harmony-like desire for the Sea Lord infected her thoughts. Normalized crazy. Enticed her to want more.

She had to resist.

Harmony forced her eyes open.

The salty water blurred her vision. She blinked.

Small fish hovered in the shade beneath the raft.

A larger fish evaded her focus.

She squinted.

Angry eyes. Dangerous purple-gray tattoos.

Electricity jolted her veins.

The monster!

She gasped.

Water clogged her throat.

She pulled herself back and slammed into the floor of the raft, coughing.

He did not follow her.

She refused to die as a dried-out, salty husk. Harmony crawled to the edge and took a deep breath. She had to be calm. Controlled. Subservient.

For Evens.

She held her breath and started to lean over to plunge in again. But before she could do so, something caught her eye.

A few feet away, the monster's forehead popped above the surface. He hovered mid-waves like a submerged crocodile. Only his eyes lifted above the waves. His nose remained beneath the water.

He studied her.

She let out her breath in a shaky rush. Her heart quickened.

This was it. He'd won. She didn't have the will to resist. Her headache hurt so badly.

He'd been destined to defeat her.

"W-well, what do I have to do?" she demanded.

His lips rose above the water line. "Do?"

"You have me. Alone." She hugged her bare elbows. Her sleeves hung from her shoulders in long strips attached by threads. "What do you want?"

"Want?" His voice rasped.

"Yes, w-want!" Hers shrilled. "You proved your point. I can't survive without you. Stop this punishment. I'll do whatever you ask."

His brow descended.

She'd made him angry. Thunderous.

Her heart thudded.

What would he do?

He searched for words. Never a good sign.

She braced.

"This is no punishment."

Of course it's a punishment! How can it not be? She swallowed the protest and waited for his wrath.

"I rescued you." His shoulders floated above the water line. Bare, knotted with muscle, riddled with scars. His voice smoothed as though he'd gotten rid of the last of the water in his throat. "You are no captive."

"Okay." She forced herself to be calm. Pretend to believe his lies. And when he transformed into an unrecognizable beast and ripped her to pieces like he'd ripped the dead fish, she would endure that terror too. "Where are you taking me?"

"Where?" He hooked a hand on the edge of the raft and gazed into the distance. "Where do you sail?"

"I don't know."

His shoulders lifted. Was that a shrug? They dropped again. "I do not know either."

"You control the wind and the water."

"I do not."

"You are the Sea Lord."

"And? You think I control the ocean surface? How would I do such a thing?"

"Use your power."

"My only power is to breathe."

"I know the truth!"

"Do other amphibious creatures possess such powers?"

Amphibious creatures? But her great-grandmother had said...

A large wave crested the raft, slapping the slats, and showered her with rebuking spray.

He had done it! Slapped her with the water!

"You are confused." He rested his second hand on the edge of the raft. His wiry muscles flexed and his brows furrowed.

In fury!

He would enter the raft and beat her.

Fear panged her chest.

She scrunched into the corner. This torture had to end, but she didn't want to die. She didn't want to—

"Please." His voice broke. Still floating, he rubbed his palm on his chest. "Do not fear me."

Had he begged the fish with that same ragged tone right before he'd dismembered it?

She squeezed her eyes shut and braced.

"Why did you summon me?" he demanded. "What do you need?"

She held her breath.

"Tell me your desire."

But she couldn't.

He would kill her.

His voice turned heavy. "I will leave you."

Silence.

Splish.

She peeped with one eye.

He was gone.

Harmony sat crisscross and mulled

The Sea Lord had said he couldn't control the wind and waves—despite evidence to the contrary. He must be lying.

Except...what if he was right?

He'd sounded so sad. Wounded, even. Her chest throbbed.

She rubbed her dress collar.

Tell me your desire.

It had been a long time since she'd told anyone her desires.

Right now, her primary desire was for a tall glass of

water followed by two cups of iced tea and a pitcher of lemonade. Pink lemonade with extra sugar.

And a thick slice of carrot cake, ten strawberry frosted toaster tarts, four pumpkin pies, and an entire Thanksgiving dinner of turkey and ham.

She'd planned to share all that someday with Evens.

"I will go to America and become a marine biologist," Evens had told her seriously on his eighth birthday. She'd scrimped to gift him a shiny new mask with bright orange plastic. He'd hugged it as his special treasure. *"I'll make them give you a work visa."*

"Oh?" She had tousled his thick, dark hair the same color as hers. *"What work will I do?"*

"You can be housekeeper in my university dorm room. But you don't have to work. You can be free. No one will ever know."

She had to save Evens.

Maybe the Sea Lord could help her.

Be brave. Tell him your desire. For Evens.

For Fab.

Heart thumping hard, Harmony knelt by the side of the raft and splashed the waves as if she was tapping on a door.

The Sea Lord arose once more.

Dark, angry eyes. Mesmerizing awareness stirred deep in her soul. Her body heated.

This time, his ears lifted above the water line.

"I'm sorry." She coughed on a dry throat. "Sorry to disturb you. I just... I...I need you to take me somewhere."

He rose above the waterline and raked his hair out of his face, exposing a long, harsh scar across his cheekbone. "Where?"

America. Anywhere in America. America, America, America.

"Haiti." She sucked in a deep breath and let it out. "I have to rescue my cousin. In Haiti."

"Where is Haiti?"

She'd asked the same question when Customs and Immigration had dumped her there. "It's the big island east of Cuba. On the western side. The eastern side is the Dominican Republic."

"How can I go there from here?"

"I don't know."

"I do not know either."

A flash of anger burned in her chest. She quelled it. Upsetting powerful men only ended up hurting her. "You have to know."

"How do I know?"

"You're the Sea Lord!"

The furious silence stretched.

She clenched her hands and released them. "So, where *can* you take me?"

"I can take you anywhere you wish."

Then take me to Haiti! She sucked in a deep breath and released it. "Do you know how to get to America?"

"I do."

"Can you take me there?"

"No."

Seriously. What was the point of making her ask if he couldn't do anything she asked him to do?

Disappointment mixed with irritation made her petulant question pop out. "Why not?"

"Because I only know the route from the deep ocean currents. Not the surface. And I did not bring my Life Tree's blossom. So you cannot transform."

She couldn't transform.

"Transform? What do you mean, I can't transform?"

"You cannot become amphibious."

"Huh?"

"To shift from human to mer, you must drink nectar from a flower of the Life Tree. Then our souls must resonate. And then you will transform."

"Oh. Wait, what do you mean, 'Our souls must resonate'?"

"We must synchronize our souls. Only once a warrior and his...his bride have synchronized can she shift into a mer."

"So, you're not going to drag me into the ocean right now?"

"You are human and would drown."

"But you're supposed to drag me to the ocean bottom and consume my soul."

"Consume? Why? And how?"

"I don't know. You're the Sea Lord."

"I do not know ei—"

"My great-grandmother said you would," she interrupted in a rush. "Every year, the Sea Lord carries off a woman of my tribe to have a child. She returns missing half her soul. That's what you do."

His jaw closed with a click. New shock burned in his eyes. "You are a sacred island bride!"

So he knew.

"That's why you kidnapped me," she reminded him.

"I rescued you," he repeated, as though she were the idiot. "What city patronizes your island?"

"Huh?"

"What mer city do your warriors come from?"

"There's more than one?"

"Of course."

"Well, how am I supposed to know?"

His lips twisted to the side with pity. "You do not review the human 'news' programs or 'internet,' do you?"

"I heard about the mer when you were first discovered, but until a couple days ago, it had as much relevance to me as life on Mars. Anyway." She rubbed her cheeks—bruised—and her knees—also bruised. "The last thing Jean-Baptiste did was radio an order to execute my cousin. I have to stop it."

"Radio? On the communications tower?"

"I guess."

"That tower broke off as your Lifet threw this life raft overboard. He could not radio anyone."

Oh, thank goodness. Relief flushed through her. Tears pricked the back of her eyes. "Are you sure?"

"Yes, very. The Coast Guard spotter announced when it happened."

"Great. Wow." She got up on her knees. "Now I have to get back to—wait. You were with the Coast Guard?"

"They asked for my aid on a different mission. I have swum for them several times."

"You weren't there for me?"

"I was there to support a sting operation on a cartel-owned submersible. During our return to port, we received the location of your gangster boyfriend."

"Ex."

"Yes. I remained alert to rescue you or any other human who fell into the water."

"But you weren't there to collect me as your 'sacred bride' or whatever?"

"No."

The coincidence was staggering. "Really?"

"Of course. Should I expect to meet a sacred island

bride, I would carry, at the very least, my Sea Opal offering."

"You didn't?"

"The Coast Guard requested I leave valuables at home."

That actually sounded plausible. Huh.

A fierce scar cut a deep, angry furrow on his brow. But he himself wasn't as angry as she'd first thought. Scars pocked the natural lines of his face and obscured his true feelings.

Maybe she had misjudged.

"My city does not limit our hunt to sacred islands," he continued, as though she needed more explanation. "We may encounter our mate on any surface. I searched for my bride from a penthouse in New York."

"New York!"

He tilted his head. "You do not recognize me? I spoke on human televisions. *Oprah. Sixty Minutes. Jersey Shore.*"

"You were on *Jersey Shore?*"

"The remake. One episode."

She snorted.

His lips curved into a shared smile.

The monster could smile?

Warmth seeped into her chest. Revitalized by the food he had brought her, calmed by his entirely normal conversation, gratitude flowed in her veins, and her ordinary, trusting nature tried to reassert itself.

She wanted to believe he had stumbled upon her by accident. She wanted to believe he worked with the Coast Guard. She wanted to believe he'd been on an episode of *Jersey Shore*. The remake.

His aura glowed a steady mauve, the same color as his

tattoos and the iridescent threads in his mesmerizing dark eyes. Reassurance flooded her veins.

Intoxicating.

He was here. Her protector, her warrior. She must seek his powerful arms, shelter in his kiss. The moment their lips touched she would be free. Once he claimed her, he would always keep her safe.

Hot desire tingled deep in her bones. Her channel slicked, readying for his possession. She wanted his claim.

No, her thoughts made no sense. She tried to shake the strange feelings off.

But her attraction to the dangerous male hummed.

She rested her palms on her knees. "Are you sure you don't steal souls?"

He hesitated.

Or maybe not. "What's, uh, more important is getting me back to land and you back to, uh, New York."

"Yes."

"So how do we do that?"

"I do not know."

Here they went again. "But you're...okay. You don't know where to sail. You expect me to know where to go."

"I push the raft," he agreed. "I traverse currents. The Coast Guard uses a navigational tool called a 'GPS' and 'maritime charts' and also 'satellites.' You have these human tools?"

"Nope." She patted the barren floorboards. "I don't even have shelter or water. Which will be pretty important pretty soon."

He ducked beneath the waves.

No.

No!

She rushed to the place he'd disappeared. "Monster!"

He was gone.

She sat back and berated herself. Harmony couldn't just call him "monster." How stupid. She needed to ask his name.

He'd come back. Right? He wouldn't strand her.

Not again.

A chunk of lawn chair sailed over the side of the raft. And then plastic webbing landed.

She fingered the shredded plastic. What—?

He surfaced. "Can you build a shelter?"

"Uh...maybe." She rotated the lawn chair pieces. "Are there poles or ropes? I can lash—"

He disappeared.

More detritus popped from the sea and landed in the raft. She pieced together a shelter, weaving the frayed plastics on rusted metal and trying not to cut herself. It had been a decade since her last tetanus shot.

The sun descended. Mist blurred the horizon once more. She positioned moisture-catchers—tarps Monsieur Joseph had taught her and Evens to build when they had still fantasized about stealing Lifet's life raft and sailing it to America—to collect fresh water.

The Sea Lord dropped two more dead fish, each the size of her hand, over the side near the others. "You now have what you need to survive?"

"Yes. Thank you."

He released the raft and turned away.

"Wait!"

He bobbed in the rolling waves.

Okay. She swallowed. "I'm sorry about before. Screaming and calling you names. I was scared and I never meant to make you angry."

"I have never been angry."

"Ever?"

"Not at you"

The sun dipped below the horizon. Harsh orange faded into a pink whimper.

In front of her floated a dangerous male. A warrior. Primal. He stirred awareness in her belly. The commanding jaw, the cut of his cheekbones, the flare of his nostrils were more deadly than any human's. And the tattoos. Dark purple—mauve—and iridescent. They shimmered like a fish.

This primal, dangerous male had rescued her.

And he claimed she had kissed him.

Well, maybe under different circumstances—in another life, when she hadn't been betrayed, exiled to Haiti, and subjected to a terrifying prophecy—maybe she would have.

Heat flared in her belly.

No!

No, she wouldn't have kissed him. Just like she wasn't wondering what his lips had tasted like. Salty? Like the ocean? Commanding? Or perhaps sweet...

Ugh! No.

"Tell me your desire," he ordered.

"I want to get to land."

"Yes, aside from that. You stare at me with an unspoken wish."

He knew. She gasped. "I, uh, just wish I could do something more useful than sitting in the raft."

"Then I will leave you." He disappeared beneath the surf.

"Ah!" She rushed to the side. But he was gone.

In the sunset distance, a long, curved shark's fin cut the water. The shark veered away from her raft. Was that the doing of the warrior?

Was he still rescuing her?

She drew the plastic shelter around her to stave off the chilly, damp wind. It worked. Her little spot created a junk nest around her shivery body.

Things were much better than they'd been hours ago.

And also much, much worse.

This Sea Lord hadn't come for her.

He didn't have ocean-controlling god powers. In fact, he and Harmony were both victims of the same storm. Both far from home. Both unable to find a way back to land.

This Sea Lord had rescued her. He stayed with her. But for how long? He could go anywhere. Dive. Leave her to fate.

And she needed to get back to land. Evens had survived Jean-Baptiste's wrath but he could still be stranded in the gang. Alone, frightened, and unable to get free.

Just like her.

SIX

Faier gave the confused female her privacy for the rest of the night and the day. Under the raft, he watched the fish from between the slats.

She took his offerings. Warmth filled his chest. He tried to crush it. She'd had no choice.

And despite how her chest had glowed as she'd learned more about him, he would not subject her to his scarred form.

Faier caught a bluehead wrasse and surfaced. In the falling darkness, he leaned over the edge of the raft to deposit it and sink back into the depths.

"Oh. Hello!" In the twilight, the female held two dead fish in her hands. Her gray-green eyes captured his with welcome. "You surfaced again. I thought you would."

"Excuse me." Faier released the raft.

"Just wait! Please."

He stopped.

"You can come in the raft. If you want." She sat on the far side of the wood, stacked the uneaten offerings next to her, and smoothed her ragged dress. "We never figured out how to reach land. I was hoping we could talk."

He did not wish to alarm her with his ugliness. Faier turned to dive.

"Wait!"

He waited.

"You, um, don't want to talk?"

"I have no idea how to reach land."

"Yeah, but we could talk about it. Get to know each other more. Maybe we'll get a great idea together. And isn't it a little, um, lonely out there? All alone?" She looped her arms over her knees. "No?"

He was used to loneliness. "No."

"Ah! Monster!" She scrambled to the edge of the raft. "Don't go."

His heart contracted. *Monster*. She had called him that before.

The description was accurate.

He obeyed her order, floating in the waves.

Her soul fluctuated dark to light to dark again. "Sorry. I'm sorry. I didn't mean to say that. I'm so sorry."

"Tell me what you desire," he said.

"Please don't be angry."

"I am not angry."

"You sound angry."

"I do not wish to frighten you, human female."

"Human female," she repeated with a small laugh. "Right. Ha ha. That's what I am to you."

He ducked his head.

"No! Mon—er, ah. I mean." She blew out a long stream of air. "I'm not scared. Not anymore. But I would like, if you aren't busy, to talk."

"We are talking."

"In the raft. I mean. I mean, um, *please* come into the raft and talk." She rubbed her elbows. "It's a little lonely up here."

He clambered into the raft.

She pushed as far away from him as possible. Her soul light plunged to black, and her gasp filled with horror. "You're naked!"

He rested one knee on the floor of the raft. "Yes."

"Wh-what happened to your clothes?"

"I left them on the Coast Guard cutter."

"Why?!"

"They restrict movement."

She stared.

He looked down at the body that paralyzed her with horror.

Thick, ropey scars crisscrossed every plane of his body. His two separate thighs, knees, calves, ankles, and long mer fins. Marks of weapons he had not evaded. Wounds that had never healed.

Despite growing a castle in Atlantis, he looked like an exile.

Embarrassing.

And, in her eyes, horrifying.

"Excuse me." He slipped over the side, into the dark, masking water once more.

"N-no. Wait." She rocked onto her knees. Her desperate request chased him. "It's okay. Please don't mind me. You surprised me. That's all."

He lingered.

Her soul light remained steady. She meant her words. She wanted him to sit in the raft subjecting her to his disfigured body.

Perhaps he could risk this. Soon, the darkness would

obscure him. She could endure his form for a short time in this twilight.

"Please come back," she begged.

He heaved himself into the raft once more. His long mer fins snapped into human feet. He crept as far away from her side as he could.

Which was his least-scarred side? He twisted in the spot where he'd deposited her fish.

The spot was empty.

He rose to leave. "I will hunt another fish."

"No!" She patted the trio of offerings she had stacked beside her, reminding him that she had deliberately hidden the offerings to lure him to the surface. "No. I am, uh, hungry for something other than fish."

"I will acquire another food. Sal. It is common in these waters. You will like it."

"Oh! But I'm hungriest for something that's not food." She gestured for him to sit again. "Please. Please."

He sat on his toes.

"Thank you. Thank you." She touched her forehead and averted her eyes. Her elevated heart rate thudded with the stress of forcing this conversation with a disgusting creature like him. "Now, I can't keep calling you—uh. Okay. What's your name?"

"Faier of Atlantis."

"Of Atlantis?" She brightened with awe. "That's where you're from? The mythical Atlantis?"

"No."

"Oh." She darkened and hugged herself like she was afraid he was going to be mad. "Um, okay. Uh..."

"Ancient Atlantis sank a thousand years ago. The Great Catastrophe when mer females died out and mankind turned on mer."

"We did?"

"Yes."

"Why?"

"The reason for the war was lost in the catastrophe."

"I guess that makes sense." She rubbed her knees, trying to forge ahead but worried about how to speak with him. "You lost your women a thousand years ago?"

"Yes. And because humans hunted us, the All-Council forged an ancient covenant with sacred islands. They saved our race."

"And that's what I am. Although my tribe's island got destroyed before I was born."

"That happened to many sacred islands. It is the reason for our revolution."

"And you are from...uh, not Atlantis..."

"Rebel King Kadir planted his Life Tree in the shadow of the ancient wreckage. His new city is also called Atlantis."

Her thin brows drew together and a hint of a skeptical smile tugged at her lips. "Did you really explain this on *Jersey Shore*?"

"I have explained it many times. Most recently to the United States Congress. Before that, to the United Nations."

"Oh. Wow. Oh!" She pressed one hand to her chest and glowed with welcome. "I'm Harmony, by the way."

"Hello, Harmony of The Way."

"Huh? Oh! It's just Harmony."

"Harmony," he repeated. "From?"

"From...hah." She smoothed her threadbare dress. "That's a complicated question. I guess I'm from nowhere, actually."

"Where is Nowhere, Actually?" he asked politely.

"It's nowhere." She snorted. Her eyes flicked to his—a brief flash of gray-green—and away. "It's not the name of a place. It's no place. I'm from nowhere."

A stab of recognition jolted him. "You are an exile?"

"Yeah. I guess I am."

"But your injuries..." They were healing. Fading from purple to yellowish green and lifting from her skin.

She rubbed her wrists. "I never would have gotten these in America. That's where I'm from originally. Omaha. The Iowa side. Well, actually, it's Council Bluffs. Right next to Omaha. It's in a landlocked state. Do you know it?"

He shook his head.

His chest froze to ice.

He should not remain here. He should not listen to her story.

He should not believe for one moment they shared a tragic past.

"It's real America," she continued in a friendly, nostalgic tone, unaware of his pain. "Casinos, frozen food, meat packing, a pipe plant. I never cared when I lived there, but after a decade in Haiti, I'd give anything to stroll into the Mall of the Bluffs and eat, like, a ten-piece KFC with coleslaw and biscuits and honey."

"You miss your ancestral foods."

"I'm not insulting your fish. I swear. My complaints must sound kind of dumb."

They did not sound dumb.

Her soul light dimmed as if she worried that she'd hurt his feelings. "Sorry. Um, what were we talking about? Oh, how to survive—"

"A certain palm frond only grew in the king's courtyard of Nerissa." He lifted his hands to illustrate its size. "Its lavender flowers tasted like your sweet raisins. And long bamboo sticks grew in every nook. They had a satisfying crunch like your potato chip." He rested his hands in his lap. "I too would give anything to taste these plants again."

"Did you get deported from Nerissa?"

"It was destroyed in a natural disaster."

"I'm so sorry." She rubbed her hands. "Losing your safe home is the worst feeling in the world, isn't it? Having nowhere to turn to. All your friends and family gone. No money, no job, no nothing."

"At times, I preferred death."

She gave his statement a respectful silence.

His torn heart swelled.

This human, Harmony, understood.

Humans did not depend on a Life Tree to survive. They did not swear fealty to a king or defend a city with their lives. Losing her Council Bluffs did not mean her blood would sicken or she would die.

But she understood.

And because of her kind silence, tendrils of healing seeped into the broken cracks of his chest. They burned where they touched his heart.

She sucked in a breath as though shaking off the melancholy. "Now you live in Atlantis. Do you like it? You have friends there?"

"Yes. And also in the rebel city Dragao Azul."

"I made friends in Haiti too. Even though I'd give anything to go home, I want to make sure my cousins are okay." She frowned. "Oh. You've been gone for days too. Your friends must be worried."

"Perhaps they will be glad of my absence."

"Then they're not very good friends," she said, coming to his defense.

"My presence on the surface has caused pain."

"What do you mean?"

"I did not find my bride in New York. So my king sent more warriors starting with Healer Balim."

Balim had surfaced to lecture humans on the healing properties of Sea Opals. The skeptical healer had also examined Faier. Why had Faier failed to find his bride? What was his problem?

Aside from the obvious, of course.

King Kadir had not expressed discouragement. No, he had worried about exposing Faier to the recently-established, deadly, anti-mer terrorist organization, the Sons of Hercules.

"Perhaps, during my absence, more successful warriors will find their brides," he finished. "And our city will thrive."

"Faier..." Her soul glowed with a soft light. "You'll find a bride."

"I do not want *a* bride. I want *my* bride."

But she did not desire him. She would never desire him.

And right now, her soul called to him. Her gaze flitted across his scarred body and a strange expression crossed his face. She looked interested. No, not interested. Hungry.

His cock pulsed.

What was this sensation? She was disgusted by his body. Not intrigued by it.

Her slender pink lips parted. Her tongue touched her lips.

He wanted to taste her again so badly his bones ached.

Faier rose and slipped into the water.

"Wait!" Harmony flung herself to the edge of the raft and held out her hand as if to clasp his arm. "Sorry. I didn't mean to offend you."

"I am not offended." He was heartbroken. And she was

in danger. He might forget her true feelings. His own desires seemed to overwhelm his better sense.

"Ah..." She lowered her outstretched hand to rest on the side of the boat. "Can you still talk?"

"Yes. If you wish."

"I wish. I really wish."

She truly wished to prolong their conversation?

He shook his head. "I am a warrior of action. Not words. I cannot give you comfort."

"I don't know." She swirled her fingers in the water. "You're doing fine to comfort me."

A strange tightness closed his throat.

He sucked in a breath. His feet unfurled into fins. Part of him wanted to dive beneath the water. Escape these tender feelings. But more wanted him to remain and feel her embrace.

"Then, what do you wish to talk about?" he replied.

"I don't know. Anything. I like hearing your voice. You're so steady." She swirled her fingers in the water again. "It makes me calm."

Tiny creatures glowed blue in the darkness. Her touch sparkled. Suddenly the creatures swirled around his body surrounding him in bright blue stars.

She rose on her elbows. "Oh! How did you do that? It's so pretty."

"I did nothing. You caused this pretty image."

"It's like all the stars have fallen into the water. I kind of want to get in." She danced her own fingers across the surface and the bright colors followed her. "Is this how you always see the ocean?"

"These creatures dwell only on the surface."

"So we're both seeing this it for the first time." She swirled the magical colors. "It's so beautiful and soothing like the ocean itself is saying, 'Don't worry. You're stranded right now but you're together. Everything's going to work out for you.'"

His throat tightened again. "My presence truly gives you comfort?"

"Of course." She smiled at him like he was missing something important. "You saved my life, Faier. I'm sorry I reacted so badly but I am sincere about my thank you. I'll never have the chance to save your life because I'm not exactly a super hero, but if I can do anything like...like if we're ever in Council Bluffs, I'll treat you to a breaded pork tenderloin."

He swallowed. "You would do this?"

"Absolutely. I also owe one to Evens and Fab and Monsieur Joseph. We're all going to meet someday in Council Bluffs. My treat."

He momentarily couldn't speak. "...You would invite me into your home?"

"Of course," she said again, tilting her head. "We're in this together now. Why are you so surprised?"

He shook his head.

"Ha ha. I know that's crazy. But if there is anything I can do, I'll try to help you."

Her lack of fear in the way she looked directly into his eyes was all the help and thanks he needed. Trust and hope sparkled in chest. He, too, suddenly felt like everything would be all right.

The sparkles faded as the night deepened but Harmony's warmth kept him near the raft. She peppered him with questions throughout the long night and then, conscious of her human eyes, he slipped away when pink touched the dawn skies. The next evening, Harmony asked him again to remain with her through the night. And the night after as well.

It was madness to return. Madness to obey. Madness to allow her soul to entwine with his when he could not stop his cravings.

During the days, Faier checked through broken slats multiple times to deliver fresh fish before she hungered.

He sorted the surface detritus for the long poles and plastic sheets she had requested to improve her human water collection and shelter.

And at night—for many nights—he engaged in warm conversation from the blue sparkles of twilight until the first light of dawn.

He refused to torture her with his disgusting appearance in daylight.

He refused to torture *himself* by allowing her any closer. He had already sworn to protect her with his life. His soul cried for more. He must have an illness to desire her when she did not desire him. Humans fell in love by accident. Mer could see another's soul light. Harmony did not desire him.

And despite their long conversations, Harmony still believed many of her great-grandmother's fearful tales.

A sacred island bride!

Faier kicked hard, testing his injured right leg as twilight approached on yet another night.

His leg collapsed.

Of all the human females he could have rescued, he'd ended up touching the one female claimed by a hostile, traditional mer city. Any of their warriors would slice his fingers off for touching her and remove his tongue for daring to address her.

He had to return her to Haiti. Then fly away. Fast. Before her warriors avenged her.

Before he cared too deeply.

Never mind that *she* had kissed *him*.

Sometimes, her gaze lingered strangely on his scarred chest, and even though he knew she could not see him in the dark, he began to imagine curious desire glowing hot in her soul light. Could she cross the raft, rest her soft hand on his chest, yield her lips once more to his taste? Draw him atop her slim body, dress bunched up around her waist, and smile with welcome while she guided his cock deep into her wet, feminine center—

No. That would never happen.

She feared his nudity and hated his scars. She'd told him so the first day. Her lingering gaze was morbid curiosity. She would never, ever welcome his touch or want him for her husband.

He shoved that painful thought from his mind.

Splish! Splish! Splish! It was twilight two weeks into their long isolation and she summoned him.

He arose with news. "I have found a current that will take us to land."

Harmony clapped eagerly. "Which land?"

"I do not know."

Her clapping slowed. "Is it 'land' like an island? Or 'land' like the Continental United States?"

He shook his head.

Her shoulders sloped in disappointment.

He'd caused her sadness.

The ocean was a vast place. The surface world, vaster. And until Atlantis had rebelled against the traditional All-Council, exposing the mer's existence to all humans, no warrior had spent more than the briefest hours on the surface.

He pushed through the sad feeling. "Do you wish to steer to the land?"

"Yeah." She sighed heavily. "Maybe we can still get home. After freeing Evens, I mean."

He felt her ache in his soul.

Harmony was an exile. Like him. She was heroically trying to rescue her young cousin from dangerous human warriors and give him a better life. Unlike his Nerissa, her Omaha/Council Bluffs still existed.

"Harmony."

She shivered. "Yes, Faier?"

"No matter where we land, I will return you to your Council Bluffs in America. I swear it."

"Thank you." She hugged her knees and wiggled her adorable unblemished pink toes. "Supposing we get to civilization in one piece, I appreciate the thought. And also thank you for listening to me all these nights, and being kind, and not dragging me back to Atlantis to consume my soul."

"Mer do *not* consume souls."

"Right, I know." She smiled softly, sharing their joke.

It made his heart clench.

He pushed through his feelings. "And, Harmony, no warrior can 'drag' you back to a city. If you do not wish to go then you must not."

Her smile faded to resignation. "I'm a sacred bride, Faier. Your explanation isn't that far off from my great-grandmother's prophecy, which makes me a hot commodity, whether I like it or not."

"Whether you like it is the most important. If you do

not like a warrior, you cannot sync souls. You will never transform. You will remain on the surface."

"Or else I'll drown."

"No, Harmony. Harming a female breaks the first law of the mer. No warrior will force you to do anything. It is dishonorable."

She snorted. "And no 'warrior' ever acts dishonorably, right?"

"Warriors have done so," he admitted, uncomfortably aware of his own wrong desires. "But even if a warrior did coerce you to transform, female mer can summon great powers. Much greater than any male."

"Oh, so *I* have the power over wind and sea? Well, heck, transform me!"

His heart squeezed. "You jest."

"I'm sorry." She hugged her knees again, her soul dimming as she hid her strength away and protected herself from hidden enemies. "It's just me having any choice is... well, it's ridiculous."

"No, Harmony." He needed her to understand for her own safety. "You *can* order warriors. You must. Even hostile warriors will obey if you bring forth your powers as a queen."

She stared at him for a long, hard moment as though her gaze were cutting through the cloaking darkness and seeing his scars. Then she rubbed the healed skin on her wrists. "I don't know how to believe you"

He straightened. "I speak the truth with honor."

She softened again. "I believe *you* would never force me."

"Not only me. Believe." He slipped over the side, into the water and ducked under to taste the current.

Chalk. Limestone. Guano.

He dragged the raft into the strong current. Fast, turbulent waves rocked the raft.

Harmony's face appeared over the edge. Wavy, anxious, beautiful. She tapped the water.

His heart shivered.

She would never be his bride, yet he had sworn to protect her. Second, he had sworn to return her to America.

His chest thrummed from the dangerous power of his unbreakable vows.

He was getting wrapped deeper and deeper into her. So when she found her destined warrior, he would ache. Only this time, the exile would be his own heart.

Her soul light flickered.

He rose, drawn like a minnow to the full moon, laid bare to surface predators. His gills shifted to lungs. He took a breath.

Her hand reached out to touch his face—and stopped. She jolted as though catching herself at the last instant and curling her fingers into a fist.

He forced himself to remain calm, as if she hadn't almost touched him of her own will, because it had clearly been a mistake. "Yes, Harmony?"

"I'll believe," she promised raggedly as if she were afraid he would disappear again if she didn't. She hugged her fist to her chest. "If you tell me to, I'll try."

"Believe in your power because it is within you," he urged. "Not because you fear me."

"I don't fear you. I fear everybody else."

"Harmony."

"Right." She sighed and scrubbed her eyes. "Believe. Ha ha. Huuuuuh."

He kicked, his fins scooping the water to keep them in

the current, the raft and its precious, damaged, frightened occupant he would do anything to soothe and keep safe.

"I swear I will try to believe I am a queen who can boss around a bunch of armed, hostile, monst—uh, guys. Warriors. I will try to believe that."

"It is important."

"Why? You're staying with me." She dropped her hands to the wood. "Right?"

He didn't know what to say.

Her soul light darkened. "Faier."

"I do not know what awaits us on this land."

"Warriors? You think hostile warriors await us?"

"Prepare yourself."

She hugged herself, her soul light dim and her voice tiny. "Okay."

"Be powerful, Harmony. Be strong."

She swallowed hard.

But he relied on her. With his injuries, he could only fight so hard. If they reached hostile territory, they would face attack.

And their fates rested on Harmony.

SEVEN

Islands appeared like pebbles on the horizon at sunrise. Harmony stared at the trio until they disappeared under the punishing shine. Her stomach panged.

Not from hunger. Faier had brought her plenty of fish, and in her desperation, the taste improved. Became familiar. Like an ancestral memory...or something.

He'd brought her weird, interconnected jellybean "sal chains." The texture was bizarre, and the taste was mostly seawater and salt.

He took care of her.

Pang.

Anxiety. That was what she felt. Her stomach rode on a roller coaster plunging endlessly down.

Be powerful. Order around armed warriors. Be strong.

Yeah, right.

Faier surfaced. "We will reach the island in daylight."

She felt ill.

"Good." She drained the droplets from her dew trap into half of a salvaged plastic water bottle. "I'm glad we'll be able to explore in the daylight."

He looked grim.

"Oh! Will you be okay? Your skin sensitivity." She gestured at the shoulders he kept submerged.

"I have no skin sensitivity, Harmony."

The way he said her name made little thrills run up her spine.

She crushed the feeling. "You don't? But you only visit at night."

"Human vision is most obscured during the night."

"Obscured?"

"In daylight, you must see my body."

Desire shot through her like a bolt.

She had seen him better than he thought in the darkness. Blue sparkling bioluminescence at dusk and moonlight had bathed him in a million stars. They had illuminated the hard outline of a male in his prime and her eagerness to see more in the light of day made her jolt with embarrassment at herself.

And now she was so comfortable with him that she'd almost reached out and cupped his cheek last night. What had she been thinking? The near-miss had wreaked havoc in her heart for hours afterward.

"Um, oh, that's fine." She tried to reassure him that she would not invade his privacy. Even though she'd already done it in the darkness. A bunch. "I won't look. I promise."

He lowered his head. "I will warn you before I must emerge."

"Yep, that's fine."

"Be on guard once we approach the inner ring."

"Sure. Will do."

"Harmony."

"Yes?"

"Forgive me." Heart-stopping mauve entangled his dark

irises. His dark gaze stole her breath. "I do not wish to subject you to any frightening sight you will find horrifying."

What?

Horrifying?

Her mouth opened and closed on its own. She tried to respond. "Hungh."

Faier ducked beneath the water.

She was alone on the raft.

The raft jerked to her left. Toward the islands.

I do not wish to subject you to any frightening sight you will find horrifying.

Horrifying?

What was horrifying?

Harmony sank and raised the cup to her lips. She sipped the droplets.

They tasted like rain.

I do not wish to subject you to any frightening sight you will find horrifying.

Do not fear me.

Please do not fear me.

Please.

Wait a minute. Wait just a gosh darned minute.

For all these nights, Faier's kind gentleness had drawn her out of her terrified shell. He'd become her support. Her friend. They were castaways together. She trusted him just like she trusted Fab or Evens or Monsieur Joseph. He had her back and she had his. Even if he did expect her to order around deadly warriors like it was no big deal. She'd already decided that even though angering powerful men terrified her, if Faier was protecting her, then she'd try.

Every morning, he'd left, and visceral sadness had

stabbed her. The night faded to a dream, and she feared Faier was her thirst-crazed delusion.

But now she understood that the reason he'd abandoned her had been her own fault.

He'd retreated beneath the raft so she wouldn't be "subjected" to his nudity. Because her terrified shriek the first day had cut his gentle soul to the core.

She had hurt him. Badly.

Hurt because of something she'd said in the middle of terror.

"Faier?" Harmony set aside her dry plastic cup and leaned over the side. "I think we had a little misunderstanding. I don't, uh...sorry!"

He didn't surface.

Harmony leaned hard on the edge of the raft and searched the empty waves.

Come back. I didn't mean it. I didn't realize you were you and I had nothing to fear.

"Faier?" She leaned.

The wooden lip bent beneath her weight.

She nearly catapulted into the sea.

Harmony jerked back, landing on the raft, and scooted to the center. Then she retreated beneath her ragged shelter. Just in case.

Was he sleeping beneath the raft? Probably not. He'd rescued her, cared for her, and he'd not once complained. He even vowed to take her back to Council Bluffs. And, unlike the others who'd given up or stopped caring, she knew he would do it.

Because he wasn't the monster she had accused him of. He was Faier.

A strong, kind, hard male with mesmerizing eyes and intricate tattoos. Always respectful of her. Always encouraging. And his lips again teased her with the wonder of how he had tasted.

Desire stirred in her nethers.

She sucked in a breath and shook it off.

Okay, so, she was no longer afraid of Faier stealing her soul *on purpose*...

Harmony concentrated on the positive.

These islands would change everything. She would apologize as soon as they landed.

Surely the hardest times were behind her.

The islands winked in and out of existence. With no reference for scale, they seemed miles away or tiny, bare boulders poking above the ocean, so small they couldn't support seabirds or insects. Not even a dragonfly.

The raft jerked and jerked again. The islands grew. Waves crashed against three bleached headlands.

Faier emerged at the head of the raft. "There is no beach. Only coral. We have no anchor. The landing will be difficult."

"Only coral," she repeated. "There has to be a beach somewhere on the three islands—"

"One island," he corrected. "Three peaks. Water over-runs at high tide."

"So what do we do?"

"Abandon the raft and swim."

She squeezed the raft lip so hard, it hurt.

He studied her white knuckles. "Do not fear me."

"What? I don't fear you." She made the mistake of glancing into his eyes and was captured.

In the daylight, he looked dangerous. The long scar pulled his brow into uncompromising dominance.

But his "uncompromising dominance" was thoughtful. Kind.

She had to tell him—

"Tell me your desire," he ordered.

A thrum of awareness shivered in her veins. Her channel contracted.

She was suddenly thinking of the wrong desires.

"Er, uh, is there no other way?" she asked, her voice thick.

"There are many 'other ways.' Other currents. Other islands."

"There are other islands!"

"In the ocean, yes."

"Oh. But not anywhere near us?"

He shrugged. "You know this region of surface, Harmony, better than me."

"I barely saw one map!"

"That is more than I have seen."

She squeezed. The waterlogged wood flaked beneath her fingers. This raft did not have long left.

But it was all she had.

"If we abandon the raft, we're stuck," she said.

He dipped his head in acknowledgment.

"I want to keep the raft."

"Good, Harmony."

"Good?"

"You stated your wish."

"Oh, you want me to state my wishes?" She laughed hysterically. "I wish I was snuggled in a big, woolen blanket with a steaming cup of hot cocoa watching *It's a Wonderful Life* while three feet of snow piled up outside my nice, new, unbroken windows. That's a wish."

His mouth quirked to one side. She amused him. Well, good. He amused her too.

The roller coaster in her belly eased.

"You express long-range desires," Faier said smugly. "Soon, you will express your true desires in every moment. And then you will find your inner confidence and rule."

"I'll order around every single dragonfly and hermit crab," she agreed, still death-gripping the shredded wood. "But for now, can we keep the raft? Is that even possible?"

"Yes."

"Great!"

"Perhaps."

She eyed him.

"The problem is guidance and momentum. I will provide momentum. You enter the water and guide the raft. We can attempt—"

"I can't swim."

His eyes widened. "No?"

She shook her head.

"But you are a sacred bride."

"I didn't know that until a couple weeks ago. Water terrified my mom."

"But *she* was a sacred bride!"

"Maybe that's why. Maybe she feared revealing she was a mermaid."

"You cannot swim. A sacred bride who cannot swim." He repeated it to himself several more times, muttering.

"So we're stuck, huh?" She sank lower into her seat. The one time she could be useful to him and she had nothing. "Sorry."

"No." He faced the islands with new resolve. "I will bring us about."

"Alone?"

He kicked hard and dove. Fins slapped the surface. He disappeared.

Oh, fins. Merman fins. She'd seen him so much as a man, she'd almost forgotten he was a mon—he could shift.

What would shifting be like? Freedom. Twirling like dolphins, wet, entwining in the water, playful and free. And useful. She could help him instead of relying on him helplessly for everything.

A dream.

The raft circled the trio of sheer, rocky spires.

Small birds nested in the highest reaches. The birds' auras glowed neutral white against the muted backdrop. Vines dangled from foliage clustered at the tips. Waves skidded across an emerging rock belt that united the three spires.

The raft plowed for the center of the rocky belt.

She braced.

The raft screeched as it scraped the coral. It halted in the center.

Land!

Faier emerged from the deeper ocean along the back side of the raft.

She opened her mouth to apologize for the misunderstanding. He didn't horrify her. She'd seen him plenty of times and...

Suddenly she really saw him. And it was shocking.

His knuckles were *coated* with scars. *Inflamed* with them. The backs of his hands looked like they'd gone through a wood chipper and been glued together on the other side.

His arms were more than a patchwork. And his chest...

His torso...

His legs...

Scars on top of scars.

The mauve tattoos beneath were intricate. But now, barely visible.

He was a mess.

How had she not noticed before?

Oh, because she'd been too busy being frightened of him the first time he'd dared to show himself. And then he'd been careful to keep her from seeing him clearly again. She'd been too busy fantasizing about his hands on her, cupping her breasts and caressing her hips, to look.

Her heart thudded. Her palms felt damp. He had done so much for her, and she'd thrown it back in his face.

Tell him.

He clambered onto the rocky shelf. "Come. Quickly."

"Faier." She stood. "I'm sorry."

"Do not apologize. Walk."

A hard wave crashed over the raft, rocking it sideways and knocking her off-balance. Water drained through the slats.

She gripped the raft in protest. "Are you sure the raft won't wash out to sea?"

"We have a short time to explore." He did not reassure her—meaning the raft *would* wash away—and his hard voice left no doubt of the urgency.

Harmony gripped the rocking raft even tighter. "Should we anchor it somehow?"

"Hurry. Please." Faier hesitated near her as if to offer his arm.

Deep jags slashed his tattoos in a rounded shark bite.

He saw her looking at the scars and jerked his arm away, hunching to cover himself. "I forgot to warn you I would emerge."

"Oh. It's fine."

"Forgive me."

"No, I'm the one who messed up because I didn't mean..."

He walked away and crossed the bleached coral toward the most prominent spire, his body a blur of muscle and movement.

She trailed off.

Harmony wanted to stop him. She wanted to tell him she didn't mind, and she didn't mean to make him uncomfortable. She wanted him to help her to the land.

But they didn't have time. She muttered her default. "Sorry."

He was too far away, and she spoke too softly to reach him.

Harmony dangled one leg over the raft and eased onto the barnacle-crusted coral. *Short time. Short time. Short time.* The coral was sharp and gritty, like walking barefoot across gravel. She picked her way to shore.

Faier clambered onto a flat boulder and stared over the rest of the island. Silent.

And naked.

Totally naked, from the top of his dark, Grecian head to the bottoms of his human feet, and every valley and mountain of muscle in between. Dark mauve tattoos covered him in an intricate web.

Including the thick cock silhouetted against his upper thigh. He was not erect, but his power made her mouth go dry.

She should—

Stab.

Needles jabbed her bare instep.

"Ouch!" She stumbled to her knees in the shallow surf.

Splish, splash!

Faier loomed over her. "What has occurred? What attack?"

She lifted her foot. Black spines stuck out of her instep.

He knelt, curled a powerful hand around her ankle, and yanked out the spines.

"Ow!"

"Forgive me."

"It's not your fault." Her foot throbbed. Pink puncture wounds darkened to red and seeped blood. They stung. "What were they?"

His angry gaze fixed on her injury for a hard moment. A muscle in his jaw flexed.

"Faier?"

He pointed to a spiny black clump on the bleached coral. "Urchin."

"Urchin? Is that bad?"

"Forgive me."

"For what? I already did."

He leaned into her. One capable arm curved around her back and the other beneath her legs. He pressed her to his sheltering chest and lurched to his feet.

She hugged him. "Oh!"

"Forgive." His teeth gritted, and he anchored his gaze on the shore.

EIGHT

Harmony held Faier tight.

Her pain and fright eased.

He was a rock. Steady, indomitable. Even his bumpy scars gave a pebbled texture to his skin over uncompromising muscle. He carried her to safety. But instead of relaxing her body pounded with increasing awareness.

He stepped onto the boulder and eased her onto the solid, wave-smoothed stone. He cupped her injured foot. "Can you heal?"

But his cock drew her attention. Before, lax. Now, aroused.

An answering tingle filled her veins.

He held her gaze. "Can you?"

Her heart stopped.

His dark gaze filled her soul. Mauve threads intertwined with his mesmerizing dark-brown irises. She was acutely aware of the sun's heat. His nearness. Her flush of sexual arousal to his question.

He frowned and released her foot—gently—to rest on the boulder.

She missed his touch.

And that realization—that she craved his touch—jolted her from her stupor. "Can I?"

"Heal. Or will you..." He broke off and looked at his large, empty hands.

"Will I?"

"Scar."

Oh. Oh, Faier. Her heart squeezed. "No." She wiped off spots of blood with her ragged sleeve. "It'll be fine with a Band-Aid."

"You will not scar?" he asked again.

"I don't think so."

He looked up to spear her with his taut demand. "Certain?"

Her breath caught.

She nodded wordlessly.

His focus intensified.

The dangerous gash marred his brow. A smaller slash crossed his full lips.

How did he taste?

Heat kindled in her belly and flooded her veins.

His gaze trailed across her parted lips and lower. To the valley of her breasts. Over the frayed buttons of her dress.

His aura *changed*. Deeper mauve. Not darker. But more intense.

He noticed her attraction. No one had ever noticed before.

Wake up.

She rubbed her palms on her ripped dress. "I mean, if it does, no one will notice on my feet."

He tore his gaze back to her injury.

Concern wrecked his expression. Like he'd failed her. "Where can I find your healing Band-Aid salves?"

"In a first aid kit." Which they had lost in the storm. "In civilization."

He rose. "I will seek it."

"Wait!"

He hesitated.

A small streak of blood marked her calf.

It wasn't hers.

"You're bleeding too." She pointed at the cuts on his fingers where he'd ripped out the urchin's spines. "Will you be okay?"

He glanced at his fingers. "Okay?"

"Will you, uh, heal?"

"I am supposed to."

"Supposed to?"

His jaw flexed again. "The sap of the Atlantis Life Tree runs in my veins. So long as it grows strong, I too will grow new skin."

"Jean-Baptiste said Sea Opals having healing powers."

"Sea Opals are the resin of a Life Tree."

"So if a Sea Opal washed ashore, then we could both heal..."

"Unfortunately, Sea Opals do not 'wash ashore.' Warriors guard them, and they only reach the surface at sacred islands as offerings to treasured brides."

She studied the island anyway.

Waves had undercut the steep, sheer cliff nearest them. Birds rustled and chirped in the foliage, but there was no way either of them could reach the top.

A strangely familiar shape was carved into the top of the cliff. Eyes, nose, and the cliff made a tuft of hair. Almost like...

"Look!"

He turned.

She pointed out the formation. "It's a face. Badly weathered, but you can see it. Hey!" She squinted at the other two outcroppings above the waves. "Are faces carved into those rocks too?"

Several minutes of study passed, broken only by the crash of surf, the caw of distant seabirds, and the whine of insects on the harsh wind.

Faier leaned onto his heels. "What does it signify?"

"I think this might be my mom's island."

His chin dropped.

She was still becoming familiar with his expressions, and this one was not happy.

"Your sacred island?"

"Er, yeah. I guess."

He studied the waves with new intensity. "You are sure this is your sacred island?"

"No."

He looked at her sharply.

"These could be the 'Three Ancestors' of water, wind, and land. They were carved into the three hillsides. Probably."

"Why do you not know?"

"My mom only talked about her island once."

"Only once…"

"The night I graduated high school." She poked at the stinging pink punctures on her instep. The star pattern throbbed red. "She got drunk for the first time ever and said my brothers' spirits were proud. That was the first time I learned I'd had brothers. She'd had a whole family before I was born. They'd all died in the storm."

"A storm?"

"*The* storm. The one that destroyed her island and forced my mom's tribe to leave."

She explained how, over generations, the sea had risen. The worst tropical storm of the century had whipped a tsunami across their village. The survivors had gathered their meager belongings and cast their fortunes across the sea.

"My mom stayed behind to lead the Sea Lords to the tribe's new location on Haiti. But she didn't. According to my great-grandmother, she betrayed the tribe."

"Betrayed how?"

"No Sea Lords are swimming to Haiti, for one thing. My mom didn't end up there either."

"You did not know?"

"Except for that one time after graduation, she talked like her life began on a beach in Miami. She reminisced about being a house cleaner in Dayton, relying on kind strangers to understand basics like how to clean—and even use—a toilet, and blaming the cleaning supplies for what turned out to be morning sickness. She had no idea she was pregnant with me."

"Humans have a 'pregnancy test.'"

"Oh, yeah, but you'd only test yourself if you had a *reason* to think you were pregnant. I mean, the way my mom used to tell it, I was like an immaculate conception. But she must have had a little clue."

"This is your sacred island." He squared his broad shoulders. "There must be a sacred church."

"I'll search too." She stood and hobbled one painful step.

"You cannot."

His rejection slapped her. She fought through the sting. "But I want to."

"It lies beneath the waves."

Oh. "It does?"

"When a sacred island sinks, the church also submerges. I will hunt it underwater."

The raft made a terrible cracking noise. It scraped against the coral but remained in place.

She took another hobbling step. Her ankle panged. "Do you have enough time?"

"I do not know."

Great. She rubbed her forehead. "So what should I do?"

"Prepare to repel enemy warriors."

"What!"

"Practice. Channel your inner confidence as queen."

"Without you?" She held out her palms to stop him. "Warriors come on land?"

"This is your sacred island."

"I believe. I mean..." Suddenly, she felt hot and light-headed. She sat with a thump and rested her head against the boulder. "Don't make me."

He knelt. "I will not force you to do anything you do not wish, Harmony."

His tone held a huge "but."

"But enemy warriors might," she finished.

"They will not. Not if you order them."

Except how would she order armed warriors? She wouldn't. It was impossible. They'd hurt her.

Once she'd been brave but then life—and Lifet—had kicked the snot out of her and now she was a tiny mouse jumping at every whiff of a cat.

"Maybe they won't visit."

"Probably they will not," he agreed. "But you have been called here. It is likely your soul has called them."

"My soul?"

"So you must enforce your will, Harmony. Do not let them insist on a course of action you do not wish."

"But I supposedly kissed you, right? Can you just tell them I claimed you or something ridiculous?"

"Yes." He met her minimizing, flustered gestures with a solid, unshakeable honor. "To my race, a kiss is very serious. To surface-dwelling humans, it is 'ridiculous.' I understand."

Her heart hurt. She kept hurting Faier when all she wanted to do was climb into his arms and stay there, sheltering him, forever. "Sorry. That's not what I meant."

"Your soul darkens with fear."

"Because I can't do this without you."

"I will protect you. I swear this."

He rested his palm on his chest. His fingers covered the scars so his tattoos looked as if they were whole. The spikes circled his heart like a compass rose.

"You are safe with me."

Her heart cracked in half, and all the pain, stress, fears of the past decade leaked out.

She hugged her elbows.

Faier wouldn't manipulate her. She'd known it as soon as she'd seen past her fears on the life raft. The tears threatening to spill out weren't because she didn't believe him. They welled because she *did* believe him.

And that was terrifying.

"Harmony?"

She shook her head, trying to bite her lip.

His breath brushed her cheek. "Harmony?"

She savored the gentle timbre of his voice. Soft, intimate. Kind. For her. It had been so long since she'd felt kindness.

Safety.

She sucked in a shaky breath. Wiping away hints of moisture at her eyelids, she apologized. "I'm sorry. My last boyfriend wasn't safe. I'm used to listening for a hint of a lie in every promise."

"I do not lie."

She laughed through her tears like a sprinkle of fresh rain. "I know. And that's something I love about y—"

Wait. What was she saying?

She coughed hard, choking on the unfinished words. *That's something I love about you.*

Faier waited for her to finish her sentence.

She cleared her throat. New tears in her eyes mixed with the old. "Um, anyway. I hope the Coast Guard makes him regret stranding us out here."

"If they do not, then you will do so."

"Me?"

Faier stood and waded into the island's tides. "Believe, Harmony."

"Yeah, right." She hobbled after him and favored her tender instep. "Sure. We'll just bring Lifet to justice. No problem."

"Yes, it will be no problem. You plan. I will return." He splashed to the ledge, dove in, and disappeared.

"Sure, I'll plot how to dismantle a Haitian gang with money, political allies, and warehouses of guns." She laughed hysterically. "We'll do it in our bare feet."

The empty, windswept island echoed her crazy laughter back at her, and she sat back down on the bumpy rock.

Deep in her heart, it was cathartic.

She'd never have the chance to bring a man like Lifet— or Jean-Baptiste, the real enemy—to justice. But fantasizing about it lifted the unending grind of fear and survival.

Her amusement died. She hugged herself and scanned the water.

Thank goodness Faier was on her side. He was a Sea Lord. He said he would protect her. And he would never, ever betray her.

NINE

Faier circled the island, searching for what Harmony would only see as a betrayal.

Fear thudded in his chest.

Was this Harmony's sacred island? Had he brought her to the single most dangerous place in the entire ocean?

There. A dark cave near the surface was too narrow to be a church entrance. He flicked his fins to inspect it anyway.

Ba-whoomph. Ba-woomph. The deadly bass note of the animal's soul jolted him backward.

Predator.

Apex predator.

He knew this deadly apex predator. What did the humans call it? It had a long, narrow body, four clawed limbs, and one long, flat tail. A land creature that hunted in water, it feasted on unwary fish and birds that perched on its rough, scaled back.

The name would come to him.

He veered from its hole.

Harmony's blood had doused the water with a tempting

scent. But now she rested on a safe boulder. Her blood had dissipated.

It would not lead this apex predator back to her.

And the predator was not the worst danger.

Faier continued his island tour.

What city was nearest to this surface location? Sireno's rebellious King Jolan pretended to be traditional, but he had refused the All-Council's bloodthirsty demands. He would shelter them.

Surely they were too far from Sireno.

Then, which city?

Aiycaya?

Faier swam. His heart pounded like the ticking of a human clock, urging him to speed.

I will protect you.

Warriors terrified Harmony. Now Faier searched for a way to make her vulnerable to them. She should fear Faier.

He searched for the sacred church. He would steal a mouthful of elixir. The liquid steeped with generations of Sea Opals would heal her injuries.

And it will transform her into a mermaid.

But only if their souls resonated.

At first, he had not thought she would ever resonate with him. He'd thought he resonated with her alone. As the nights and days passed, he wondered. She seemed closer. And just now she had become aware of his desires. She'd gazed on his hard cock and her pink tongue had touched her lips with interest. More than interest, her soul light had flared. She'd shared his desires.

His cock throbbed with welcome heat.

Was it possible? Had she begun to look past his scars and see the warrior within?

But now he searched for elixir that would destroy

Harmony's trust. Yes, it was to heal her, but she feared being dragged to the bottom of the sea. If she never drank the elixir she would never transform and she would not descend.

So he must tell her before she consumed the healing elixir. Even if she refused to drink it. He must not lie. He would bring her the elixir and tell her the risk.

Unless she had succumbed to her injuries. Many sea animals poisoned humans. Box jellyfish. Portuguese man-of-war. Blue-ring octopus. He had not memorized all.

Her foot and ankle had swelled.

Were urchins fatal as well?

If she became so ill that she could not communicate —if she were dying—would Faier respect her wishes? His heart thudded hard. No. Even though it would destroy this fragile trust growing between them, he could not let his soul mate die. He would feed her the elixir against her will.

Even thinking about betraying her made his chest clench.

Faier swam harder. His right leg twinged with the first warning signs of a cramp. He'd overextended by pushing the raft onto the shelf.

Harmony cannot swim.

Faier surfaced.

The second spire was forbidding and steep. Was it carved into a profile?

Perhaps.

Claw marks showed the apex predator hunted here. It attacked low-level prey.

Like Harmony...

Faier submerged and kicked to the third pillar. He lifted his head in passing—first to check for Harmony, then to look for the carvings—and now the raft surged between them, blocking his view.

Except it wasn't.

The raft coasted over the shallow rocks. The tide flooded in! Harmony hobbled across the dangerous, urchin-infested white coral after it. She winced.

She was bleeding again. And the waves carried her blood off the shelf in both directions over the water.

He kicked out of the surf to scream. Water choked him. His right leg cramped. He fell back, sealed his lungs to human, and shouted just before he submerged, "Harmony!"

She paused.

Water closed over his view.

He struggled to the surface, massaging his stabbing calf with one hand.

The raft broke free of the rocks with a shriek.

She hurried after it.

"Harmony!"

She paused again.

A long green log swam toward her.

The apex predator.

His blood ran cold. "Harmony!"

She hobbled closer and closer.

He dove, transitioning to mer, and kicked through the pain.

Life Tree, give me speed. Do not let me be too late.

TEN

Harmony chased the raft, cursing and crying.

Her foot hurt, her throat hurt, and Faier was taking an awfully long time. Long enough for the tide to change and the raft she needed for survival to float away.

She hobbled around the long spikes of the urchins and lunged for the raft—and missed. It was way too heavy for her to control. Her soaked, ragged dress clung to her knees.

Maybe he'd found something exciting.

A secret door that opened into the Mall of America food court.

Two kids selling fresh pineapple juice.

An old lady hawking thick sausage paté. A young, cool guy selling a calorie-dense, blended spaghetti shake. This kind of meal-replacement shake—as in, a full dinner plate was dumped directly into a blender—was found only in Haiti...

One tall, frosty glass of tap water.

Sure.

She lunged again.

A wave knocked the raft into her knees.

"Ack!"

She fell on her butt.

Her dress buttons ripped down the front. Her breasts flew free.

Great.

Just great.

The raft drifted in the opposite direction, scraping coral on the way. Its main support beam tore loose. The raft hung up on the coral and rocked.

A strong wave would lift it right out to sea.

She timed the waves and stood when one gave her a good push, then teetered on the sharp coral. Her dress flapped.

Harmony hugged her chest.

The raft support beam shrieked. Wave after wave yanked the slats apart wider and wider.

She had to get it off the ledge before the whole raft fell to pieces.

Harmony hobbled toward it.

If the raft floated out to sea, then what should she do?

Get in?

She couldn't live on this island. There was no spring. No stream. No well. No water whatsoever, as her parched mouth and dry throat reminded her. No food, grumbled her stomach. She'd eaten and drunk nothing since Faier had left, and that was another reason she tracked his absence.

No food, no water. Nothing to make a shelter. *Nothing*.

Maybe Faier could fish as he had on the raft. Maybe she could set up another dew catcher as Monsieur Joseph had taught her. Maybe she could survive.

But her ancestors had abandoned this island for a reason.

One solid wave from a mild tropical storm would wash over the whole island. The sea could sweep her away at any moment, even in her sleep.

A wave knocked Harmony forward. She fell on her knees. Her dress ripped clean apart.

Okay. Now it was a robe.

Wind and waves crashed. The raft squealed as the second support beam frayed.

She pushed herself up and slogged to the disintegrating raft.

A faint echo reached her. "—ony!"

She straightened and looked behind her. "Faier?"

Nothing but horizon, island, and empty ocean.

Huh.

She turned back to the raft.

On the other side, a long, dark, slimy green log drifted.

Finally, good fortune!

So, there was driftwood. She'd rescue the raft, somehow, and Faier could use the driftwood to repair the...

Wait.

Neutral white glowed around the log's edges.

Aura. The log had an aura.

She squinted.

Neutral white?

An animal.

A long, greenish-brown, partially submerged, log-shaped animal...

Danger.

She backed away just as the log—no—the massive crocodile lunged. *Roar*. It stomped on the raft as it surged for her face.

She froze.

Teeth. Snapped. An inch from her nose.

The raft collapsed in half like a bear trap. Wood smashed together over the crocodile's back and shattered.

The crocodile whipped away from her in surprise.

Its tail whooshed the air in front of her.

Her shelter tangled its feet.

It attacked the shreds of plastic and bits of crate in the shallows. Its anger echoed between the three pinnacles. *Roar!*

Harmony stood stupidly while the crocodile thrashed in fury. She felt nothing. Just an electric coldness.

She.

Couldn't.

Breathe.

Something dark erupted from the deep water next to her. An arm hooked around her waist. Dark head. Scars.

Faier.

He dragged her away.

The horizon rotated. Sky underfoot, sea overhead.

She plunged under water.

The shock of the cool jolted her out of her stupor. She struggled away from the surface where the crocodile was making so much noise splashing and roaring.

Her dress separated into fibers around her.

She was nude.

The crocodile was coming!

Panic seeped in.

She had to outswim the crocodile, and she had never learned how to swim.

The roaring and splashing dropped silent. The crocodile had escaped its entanglement. It chased them with the opening music of a horror movie.

Ba-whoomph. Ba-woomph.

Her heart jumped into her throat. Her chest trembled.

Faier gripped her shoulders. His dark, mauve-threaded eyes focused on her. His mouth was closed. But she heard his soft voice inside her chest, right behind her heart.

"Go."

He released her and kicked for the diving crocodile. An indomitable warrior, he faced the charging reptile barehanded.

The crocodile slashed his chest. Red marks appeared, and blood puffed in the water. He kicked his big fins and flew over the crocodile's bumpy back. The crocodile twisted after him. He outpaced its turn, straddled the beast, and looped his arms around its neck in a chokehold. The crocodile rolled. Faier rolled with it and then broke free.

The crocodile swam after him, leaving her.

This was how he'd earned the scars. He battled the deadly monster with grace. He led it out to sea.

Her heart calmed. Faier would get away. She had to wait for him to come back and rescue her.

Rescue her from being underwater.

Right.

Harmony held her breath.

But...huh.

Did swimming always feel so...freeing?

The entire ocean spread around her. Floating in the middle of it felt natural. She didn't even need to breathe. But that was crazy, wasn't it? She must breathe.

Harmony wiggled.

She didn't ascend. Her human toes looked so little in comparison to Faier's long fins. The surface remained far away.

But she wasn't too worried about it either.

Why wasn't she worried? Panicked? Drowning?

It made no sense.

She had to be dreaming.

Faier returned. He'd led the crocodile far out to sea. Now he searched the surface of the water, his two long fins propelling him quickly. He didn't see her. So he looked down.

He flew to her. Concern glowed in his aura.

Blood flowed from long slashes across his chest. Scars obscured his compass rose.

He cared.

Her heart contracted again.

She had once called him a monster. Beneath those surface scars, he was a good man.

At least, in this dream world where she was floating underwater like it was no big deal, he was a good man.

"Harmony." He stopped in front of her. Sunlight glimmered from the surface behind him. His concern morphed into confusion. Even with his mouth closed, his voice reached her. "You are alive."

She heard him inside her chest, in a cavity behind her heart, and answered in the same natural, closemouthed, chest-vibrating way. "You saved me."

His brows shot for his hairline. He jolted, both palms open, his entire body electrified in surprise.

Was her gratitude really so surprising? She needed to fix his surprise by expressing her gratitude more.

The air—or water?—between them grew warm as she drifted into his orbit.

"You saved me again." Harmony touched his scarred forearm. "And I'm sorry I made you feel bad. Your scars don't bother me. Not at all."

He looked at her touch without seeming to understand. "Scars? But...you..."

She rested her fingertips lightly on the teeth marks.

Fresh cuts too. Angry, red slashes he'd gotten from saving her.

Again.

"Me?" She floated closer, giving in to the wish that had called her soul forth this entire time.

He drifted back, not understanding her intention, his surprise giving way to a slight frown. "Yes, you..."

He said they'd kissed? No, that she had kissed him? Well, this time, she would remember.

His lips parted as if he were about to take a breath and ask her what she was doing. "You are a—"

She aimed for his mouth and brushed his lips.

They kissed.

Lips touched, the briefest union, and parted again. Sparkles flickered in her veins like the blue luminescence from her fingertips stirring the ocean in the twilight. She felt happy, for the first time in forever, and *alive*.

His lips cracked open. "Harmony."

Was he trying to draw back?

Normally Harmony would let him. She never took the initiative.

But Faier was different. He held himself back, taking care of her, still protecting her. In the dream world, his control drove her wild.

She pushed forward, her tongue thrusting into his too-willing mouth.

He groaned in his chest, the same way he spoke. "You kiss me. Remember this time."

"I'll never forget. I want to do everything to you."

Heat seduced her mouth. Hunger curled in her belly and dragged her forward. She wove eager fingers into his locks of dark hair and meshed his lips with hers. Wet heat mixed with the salt of the ocean.

He tasted like freedom. Like water. Like life-giving rain.

She sucked him in, consuming all of him. A primal warrior whose aura glowed with addictive heat. A friend and ally who had become so much more.

"No," he said, low, his control holding on by a thread. "Your soul is not mine."

"Isn't it?" She pressed her chocolate-kiss nipples to his hot chest and canted her hips, writhing. "Don't you feel what I do?"

He did feel what she did. His control broke.

His arms tightened around her back. His biceps flexed. His fingers lowered, feeling the shape of her nude body pressed to his. The curve of her waist. The flare of her hip. His fingers dug in.

Her pussy throbbed. She moaned, giving herself to him, finally sheltering in his arms the way she'd dreamed since the moment of their first meeting.

His large, steady thigh nudged between hers.

Yes.

She wrapped her thighs around his and writhed. He was her protector. Her warrior. The motion dragged her throbbing clit across his taut muscle. She disappeared into pleasure.

He growled deep and kissed across her jaw, down the column of her sensitive neck to her breasts. Possessing her just the way she wanted.

She arched, guiding him to her dream.

He dragged one nipple into his mouth. Pinpricks of desire lanced her throbbing pussy.

She tangled her hands in his hair. *More.* She wanted so much more.

This was the best dream ever—

Someone shouted. Arms ripped her away from Faier.

She thrashed.

Faier cried out. "Swim to the land!"

But she couldn't swim anywhere. Enemy warriors holding long tridents, bristling with daggers and inked with strange tattoos, surrounded them.

One held a sharp blade to her neck.

ELEVEN

Faier bashed the dagger from the idiot warrior in teal and white tattoos who threatened Harmony.

That warrior dropped his blade and tumbled back with a cry.

Other warriors flew around them in a hunting formation.

Harmony hovered, frozen.

He dragged her into his arms under his protection. "You will not *dare* attack a sacred bride!"

The new warriors slowed. They circled for an opening to separate him from Harmony.

Faier evaluated the war party. Three low-level warriors. Two leaders. All armed with long, sharp tridents and short bicep-bound daggers.

Standard escort for a sacred island bride.

Faier's blood pumped. Harmony's taste lingered on his lips. Her acceptance heated his chest and her arousal pulsed in his hard cock.

No one would take her from him.

The youngest, least-experienced warrior—by the

simplicity and barrenness of his tropical pink tattoos—spoke to them. His words vibrated in his chest. "*Aiycaya a n'aila l'ai no ana pu?*"

Harmony's arms tightened around Faier's neck. "What's he saying?"

"I do not know."

"What? How can you not know your language?"

"It is not my language," he explained with soothing patience he did not feel. "It is the language of your tribe."

"Oh. My tribe? Then they are…?"

"Warriors of Aiycaya," he guessed.

Her mouth snapped shut. Her soul light darkened in fear.

The youngest warrior darted to her. "*Aiycaya l'ai no ana pu?*"

She hid her face in Faier's shoulder. "Eep!"

The young warrior growled low in his tropical pink chest. "*L'ai no ana pu!*"

Faier's chest thrummed with readiness. "Calm. You frighten her."

One leader—sharp featured, with mango tattoos—made an irritated comment. The young warrior's eyes flashed with embarrassment.

Thud. Behind Faier, the idiot teal-and-white warrior thumped Faier's calf with the hard butt of his trident.

An opportunity.

Faier whirled and hooked the trident in his elbow.

Harmony shrieked.

Faier continued his whirl and dragged the idiot warrior in a circle. The warrior fought him like a hooked skipjack. Faier slammed him into the other two.

The tropical-pink warrior kicked free.

Faier shoved the others back.

They caught themselves, glowed with fury, and attacked.

"I have a bride!" Faier snarled, bracing to protect Harmony.

The second leader, with intricate blue-green tattoos, dealt a short, clipped order.

Both warriors ignored him and charged.

The mango leader snapped.

They pulled up like he'd grabbed their hair.

So, the sharp-featured mango warrior was the true leader. The blue-seas warrior was a lesser leader trying to assert authority. And the young hot-pink warrior berating the insolent warriors and fawning over the mango leader was...

What was he?

The hot-pink warrior darted to them once more. He moved without discipline. And he alone addressed Harmony. "*Su ala no laina a. Tu su la no.*"

A bad feeling pooled in Faier's chest.

She almost strangled Faier in her tight grip. "What does he want?"

Faier did not understand any words, but the warrior's body language was unmistakable.

"Something he will never have," Faier growled.

"Me." She swallowed. Her hands shook. "Sorry. I'm supposed to order them. But I don't know how."

"Tell them."

"Just tell them? They'll listen? Are you sure?"

"You are powerful."

She moaned.

"*Salana na ala no.*" The youngest warrior held out his hand to Harmony.

She stared at his outstretched hand in horror. "No..."

"Believe," Faier insisted.

He evaluated the escort for another opportunity. Their coordination was not good. He could...hmm...

The young warrior continued to lure Harmony, ignoring her mounting distress. "*Asa la sana pu?*"

She shrieked. "Leave me alone!"

The hot-pink warrior looked startled and then offended.

Faier stroked her shoulder, calming and protecting her. It was a start.

The hot-pink warrior regrouped his warriors, and they muttered among themselves.

The blue-green leader articulated one word. "English."

The hot-pink warrior dismissed him and jabbered on in their language.

"Are they going away?" she asked Faier.

"For the moment."

"Now what are they doing?"

"They are debating whether to speak to you in English."

She blinked. "They speak English?"

"Yes."

"Seriously? They understand what we're saying? Right now?"

"English is the common language of warriors."

"So why are they pretending they can't understand?"

"They do not pretend. The warrior speaks to you in his city's language of brides. Changing to English forces him to admit you are not his city's sacred bride."

"Ugh." She shuddered and rested her chin on his shoulder. "Lifet used to speak Kreyòl when he didn't want me to know what he was saying. It's torture."

"Tell them."

"Tell them what?"

"Speaking a language other than English is torture."

"What good will that do?"

"They will speak English."

"Okay." She swallowed hard. Her vibrations turned ragged and her soul light darkened. "Tell them. Just tell them. Okay."

The hot-pink warrior bowed to Harmony and yammered in his language once more.

"Um." She swallowed. "E-excuse me."

The hot-pink warrior talked over her.

She turned her tremulous gaze on Faier. "I tried."

"Again." Faier nudged her encouragingly. "Order them to speak English. What do you fear?"

"Do you see all those knives and spears?"

"They will not injure you. Believe."

"B-believe." Her light dimmed further. "S-sure."

The hot-pink warrior snarled at him in English. "Do not harass my sacred bride. I will kill you!"

"Speak English," Faier returned on Harmony's behalf.

"We speak the sacred language."

Faier waited.

Harmony hid her face, terrified beyond her limit.

Faier answered, "She does not."

The hot-pink warrior's mouth flattened with disbelief. "She *is* my sacred bride." He puffed out his narrow chest. "I am King Kayo of Aiycaya."

"King!" Faier had seen a lot of kings. This young male could not lead a hunting party, much less rule a city.

Harmony lifted her head. "King?"

"You, sacred bride, accept my offering and come with me." King Kayo reached into the woven bag at his slender hip and held out a large, pearly mating gem.

Faier's heart stung. He should have defied the Coast

Guard and carried his offering to give to Harmony. His arm tightened around her.

Harmony stared at the king's offering. "That's a Sea Opal."

"Yes, my sacred bride. It is my gift to you."

"No." She rubbed her forehead as though she experienced sudden head pain. The fog cleared from her eyes, and heavy resignation replaced it. "No. It's not for me. I don't want to go with you. Don't make me go to the bottom of the sea and consume my soul."

"Consume your soul?" King Kayo tilted his head. "I will care for you. You will join with me and give me a young fry."

She again turned to Faier. "Tell me what to do."

"Tell him no."

"I did."

"Again—"

"Release her, exile!" King Kayo raised his trident in warning. "If you do not unhand her I will kill you!"

She whipped to King Kayo. Fear wrapped her in paralyzing bindings.

Faier ignored him to reach her. "You can order—"

"Silence!" King Kayo shook his trident again. "You agitate my sacred bride. Do it again and I will end you."

Harmony's shut her eyes tight. "No..."

Faier straightened, sheltering her with his arms. He'd encouraged her to issue orders because he was used to Queens Lucy, Aya, and Elyssa commanding armies. They would defy the All-Council itself without fear.

Harmony had just escaped a relationship that had bruised more than her body. She was unable to command these five armed warriors. He asked for too much and it was breaking her.

Faier growled at the king. "Leave us."

The king laughed. "Leave you? Yes, beg me for your life. You know how this futile standoff ends."

"I will not ask again."

"You wield no weapon, exile. And you are tired, weak, and malnourished. There is one of you and five of us. I will send you into the Blacknight Sea with my own trident and there is nothing you can—"

Harmony pushed off of Faier and shrieked. "D-do you promise not to hurt him?"

"Hurt who?" Faier asked, his arms now strangely empty.

King Kayo also looked confused. "The exile will not hurt me, my sacred bride."

"No." She almost couldn't speak she was so terrified. She gestured behind her at Faier. "Him. If I go with you, do you promise not to hurt him?"

Faier's heart sank. "Harmony. Do not go with this king."

"B-but..." She rested a trembling hand on Faier's forearm. "Maybe it's for the best."

"What is for the best?"

"He wants me." She swallowed hard. "N-not you. S-so if he takes me then you can—"

"No." He rejected her flatly.

"What choice do we have, Faier?" She vibrated with helpless fear. "Tell me. Right now. What choice do we have?"

"I will fight to the death to—"

"No! You can't." She choked on a sob. "I can't lose you, too."

"But—"

"Evens is kidnapped. Monsieur Joseph is crippled."

Harmony's palm pushed against Faier's forearm. "I can't let you die. Not when I can stop it."

She was trying to be heroic.

His heart clenched.

Unsettling, jittery fear seeped into the black hole in his belly. His scars pulsed. His injuries twinged. Without Harmony he had nothing. He had no city, no Life Tree, and he would die alone.

"I cannot let you make this sacrifice," he said quietly.

"You have to." Her soul darkened. "It's only a little while. And it's not my life. It's my b-body. And womb. And s-soul."

His fingers loosened.

She drifted out of his grasp and began to turn, wretched and horrified, toward King Kayo.

"No." Faier kicked forward to reach for her. He'd rather die than—

A trident blade flashed over his forearm. He jerked back. The blade slashed the water and cut the back of his hand.

The other two warriors had crept closer. Now Harmony was clear. They attacked.

Harmony shrieked and hugged herself.

King Kayo swam in front of her as a protective buffer.

The teal-and-white warrior thrashed to bring his blade up again.

Faier rolled over that warrior's back. Blades scraped his arms. Blood scented the water.

The more cautious bright-yellow warrior jabbed his trident at Faier's midsection.

Faier jackknifed.

He overextended.

Faier grabbed the trident and yanked. The bright-yellow warrior struggled for the long handle. Faier smacked the blunt end into his nose. He grunted in pain, and his nose bled. Faier kicked hard and bowled him over. He still kept a hold on his trident with both hands.

The dagger at his bicep passed Faier's face.

He grabbed the pommel and yanked the blade free.

Now he was armed.

The bright-yellow warrior cupped his nose with one hand.

The more aggressive teal-and-white-tattooed warrior put his head down and his trident up.

"Chiba. Kusi," the blue-green leader snapped. "Stop your attack."

The teal-and-white warrior barreled toward Faier.

"Kusi!"

Faier parried his headlong attack with a neat swipe of his blade and rotated to face the yellow Chiba.

"Stop. King Kayo did not order your attack!"

"It does not matter, Xarin." The young king eagerly watched the fight. "This will end soon. Right?"

"I am not sure."

Cautious Chiba dropped his bloody hand to his trident and flew at Faier. Behind Faier, Kusi once more charged. Faier rolled around both their attacks, tangled the two tridents, and kicked. Kusi's third tine snapped off in the clash. Faier dove and collected it.

Now he had two weapons.

"He is arming himself," the blue-green leader, Xarin, pointed out.

"We will take those weapons away once Chiba and Kusi finish practicing against him. Right, First Lieutenant Tibe?"

The mango warrior's thin lips sharpened into what could be a smile. "Of course, my king."

While the young king eagerly watched the fight, Harmony hunched in on herself like a dark spot in the middle of the ocean. "Leave him alone!"

Curse these warriors for hurting and frightening her.

He had to reach her. "You are not so helpless. Believe."

She straightened.

Faier parried the next attacks, watching for his opportunity to reach out to her and help her escape. *You have choices.* He needed to figure out how to show her the way.

She looked up at the surface.

Yes, the surface. She could escape to land.

Faier parried another slash and thrust his knife beneath Kusi's blade. The aggressive warrior evaded. Faier twirled beneath Chiba's trident and switched hands with his blade.

His right calf twinged.

Harmony wiggled. Her little human feet wobbled.

Faier concentrated on giving a good fight. He would distract King Kayo while she snuck—

"Hey!" Harmony vibrated hard, her shout echoing in the water. "I'm escaping! Leave him alone! Look at me!"

Curse it.

She moved so slowly and inefficiently, King Kayo barely noticed.

"Hey!"

Bah-woomph. Bah-woomph.

Faier avoided Chiba's slash and looked up.

The crocodile had returned. It floated on the surface like a log.

Harmony shouted at the king and the other warriors. But they all ignored her. She sounded scared and frustrated like she was going to cry.

She swam underneath the crocodile. "Hey, crocodile! Attack these mermen, okay?"

It rolled. Its claws slashed her hair.

"No!" Faier broke free of the attack and kicked for her. His right leg twinged more painfully. "You are not skilled enough to evade the crocodile. Stop!"

Her soul light brightened and darkened. She was even more terrified and still trying to save him.

His torn muscles spasmed.

"Kusi. Chiba." First Lieutenant Tibe jerked his chin. "End this."

He tried to kick through the cramp, but he couldn't evade attacks, rescue Harmony, and endure his old pain. He punched his calf, trying to free the frozen muscle.

King Kayo laughed and lunged forward. He brought his trident to Faier's neck. "You stop, exile."

Kusi and Chiba grappled with Faier and recovered his stolen blade. Their daggers bit into his back and bottom.

Faier clenched his teeth. "Save her."

Xarin swam between Kusi and Chiba. He disarmed and bound Faier. But Faier secretly held on to the fragment of tine.

"What?" King Kayo grinned.

"From the crocodile."

The king finally followed Faier's bound gaze and exclaimed.

The crocodile dove and opened its toothy maw. Harmony scrambled away from its jaws.

King Kayo kicked hard. His trident extended, he rammed the beast.

They tumbled over and over in the water. The crocodile thrashed. King Kayo evaded in a blur of hot pink and masking bubbles. Deadly blades crossed impenetrable hide and eviscerating claws.

Behind Faier, Xarin kicked toward the fight.

First Lieutenant Tibe stopped him. "Xarin."

"King Kayo needs help."

"Nonsense. Give him his glory."

Xarin crossed his arms. His gaze locked on the distant fight.

The water stilled.

Harmony was alive.

Faier's heart calmed. His wrists flexed in the tight binding. He positioned the tip of the stolen trident tine to rub it. The bindings frayed.

He could still get free.

King Kayo flew to them, exultant. The dead body of the crocodile plowed the water, speared on the end of his trident. He cupped Harmony to his side.

A conquering king.

Harmony's soul dimmed, and her hands covered her eyes.

"Ah." First Lieutenant Tibe smiled, arms out to greet the returning young male. "King Kayo, expert fighting, as usual."

"I slew the monster and defended my sacred bride." His chest glowed with eager approval. "Not even my father accomplished so many honors in one journey."

"You are right, my king."

The king frowned. "What are you doing there, Xarin?"

Xarin stopped, the crocodile half onto his trident. "Freeing your trident."

"Taking my prize?"

The other warriors snickered.

"To free your trident," Xarin repeated stiffly over the snickers. "So you will have weapons free to comfort your sacred bride."

"Comfort?"

Xarin pointed. "Your sacred bride."

"Yes, I know that is my..." He suddenly noticed Harmony's desperation. "Do not fear, my sacred bride. I have vanquished the monster."

Her shoulders hunched.

"That upsets her," Xarin said.

"I see that," King Kayo snapped. "We have lingered too long on the surface. That is why she is scared. We must hurry to the Life Tree to marry. Xarin, you carry my trophy."

Xarin finished freeing King Kayo's trident, bound the crocodile's legs to its body like a long torpedo, and looped the end of the rope to drag it through the water.

"Tibe. Are you ready?"

"Journey without me." First Lieutenant Tibe gripped his trident and approached Faier coldly. "I will finish the exile and join you."

Harmony's hands dropped. "Finish the...? No. No!"

Her voice edged into dangerous hysteria. The bones in Faier's chest vibrated painfully.

King Kayo stopped. "My sacred bride, do not be alarmed."

"You have to let him go."

"Let him go?" King Kayo laughed. "This male is a dangerous exile. He has committed an unforgivable dishonor against Aiycaya. We cannot let him go."

"But...but..."

"Do you pity him? He tricked you."

"He didn't trick me. You tricked me!"

"This exile transformed you into a bride and lured you to the open waters where you cannot survive."

"He saved me." But she sounded less certain. "Faier? Why *am* I underwater?"

Faier paused his subtle motion of sawing the bindings. "I do not know."

"How—"

"He lies," King Kayo interrupted flatly. "He stole elixir from this island and fed it to you."

"Elixir? You drugged me?"

Mistrust darkened her heart and her soul.

Her doubts ripped his heart out.

"I did nothing against your wishes," Faier said, hurt.

"Another lie." King Kayo waved his trident at First Lieutenant Tibe. "Execute him."

First Lieutenant Tibe's teeth gleamed. He bowed. "My king."

"Execute!" Harmony pushed away from the king. "No."

Surprised, King Kayo let her go. "My sacred bride, it is necessary to—"

"No!"

"Do not be distressed. He is only an exile."

"But he's already injured!"

"That is common of exiles."

While they argued, First Lieutenant Tibe moved his long trident blade in front of Faier. Slow, controlled. "You move well for an exile. Where were you from?"

Faier followed the movements to gauge Tibe's skill. "Why should I tell you?"

"Because soon it will not matter."

Tibe's arm flashed. *Wham.* The trident lodged in the point of Faier's jaw, its tip protruding to the underside of his tongue.

"Well?"

Blood and pain blinded Faier.

His jaw throbbed. Tibe had speared him like a fish.

Time. He needed time.

Faier's chest vibrated. "Nerissa."

"Nerissa?" A new light gleamed in the first lieutenant's cold eyes. "You must be the last survivor. Let me change that."

He yanked the blade free.

Faier bent over. Salt water invaded his mouth from the wrong direction. His wound stung.

"Faier?" Harmony's cry reached him through the fog.

Someone yanked his head up. He cracked his eyes open.

Tibe's sneer was audible as he raised his voice. "My king, take your sacred bride away."

"But—stop. Stop! Faier? They're not listening to me. You said they would listen. Faier!"

The bindings were still too tight. Faier sawed faster. He had no intention of dying.

Harmony screamed. "*Stop!*"

Her high pitch was ocean-shattering.

A dark reverberation of horror echoed in his chest. Somewhere, a Life Tree had been pulled up by its roots and groaned a death cry, dooming its city and all its mer. His tear ducts prickled. He wanted to throw up and cry.

He shuddered.

The other warriors also curled in on themselves. Their soul lights fluctuated dark to light. The king swallowed convulsively. Even Tibe lowered his trident, jaw working, and looked unwell.

Harmony's fearful darkness eased.

Dragged to the absolute edge of desperation, she issued her first wobbly order. "Don't you hurt him."

Faier wanted to cheer.

He choked on blood.

The warriors collected themselves, shaking their

muscles and cracking joints. They did not cheer her for exercising her powers. No, they ignored her.

She was right. He had lied to her.

He had spent so long with rebels who listened to their females that he had forgotten how badly traditionalists behaved. Or perhaps Aiycaya ignored its brides more than the other cities.

From the moment he'd brought Harmony to this island she had been in terrible danger and now he had failed on every level to protect her.

His soul wept.

First Lieutenant Tibe pointed his trident at King Kayo. "This is why you should have taken away your sacred bride."

The king flushed. "We were leaving. You moved too quickly."

Tibe's lips curled in a snarl. "Leave us now."

King Kayo supplicated Harmony. "Come, my sacred bride."

She hugged herself, shaking with fear and anger. "No."

"Your destiny lies with me."

"No, no."

"But you must—"

"No! Look." She swallowed hard and faced the king with noble sacrifice in her eyes. "I already said I would go with you. As your sacred bride even."

Faier's chest squeezed.

"*If* you promised not to hurt him." She glared at the hot-pink male. "Okay? Do you understand?"

The male understood, and he looked at Faier strangely. "I understand your words."

"So? Your answer? Will you agree?" Her voice shook.

Faier couldn't help himself. His chest vibrated. "Do not join with him."

"No, Faier." She whipped to him. Fearless, unflinching, she looked past his scars and straight into his eyes. Into his heart. Into his soul. "I don't understand if you drugged me or if it was an accident."

He shook his head. He had done neither.

"But you've only tried to help me, and I can't watch you get hurt like Monsieur Joseph or my cousin or..." She swallowed again. "I can't fight these guys. I can't even swim. My one idea to distract them with the crocodile backfired and got you caught."

He shook his head again. She had not distracted him. His body had failed.

"But being a useless prize who sits on a shelf, helpless, is something I can do." She saw his refusal and her vibrations broke. "I don't want this either. If you have another idea, tell me now."

He needed her to save herself. Not worry about him.

But she was exactly the same. She wanted to save him and not worry about herself.

No, Harmony. Please. I could not live without you You must save yourself.

She turned to King Kayo. "Promise you won't harm Faier. Promise you'll let him go."

King Kayo shrugged. "I will not harm him."

"Okay." She squared her shoulders. "Okay, then. I'll go with you."

Faier's heartbeat thudded in his ears.

The battle wasn't over.

She wiggled her small human legs and feet, barely moving. The king flicked closer and folded her into his arms. She rested her forearms on his chest to keep a distance between their bodies.

Watching her choice ripped Faier's heart in half.

"Harmo—"

Tibe wrenched Faier's head back. His jaw radiated pain. "Silence."

Harmony struggled in King Kayo's arms. "You promised not to hurt him!"

King Kayo looked surprised. "I am not."

"Your people are."

"He fights his fate."

"You're supposed to let him go!"

"My sacred bride, that is impossible."

"But you promised!"

"I promised not to cause harm. And I am not." His cocky tone and attitude said he had only agreed to the part of the promise he'd intended to keep. Now, he acted as though he had won. "I keep my vow."

She wilted. Her power drained into the ocean. She whimpered, losing her energy just like she had during their first meeting in the storm when she'd half-rescued herself and then given up.

"You have to let him go. It's all I ask. I beg you."

Faier's heart broke.

King Kayo swallowed hard. His voice sounded rough yet noble in his chest, mature for his years, and finally like a king. "An exile cannot terrorize our sacred islands."

"He's not. I swear. He's not."

"It is our law, sacred bride."

"You're the king."

"And even I am the law's prisoner."

"Please," she whimpered. "Please."

He placed a gentle arm around her shoulder. "Come this way. Your destiny awaits."

"No." She resisted with a helpless moan. "No..."

Xarin squared his shoulders. "King Kayo. Perhaps your sacred bride will accept his fate after she understands his crimes."

King Kayo's expression hardened. "I have explained them."

Xarin stiffened to match and spoke even more formally. "I meant after a judgment of the elders. A traditional trial."

"For an exile?" First Lieutenant Tibe said with disgust.

Chiba and Kusi snorted.

King Kayo matched his opinion. "Delay is unnecessary."

Xarin's hands clenched his trident. "Perhaps...for the sacred bride...a slight delay will be calming..."

King Kayo ignored that reasoning. "He is an exile! It is not as though a city will avenge his death."

"Yes." Harmony's soul brightened. "Yes! Faier's not really an exile. He's from—"

"Look, my sacred bride already feels better." King Kayo lifted his chin at Xarin arrogantly. "Your suggestion is unnecessary, *Second Lieutenant*."

The blue-green warrior's brows drew together with worry, and he bowed. "My king."

"Come, my sacred bride. Xarin. Kusi. Chiba."

The other warriors flew to him.

Harmony struggled. "But— You don't—"

"First Lieutenant Tibe, we will go ahead."

"Listen to me. Faier isn't an exile! He's—hey!"

The king pressed Harmony to his side and kicked.

She argued desperately.

King Kayo chatted over her with Chiba in his language.

First Lieutenant Tibe turned to Faier. "I suppose I should ask a few questions. Such as, what did your sacred bride mean when she said you were not an exile? Will your death loose the wrath of another city on our heads?"

Faier strained against the sawed bindings.

They loosened. Not enough.

"But..." Tibe lifted his trident. "I do not care."

Tibe whirled his trident.

Faier broke the bindings.

Tibe's trident aimed at Faier's center.

Faier twisted to escape...

Not enough.

Stab.

Tibe's trident buried deep into the left side of Faier's abdomen.

That entire side of his body turned cold and then lit on fire.

Tibe yanked the trident out.

Pain lanced him again. His blood flooded the water. He cupped the wound. His life leaked out between his shivering fingers.

Tibe aimed at the center of Faier's chest. "Let us try that again. Without the twisting."

Faier's body shook.

The blow was mortal.

He was dying. Like an exile. Alone.

In the distance, Harmony screamed.

<h1 style="text-align:center">TWELVE</h1>

tab. Stab. Stab.

Harmony's left side split open. Her insides leaked out.

She released King Kayo and grabbed her whole, unblemished waist. She wasn't hurt. But her muscles tensed. She was being ripped open. *Stab.*

She arched her back in agony.

Her scream erupted from her soul.

Around her, the warriors flurried.

"My sacred bride!" King Kayo's face wavered in and out of focus. "What is it? What attacks you? My sacred bride!"

The agony continued.

She couldn't stop screaming.

And then she didn't want to.

Listen. Hear me, she silently begged the warriors.

"Calm, my sacred bride. I beg you!"

No. I refuse.

More flurries of activity.

"Why have you returned?" The hooked nose of the mango warrior named Tibe wavered into focus. "Ah. My king, her pain is not surprising. The exile fed her elixir. She transformed because they entangled their souls. We sever that connection with his death."

"But she is innocent. The exile deserves death."

"Law must prevail."

The blue-green warrior, Xarin, spoke. "There is another way. Delay judgment to—"

"I told you to be silent, Xarin! You are not king. I am king!"

"My king." The teal-and-white warrior, Kusi, hugged his chest. "Make her stop."

"The scream is agonizing," pineapple-yellow warrior Chiba agreed.

"She will stop screaming when he is dead," Tibe said. "I will end him."

"Wait, First Lieutenant Tibe. If her sadness increases any more, she may never produce a healthy young fry."

"King Kayo, that tragedy may happen, but justice must be served. Even a king is not above the law."

"Yes. You are right. Justice matters... No."

"I am ending him now, my king."

"Stop! All of you stop. My sacred bride cannot carry such hurt. This is too painful."

"The law—"

"The law of the mer is to not injure sacred brides. They are sacred! Harming the exile harms her. We will disentangle their souls another way!"

"But, my king-—"

"You, Xarin, bind his injury. We will disentangle their souls at the Life Tree. My sacred bride will calm!"

The ocean fell silent.

The pain receded to a dull, throbbing ache.

Without meaning to, she stopped screaming.

Her breath wouldn't go in. Oh, she was underwater, so of course it wouldn't. But she felt stunned, as if someone had slammed her into concrete and knocked the breath right out of her.

King Kayo's worried face swam into focus. His brows lifted. "My sacred bride. You have quieted."

Beyond him, Xarin tied seaweed around Faier's waist.

Faier looked woozy and sick. Blood clouded the water. He rested his hands on top of the bandage.

Tibe complained. "You should not waste our bandages on an exile."

"I 'waste it' on my sacred bride," King Kayo sniped. "Hurry now to the Life Tree."

She looked over his shoulder at Faier. "Are you going to leave him like this?"

"No," the king said.

Relief eased her heart. Even if the crocodile was dead, Faier wouldn't survive alone with such a terrible injury.

"We must ensure he is dead ourselves."

Her stomach rolled.

King Kayo caught himself. "After the judgment of the elders."

The other warriors floated around Faier. They attached a noose to his wrists and pulled him through the water. Down, down, into the deep.

Descending into the ocean felt like flying. Soaring underwater into an endless blue sky. Not blue in the usual sense, but clear, like air, and she saw for miles. Probably to the sea floor. If she squinted, she could almost see to the glimmering surface, even though that view grew congested with layers upon layers of shimmering fish.

Fish swarmed them, enmeshing the mer into the sea in a

way humans never would be. Tiny see-through creatures and schools of giants twice her size, hundreds deep.

Every fish made its own particular noise and glowed with soft light. Sponges, minnows, sprites. She had seen these white auras before on land animals. The undersea animals glowed the same. She'd never heard the music.

Each fish announced itself with a bass "whoomph" or a high pitched "waw-waw." New Age flute and panpipes, like what used to float out of the scented crystal-filled shop near her mom's apartment. Peaceful, soothing, natural.

Along with the occasional "Na-na, na-na" *Jaws* music as a large, multitoothed denizen swerved close. One particular nasty big fish with crooked teeth tried to chomp the dead crocodile—and then blood-streaked Faier. Xarin whirled and slashed it with his trident. It swerved away.

The warriors swam in formation: Kusi in the lead, then Chiba and First Lieutenant Tibe around her and King Kayo, and Xarin in the back dragging both Faier and the dead crocodile. King Kayo's two trophies. The warriors chatted in their tribal language, excluding her again. Where was her translator, Evens, when she needed him?

Oh, Evens... She hoped he was safe. He knew English thanks to her, French from school, Kreyòl because everyone besides her spoke it, and the tribal language from his mom. She missed him so much, it hurt.

At the appearance of the crooked-tooth giant, the warriors grew more animated.

Xarin made a comment in the tribal language. King Kayo snarled. Xarin darkened and fell silent.

The other warriors snickered.

King Kayo told Harmony in English, "You will stay here with Xarin while we hunt."

Sharp fear streaked into her. He was abandoning her in

the middle of the deadly ocean! She gripped his shoulder. "What?"

"We hunt the bluefin." He pointed his trident at the big fish lingering for another chance to attack. "The blood has lured it. Wait here. It is a wild fight."

He released her.

The woolen ocean water wrapped a strange blanket around her. Rather than feeling cold, the water felt thicker the deeper they swam. Now it thickened to syrup.

She couldn't move.

"King Kayo!"

He returned to her elbow. "What is it, my sacred bride?"

"I can't swim!"

"Do not swim here. Float."

"B-but I can't—there are so many—is this really safe?"

"So long as no predators come."

"Ah! What if more predators come?"

"Xarin will protect you."

"But he's already protecting Faier."

"He will drop the exile to protect you. Oi, Xarin! Do not let those sucker fish damage my trophy."

The blue-green warrior swept his trident over the crocodile and dislodged multiple slender fish. They flew like a cloud of flies and landed again.

Some latched on to Faier.

He only brushed one from his face. It fluttered and then suctioned his cheek just below his closed left eye. He did not wave it away again.

"My king." His favorite lieutenant, Tibe, sidled close. "We must hunt now or lose our chance."

"No!" She grabbed on to King Kayo. "It's too dangerous!"

Tibe lifted his shoulders. "If your bride doubts Xarin's abilities, I will guard her, and Xarin can hunt with you."

"No, Tibe, you are much more fun to hunt with. Xarin whines at me to not take so many risks."

"You are capable of many great achievements, my king."

"Exactly. You understand." King Kayo rested his calming hand on hers. "We will go a short time."

"But..." In the distance, another tiny bluefin appeared. She pointed, triumphant. "There's another one!"

He squinted. His tone wavered. "Eh...it is very far away..."

"It's not safe to leave me here."

"Very well. Tibe will—"

"With anyone!"

"—keep you safe." He vibrated in his chest to call the warrior back. "Ti—"

"No!" She grappled with him, and his chest vibration cut off. "That man *stabbed* Faier."

"On my orders."

"And ever since we stopped, the cloud of little fish has grown. And look. Now's there's bigger fish. Soon, you won't have any trophy left."

He wavered.

"And I can't swim," she repeated. "At all."

"You are a sacred bride."

"*At all.*"

He frowned. Just like Faier, he couldn't believe she hadn't been taught the basics. "You will be fine."

"But—"

"My king!" Tibe waved. "We must hunt."

"Coming." King Kayo removed her hands and held her at a distance. "Remain here."

Protestations silently died in her mind.

She watched him kick away.

Okay. Yes, she was terrified. But she didn't want to be useless. This was an opportunity.

She turned and kicked for Faier.

He noted her approach. As did Xarin. But the blue-green warrior was too busy slicing at small invaders. He did not try to stop her.

She reached Faier and shooed away the parasitic fish. "I'm sorry. I'm so sorry. I did everything wrong. I never wanted you to get hurt."

His aura brightened and his chest vibrated. "Do not injure yourself with regrets."

"I didn't. You did. I'm sorry." She floated in front of Faier, rubbing her healed wrists. "If I'd met you before Lifet I think I could have done it. I could have ordered them. I'll try again."

He regarded her with comforting calm. "Do not fret. Your bruises are healed on the outside, not within."

Tears pricked her eyes. He understood and forgave her. She swallowed hard. "Tell me what to do."

"Stay with the king." He flicked an unsteady gaze beyond alert Xarin to where the hot-pink male conferenced eagerly one last time with Tibe and the others. "He is young but will not cause you harm."

"Okay. But how can I help you?"

A flicker of dry amusement crossed his pained face. "It may be too late for me."

Her heart squeezed. She brushed away the lingering parasitic fish and hovered her hand over the bandage, wishing she could do something, anything. "No, Faier. You have to tell me. Whatever you say I'll order them. I'll make them obey me."

His aura gleamed. "Grow strong."

"But what do I say?"

"State your desire."

The king glanced back at them once more, noted that she had moved, and flew to her, casually dragging her away from Faier and back to the empty place he had left her. "Remain here."

He let go.

The protestations sounded in her heart again. This was unsafe. She was at risk. Faier was in danger. He was acting irresponsibly.

No. I refuse.

Listen.

Hear me.

"No," Harmony said.

King Kayo was already two kicks away before he checked. "What was that?"

"I said no."

His brows lifted.

The word had just popped out. She couldn't believe it herself. Her heart shot for the surface while her arms trembled. "I mean, uh, well, I won't remain *right* here. I will go over to, uh, Faier. And Xarin. For protection."

"Do not go there." King Kayo's brows lowered in consternation. "Physical contact increases your connection. You will entwine your soul more with the exile."

"Yeah? Well, he never left me." She pushed that tiny leverage. "Except when I asked him to."

King Kayo's frown deepened. "You are *my* sacred bride."

"So, then, isn't it even more important you don't leave me alone on my first day in the ocean? It's terrifying. Can't you understand?"

He took an adversarial stance. "Why do you not understand that you will be safe? Why is my word not enough?"

"Please."

"Please what?"

Seriously? Why did she doubt his word?

He lifted his chin and pouted. It was like arguing with Evens, before he understood how the world worked.

Harmony swallowed her accusations. She had to reach King Kayo's heart. His aura glowed energetically as Lifet's once had.

She returned his question. "Why is my fear not enough?"

King Kayo reluctantly drew her into the travel position snugged against his side. "This is disappointing."

"Thank you." She clung like a limpet, one of the tide-pool shells Evens had pointed out to her. "Thank you."

"My king?" Tibe returned with the others. "You are not hunting?"

"My sacred bride is too afraid."

"I have offered—"

"Yes, I know. She is reassured by no protection but mine."

The sharp warrior regarded her with cold eyes. "She does not know our ways."

"That is why I must reassure her." King Kayo puffed out his chest and kicked. "I will hunt as soon as we perform the marriage ceremony!"

The other warriors fell into their positions. Xarin moved more slowly, as though he were tired. But he dragged Faier and the crocodile carcass clear of the clouds of parasitic fish.

And now she had a future to fear. *Marriage ceremony.* What new horrors awaited in the mer city?

Perhaps the answer would never arrive. They journeyed

forever. And when she wasn't studying fish, she studied the warriors.

Her life depended on it.

King Kayo's aura shone bright and cocky like young Lifet's, but even more rash. First Lieutenant Tibe auditioned for the role of Jean-Baptiste. His bitter mango aura was not filled with malice, only brutalized efficiency.

But even if she couldn't see auras, she would know he was dangerous.

He looked at her and Faier as if they were problems to be solved, not living souls. If Tibe had been her destined husband, she would not have tried to create a distraction by antagonizing the crocodile. She would have thrown herself right into its mouth.

Xarin was the blue-green of the sea, reflecting jungle. He was the long-suffering second lieutenant who threatened King Kayo by being good at his job.

Pineapple warrior Chiba constantly checked his weapons. Faier had stolen one of his knives in combat. His continuous tapping and fidgeting showed an attention deficit.

Kusi's tattoos were beautiful teal and white foam on a shallow ocean. The opposite of Chiba, he concentrated too hard. Whenever someone called to him, they had to shout four or five times before he jerked his head up and responded.

Faier, miraculously, remained conscious. Falling on the end of his line, being dragged, and waking up again, his aura fluctuated as he faded.

He didn't deserve this.

Had he drugged her? She had trusted him. The question tore at her heart.

And what of her own aura?

Emotions colored her aura with horror, worry, and relief.

Relief?

Yes, relief. The inevitable had happened. The prophecy she'd tried to avoid, the fate she'd run from full speed, had caught her like a rogue wave. Now, she tumbled in its fury.

But if she were here voluntarily it would be kind of adventurous.

The craggy mountains and valleys of the ocean bottom passed by her eyes. Mass crab migrations, clouds of flounder, long ribbons of eels, and hundreds of strange and wondrous creatures exhilarated her. A distant octopus the size of Lifet's yacht gurgled eardrum-scratching noises as it traversed the sea floor. The ocean was well lit. She saw —and heard— animals and rocks for miles. It was almost fun.

So long as she and Faier didn't die...

New warriors emerged from the distance and greeted their party. They called out in their language. Far on the horizon, a tiny pinprick gleamed like a distant sun in the noonday sky.

The warriors aimed for it.

"Is that...?" she asked.

"Aiycaya," King Kayo confirmed proudly. "The Life Tree. Welcome to your new home, my sacred bride."

The Aiycaya Life Tree glowed brilliantly. Beneath it, the ground was colorful and full of life—fish, coral, floating sponges; an undersea forest thickening with vibrancy as they approached its epicenter. With the explosion of life came a matching explosion of music from their gleaming souls.

The mer city was embedded in the ocean floor like a giant submerged candelabra. Each sphere was a massive green bulb anchored to the seafloor by a long, slender column. They grew in concentric circles.

In the center arose the thickest and most magnificent column. It ended in a bulb that had burst open, petals wide, to reveal a dais holding the pure, holy, white Life Tree.

It produced the light that the city and ocean used for growing.

King Kayo reached the first line of spheres.

Mer flowed in and out of the entrance holes, and she suddenly realized the scale. The spheres were ancient and huge. Apartment-building tall. As they continued through to the inner circles, the spheres grew larger and more impressive. They passed a strip-mall-sized palace closest to the Life Tree.

"My castle," King Kayo announced. "You will never leave it."

So, it was to be her prison. At least her prison would be large...

He rounded the curve.

A pure, holy silence fell over the city. No fish souls or warriors' shouts disturbed the heart-calming peace. It muffled all the sounds. The stillness was acute but comforting, like the way sound was muffled on foglit winter evenings when houses glowed with warmth and empty roads were blanketed by freshly fallen snow.

Harmony expected to squint like looking into the sun. But the leafless, white, winter oak was pearly and gentle on her eyes. Its branches stretched toward the surface, bare and dormant, waiting for spring. It rested on mounds of pearls. Those same pearls dripped from the tree's crevices, hardened, and tumbled to the dais with tender clinks.

Sea Opals. Hundreds and hundreds of massive, healing Sea Opals.

New warriors relieved Xarin of the king's trophies. They took the crocodile to display and dragged Faier away from the Life Tree to the distant ocean floor.

She watched him go helplessly.

Faier had a better color. Still wrecked and pained, but maybe, just maybe, he'd survive.

Until the judgment...

THIRTEEN

Faier was not dead.

For the umpteenth time in his life, he reflected on that fact with surprise.

An undersea volcano had destroyed his city. Raiders had disfigured him to the point that the Rusalka elders had not believed he would recover. Different raiders had snuck into Atlantis and attacked by surprise. He had escaped the jaws of an ancient megalodon.

He rubbed the bite marks on his forearms.

His punctured jaw ached.

But nothing like the gaping pain in his side.

The Aiycaya warriors brought him to a prison below the city. Spiky coral enclosed barren rock. Outside, the deep sea forest grew wild and untamed.

Xarin positioned himself outside. One lone guard. The rest ascended to watch the king marry Harmony.

Faier's heart hardened to stone.

He must have healed. Imagining her marriage agonized him more than his torn side.

Harmony did not wish to belong to any warrior. He

almost tasted her terror. Yet she had sacrificed herself to save him.

He would give anything to return to the time when she'd been safe.

No.

He *would* save Harmony. He would return her to her beloved Council Bluffs.

No matter what.

Chiba returned with an elder bearing coral-pink tattoos, and Xarin led him into the prison. "Healer Hobin. Faier is here."

"Faier, eh? So, he still has a name." Healer Hobin knelt on the barren rock and unrolled his woven seaweed bag. "He is bound! Let me cut these bindings…"

The bindings fell away. Blood flowed into Faier's arms with needle-sharp pains. He flexed his wrists and his fingers. Newfound freedom…

Xarin watched him. Faier, not the healer. And when he noticed Faier's returned gaze, Xarin changed his grip on the trident to let Faier know that if he moved, Xarin would stab him through the heart, and this time, his injury would be fatal.

Faier rested his hands on his knees. Palms up. Surrender.

For now.

Chiba twisted his trident restlessly. It slipped through his nervous fingers and clanked against the rock.

Faier watched it.

Xarin watched him.

Chiba grabbed the trident and straightened. Then, he again tossed the metal back and forth between his hands.

Xarin snapped, "Chiba."

The pineapple-yellow warrior stiffened. "Second Lieutenant."

"Guard the entrance."

"Sir."

Hobin removed the seaweed binding Faier's injury. "Be strong, exile. This will hurt."

Faier had been through this before. He tensed.

Balim had always rolled his eyes with a sarcastic *"What heroic idiocy have you performed this time?"* He'd been unable to joke when he'd visited Faier on the surface to conduct his last examination. That was how Faier had known he'd worried King Kadir. He'd disappointed Balim too—

Pain lanced his abdomen a second time.

He grunted. It was not as horrible as Harmony's screams. He'd survive.

"Hmm." Healer Hobin probed the injury. His fingers caused new slices of agony. "This happened on the surface? And you traveled here?"

Faier gritted his teeth to endure.

Xarin answered, "Yes."

"Hmm," Healer Hobin muttered to himself. "Closed up already. Unusual healing in an exile."

"Hobin." Xarin switched to the tribal bride language of their sacred brides to prevent Faier from understanding. *"Na alu la nu oo a alu?"*

"No, he most likely *is* an exile. Look at these scars." Healer Hobin continued speaking in English, not apparently noticing the language shift, as he traced the deep stitching across Faier's right calf. "These are old. Only an exile with no Life Tree will have such old scars. But his new injuries are healing. These slashes across his chest—a crocodile's claws—are days old and yet they are disappearing into his skin. And this stab wound... Sap is active in these wounds. A Life Tree is healing him."

"Which?" Xarin asked.

"I cannot say. It is strange. Perhaps a new Life Tree has just now accepted him."

Xarin focused on Faier for a long moment. His eyes narrowed. "Our Life Tree?"

"No. It happened a short time before he fought you."

"How could he journey so swiftly from another Life Tree?"

"It is strange," Healer Hobin agreed. "Well, Exile Faier? How do you explain your injuries?"

There was only one explanation. But it made no sense.

Somehow, after Harmony had kissed him for the second time, the Atlantis Life Tree had activated. It now healed his wounds. But only his newest wounds. That was strange.

If true, Harmony *was* his bride. The healing proved it. And yet she married another.

FOURTEEN

Harmony waited to marry King Kayo.

The headache that had been stabbing her temples since the storm abated. Her stomach growled.

She was coming to life.

Just in time to lose Faier and everything.

King Kayo swam to the edge of the dais and released her. "Now, we marry. Elder Wida! Where is the Life Tree blossom that will bind my sacred bride to me for eternity?"

A large, bald elder decorated with bone-white tattoos rumbled in a deep voice, "It has not yet grown, my king."

"Ah. Yes. We will marry, and then it will grow."

"For certain."

"Call all warriors to attend the ceremony."

"Yes, my king."

"King Kayo." A much older, bony warrior with thin, pinched cheeks and a narrow nose bowed. "You have returned successfully. I cannot believe it."

"Elder Bawa." King Kayo puffed out his chest. "This is my sacred bride."

"After so many years. What an honor." The elder bowed to her. His muted orange tattoos were thick and intricate. "*Ana l'ai o pu ala na la.*"

"She speaks English."

"English?" Elder Bawa blinked and frowned. "But, my king... *No l'ai ana so la una ee.*"

"English," he confirmed. "And yes, I am certain she is a sacred bride. She was on the sacred island. I defeated the exile who had already transformed her, *and* I killed a deadly crocodile. See my trophy?"

Other warriors clustered around the crocodile corpse, examined his trident stab, and picked off a few pesky crustaceans.

Elder Bawa barely glanced at it. "Already transformed her? Then, you did not feed her elixir yourself?"

"We had none."

"None? The other islands—"

"Yes, we went to the seven ancient sacred islands you requested. No humans have lived on any for decades or centuries. We found nothing."

"And yet, she had transformed already..."

"How lucky the exile fed his elixir to her first."

"Lucky? But my king! Her soul resonates with him now."

"Yes, for now. But that will soon change."

Elder Bawa's aura darkened to burnt orange in agitation. "Are you *certain* she is a sacred bride?"

King Kayo, still beaming at his accomplishments, tilted his head. "What other female would I find transformed within the sea?"

The elder's mouth flapped. His aura darkened and lightened again. "There is a...rumor...that a rebel city... perhaps...contacted *modern* females."

"Modern females? What are they?"

"Females who do not dwell on a sacred island. They dwell elsewhere on the surface." The elder made an impatient noise. "On land."

King Kayo's smile slipped to shock. "Exposing mer to mainland humans violates the ancient covenant."

"Yes, well, that is why they are rebels."

"So, females on the mainland wish to become our brides? How many?"

"No, do not imagine. They are anathema. The ancient covenant forbids them." Elder Bawa harrumphed and straightened the daggers dangling from his biceps. "But if you did not transform her, perhaps she is a modern female transformed by a rebel to trick you."

King Kayo shook his head.

"Yes, my king, it is a real possibility. She could have transformed in Atlantis or...or Sireno and swum across the—"

"She cannot swim."

"That is more reason she may be—"

"She is my sacred bride."

"But—"

"You will *not* deny my right as king."

"No, but you cannot risk our status with the All-Council."

"I have done nothing wrong."

"She could be dangerous, my king. Rebel females are demanding and...well, she could...er, she could be a dangerous—er, danger."

"A dangerous danger?" King Kayo regarded him skeptically. "Speak what you mean."

"It is nothing, my king. A slip. A rumor."

"And?"

"Some modern females have...eh...used weapons against their kings."

"She cannot lift a trident."

"Not ordinary weapons."

"Explain."

"Ah...it is difficult to... City-disrupting weapons. One modern female killed the Sireno Life Tree."

"Sireno still stands."

"A new Life Tree was planted."

"Hmm. What human weapon did she wield?"

"She used no human weapon. She...eh..."

"Elder Bawa, I grow tired of your hesitation. Explain yourself succinctly. Is my sacred bride a threat to the city and our Life Tree? And if so, why?"

Elder Bawa eyed Harmony.

She hugged her elbows.

He frowned greatly. "Eh...it is a rumor only. Nothing to concern yourself with, my king."

"Then I shall not concern myself." King Kayo turned his back on the elder.

Elder Bawa glared at Harmony.

She shrank away from him.

"Elder Yane!" King Kayo waved to an elder with sunstar-yellow tattoos arriving with a phalanx of warriors. "Has everyone gathered for the ceremony?"

"Almost, my king."

"Come look at this crocodile! It dared to threaten my bride." He glanced sideways at the irritated Elder Bawa. "I let nothing threaten what is mine."

Elder Bawa held his gaze for a long moment.

Warriors gathered to congratulate the king and admire his trophy. King Kayo returned their congratulations with kind cheer. Although he was young, his warriors regarded him with affection and respect. He ruled happily here.

But danger lurked in high places.

Lifet would have made his people speak so he understood. King Kayo didn't seem interested. Elder Bawa and his favorite lieutenant, Tibe, got away with too much.

There was still purity in King Kayo's aura that could be saved.

If she tried...

Elder Bawa drifted to the back of the crowd and sidled close to First Lieutenant Tibe. His words were difficult to hear over the chattering, but it helped that the elder forgot and spoke in English.

"How dare you allow the king to return with this strange female?" Elder Bawa demanded of Tibe. "She may be a rebel queen."

"How should I know what she is?" Tibe returned coldly.

"This is why I told you not to allow any exiles. And yet you have returned with one. And a strange female! Who knows what they will tell King—" Elder Bawa caught Harmony's eye across the crowd, startled, and hunched away from her. "*Na ala ta ailu kor*, Tibe."

First Lieutenant Tibe's cold gaze swept over her. He answered in his language. But the cryptic words gave her a chill.

I will take care of it. That's what it seemed like he said. She didn't actually understand the tribal words, but his tone and body language gave her no doubt.

He was ruthless. Efficient. Brutal.

Fear lanced her.

King Kayo thought she was a sacred bride, but

Harmony and Faier knew she wasn't. What would happen when King Kayo found out the truth?

She'd thought the worst was behind her, but she'd been so wrong.

The worst was just unfolding.

"My sacred bride. Come." King Kayo clasped Harmony's hand and tugged her across the mounds of Sea Opals toward the trunk of the Life Tree. His eyes flashed with excitement. "We marry now."

We marry now.

Harmony followed King Kayo across the smooth, tinkling pearls.

She had to marry him, or else he would know she wasn't a sacred bride.

He would know and...

What? She would die?

Harmony swallowed.

Where was Faier? Had they taken him to the doctor? Was he getting medical treatment and food and water?

She would give anything to have him beside her, holding her hand, telling her in his calm way that everything would be all right. Or, if it wasn't, then being stoic because he wouldn't lie.

Except when he'd drugged her.

Had he?

If he hadn't, who had? And when?

She couldn't suspect Faier. They had been through too much. He had saved her. And his aura was good and gentle and noble and enticing. He lit her soul on fire and he urged her to make her own choices and he unshackled her to be the powerful woman she'd once been. He lifted her up from the darkness and showed her sunlight.

He never would have taken her choices away and forced drugs down her throat. It wasn't him. He couldn't have.

But logically she didn't have anyone else to blame.

If she hadn't been drugged with elixir, she also never would have been forced to the ocean bottom. King Kayo had no elixir or nectar. He couldn't have transformed her. She'd have been stuck on that isolated, barren, waterless island.

Or maybe the fault was hers. Someone had drugged her *and* her soul had resonated with Faier's so much that she'd transformed to grow gills, see long distances, and speak with chest vibrations.

It must have been the sizzle from their kiss.

King Kayo knelt at the base of the Life Tree and touched the bark with his fingertips. He bowed his head. "I, King Kayo of Aiycaya, marry my sacred bride. Shower your blessing and healing on our union so our joining will swiftly produce a healthy young fry."

A gentle tinkling like wind chimes filled the ocean. Up close, the bark gleamed as if she gazed upon fine jewelry.

King Kayo stood and gestured to her. "Now you."

This was it.

Marriage.

She bounded forward.

He caught her to keep her from smacking into the branches. "Careful, my sacred bride. Do not damage the Life Tree."

"Sorry." She released his helpful hand and knelt at the base, just as he'd done. She rested her whole hand on the trunk.

A gasp erupted behind her.

"Release the Life Tree," King Kayo said tightly.

She lifted her hand. "Oh. Sorry. I thought you touched it."

"Just the fingertips. Caress. Gentle."

She touched with just her fingertips.

Honestly, the Life Tree felt like a tree. Not fragile glass. It felt warm and alive and smooth and...

Calm acceptance filled her heart with relief.

She had arrived.

The Life Tree had been waiting for her. All this time. She was here. This was home. She claimed her destiny. No matter what happened before or after, for this one holy moment, she communed with the ancient Life Tree.

And it was perfect.

Had her mother felt this once too? Had it calmed her grief?

King Kayo rumbled behind her, "Speak the vows, my sacred bride, so we can join."

No.

"I..."

The Life Tree tinkled on an imaginary breeze.

I refuse.

The Life Tree supported her true desires. Desires buried deep within her heart. Everything would be okay. Strength flowed into her veins. Maybe she truly was how Faier saw her. Powerful. Vital. Alive.

"I present King Kayo..." the king prompted.

"I'm sorry, King Kayo."

"No, no. 'I *present* King Kayo.'"

Harmony turned and faced him. She braced for his reaction. "I can't marry you."

FIFTEEN

I can't marry you.

Harmony's words caused the king to still with shock. She tensed.

Now was when he would hurt her.

But King Kayo was not Lifet. He still had a heart. King Kayo did not darken with fury.

No, his aura flickered with hurt, sorrow, and fear.

Fear?

King Kayo dropped to her level and vibrated urgently. His quiet words did not reach the crowd of warriors ringing the Life Tree. "Yes. You can. *You must.*"

Harmony twitched.

Normally, she would hunch in and give up. Fearful. Who did she think she was? Standing up to a king? He would only ignore her and force her to do what he wanted. Her resistance would only cause her to get hurt.

But strength flowed up her arm and into her warm chest the way the sap of the Life Tree seeped into her cracked heart.

She faced King Kayo as if she were equal to him. As if

she could make demands and he could obey or at least listen.

As if, for just one moment, what she did *mattered*.

"I can't," she repeated, firmly but quietly so only he would hear. She didn't want to embarrass him in front of his subjects.

He leaned close, relieved to keep their argument quiet, and carried on. "Because your soul still entwines with the exile's?"

"No."

"It will entwine with mine. Soon. I promise you."

"That's not the reason."

While they had their muffled argument, a small green octopus about the size of a kitten curled a tentacle around the lowest branch of the Life Tree. Unlike the other fish who produced pleasant New Age music, she yowled like a cat crossed with an angry seagull. *Gwowlll. Yogwowwl. Agwowwl.* She studied Harmony curiously.

"You will acclimate to the mer world," he promised her intently and quietly. "It will happen quickly."

"I think it's already happening, actually." She sat criss-cross, with her fingertips still touching the Life Tree.

"I will help you."

"Thanks. I think."

"You think? What does this mean, 'you think'?"

"It means...uh..."

The little octopus crept over the roots of the Life Tree and explored Harmony's outstretched thigh. Its eardrum-curdling noise was so ugly, it was cute.

"It means I'll be grateful for your help *and* I'm on guard in case you try to dump me off somewhere to do something more fun."

He jerked his chin in, affronted. "I would not do that."

"You tried to leave me on the journey."

"We needed the meat and you were probably safe."

"Probably?"

"From now on, you will live within my castle. You will never leave it. My castle is safe. Absolutely safe."

The little octopus looked up at her several times to make sure she would not move and then it crawled onto her lap. She stroked its rubbery texture. It curled one tentacle around her index finger.

"Absolutely safe. Huh. That's much better than 'probably' safe."

He huffed. "Forget the past. The moment is gone. You should not think about it."

Now she was irritated. "How can I not think about it? I begged you not to leave me. I cried."

He knelt stiffly, hands on his bent knees. "And that is why you will not marry me? Because you do not trust my ability to protect you?"

"That's still not the reason." She gathered her courage. "I heard what you said to Elder Bawa and...I'm not a sacred bride."

"That is a lie. Observe." He pointed to the octopus. "My house guardian resides in your lap. She recognizes you as the female who belongs in our castle. You are a sacred bride."

This was his pet octopus? Huh. "She sounds like a box of angry seagulls."

"House guardians are not attractive singers, but they are formidable protectors."

"What's her name?"

"She is a house guardian. She has no name."

Harmony tugged her little tentacle. The octopus

gnawed on her fingernail with her tiny beak. "Well, I can explain this."

"You are a sacred bride."

"My mom was a sacred bride. My whole tribe had to leave that island. You saw why."

"And you are a—"

"I was raised on the mainland."

He tilted his head. "You are a modern female?"

"I guess. A few weeks ago, I met my tribe. And my great-grandmother told me that marrying you was my destiny."

"Then you *are* a sacred bride."

"But I wasn't raised on the sacred island. Is it okay?"

"Is it?"

"Are you asking me?"

"Yes."

She snorted. "I don't know your rules."

"Because you are a modern sacred bride." His lips quirked to the side. "It is fine. We will not tell Elder Bawa. You came to the sacred island to marry and give me a young fry."

"But—I didn't go there to—I was shipwrecked. I was fleeing somewhere else. I don't know how I ended up at the sacred island."

"The Life Tree guided you." He looked up at the branches. "It sensed your presence and pulled your soul."

She squinted up at the pure gemstone brilliance. Faier had said something similar. "The Life Tree controls the wind and the waves?"

"Perhaps." He returned his gaze to her. Pure and gentle and without guile. "How is any warrior united with his sacred bride? There are as many humans on the land as stars in the sky. And yet, one female makes her way to the city and drinks her husband's Life Tree blossom nectar. Their souls entwine for all time."

"That's beautiful."

"It is the Life Tree's power."

His poetic words lulled her to calm. For the first time, they both spoke from the heart.

"And," she straightened, "actually, the one who guided the raft was Faier."

King Kayo scowled. "The exile."

"He's not an exile. He's a warrior who... He assists with the... Um, he rescued me from the storm. He fed me and kept me from starving."

"If you were starving, he did not feed you well."

"I could say the same about you."

He blinked. "You are hungry now?"

"Yeah." Her stomach growled again. "I'm hungry now."

He gritted his teeth. "But you must marry me."

"I can't!"

"Because of the exile..."

"For the umpteenth time, he's not an exile."

"Then what is he?"

"He's a...fine. I'll tell you. Even though I'm not sure he'd want it." She lowered her already quiet voice. "He's a citizen of Atlantis and another city. It starts with a D."

"Dragao Azul."

"Right. He's the opposite of an exile. The only exile here is me."

But once more, King Kayo wasn't listening. "He's a rebel. All those scars. They must live like sharks fighting for every mouthful. No wonder he kept you weak and dependent. He starved you."

"He didn't!"

He glanced behind them at the warriors and made the lower-your-voice gesture. "Calm, my sacred bride."

"Sorry," she whisper-vibrated. "But, I mean, what if I am a 'dangerous danger'? What would you do then?"

"Take you to the surface."

Her heart dropped. "Seriously?"

"Yes."

"Then take us!" She almost strangled herself in her urgency. "We're both extremely dangerous—"

"Silence." He stopped her with a deadly expression.

Fear punched her belly.

"You do not understand what you say. But *never* say these words to any mer *ever again*. Not if you value your rebel's life or your own."

She hugged herself with one arm. "I'm sorry. I'm sorry. Please don't hurt me. I'm sorry."

His brows smoothed and he started to reach out a hand to touch her trembling arm.

She tensed for the blow.

He stopped, shocked. In the same hurt tone Faier had once used, he said, "You fear me."

She nodded jerkily, not trusting her voice or her words. Her octopus stroked her softly.

He lowered his hand to rest on his knees. "I would never hurt a female. You are safe in Aiycaya."

She dared to point out the inconsistency. "But you just said—"

"Because Elder Bawa lectures me so." He looked chagrined. "He might bore you to death. But do not give him reason by pretending you are dangerous."

"If you'll just return me and Faier to the surface—"

"Your case and the rebel's are different. You will return to the surface after bearing my young fry. He never will."

"Never?"

"He must face the punishment for his crimes."

"But he didn't do anything wrong…" Her heart sank. "Isn't there anything I can do? Any thing I can say or offer? Any way you can let him go?"

King Kayo's expression ended her quest. Despite tears and begging and bargaining, he was unmoved. Harmony could trick him into letting her go. Faier would be held and then executed.

Harmony communed with the little green octopus while she dealt with this blow.

Faier had remained with her all the weeks she'd been stuck in the raft. Even though it was dangerous, and he could have abandoned her at any time.

She would remain here with him. Somehow, she would save him. They would escape together.

Or not at all.

"Let me know if you change your mind," she said heavily. "If I can do anything to free Faier, anything at all, tell me."

"I do not know that I would tell you," he returned, somewhat bitter. "I already know you as a female who breaks her promise after I have kept mine."

She jerked up. "What promise?"

"On the surface, you promised to marry me."

"Well, you promised you wouldn't hurt Faier."

"And I did not hurt him."

"Your men did."

"I did not vow to stop my men."

"That's what I wanted!"

"You made a mistake. I spoke the truth. You misunderstood."

"Well, so, you misunderstood too. I only promised to travel with you. I didn't promise to marry you."

"But a sacred bride's purpose is to marry."

"Too bad. 'You made a mistake. I spoke the truth.' How does that feel?"

He flexed his jaw. "A sacred bride's purpose is marriage to produce a young fry."

"My purpose was to save Faier. I haven't gotten what I want, so I don't see why you should get what you want."

"But I am the king. There is no worthier male. The elders chose me."

"I did not."

He twitched. Anger darkened his aura. Dangerous, for the first time. He glanced at the crowd behind them, waiting patiently to finish this ceremony, and then he vibrated his quiet question with a biting tone. "Is it Xarin? Is that the male you choose?"

Xarin?

The heck?

"No," she said.

His shoulders lowered.

"Are you okay?" she asked.

"Many have said he should be king. If my sacred bride chose him also..." He shook his taut muscles and rolled his neck. "Then. You cannot marry me."

"I'm sorry."

"Your soul enmeshes with the rebel's."

"I guess. Yes." She straightened. "Please don't hurt Faier. He really did save my life. If I can just change your mind—"

"The elders judge exiles. Since he is no exile, they will not judge." King Kayo lifted his chin. "Aiycaya is a traditional city. We will obey the tradition."

"Oh, thank—"

"The All-Council mediates disputes between cities. We will await the All-Council's ruling."

She swallowed. "When will that happen?"

"We must convey our request at our Echo Point. Then await their judgment in return. It will be a little time."

She wouldn't get a better offer. The delay gave her more time to learn about the mer, about Aiycaya, and about King Kayo.

But that didn't mean she felt great.

"So, just to be clear, none of your warriors will hurt Faier? Not you, not Tibe, not your warriors, *not anybody*?"

"No one in this city will injure Faier until after the All-Council ruling."

"If we are having another misunderstanding, I will never trust you ever again. Ever."

"I am a male of my word," he insisted.

"And I want to repeat, right now, that I have no feelings for you. There is no way we can ever marry."

"I have a year to change your mind." He rose and held out his hand.

"A year?"

"According to the ancient covenant, if after one year our souls still do not synchronize with resonance, then I must return you to the surface."

"And what about young fry?"

He raised a brow as if she were crazy. "If our souls do not share resonance, then how can we produce young fry?"

She didn't know how to answer.

He gestured below his waist to his flaccid cock.

His. Flaccid. Cock.

He was naked right now.

And she was naked.

Right.

Now.

Her dress, which had been threadbare before she'd run off into the jungle for a week and then hadn't gotten any nicer after Lifet's beatings or the storm, had finally disintegrated on the surface. She, like Faier, had been naked under the water this whole time.

This. Whole. Time.

And so was King Kayo. The bright pink tattoos that shone, iridescent, like scales on a reef fish, also coiled around his flaccid male member.

As did the tattoos on the mermen floating respectfully in the distance. And the males in the war party who had escorted her from the surface to the ocean bottom. Chiba and Kusi. Tibe. Xarin.

She hadn't noticed. Her brain had willfully blinded her. The warriors were muscular, and some were even handsome. But she didn't see them as men? Huh.

Harmony looked up to King Kayo's face.

And it happened.

His aura gleamed like a reflection off pink chrome, and she sort of forgot he was naked until she forced herself to think about it. Totally naked.

So then it was the same for him?

"You can't impregnate me because our souls don't resonate."

"Of course."

Oh, thank goodness. What a relief.

He tilted his head. "Is it not the same for humans?"

"It's not the same." She suppressed her hysterical laugh and took his offered hand, rising. The little octopus spilled off her lap, and the Sea Opals tinkled. "It's so not the same."

"I see." He lifted her to her tiptoes and, still keeping his voice low, murmured, "You will tell everyone we are married now. That way, no other male will try to steal you."

Her heart lurched. "That could happen?"

"It is the most common reason for intercity warfare."

"But I thought you just said no warrior could impregnate me unless our souls resonated."

"Many warriors steal a bride hoping their resonance will grow."

"But—but you said the Life Tree magically draws a warrior's sacred bride!"

"Yes, but not always for the warrior who has gone to fetch her."

More questions buzzed in Harmony's mind as King Kayo tugged her off her feet. Worry invaded without the steadying calm of the Life Tree beneath her fingers.

Tinkle. Tinkle.

Ah. She could still hear the clinking of the Sea Opals and the Life Tree's calming, muffling silence.

King Kayo swam her over the expectant crowd. He raised their linked hands. "My sacred bride!"

The warriors cheered. They had heard nothing of the argument.

Elder Wida smiled beatifically and clasped King Kayo's arm. His deep voice rumbled. "You have done well, my king. Your souls glow the same color! A flower will surely blossom now."

"Yes." King Kayo smiled with closed teeth. "Indeed."

The other warriors rushed to offer their congratulations. They spoke to King Kayo, ignoring her, and most forgot to use English. She teetered so much on edge her shoulders ached with boredom and exhausted.

Her stomach growled.

"Tell me the honeymoon has food," she muttered near King Kayo's back while she floated behind him.

"Yes. Let me speak to Tibe a moment."

King Kayo spoke in his language to his first lieutenant. She swore she heard *Atlantis* and *Dragao Azul* intermixed in his words. Tibe held her gaze coldly. Then his gaze narrowed as he pulled back.

"Now! We will have a great feast." King Kayo drew her into his arms and waved to the crowds of warriors. "Come with me to celebrate the first marriage since old King Aka's reign!"

The warriors cheered and followed.

But she couldn't ignore the dangerous gaze of cold Tibe.

Or how he turned away and swam toward the prison...

SIXTEEN

"Impressive healing for an exile," Healer Hobin said again as he rested his hands on his tools. "You are, as you stated, an exile?"

Faier stared down the healer without fear. His injury felt better. "I never said I was an exile."

Healer Hobin swallowed. "I see."

The prison was cold and quiet as other warriors attended King Kayo and Harmony's wedding.

Faier had to get free. He had to save her. He needed just one opportunity.

Xarin's fingers tightened on his trident. Anger darkened his soul. "You claimed to be from Nerissa."

"I am."

"Nerissa was lost."

"It was."

"Then you lie!"

He held the warrior's blue-green gaze and changed the subject. "You have a young king."

Xarin blinked.

"I am surprised you do not have an older, more skilled leader."

"Yes, perhaps, but King Kayo is popular." Hobin applied a stinging salve to Faier's abdomen. "His father, King Kamuy, was a great hunter and patient ruler. His son... well, King Kayo does enjoy hunting."

"Hobin," Xarin said quellingly.

"He relies on Elder Bawa and First Lieutenant Tibe to manage. And the other elders, of course. It is not surprising since King Kamuy himself was never groomed for succession."

Faier latched on to that detail. *Opportunity*. "King Kayo's father was not the intended successor?"

"Oh, no. Xarin's father, First Lieutenant Xawey, you might know, was the intended. Everyone was so surprised when the old King chose ordinary Warlord Kamuy."

Xarin hissed in his chest. "He does not need this knowledge."

"Ah, he will not keep it for long. The judgment will happen soon after the wedding feast. Shame to heal so well." Hobin finished his work and retied the seaweed bandage. He rested on human heels. "Once the elders judge, they will disfigure you and throw you into the vent."

Yes. That was why he needed to create an opportunity now to steal a weapon, overpower the guards, and escape with Harmony.

Faier's heart squeezed and relaxed, squeezed and relaxed.

"There. I completed my handiwork." Hobin floated. His feet elongated into fins. He kicked backward. "You will live."

Faier would live.

He had to make it count.

Furious commotion at the entrance interrupted his thoughts.

Xarin frowned, turned, and exited. Beyond the entrance, tridents clashed and shouts vibrated.

Ominous.

"That cannot be good," Healer Hobin muttered and floated toward the entrance.

First Lieutenant Tibe burst into the prison with Chiba and Kusi floating right behind him. All were armed. Tibe aimed two tridents at Faier.

Faier rose. Arms loose, ankles still sore from being bound for the journey from the surface.

"No, no. Do not move!" Healer Hobin shouted at him in a panic. "You will reinjure your wound. Xarin!"

Xarin flew into the prison and aimed his trident at Tibe without hesitation. "First Lieutenant Tibe, King Kayo did not authorize you to enter."

The first lieutenant waved one trident at the exit. "Xarin, go outside."

Xarin didn't move. "The exile awaits the judgment of the elders."

"Outside."

"King Kayo ordered—"

"Outside, now! *Second Lieutenant*."

Xarin stiffened. He clenched his trident tight to his side in a grim gesture of obedience. "First Lieutenant." He flew out the exit, but his form remained visible in the portal.

"Tibe..." Healer Hobin's tone lilted in warning. "He is not healed..."

"Healer, this is no matter for you. Out."

Healer Hobin joined Xarin reluctantly.

Faier faced the new warriors empty-handed. His heart thudded. Blood pumped swiftly through his veins.

"Faier of Atlantis." Tibe pointed his long trident at Faier's chest. "And of Dragao Azul. I judge you a notorious rebel. You and your 'sacred bride.'"

Faier flexed his empty hands. "Leave her alone."

"King Kayo has seen through her lies. He will end her with his own blade."

Fury burned in Faier's chest. "Then I will kill all of you!"

"Try." Tibe tossed Kusi's broken, two-tined trident. It landed on the bare rock in front of Faier with a clatter. "Fight me. But I assure you that you will die."

HARMONY COULDN'T GET Tibe's cold gaze out of her mind, even though she should concentrate on the wedding feast.

King Kayo swam, with her pressed to his side, to his castle and zipped through the doorway—a vast tunnel with arched ceilings—and burst into a giant inner hollow of the sphere.

At the base, a lush garden grew in tended lots around a pedestal. King Kayo identified the small, palm-sized bean in the center as a seed of the Life Tree.

Holes pocked the vast inner walls. Each doorway led to secret corridors.

"That was my father's favorite wing." He pointed at a twisting cavern etched with drawings. "It goes to the castle's heart chamber. The king before him favored those chambers nearest the courtyard. You choose whichever rooms you like."

"Where's the pantry?"

He snorted. "Indeed. Here." He flew her to the pantry.

The movement of warriors blocked the large corridor as they set out stores for the feast. From the procession, King Kayo snagged a small wooden box. He removed the planks. Inside glistened a delicious fish steak. He unsheathed the dagger from his bicep and cut a slice.

"Here is festival meat." He handed her the slice—big enough for both hands—a little sadly. "Someday, we will eat this again. When I wed my true bride."

Who would be someone else.

She stuffed the meat in her mouth without responding.

Smoked salmon and Thanksgiving turkey and Christmas ham fresh from the oven and smothered with gravy. Heaven.

King Kayo abandoned her and swam to a cluster of elders in the middle of the courtyard helping to oversee the feast. They conferenced.

Harmony felt alone and afraid. But surely no one would hurt her in this wedding feast in front of King Kayo.

She tried to control her fears and scarfed big, juicy bites. Her meat disappeared in seconds. And then, since more remained in the box, she pulled out the second half. Mmm! Rich, savory, satisfying. She licked her fingers and then licked the box.

Had Faier gotten to eat anything like this? He must be starving as well. She should smuggled him some of this. As soon as King Kayo finished his duties with the elders and returned to her, she would ask.

They seasoned the wood with gravy...

She collected a plank and chewed on it. Mmm. Could she eat it?

"Er, Sacred Bride." A shy warrior held out his hands to take the empty box. "I must take your... Did you eat all that festival meat?"

She spat out the plank and linked her fingers in front of her chest. "Um...yes? Did you have any more?"

"Excuse me. I must not speak to..." Then, he blinked. "You are still hungry?"

She nodded.

"There is...uh..." He looked up at King Kayo, still conversing with the elders about his hunt, and then he lifted a long vine beside her and plucked off a line of pods. "These are succulent. And here, these grasses, humans have said they are very palatable."

She followed the shy warrior.

He gave her a short tour of the garden. She filled the box for Faier and stuffed her mouth. The pods mushed against her tongue, creamy and filling, like garbanzo beans. The long fronds crunched like lettuce.

"And the rest of the meat is that way." He pointed at the corridor. "Festival and ordinary meat."

She noted it, storing up her knowledge as she continued to pop food into her mouth. In Haiti, there hadn't been fancy food, but there had always been enough. Cooked fresh through backbreaking labor, simple and tasty.

For the first time in years, she didn't salivate over the thought of biting into a puffy slice of snow-white Wonder Bread.

"Anything else?" the warrior asked, edging away.

"This is great. Thank you."

"You are welcome, Sacred Bride..." He frowned as though searching for her name.

"Harmony," she supplied.

His brow cleared. "Sacred Bride Harmony."

"And you are?"

"Warrior Zaka of Aiycaya."

"Yes. Warrior Zaka." She smiled around her mouthful.

Hey, she could now eat and talk at the same time. "Nice to meet you."

"Nice to meet you. When you finish using that box, please allow me to take it."

She clutched the full box of legumes. "You need this?"

"My role here is packing the king's meat. He hunts often. We are always in need of—" He broke off. His brow lifted in sudden realization. "Do not give it until you finish! We can make new boxes. I did not think. Please forgive me, Sacred Bride Harmony."

"Oh, sure. No problem."

"Here. Have a second box. No, have three." He stacked two more meat boxes atop her legumes.

She didn't complain. "Thank you."

"Yes. I—"

A shout of anger interrupted them.

"What do you mean, First Lieutenant Tibe interrogates my prisoner?" King Kayo's chest vibrated with fury at the elders, silencing everyone nearby. "That was not my order!"

Her blood ran cold.

"You were busy with your wedding," Elder Bawa murmured. "We did not wish to disturb your sacred bride at that most important ceremony. Why are you upset? We have done this as a favor."

"First Lieutenant Tibe interrogates too roughly!" King Kayo caught her eye. "If he injures my prisoner, you, Elder Bawa, will accept responsibility!"

"My king, please calm. He is only an exile."

"Why do you call him that, Elder Bawa? I told you just a short while ago that I had learned he is a rebel from Atlantis and Dragao Azul."

Elder Bawa blanched. "Excuse me, my king. I had forgotten that...yes, I had meant to keep the information from upsetting the other warriors...and...from embarrassing you! It is one thing to bring a dirty exile back to our city instead of correctly dispatching him in the field, but you must not risk infecting our city with a nasty rebel. I did not wish to embarrass you."

"And that is why you ordered Tibe to interrogate?"

"My king, I do not order First Lieutenant Tibe. You issue his orders."

"And I did not order him to interrogate my captive!" King Kayo gestured to several warriors, including Zaka, and they flew to him.

"My king, where are you going?" Elder Bawa called.

"I will conduct any interrogations!" The king and his warriors exited.

"Your wedding feast is here!" Elder Bawa vibrated with exasperation at the empty passage. "Do not behave like a child."

She prayed King Kayo was not too late.

Tibe was dangerous. But Elder Bawa poisoned King Kayo by undermining and lying to him. And she knew where poisoning led.

Harmony rubbed her wrists. They were no longer bruised, but she would never forget the terror of being manacled by the man she'd once loved.

Elder Bawa murmured to a warrior with thin features and ice-blue tattoos.

She strained to hear over the crowd.

"...go quietly and answer no questions." Elder Bawa's chest vibrations just reached her. "Quietly, Warlord Sao."

Warlord Sao nodded once, dropped his food half-eaten and gathered several warriors.

Elder Bawa turned to her with smug satisfaction—that wavered when he noticed her looking back at him. He took the icy warrior's place in the feast, drew everyone's attention, and made what sounded like toasts in their language accompanied by lots of cheering.

The ice-blue Warlord Sao swam to Harmony.

Cold shivered in her veins. She hunched in the isolated pantry.

He stopped right in front of her.

Oh, no.

He released a bundle of seaweed rope. His vibration was icy as his tattoos. "Put that on."

She hugged the food boxes to her chest. "Why?"

"Do not speak."

Her heart thudded. Faier had promised these warriors would not harm her. But Elder Bawa made her nervous.

I will take care of it.

She'd feared being left alone in the dangerous ocean. But inside the city seemed even more dangerous—and inside the castle of her supposed husband, the king, was the most dangerous of all.

The seaweed floated like the ropes Xarin had used to bind Faier and drag him.

"Wh-what is it?"

Warlord Sao refused to answer.

The four warriors behind him remained at stiff attention.

She swallowed. "I want King Kayo."

"Put the harness on *now*." His tone was even more clipped.

She had no choice. They could overpower her. They could punish her. Or worse, they could punish Faier.

Harmony curled her hands around the hard corners of the boxes.

She had no choice. She had no choice. She had no choice.

Just like always.

She—

Tinkle, tinkle.

The soothing calmness of the Life Tree flowed through the castle walls and into her heart. Her desperate beat of panic soothed into calm.

Yes, they could overpower her, punish her, or worse.

And yet, she still had a choice.

I refuse.

Harmony straightened and grabbed one of the seaweed ropes.

The ice-blue warrior looked relieved. "Wrap that end around your waist."

She vibrated loudly. "No, I won't, Warlord Sao!"

He went still with shock.

"I won't!"

Her vibrations cut through Elder Bawa's toast. The cheers died. Warriors craned to see inside the pantry.

Warlord Sao narrowed his gaze. "Sacred Bride, please—"

"I'm not putting on any harness until I see Faier or King Kayo." Still holding the rope, she crossed her arms over her chest. "And if you try to make me, I'll scream."

Warlord Sao clenched the seaweed with new conviction. "Quiet."

"No!"

The murmurs outside increased. "What is happening? Where is Warlord Sao taking the king's sacred bride?"

Warlord Sao looked across the feast at a red-faced Elder Bawa.

Elder Bawa gestured for him to act.

The warriors ranged around her picked up different ends.

She screeched. "Don't touch me!"

"Touch? Warlord Sao!" Two elders—sun-gold Yane and bone-white Wida—approached the doorway. "You will not touch another male's sacred bride."

"No. I will not touch." He fingered the seaweed cable as though he would loop it into a lasso.

"Come out."

Warlord Sao did not leave. "I have orders."

Elder Yane's smile was strained. "They will wait. This is a wedding feast. Come out at once."

"I will not touch," Warlord Sao insisted.

"Only an idiot would try to bind a bride against her will —inside close quarters—and swear they would not touch her. And on her wedding feast," Elder Yane said, disapproving.

"You have earned my contempt," Elder Wida boomed. "If the king does not cut off your hand, I will."

"He will not cut off my hand." The warlord's eyes flashed. "I act on his orders."

Everyone looked relieved, as if they believed Warlord Sao.

"No way," she protested. "He didn't order you to do anything."

The elders stared at Warlord Sao, flummoxed.

"King Kayo doesn't want me tied up. Ask him yourself."

Elder Yane frowned. "Warlord Sao is very honorable. He does not lie."

Warlord Sao lifted his chin in triumph.

Harmony braced.

She didn't want to be a victim anymore. She didn't want to get thrown overboard or deported or pushed around.

But she was all alone. Again. She had no—

The little green octopus flew into the pantry and twirled beside her as though her fear had summoned it.

Oh. Thank goodness. Even though the octopus was tiny it shored up her heart. Now they were two against five hardened warriors and the others outside.

Harmony refused to give in even though didn't know if she would survive.

SEVENTEEN

Faier did not attack wildly.

The first lieutenant defended carelessly. Faier's first calculated swipe caught him by surprise.

"You disgusting rebel." Tibe vibrated with amusement. He took his time swimming back and forth before Faier, enjoying stalking him almost as much as he enjoyed flaunting his power in front of seething Xarin. "A sacred bride's pity will not save your scarred hide. You will die."

Faier measured his dexterity and reach. "I survived your last 'mortal' attack. You must work harder to kill me."

"Very well." He slashed.

Faier kicked hard. He rolled over the slash.

Tibe reversed directions. "Ha!"

Faier twisted—agony in his side—out of the blade's path and brought down his borrowed broken trident.

Clash.

Their tridents locked.

The motion stretched his abdomen. Pain stabbed him, and his side throbbed. Hot blood seeped from the bandage.

Tibe yanked back and paced before Faier again. A mild

frown touched his brow, but his cold smile remained fixed on his mouth. "Your endurance is astounding. Rebel warriors must live hard, pained lives."

"I would endure any hardship to honor *my* king." Faier closed a hand over his bleeding, throbbing injury. One-handed, he leveled his two blade tips on Tibe. "Even converse with you."

"Then I will stop talking and start killing." Tibe slashed.

Faier backed out of his reach.

Tibe darted after him.

Faier's back hit the coral. Tibe thrust for his weak abdomen. Faier whirled away. Tibe's trident jammed into the coral and chipped it.

Tibe reared back, surprised to have missed Faier twice, and focused. "You are still conscious."

"You are still dishonorable."

"I have honor." He backed Faier across the pen. "I am the most lawful warrior in this city. Ha!"

Faier used minimal evasions so each attack looked like it would hit him and then he escaped at the last moment.

He did not have endless stamina. He needed to draw the first lieutenant into a trap.

And that would not be easy.

Tibe broke away. Chest heaving as the water flushed through his lungs, he recaptured his casual smile.

"I see our hospitality has been too kind to you." He straightened his shoulders and gestured to his obedient warriors. "Tire him."

Chiba and Kusi swam forward.

Kusi thrust for Faier's vulnerable abdomen.

Faier kicked to the left.

Chiba slashed for his weak leg.

Faier whirled around his trident and slammed both ends to block.

His side throbbed.

Kusi and Chiba pushed and broke off, circling like sand sharks, and then dove in for the next attack. He kept atop of them by sheer will. But Tibe had been smart. Faier could not fight them all. He would break.

A mistake right now meant death.

Rescue Harmony.

He could not bear a mistake. Faier fought on.

A commotion erupted at the front of the prison. Faier focused on the two warriors, especially single-minded Kusi, because they did not break off.

King Kayo led in a new group of warriors. Xarin and Healer Hobin ranged behind him. "Stop this interrogation. Stop it right now!"

"King Kayo." Tibe straightened but did not call off his warriors. "Why are you here?"

"I did not give permission."

"Oh? But I have never needed your permission to interrogate criminals before."

"I do not wish this warrior killed."

Kusi barreled into Faier.

Faier kicked hard to escape his tackle. The warrior's trident slashed a new line across his abdomen. The bandage unraveled, and the hot ache increased.

Kusi scraped the wall, veered, and followed Faier.

King Kayo snarled. "Stop Kusi!"

Xarin moved to intercept. Kusi kept his head down. Xarin braced.

"Not you, Xarin."

Xarin hesitated and then obeyed.

"Tibe! You call him off."

"My king, you know how difficult it is to stop Warrior Kusi once he—"

"Now!"

"Really, my king, there is no need to interrupt. He secures our city. This rebel is toxic to—"

"Fine. I will do it myself." King Kayo turned away from Tibe with exasperation and flew at the dueling warriors. "Kusi. You listen to me. I am your king!"

Faier dodged Kusi's wild attack.

His weak leg wobbled but did not collapse.

Kusi's trident flew past Faier's waist.

King Kayo floated within arm's reach. His attention was off Faier and focused on Kusi. And the other warriors were too far away.

Opportunity coalesced into action.

Now.

Faier kicked to his strong side and trapped Kusi's trident between his bicep and chest. Kusi yanked—a trainee mistake—and Faier used his own momentum to fly over both his and the king's heads. He exposed his back to the disorganized warriors. They did not attack when they should have. Faier whirled to his prey.

He locked his forearm around the king's neck.

The other warriors shouted.

Xarin shoved Kusi out of his way and flew at Faier with deadly fury.

King Kayo wheeled in Faier's choke hold, dragging Faier out of danger. "What is the meaning of this? You dare attack me?"

Faier brought the sharp middle blade of his trident to the king's soft underjaw. "Hold."

King Kayo froze.

Xarin also held. Murder burned in his gaze.

The other warriors pulled up sharply.

The king gripped Faier's forearm. He breathed through the gills in his lower back so Faier's hold did not endanger him. Only the sharp blades were the real risk. But Faier's grip immobilized him, and crushing a human's voice box caused harsh pain.

Faier spoke quietly. "Bring me Harmony."

The king growled. "What?"

One warrior whirled and flew out the exit.

Did he think to raise the Aiycaya army? Let them come. Faier would fight them all for Harmony.

He tightened his grip. "Your so-called sacred bride. Is she safe? Have you hurt her? Where is she?"

"You will never see *my* sacred bride again."

"Then neither will you." He ground the tip of the trident into King Kayo's jaw. Blood burst into the water. The king grunted.

An elder shrieked, "Do not touch our king, exile!"

"I will threaten much more if someone does not bring her, safe and unhurt, right now!"

Xarin jerked his chin at several warriors without ever taking his eyes off Faier. Those warriors exited.

King Kayo struggled against his grip. "You will not leave this prison alive."

"Worry about your own life if you have harmed her."

"Harmed her?" King Kayo continued to struggle. "What monsters do you think we are? To harm any female, much less a sacred bride. You are the monster, rebel scum. We are traditional in Aiycaya. Why would you ever think otherwise?"

Faier locked gazes with the first lieutenant.

A small smile touched his harsh mango-glazed features.

Deep within Faier's heart, a kernel of wisdom told him she was still alive.

He would not rest easy until he had seen her—unharmed—with his own eyes.

"Modern females must not want husbands," the king growled, still struggling. "Rebels are desperate. You belong to two cities and still steal *my* bride."

Faier couldn't help the small smile.

The king jerked on his iron forearm. "You laugh at me."

"There are more females on the land than stars in the sky."

"And yet none of them have become your bride."

It was true.

But that did not matter. "Soon, all our warriors will surface and claim *willing* brides."

"All at once? How stupid. Raiders will overrun your cities."

"Warriors who already found their queens will safeguard our cities."

"Queens!" King Kayo barked a laugh. "The rebel cities have queens? Queens of legend, I assume, who fight off mighty armies with ease and command the very water of the ocean, like those in my father's sleepy stories of before the Great Catastrophe?"

Elder Bawa burrowed through the assembled guards and tore into the standoff. "My king! My king, I have just arrived. You must not listen to the rebel. He lies!"

"Lies about what, Elder Bawa?"

"Everything, my king. You must not believe him!"

"Just now he tells me all their warriors will seek brides and leave city defense in the hands of 'queens'!"

"Yes, well, but...powerful queens are no reason to break the ancient covenant," the elder refuted, accidentally confirming they did, in fact, exist and they did, in fact, wield shocking powers. "No, my king. Any female who is not a sacred bride *must not* be exposed to the mer. The rebel 'queens' are anathema, modern females who overstay the limits of the ancient covenant and do not return to the safety of land where they belong."

"They stay?" he repeated, focusing on a point many warriors cared deeply about. No warrior wanted to return his soul mate to the surface and be separated from her forever, traditional or rebel. "For how long?"

"All air-breathers pine for the surface, my king. Holding them beneath the waves damages females. These so-called queens are tragic figures parted from—"

"Forever," Faier interjected. "They visit the surface frequently and return."

"They return! How many times do they return?"

"No, King Kayo, do not listen. No honorable warrior should take pride in trapping a female or in leaving the defense of the city to her. She should surface after fulfilling her duties to provide a young fry. That is the rule of a traditional city. These rebels forget their honor simply because our race has dwindled to dangerous levels."

Everyone looked at the red-faced elder. He had spoken far, far much too much without realizing.

King Kayo addressed Faier soberly. "How many of these queens exist?"

"My king, you must not listen to—"

"Hush, Elder Bawa. Rebel, explain."

He answered despite still holding the king in a deadlock. "In Atlantis, three. In Dragao Azul, five."

"And every modern female who enters a rebel city becomes a queen?"

"As soon as she learns to channel the Life Tree, forms her fins, and embraces her powers."

"Form fins! Now I know you are lying. And yet you would claim such females still birth healthy young fries? And there is no fighting? Among queens? Or warriors?"

"Only to be the next male chosen to surface and find his bride."

"You said all warriors may surface at any time."

"Soon."

"Why are they waiting?"

"My king!" Elder Bawa glowed so red, a vessel in his forehead throbbed. "It is dangerous to speak with the rebel. Their tongues are made of shiny metal forked with poison."

"Elder Bawa." The king glared. "Do you think I believe every word I am told?"

"Eh..."

"Am I so weak-willed?"

"No..."

"Good. Silence. Rebel, why are the warriors waiting?"

"King Kadir rebuilds the platform connecting the surface to Atlantis."

King Kayo blinked. "Your king rebuilds ancient Atlantis? Madness. He risks the wrath of mainland humans. His warriors could find anathema brides on any beach."

"He wishes for his Queen Elyssa and their young fry Prince Kael to play easily on the surface with her human family."

"Another 'queen,'" King Kayo mused. "Very well, pretend I believe all this. Dragao Azul is also waiting for the Atlantis platform to rise? They are far away."

"No. They fight a human terrorist organization, the Sons of Hercules, that strikes any warriors who arise."

The occupants of the prison tensed.

"Those are the first words of your story I believe." King Kayo boldly broke the tension. "Our ancestors formed the ancient covenant for our protection. Dragao Azul's King wisely restricts surfacing."

"Queen," he corrected.

"What? A queen rules Dragao Azul?"

"All warriors also rule."

"That is not rule. That is chaos."

"Decisions are made slowly. But they *are* made. The last sacred bride of Dragao Azul insisted on this 'democracy' as her condition to remain as queen."

"You are confused. Is Dragao Azul ruled by a sacred bride or by a queen?"

"The last sacred bride embraced her queen powers, drove out the All-Council army, and liberated the city. Now she remains as queen."

Faier's quiet pronouncement silenced all in the prison. Elder Bawa burned red, melting the orange of his tattoos. Xarin and the other warriors listened with confusion. Tibe fingered his trident as though studying an all-new threat.

"Liberated? You mean she turned it to a rebel city," the king argued. "And that is why you are its citizen. Because you led the rebel army from Atlantis to Dragao Azul."

"I led only the queen."

"Lies." He clenched Faier's forearm. "Elder Bawa, now I know why you did not wish to tell me about the rebel cities. The All-Council suffered embarrassing defeats. Instead of owning their failures, they pretend the queens of legend have returned."

Uneasy chuckles emerged from the taut warriors.

Elder Bawa grimaced, attempting to share in the joke. He knew Faier spoke the truth. And he had fed the other warriors—including the king, the other elders, everyone—a dismissive stream of lies.

Breaking the ancient covenant and leaving the All-Council was deadly.

But the alternative was worse.

"And this is your intention in Aiycaya," the king continued, growling low in his chest. "You 'liberate' it by murdering me."

"I have never attacked a king."

"Until now."

He kept his grip locked tight. "There is an easier way to destroy Aiycaya. You are a young male, King Kayo."

"I am old enough," he snarled.

"And yet I have seen no young fry. No trainees. These males wear intricate tattoos. More intricate—and experienced—than yours."

"At least my tattoos are not defaced!"

"In another generation, you will lose your elders. And in another, your warriors. And finally, all that will remain of 'traditional' Aiycaya will be you. I do not have to murder you. All I must do to destroy 'traditional' Aiycaya is leave you alone."

"Lies," the king returned. "We are faithful, honor the ancient covenant, and find our sacred brides. Starting with yours."

A bright light glowed overhead through the mesh lattice of the coral prison. Little glimmers lifted his heart. What was that faint glow floating down?

Harmony!

His heart thudded hard.

"You will never escape justice, rebel," the king snarled. He had seen Harmony too.

Faier did not respond.

Her light moved closer. The warriors at the entrance parted. They'd wrapped her in a harness used for transporting warriors too injured to swim alone. It was a common way to move sacred brides and obey the rule that only their husbands touch them.

The warrior pulled her into the center of the prison. He released her and returned to float by Xarin. He shyly avoided eye contact.

Harmony's soul glowed. "Faier. You're alive!"

His heart swelled. The crackles in his chest burned. Truly, she was his bride.

And she'd married King Kayo.

Harmony tugged the harness knots. Three wooden boxes of aged meat were tangled in the lines. They wrapped around her legs and knotted.

She already had three boxes of food for the journey? Good.

"Stay in the harness." Faier addressed the shy warrior. "Gather four more warriors and convey her to the surface."

Harmony stopped.

"I will end you," the king vowed, renewing his struggle. "I will chase after you as soon as you leave here. You will not escape me."

"I will stay," Faier told him. "You convey her safely."

The king choked.

Her soul glow dimmed with unhappiness. "Faier."

He could not let her feelings distract him. "Take her to Haiti."

The shy warrior looked at Xarin.

Xarin gripped his trident and awaited the orders of King Kayo.

The king exploded. "You dare expose my warriors? To modern humans?"

"I do not care about you."

"No, Faier." Harmony glowed brilliantly. "I won't leave you here."

"You must. It is not safe for you here."

The king snarled and writhed, slicing his own jaw on Faier's blade. "How dare you! I protect my sacred bride with my life!"

She shook her head, insisting she would remain with him, but he had to convince her. "The king will not protect you."

"Rebel scum! Release me at once. I will fight you! *She is mine*."

She wavered uncertainly. "You were the one who said he wouldn't hurt me."

"I lied."

She jerked her chin. "You never lie."

"I have lived outside traditional cities for too long. You are only a trident or a net to him. He does not see you as a person."

"Of course I see she is a human," King Kayo snapped. "A helpless, defenseless human."

"Not as a human. *A person*. A living female with desires and dreams," Faier clarified. "He does not even know your name."

She blinked.

The king's mouth opened and then closed. A remnant of surface-dwelling. He gritted his jaw. "Yes. I know this. She is my sacred bride. Of course I know her name."

The silence stretched.

Harmony frowned at the king.

The shy warrior spoke. "The king knows her name. It is Harmony."

Everyone turned to him.

"Ar-mo-nee?" King Kayo repeated. "What name is Ar-mo-nee?"

"Harmony." She let out a puff of water and rubbed her cheeks. "Oh, goodness. Wow. We even got 'married'..." she made finger gestures, "...and you didn't ask my name. That's rude on the surface."

"It is rude anywhere," Faier confirmed.

"I just...you...there was never a... The rebel interrupted our introductions!"

"Real mature to blame someone else."

"But—"

Xarin's voice intruded, low with disapproval. "Warrior Zaka, why do you know the sacred bride's name? No warrior must touch *or address* the king's sacred bride."

The king shouted at the shy warrior, "Yes, Warrior Zaka! How dare you speak to my sacred—er, my Harmony?"

Warrior Zaka held up his hands. "I did not mean to—"

"How dare you ask her such an intimate question?"

"I told him," Harmony said.

But her statement disappeared in the disapproving rumble from warriors and elders.

"Banished!" The king released Faier's forearm to point to the exit of the prison. "To the Life Tree. Replace Warrior Luin on patrol there. His punishment is yours."

Warrior Zaka hung his head and swam, his soul light dark, for the exit.

King Kayo heard him well enough. "Insolent rebel! I just told you I will defend her from any injury to her body."

"But not in her soul."

"Her soul!"

"There are many ways to injure a female," Faier told him. "Lying is one."

"You didn't lie on purpose, Faier," Harmony said, brightening with hope. "You made a mistake. I make those all the time."

"Go to Haiti," Faier urged. "Once you are safe, I will find you and keep my vow. I promise."

Her brow cleared. "I know you will. But I can't. I'm not leaving here without you."

"Harmony, you do not need me. Complete your rescue yourself."

"No. I still need you," she insisted, making his chest hurt. "I will never stop needing you. We're rescuing each other now, okay? We have to both go. Together."

He had rescued many people. Humans with the Coast Guard. Mer in his previous cities. All had been grateful. After the rescue he was no longer needed.

Harmony was different. "You...need me?"

"Yes." She glowed with promise. "I can't get rescued you."

A harder truth choked into his happiness. "Harmony, you must go alone. I am too injured to swim with you."

She shook her head.

"Yes. You must."

"The journey will take days," the king argued, trying to break between them. "Stupid exile, you will not hold me prisoner for days or weeks."

"To protect Harmony, I would wait years."

Harmony covered her mouth. Her soul flared with feeling. She reached for his—

"But I will not." Tibe lofted his trident. "No warrior insults my king. Now, die."

The mango-tattooed first lieutenant kicked forward with deadly intent. Warriors Chiba and Kusi flew into line behind him.

King Kayo stiffened. "Wait, Tibe."

"Tibe, stop!" Elder Bawa shouted. "Do not risk the life of our king!"

Faier kicked backward, dragging the king away from the first lieutenant's deadly strike.

King Kayo held on dumbly, neither fighting nor assisting. "We are negotiating!"

"You had the chance to free yourself," the mango warrior said coldly. "Now I will free you."

"Stop! I do not wish for this. Do not help me!"

"I should have killed you on the surface." Tibe veered to follow Faier. "Every moment you are alive wastes my time."

"Do not test me, First Lieutenant." Faier flew backward fast and hard. His side ached. But thanks to Harmony, he felt strong. "You do not know what I am capable of."

"Oh?" Tibe bunched his muscles and lofted his trident to strike. "Show me."

"Tibe!" the elders shouted. "No!"

The first lieutenant thrust at King Kayo's chest.

The strike centered on the king's heart.

Faier watched the blade tines approach as the other warriors and elders screamed. Harmony froze in horror. Xarin roared and flew to attack Tibe.

But he would be too late.

Everyone would be too late.

King Kayo stiffened in Faier's arms.

Curse it.

Faier twisted again—agony—and pushed King Kayo out of the way. King Kayo fell backward.

Tibe's trident spear lanced the water over his face.

King Kayo's eyes widened.

Faier gripped his throbbing, hot side and kicked hard.

Tibe blocked his path and slashed at Faier. Faier brought his trident up and met Tibe's attack.

Too slow.

The long tine of Tibe's trident scored his cheekbone.

Faier jerked back.

Pain.

His blood salted the water.

Faier slashed up. Their tridents tangled.

Tibe pushed. "Disgusting rebel. Where is your honor?"

But Faier was angry. He pushed back. "That is a question you should ask yourself."

Tibe growled.

He dropped the butt of the trident and swung it at Faier's belly.

Faier kicked out of the way.

Into a wall of seething warriors—and the king.

King Kayo lifted his trident. "Drop your weapon."

EIGHTEEN

Faier lowered his trident, his gaze flicking back to Harmony, and the fear there stabbed her in the heart.

She couldn't breathe.

The warriors swarmed Faier, taking his trident and binding him.

Good thing she hadn't been convinced to leave him for Haiti. Tibe would have lost his patience and attacked before she was even out the door.

She was the only leverage they had. Somehow she had to figure out how to use herself to save him.

Tibe floated to Faier and raised his trident.

"Don't hurt him!" she cried.

The mango warrior she hated rammed the butt of his trident into Faier's bleeding injury.

Faier arched and roared in pain.

Xarin whirled between Faier and Tibe, edging the first lieutenant out of his way, while he continued to bind Faier so he could not vibrate a single word, not even a scream. "Warrior Luin. Call Healer Hobin."

Warrior Luin, with thin red tattoos, swam for the exit.

"Do not bother." Tibe sneered and raised his trident again. "We kill him now."

"No!" Harmony shrieked.

Just as before, the word popped out of her mouth before she could stop it.

King Kayo's gaze flicked to her.

"No, you promised!" She shoved free of the harness—which she'd entered the moment Warrior Zaka had told her Faier was holding King Kayo hostage—and wiggled her tiny, stubby human feet like crazy to reach the distant mob. "You promised the All-Council would judge Faier."

King Kayo rubbed his throat, winced at the forming bruise, and glared daggers at Faier. "I promised."

Tibe's head reared back. "Wait for the All-Council? No. You must show your strength by immediate execution."

"I gave my word, Tibe."

"Aiycaya cannot be weak."

"I promised Harmony."

"Who cares about a sacred bride? She does not know our ways. This is for the good of our city."

King Kayo regarded Tibe with a dark arua.

Tibe's lip curled in a silent snarl. "Other cities will attack. Rebels and exiles will flood us. We do not have the warriors to fight them. You would endanger our city because of one misguided promise to a sacred bride?"

"Tibe."

"The insult cannot stand. We must enforce our laws. Do not pity this rebel. He attacked a king!"

King Kayo nodded slowly. His grip tightened on his trident. He closed his eyes tight and opened them with new anger. Anger directed at the wheezing, trembling, defeated form of Faier.

Because of her.

And there was nothing she could...

Tinkle. Tinkle. Tinkle.

"So did you," Harmony said clearly.

King Kayo stopped. "Harmony. Wait quietly."

"'He attacked a king.'" She repeated Tibe's words. "And so did you."

The king's eyes narrowed.

Then the realization struck him. His brows lifted. He stared at the trident in his hand as if seeing it for the first time. Then he looked at Faier. And, finally, beyond Tibe to her.

Tibe hadn't heard her. Or if he had, he hadn't paid attention. He gestured for the king to continue. "End him, King Kayo. He tried to kill you."

"So did you," Harmony called, louder and clearer.

Faier looked over at her. Through his cloudy aura of pain, he still heard her. And despite her hesitation that had so badly hurt him, he smiled.

The smile stung her chest.

I will save you.

King Kayo's trident lifted, and the blade pointed at Tibe's chest.

Tibe looked up. "What?"

King Kayo vibrated with firm anger. "You also tried to kill me."

Tibe's thin lips parted. His eyes widened. "I?"

"When you flew with your trident. It would not have stabbed his chest. It would have stabbed mine."

His mouth snapped shut, and his chest vibrated with cold fury. "This, then, is what you think of me?"

King Kayo gripped his trident more firmly. "The blow would have been mortal."

"And you think I would kill you? When a deadly rebel already chokes you, you think I would rather stab you myself?"

King Kayo glanced at Faier's sliced abdomen, which Tibe had continued to strike. "I saw the angle of your attack. If he had not moved, I would be dead."

"Twelve years."

King Kayo hesitated. "What?"

"Twelve years I have been your first lieutenant. I have advised you. Guided you. Given you my wisdom, my blade, my life. And now, you question my loyalty."

"I saw the angle..."

"And you think I had not the wisdom to calculate my opponent's weakness, use it against him, and ensure I would not harm you in my attack?"

"So you..." King Kayo blinked. "You knew he would move and your trident would not strike me...and so you...hmm..."

Tibe grabbed King Kayo's trident just beneath the fork and brought the sharpest tine to his neck. "If you doubt my loyalty, then take my life."

King Kayo closed his eyes. "Tibe..."

"Take it. I do not need it."

"Tibe."

"Now." He jerked the blade across his own throat. It scratched and drew blood.

"Urgh. No!" King Kayo dragged his trident away and glared at the mango warrior. "I believe you. You are forgiven. Do not give me cause to doubt again."

"My king, it is not I who cause doubt." He pointed at Faier. "It is the rebel whose life you must end."

King Kayo returned to Faier with resignation. His brows lowered along with his trident.

"No!" Harmony wiggled faster toward the group. It took forever to reach them. She was a little closer. "No, you can't!"

"Now." Tibe jerked his chin. "Administer justice."

"King Kayo! This isn't justice."

King Kayo wrinkled his nose and whirled on Harmony with irritation. "It is justice!"

"It is not."

"It is."

"It is *not*."

"It *is*." King Kayo returned to Faier, snarled at the bound warrior, and repositioned his trident. "The sentence for attacking a king is immediate death and dismemberment over the nearest vent. You will not be sung. You will not be remembered. You will not be honored. I sentence you to—"

"Faier saved your life!"

King Kayo bit down on a snarl and whirled to face her again. "What?!"

"Faier saved you."

"I do not... How...?" He looked at Tibe.

"Your bride is confused." Tibe turned away from her. "Carry on."

"I'm not confused." She kicked harder.

Elder Wida scratched his white-tattoo-swirled nose, his voice booming. "Her words are odd but lucid."

"Her words are hysterical."

"Yes, my king." Elder Bawa swam forward, inserting himself as a new authority. "Your bride is hysterical from being outside your castle so long. She is an air breather who cannot handle the stress of the mer environment. Remember that your mother never once left her castle the entire time she was in Aiycaya. Even those extra months."

They regarded Harmony with pity.

Faier's chest vibrated. Muffled by the ties. She couldn't hear.

King Kayo leaned in, frowned, and shook his head. He couldn't hear either.

Listen.

"Do not listen to her," Elder Bawa blurted.

Tibe agreed. "Ignore her."

King Kayo turned his shoulder against her.

They wouldn't listen. And she couldn't make them.

She couldn't...

The warmth of the Life Tree swirled around her again even though it was far above in the city. She shivered from her toes up to the base of her neck and tingled all the way down. Clear righteousness filled her.

"Fine. Don't listen to me." She jabbed her index finger at Tibe. "Listen to him!"

King Kayo looked at his first lieutenant.

"I told you to execute him," Tibe said smugly.

"Tibe admitted he aimed to kill you," she corrected.

King Kayo's frown deepened.

"I did no such thing," Tibe declared.

"He 'calculated Faier's weakness' and 'used it against him.'"

The other warriors murmured.

"What is your meaning?" Elder Wida asked with a deep bass rumble.

"Faier's 'weakness' was that he would not let you die." She spoke to King Kayo. "Faier saved your life."

King Kayo's brow furrowed so deeply, his eyebrows almost receded into his hairline. "That makes a strange kind of sense."

Elder Yane and Elder Wida also nodded.

Elder Bawa pursed his lips, searching for the argument.

"No." Tibe shook his head. "I freed you from the rebel. He *threatened* your life. I saved you from him."

"By striking a mortal blow at me," King Kayo intoned. "And trusting the rebel would move *me* away from your strike."

"He moved out of the strike," Tibe insisted. "His bravery faltered before my blade."

"And your blade was aimed at King Kayo's chest plate," Elder Yane said. "It upset me. I would never advise my warriors to perform such a reckless attack."

"Because I knew you would not be hurt! He shied away. The rebel did not commit to 'win at all costs.' He is as weak-willed as Xarin!"

Xarin glared at the mango warrior. "Upholding mer law is no weakness."

King Kayo tensed. "Stop this argument."

"You would let raiders destroy our city before you compromise on 'principle,'" Tibe sniped at Xarin. "That is why you are second lieutenant. So a true warrior with strength can ensure the city's safety."

"I would not entrust my king's life on the morality of an unknown rebel."

"For the last time, I knew he would yield!"

"Because it would have been much better for him if he had not. After a king's death, how much more easily could the rebel have taken his sacred bride and escape—"

"Enough!" King Kayo vibrated to a shout. "Xarin, secure the prison."

"The king's sacred bride," Tibe corrected with a growl, prowling in front of Xarin and preventing him from carrying out King Kayo's orders. "How dare you mistake his bride for a rebel's sad, sickly female?"

"Move," Xarin growled.

"You dare to order me? Second Lieutenant?"

"The king issued a direct order, First Lieutenant Tibe. You are in my—"

"Silence!" King Kayo roared. "Xarin! Go. Now."

Xarin eased around Tibe, trident at his side and refusing to show his back. He led the warriors and most of the elders out. They streamed past Harmony. Only Elder Wida and Elder Bawa remained.

"Such insubordination." Tibe lowered his trident.

"Tibe, go with Xarin," the king snapped.

He looked startled and then stiffened correctly. "Yes, my king." But he did not float away.

The king didn't seem to notice. He raised his voice loud enough to vibrate to the entrance. "And summon Healer Hobin!"

The vibrations echoed in the barren prison.

An older warrior with coral-pink tattoos flew in. He knelt and tsked over Faier's injuries. "They muffled you. Suppose I replace the bandage..."

Harmony reached Faier's side. Finally! She hovered behind the healer.

Faier focused on her.

She looked into his pain-darkened eyes and promised, once more, that she would save him. Together.

King Kayo turned to his elders. "Elder Wida. You have prepared the hunt?"

"Elder Yane assembled the nets and harpoons."

"Good. We will soon launch."

While the healer worked, Harmony noticed her small green octopus squeezing through the coral wall. She walked down the wall to the floor and crept close.

"Elder Bawa. When will the All-Council representative arrive?"

The elder harrumphed. "It is too early to hear, my king."

"I want to know before they arrive."

"My king! I can fully prepare the city for the All-Council representative. You should focus on your bride."

His lids lowered to half. "I am."

"And on your hunt! Do not distract yourself with All-Council matters. As you know, there was no greater hunter than King Kamuy."

"Yes, I said I would hunt."

"You have taken after King Kamuy in almost every way. He supported his warriors even on his deathbed. He would not abandon his warriors for small, trifling, unimportant All-Council business."

King Kayo gritted his teeth. "Does it sound as though I am abandoning my warriors?"

"A king must never rest easy. No matter how tired. If a deathbed will not stop your father, then you too must focus. Do you not want to be seen as the greatest king?"

"Yes. Of course." He turned his shoulder to Elder Bawa. "You carry on."

"Thank you, my king." Elder Bawa looked at Tibe meaningfully behind King Kayo and swam to the exit.

The healer finished rebinding Faier's wound and rose. "Rest now. No more sudden movements until you heal. Or you will mortally damage your insides."

Faier closed heavy lids and forced them open again.

"Can't you untie him?" she begged. "It's cruel to leave him so he can't even speak."

The healer glanced at the king. "He attacked a ruler."

"After Tibe attacked him!"

"A misunderstanding," King Kayo dismissed.

Fury welled in her body and heated her cheeks.

What.

The.

Heck.

Healer Hobin rolled up his tools and swished to the exit, passing the slow-moving Elder Bawa and disappearing into the sea.

Harmony felt pissed.

"What is with you mermen and your 'misunderstandings'?" She glared at the remaining four. "*Are* we speaking the same language? Or are you a bunch of truth-twisters who don't own up to your lies?"

Tibe's voice snapped with cold. "King Kayo. It is time to put away your confused bride."

King Kayo nodded at the elder. "Elder Wida. See my bride back to my castle."

Elder Wida collected the seaweed rope harness.

"No," Harmony said. It came more easily.

King Kayo blinked. "Harmony?"

"I'm not going back to the castle." Harmony sat cross-legged next to Faier, bouncing on the hard rock. "I'm staying right here."

"You must leave."

"I refuse."

King Kayo descended to the rock and knelt to her level. His vibrations dropped to intimate concern. "I will not endanger your rebel. My vow is unbroken."

"I'm still staying here," she told him.

Faier's eyes flicked between them. His aura darkened.

"There are no comforts," King Kayo protested.

"Sure there are. I've got my 'house guardian' over there." Her stomach growled, and she pointed to the three boxes she had forced Warrior Zaka to tie to the harness. "And I've got my food."

"A sacred bride cannot dwell in prison." King Kayo's aura fluttered with hurt. "You reject my castle?"

"I would rather be with Faier in prison than in a thousand castles alone."

"You will never be alone."

"That doesn't exactly help. You got mad at Warrior Zaka and he was only ever nice to me. Prison feels safer."

"Safer than my castle?!"

Elder Wida vibrated with a low, throat-clearing rumble. "I believe I might know the root of your sacred bride's fear, my king. Just after you left the wedding feast, Warlord Sao attempted to take her."

"Warlord Sao?" King Kayo reared back. "Take her where?"

"He would not answer. Moving her was not your orders?"

King Kayo whipped to Tibe with accusation in his expression. "You ordered your top warlord?"

His first lieutenant returned his gaze coolly. "To do what?"

King Kayo looked beyond him to the back of the still-lingering elder. "Elder Bawa!"

The elder jolted. "I am leaving, my king!" He flew out.

King Kayo grimaced. "I will ask Warlord Sao myself."

"Sao has already left the city. He clears the hunting route of exiles." Tibe turned to Elder Wida. "Remove his sacred bride."

Elder Wida looked straight back at Tibe. "First Lieutenant, I did not hear the king issue that order."

"He needs to." Tibe glanced at King Kayo. "The hunt begins. Now."

King Kayo looked down at Harmony.

She crossed her arms tighter.

He sagged, exhausted, and scrubbed his face. Then he motioned for the warrior and elder to leave. "She will stay."

"With the rebel?" Tibe's normal certainty fell to shock. "But, my king—"

"Our city is well patrolled. She will be safe enough here."

"She insults you. She disgraces your castle."

"Tibe. Please."

"You cannot allow this insubordination to—"

"My bride needs time."

"She will have all the time she needs *inside* your castle." Tibe hovered over her and barked, "Your king gave you an order. Do not disrespect the king's orders!"

She glared right back. "I am not his warrior to order and obey."

Tibe's eyes widened. "You dare—"

"And decisions about me are *his* to make. Not yours."

Shock and then wrath darkened Tibe's aura to deadly.

He was the true danger. Like Jean-Baptiste, he twisted reality to suit his desires and forced King Kayo to come along. Now, she stood in his way.

Harmony hunched closer to Faier.

Her little octopus flew in front of her, tentacles balled into warning fists.

Tibe's lips peeled back from his teeth. "You dirty, surface-dwelling—"

"Tibe," the king growled. He lifted his trident in warning. "Do not threaten my sacred bride."

Tibe pulled himself back from the abyss. Barely. "My king, when you chose me as your first lieutenant, I vowed to let no one disrespect you. Not even your sacred bride."

"I do not feel disrespected."

He blinked. "But...she..."

"Go."

"She is flouting your orders."

"And you are frightening her. Can you not see that much?"

"One who disobeys me should be frightened."

"First Lieutenant—"

"Because you order it, my king, I obey." Tibe wheeled away. "Xarin will lead the first phalanx of the hunt."

"Leave Xarin at the prison. He has shown adeptness as a guard."

"My king, I do not think the prisoner deserves such a talented hunter."

"Tibe, I order you to take another warrior. Do you hear me?"

Tibe flew out the exit without answering.

King Kayo looked up at the remaining elder. "Elder Wida? You were leaving?"

"Yes, my king." He reluctantly flew out.

Then, it was just her, King Kayo, and a bound-silent, still-injured Faier.

As though knowing it was finally safe to do so, Faier closed his eyes. His head tipped and his lips parted. If air moved in and out of his lungs, she was sure he'd be snoring.

King Kayo descended again to Harmony's level. The hot-pink accents in his eyes glowed with promise. "I will discover Warlord Sao's motives. You *will* be safe in my city."

"Thank you."

"I will assign you more guards. Trustworthy guards. Even, if you demand it, Warrior Zaka."

"Okay."

"We patrol our borders, but there is still a risk. Will you

not return to the castle? It has thick walls. The heart chamber is reinforced."

"I'm not afraid of walls. I am afraid of the warriors who lie and undermine you."

His jaw clenched. "Xarin is—"

"I mean Tibe. And Elder Bawa."

The anger drained out of him. For the second time, he looked exhausted. Beyond wrecked with tiredness. His shoulders sagged, and the deep furrows in his face made him a much older, world-weary male.

"Elder Bawa has always treated me like a child."

King Kayo rubbed his forehead. Red vessels swelled in his bloodshot eyes.

"But he is our representative to the All-Council. He has the most knowledge of their laws and ways. In my father's time, he devised a petition to reconnect with our sacred brides. And we are so close now. Your rebel is correct that our city is failing and we are only a few generations from dissolution. I will not distract Elder Bawa from the work that holds so much importance."

She respected King Kayo's mature attitude. He had put more thought into the dynamic than she had realized.

"And Tibe?"

"Tibe is Tibe." King Kayo rose. His human feet extended into long fins. His gaze fixed beyond her on sleeping Faier. "Rest well, rebel. I leave my sacred bride in your care."

King Kayo kicked for the exit.

"His care?" Harmony rose onto her knees. "Then won't you at least untie him?"

He disappeared out the exit.

Oh, jeez.

She struggled with the bonds but they were tied in such

a way that she couldn't even wedge a finger under them. She tried until her fingers bruised and then she didn't know what to do.

"I won't leave you," she promised sleeping Faier. "I couldn't save Evens or Monsieur Joseph or even Lifet. But I will save you. We're going to figure this out together."

It might have been her imagination but she thought his chest rose and fell a little easier.

This day had been a million years long. Harmony laid her head in Faier's lap. He didn't wake up.

She had to think. How could she get Faier out of here alive? Tibe would murder them as soon as King Kayo turned his back. Elder Bawa was just as bad. A bunch of other warriors were under their control rather than King Kayo's. And King Kayo was in denial. Especially about Tibe.

His hunt wouldn't last forever.

She had to think. Plot. Strategize.

For just one second, while she was wracking her addled brain, she closed her eyes...

NINETEEN

Something gnawed on Faier's wrist.

Sharp pricks—*pinch*—and real pain, as if a small animal was chewing off his skin, and snarling.

Danger.

"Ngh!" He came awake with a shudder. His side twinged. But there was no stabbing pain.

He searched for the source of his unease.

Harmony's head rested on his bent knees. She lay on her side, the gentle swell of her hips and breasts undulating against the harsh prison floor.

Relief mixed with impending doom like two colors of oil on water.

Pinch.

He grunted. It felt like his tendons were separating. He strained against his bindings.

Shhhip. His wrists separated. The seaweed cables frayed apart.

He flexed his strained shoulders, brought his hands around to the front, and twisted them. Pain and heat radiated up his forearms. Pins needled his fingertips.

He strained to look over his shoulder without disturbing Harmony.

A small green tentacle waved in the corner of his eye. The unmistakable gurgling of an atonal, but otherwise pleased, house guardian scratched his eardrums.

Pinch. Pinch. The binding at his ankles loosened.

All bindings loosened. He expanded his lungs, flushing in fresh water. His mind cleared.

Neat bites on his wrist reddened where the house guardian had pinched him. Beneath, the wounds of his last battle with Tibe had closed. Swollen and dark, they were not as painful.

Strange.

He leaned forward to lift the bindings to a better angle for the house guardian and to reduce her bites.

"Freeze, rebel." Warrior Luin—that was the name—startled as if he'd been snoozing on guard duty. He thrust a trident in Faier's face. "I do not know how you got free, but release the king's sacred bride and remain still, or I will—I will end you!"

Red lines, thin with inexperience, inked his skin.

"Shhh." Faier lifted his palms in surrender and gestured at prone Harmony. "She is sleeping."

"Yes." His throat apple bobbed. "I could not make her move. But you can! No warrior may touch another's sacred bride. But you will die for your crimes!"

"Please lower your voice," he murmured.

To no avail.

Harmony stirred, rising and yawning. She saw the trident and froze. Her soul light darkened. "What do you want?"

Warrior Luin didn't answer. He looked at Faier.

"He wants you to move away from me," Faier said

wryly.

"Why doesn't he just say so?"

"Because they forbid speaking to another warrior's sacred bride in a traditional city. It is a safeguard to prevent another warrior's soul from resonating with a sacred bride and changing her allegiance."

"That's not happening." She dismissed Warrior Luin with amusement. "No way is he stealing my 'allegiance' from the king."

Faier's heart squeezed.

Her soul *had* resonated with the king's. They were very similar. He listened to her. In this short time, their souls flared the same color.

And she had earned the approval of a house guardian. This city called her soul. This Life Tree.

King Kayo.

Not Faier.

"Oh, yes! You're awake. I'm so glad you're okay!" She flew into Faier and wrapped him in a thrilling hug.

He grabbed her arms as he fell back, over his still-tied ankles, and bumped his head on the ground as he rotated with her. Her softness filled his arms and her joy filled his soul with rightness. "Thank you, Harmony."

Warrior Luin protested. "You must not touch. He is not your husband."

"Huh? Oh." She kicked her feet and finished the somersault so he rested on the floor again. So close, they could almost kiss.

Then, she glanced at the other warrior and floated back. "I was so worried. I begged them not to hurt you, but they wouldn't listen."

"I know."

"Only Xarin even heard me. Oh, no. You're hurt again."

She touched the scar running across Faier's face from his temple to his nose.

The red-limned Warrior Luin protested again. "You must not touch."

"We touch on the surface."

"A sacred bride must not. You disrespect King Kayo."

"And you disrespect her," Faier reminded him. "No talking."

He reddened like his tattoos. "Silence, rebel prisoner!"

"Okay, okay. Calm down, Warrior Luin. It's true that I don't like to break rules."

"Then you should return to the king's castle," a lime-green warrior who floated in from the entrance called.

She turned. "Is that a rule or tradition?"

"Tradition *is* a rule, Sacred Bride Harmony."

"Hush, Warrior Poro. Do not speak to her. She is a sacred bride."

"I know she is, Warrior Luin. I can see with my own eyes."

"Then do not speak. *S'ai ala oo, Poro.*"

"*Ti kanis, Luin.*"

Both warriors bickered in their own language. Their inexperience swayed and confused them. Perhaps the only warrior with less experience was their absent King.

The city was in desperate straits.

"I appreciate the truth," she whispered.

"I will always tell you the truth, Harmony."

"Yeah, I know. You've told me plenty of things I'd rather have not been true." She looked at the other warriors. "Here, I don't know who to trust."

Warrior Luin swallowed.

"You can trust King Kayo," the lime-green Warrior Poro

assured her. "You are his treasured sacred bride. He will treat you honorably."

"You like the king," she noted. "He seems young."

"The youngest warrior," Warrior Poro agreed, talkative. "His father should have lived longer and trained him thoroughly."

"I'm sorry. What about Tibe? What's his story?"

"He—"

"You must ask King Kayo." Warrior Luin nudged Warrior Poro. "We must not speak to his sacred bride."

"I'll ask, but I wish you would speak to me. Otherwise, it will be a long, lonely year."

Warrior Poro sought her gaze. "Sac—"

"Tut." Warrior Luin blocked his view and clinked his trident against Poro's.

They lapsed into silence.

Ocean sounds filled the chamber. The house guardian's yowls mixed with pleasant fish songs on the other side of the prison walls.

Harmony's soul light wavered.

"You are right," Faier said, drawing her attention back to him. "Insist on speaking as you wish. Flex your will."

She suppressed a smile. Her soul glowed with amusement she concealed from her face. "You always say crazy things."

"Crazy things?"

"As if I could control my destiny when I am as much a prisoner as you."

Both warriors gaped. Did she consider herself a prisoner? She shocked them.

"You are no prisoner." Faier voiced their confusion. "The king asked you to return to his castle. Yet here you are. You controlled your destiny."

"Well...but...you're still tied up."

"The reason I still live is you. Believe."

"I wanted to save you." Her soul light brightened to blinding, and her eyes reddened with feeling. She swallowed. "Okay. Um, can we untie your ankles?"

Warrior Luin snapped out of his stupor. "No one can untie you. First Lieutenant Tibe's orders."

"Maybe you should ask the doctor."

"First Lieutenant Tibe's orders overrule everyone."

"King Kayo's orders are for Faier to heal. He'll heal better if he can rest. So untie him."

Again, the warriors looked at each other.

"King Kayo will listen to reason," she said. "I mean, look at me. Here I am."

Warrior Poro muttered something in his language. Warrior Luin's eyebrows shot for the ceiling with surprise. They chatted again in their language.

Harmony broke in. "Yes, the king told Tibe to leave instead of forcing me. Why is that so surprising?"

They both jolted and stared at her in shock.

"You learned their language?" Faier's heart sank deeper. "Already?"

"Oh. That was in their language?" She thought about it. "I wouldn't say I know the words. But I kind of got a feeling of the meaning. Somehow."

Knowing their language would be useful to escape their captors.

Except it meant she resonated more and more with the Aiycaya Life Tree and its king.

She rose and bounced to Warrior Poro. "Well, have you at least given him food?"

"We must not, Sacred Bride Harmony." Warrior Poro ignored Warrior Luin's "silence" gesture. "Tibe ordered—"

"He's supposed to heal."

Again, the warriors seemed nonplussed.

Her small house guardian flew around her and tangled her tentacles playfully in Harmony's hair.

She knelt to untie him.

"You must not!" both warriors protested.

"First Lieutenant Tibe ordered..." Warrior Luin repeated weakly.

"I'm sure he only ordered *you* not to do it." Her fingers whisked against his ankles like fluttery kisses. "No way did he say a sacred bride couldn't untie Faier."

"He did not specify..."

"So, that's fine, then." She hummed.

The warriors argued in their language, eying her furtively.

He enjoyed her light touch on his bonds.

At least he could have that much.

Soon, he would be free. He flexed his ankles. How would he disarm the two warriors? With the least harm?

Because of Harmony...

"Huh." She kicked to his front. "I still can't untie the knots. They're too tight. Are you okay?"

His toes were numb.

He flexed them. "Thank you for trying, Harmony."

Another pinch tickled his fingers.

He startled badly. What creature had snuck up and—oh, yes. His ears were again insulted by her off-tone yowl.

"My octopus!" Harmony wiggled her fingers. "Good luck. They're tight."

The house guardian's small tentacles teased his bonds apart, and her hard beak sawed.

Faier tried to focus on her happiness. But it knifed his side. "You communicate well with this city's king?"

"Oh... He's okay." She waved one hand and rolled her eyes in exasperation. "He doesn't listen. But I got through at the end."

Faier's bonds loosened. He flexed his ankles. The house guardian wiggled.

"Can I get you food?" Harmony turned to Warrior Luin. "Please bring in my lunch."

Warrior Luin protested. "It is against First Lieutenant Tibe's—"

"To give me my lunch?"

"Oh. For you... Then I guess..."

He returned with the three small boxes. Harmony reached out. Luin let go and jerked back to avoid touching her.

She opened the top box to display flavorful aged meat.

"I've eaten so much." Harmony pulled out a slice and offered it to Faier. "It's really good. As a thank-you for feeding me on the surface, I want to feed you."

Both warriors protested. "No warrior may feed the exile!"

"I am no warrior. So, that can't be against orders, can it?"

The warriors looked at each other. No one had ordered them to stop the sacred bride from feeding the prisoner.

Her soul flared as she looked back at Faier and handed him the hunk. "Go ahead."

He chewed the delicious sustenance.

"Here." Harmony handed him another hunk for his free hand. "Eat up."

Both warriors edged back and forth, muttering and gazing at the entrance, as though awaiting a furious superior. Here were the prisoner and the king's sacred bride sitting in the middle of the prison enjoying good meat. And

Faier was starving. His last human food had been a cup of coffee and a chicken sandwich on the Coast Guard cutter hours before they'd hit the storm. He'd eaten fish underneath the raft. Then, his injury, and nothing.

Health flowed into his veins and revitalized his body.

Harmony studied him critically. "You look better. Your scars, I mean. They're less angry and more...scar-y."

He flexed his shoulders and his arms. And then his legs were free, and he flexed his toes. "Yes, I feel better."

The house guardian darted between them and rotated in a happy circle.

Harmony handed the king's house guardian her own hunk of meat. "Good girl."

The warriors both dropped their jaws.

"House guardians forage for scraps," he noted.

"Well, she freed you where I couldn't." Harmony handed the pleased house guardian a second chunk. "So, it's only fair she should share the reward."

He stretched his aching legs and remained in human form to lull his guards into false security. "You eat well in Aiycaya?"

"Here! Vegetables." She opened another box filled with an assortment of revitalizing legumes. "It's weird, but this place feels familiar. Like I've been here in a dream. But..." her soul light fluctuated to dark and light again, "...I came here to ask you about that."

"Me?"

"You." She rolled onto her knees and rested her hands on her thighs. "Did you give me elixir?"

He stopped chewing.

"You never lie. Right?"

He choked. Her doubts cut into his already hurting heart. "Harmony."

"I know you would've done it to save my life," she said in a rush. "Really. You didn't want to tell me after you found out how scared I was. You've always helped me. I just have to know."

He answered truthfully. Even though his past wishes filled him with shame. "I wished to give you elixir. But I had none."

"Nothing? Not even by accident?"

"You doubt me because of my disrespectful thoughts."

"Thoughts? Oh, no, I'm asking about logistics here. The Aiycaya warriors said there was no elixir on any of their islands *and* they didn't have a Life Tree blossom, so there's literally no way they could have transformed me. So, how *did* I transform? If not them, then...?"

"I had many disrespectful thoughts, Harmony."

"But thoughts are...I mean, I couldn't have spontaneously transformed, right? It's impossible. Nobody would ever drown."

"Transforming to marry a warrior was your greatest fear. Even so, I swam around your sacred island searching for the elixir. I found none."

"Neither did they. That's what I'm saying."

"I wished I would have had my blossom when the crocodile attacked you and our only choice was to lose the raft and dive. I thought you would die."

"So did I. And I drank nothing on that island. So how did I transform? I'm a little confused."

"But I did not have my blossom or my Sea Opal. I did not expect to meet my mate on the rescue mission for the Coast Guard."

She froze. Her chest light grew bright and then dark and then shivered and shuddered. Finally, they were in sync. "Your mate? I'm your mate?"

Yes.

But no. No. No.

His mouth opened and closed.

She waited expectantly

He felt like a hunter who had brought the greatest catch to his bride only to overhear she hated hunting.

His heart turned over. Cold warred with heat.

You are my mate.

Even though she did not love him. Even though he was a monster. Even though she turned away from him and synchronized her soul to the king.

He had long ago known he would never find a bride. And now, with Harmony before him, he was the closest he would ever come.

And still an infinite sea parted them.

It would be easier to lie. More convenient for her. Less damaging to him.

But Faier was not a warrior who lied.

"Yes. You are mine."

TWENTY

You are mine.

Faier's powerful claim heated Harmony's chest. Surprise unfurled like the petals of a flower opening to the sun. Her sun was the mauve threads in his eyes, the ruined lines on his rough skin, and the fierce glow of his aura promising her what she already knew: He was her one.

He looked away and rubbed his wrists. "Forgive me."

"No, I..."

He winced and avoided her gaze. "Please."

Funny. He looked uncomfortable. Had he not meant to confess?

Huh. Harmony worried all the time, yet Faier, in the worst situations, looked calm. As if being bound and hit by furious warriors in revenge for holding their king hostage wasn't so bad; he'd seen worse and wasn't worried.

Seeing him uncomfortable was refreshing.

"Why didn't you tell me?" she asked

"You did not wish to become the husband of a merman."

"But that's... My wishes are separate from your feelings."

"No."

The bubbles of surprise popped once more. "No?"

"A bride must desire her husband. Her desire increases his desire. But you do not have these feelings for me. So I should not harbor these wishes for you."

"But you do."

"I want you for my mate." He blazed at her for one pure moment and then died away. "I am sorry."

"I'm not."

He looked up again. He didn't understand.

Her feelings bubbled up in her chest, unstoppable.

He had never looked so beautiful. His shining aura remained steady. Strong. He was a rock in any storm.

Literally.

She caressed the little ducktail at the back of his neck.

He stilled.

The feathery lock was soft and curled around her index finger just like she'd imagined. A rush of heat filled her belly with pounding longing. Her breasts tightened with need.

No one stopped her. The guards had returned to the entrance and peered out. Something distracted them.

Good.

She leaned in. "I do feel desire, Faier."

The mauve threads in his eyes gleamed.

She waited for him to understand. Wrap confident fingers around her nape. Draw her in for the kiss that claimed her.

But he looked down and flexed his scarred knuckles. "You feel desire for your husband—"

"For you."

He avoided her gaze again. He didn't believe her.

She leaned in and pressed her lips to his.

No reaction.

Her mouth nibbled his. His lips were firm and flat and also slack with shock.

He was no player but a kind warrior who just wanted love. She had kissed him how many times? And always drawn away when it mattered. No wonder he couldn't believe in her now.

Now, finally, she could look outside herself and give him that love.

He responded—

"Escape! Swim! Fly!"

Warriors Luin and Poro yelled across the large space.

She and Faier jolted apart. Even though she'd been expecting their shouts, the panic made terror squeeze her chest.

The warriors dove toward them and shouted, "Flee! Enemy! Flee!"

A strange shadow covered the entrance.

Warning delivered, the warriors turned and flew to the shadow, tridents flashing, war screams echoing through the water.

Faier wrapped his arms tightly around Harmony. "Hold on to me."

She did.

He pushed off the bare floor. His human feet shifted to long fins. He kicked. They zoomed deeper into the prison, away from the entrance. Her octopus flew at their side.

Looking back, between Faier's powerful fins, she saw the shadow. A giant speckled red-and-blue fish charged the prison. Its ice-pick teeth chomped at the warriors.

It crashed into the entrance.

The prison shuddered. Coral flaked like paint chips.

The warriors scattered. They hooted and screamed, trying to draw the fish away.

Warrior Luin threw his trident.

The monstrous fish batted the sharp spear away and dove at the now-unarmed merman.

He retreated into the prison. Too slow.

The fish's teeth snapped on the tip of his fins.

He screamed.

The fish released him. Warrior Luin kicked with ragged fins to escape. The fish bashed the portal entrance, struggling to shoulder its way in to trap them.

The front entrance crumbled.

The fish nudged chunks out of its way and wiggled deeper.

"Faier. It's coming!"

Faier skimmed the ceiling. Her octopus scrambled out a small gap. But they couldn't get through.

No exit...

The fish struck again. *Wham.* A shock wave rolled through the water.

The coral fractured.

Snap.

The floor cracked, and the walls screeched as they shifted.

Her heart lodged in her throat.

Faier tracked the largest crack in the ceiling. It met other cracks, and a chunk the size of a minivan broke free and hurtled to the floor. The water clouded with dust. He dodged the choking debris and fought the current sucking them under the collapsing structure.

Warrior Poro's shouts grew more distant—and more desperate.

Faier flew free.

The water cleared.

In the distance, the giant fish thrashed in the collapsed prison like Godzilla storming the wreckage of Tokyo. More warriors surrounded the fish. It scattered them, an angry fighter jet dispensing spine-cracking bites rather than bombs.

"You can escape," Faier told her. "The warriors are distracted. Perhaps long enough for you to reach land."

"What about you?"

"I am too injured." He touched the wound Tibe had hit again.

Firmness filled her chest. "Then I'm not going either."

"You can cross the open ocean alone."

"I'm not leaving you here."

"Harmony. If you channel your queen powers you can cross."

"Even if I could, I wouldn't leave you. So what do we do?"

He held her to his hard chest. "Perhaps in this forest..."

The giant fish shook off nets, ignored the war party, and flew after them.

"It's coming," she moaned as the fish loomed over them.

Faier darted left. It whipped right. The wake pulled them into the spiky coral bed. He contorted, and her shoulder skimmed the bed without breaking skin.

"We cannot outrun it," he grunted. "Seek a place to hide."

"Hide?"

Faier dove for the sea floor.

Corals grew on top of each other, tangling into spires. He wove between them. She felt like she was looking through a treetop layer of an oak forest. It was difficult to see through the twisty branches to the true ground.

A gap between coral flashed. "Ah—"

They passed it.

Faier rolled. "What?"

"Never mind." The pocket had been too small for them both.

The monstrous fish roared.

Smaller creatures fled far below.

Faier dove. "Hurry."

The giant roared again. It gained on them. Its long, sharp teeth snicked at Faier's fins.

A slender fish darted between two broken-off coral spires.

She pointed. "There! A gap!"

He wheeled.

The giant fish flew over them.

Faier reached the gap. It was too shallow. He pushed her into the crevice and faced the charging giant.

Barehanded. Like always.

No.

There was a narrow bottleneck beneath her.

She scrabbled for his fingers and hooked his hand. He looked down in confusion. She yanked him into the crevice while she wiggled into the bottleneck.

The giant fish chomped the spires and smashed into the coral. *Crack.*

Hard stone clawed at her shoulders and shin. Coral broke off around her. Then she was through the bottleneck. Faier squeezed after. His blood flowed again. He flew around the larger pocket and scanned for enemies.

She shuddered in shock.

They'd made it.

The giant fish roared and bashed into the crevice,

breaking all the way into the bottleneck. Teeth snicked inches from her nose.

She jerked back with a shriek.

Faier hooked an arm around her waist and pulled her down. Beneath him, another narrow tunnel led to the "forest" floor. He studied the tunnel. His nose was bleeding.

"You're hurt again," she said, shaky.

He brushed it off. "The tunnel is clear. Descend."

She kicked on her stubby human feet. Moving took an embarrassingly long time. "I wish I had fins."

"I will show you how to make them."

Her chest lifted. If she could make fins, then she could help next time. She entered the tunnel.

Overhead, the giant fish roared and bashed the bottleneck like a grizzly dragon attacking concrete. The walled coral was too thick for it to break. It roared again and then the sound grew faint. It flew away.

In pockets of the coral around Harmony, small rainbow shrimp—or lobsters? They clicked little claws—scooted about. They were slender, the size of her thumb, and they buzzed as she passed through the tunnel like friendly hummingbirds coming out to say hello.

"Hello," she said aloud, her chest vibrating.

They hovered.

She rotated as she paddled, swimming through a shimmering rainbow tunnel, and exited into a quiet glade.

Faier turned away from the dangerous fish and entered the tunnel after her.

Her heart calmed. Now they were safe—

"Harmony?" Faier froze mid-tunnel. He stared at the small crustaceans with astonishment. "What did you do?"

"Do?" She reentered the tunnel to meet him.

"Stop." He swallowed hard, horror creeping over his

features. His jaw worked. "Do not approach these mantis shrimp."

"Why? They've been fine. Come on."

He didn't move.

One braver rainbow-colored miniature lobster floated between them. It regarded her with beady eyes and then rotated to Faier.

Faier stiffened.

"It's seriously fine," she insisted, and reached up to—

Click. Click. Click.

BOOM.

A long pin, like a bee's stinger, stung her in the center of her chest.

"Ow." She rubbed the spot.

Three more floated out to join the first.

Click. Click. Click.

Faier's eyes widened.

She reached past them and grabbed his hand again. "Come on."

BOOM. BOOM. BOOM.

Stings lanced her chest. Thumbtacks punctured her heart like the worst pain of her life.

Faier jackknifed. His body scraped the tunnel sides.

More mantis shrimp poured into the water like an angry cloud of killer bees. Their warning clicks filled the narrow space.

He twisted in agony.

No. No!

She screamed at them. "Stop it!"

The lobsters scattered. The water cleared.

Faier huddled in his protective hunch.

She paddled laboriously and yanked him to the glowing forest floor. The shrimp buzzed at the tunnel entrance.

Faier uncurled. Red welts, like inflamed insect bites, marred his chest. He rubbed them and watched the buzzing shrimp with shock. "Incredible."

"I know! What were those things?" She rubbed her own matching welts.

"Mantis shrimp. That is the human name." He cupped a long scratch from elbow to shoulder. New injuries scraped his ocean-waves tattoo. "This deep-sea variety is angry. They kill mermen. And you swam through their nest so bravely."

"You mean so stupidly. I thought they were pretty."

He gaped at her. "Pretty? They are deadly."

"Yes, well, anyway." She didn't deserve the respect shining in his eyes because she hadn't really done anything worthy of respect. "Where are we?"

He retracted his fins and rested on the coral floor. "For the moment, safe."

"For the moment?"

"Aiycaya cannot let us escape. They will destroy the mantis shrimp nest if they must, sacrificing many males. But for the moment, they must fight a Trench Jack. They will not come for us."

So *now* they were safe.

For the moment.

She joined him on the coral floor. It felt bumpy on her toes, but not jagged like the reef at the sacred island, and the floor itself glowed with life. She bounced in an electric wonderland.

Small and large stands of coral grew like a real forest. Each stand illuminated the ocean with its own neon cheer. Little blue worms shimmered like flower petals on a breeze. Scores of silvery fish darted around them, and larger, multi-colored fish fluttered like butterflies or darted like small birds. Long ribbon eels drifted across the forests around her like blades of grass caught by the wind.

The whole hidden grotto felt summery and wistful and vibrant. Like breathing in the air from still, cool, ancient forests untouched by man.

She moved her diaphragm to inhale the water and pushed it through her gills. "It's beautiful."

"A much nicer prison," he agreed.

"Perhaps we can leave this way." She bounced around a winding curve.

Faier followed. "This direction passes beneath the Life Tree."

"No wonder I like it." She touched the bulges and knots of the great Life Tree's stem and roots anchoring it to the sea floor beneath brambles of coral. "But I hope we find another exit. I don't want anyone hurt by the mantis shrimp."

His aura changed intensity, signaling dark thoughts he hid from his impassive face. He brushed at his new injuries.

Oh. He probably felt betrayed again. These Aiycaya warriors wanted to kill him. No wonder his feelings were hurt.

She grabbed his fingers and linked hers. "I want to rescue you."

He looked up. "Rescue me?"

"It's been a long time since I could do anything for myself, much less for another person. And now I want to do more."

His brows lightened along with his aura. He swelled with pride and hope. "You begin to believe."

Her own chest squeezed. "Yeah, well, I'm trying."

"That is wonderful, Harmony."

"And I, uh, want to transform so the next time I can help you."

He stopped and lifted his foot. Bumpy scars effaced his swirled tattoos. Otherwise, it was very, very human.

"You must—I am told—gather your 'strength of personhood' and flex."

He flexed his toes toward the floor and then toward the ceiling.

His toes elongated. The skin between stretched into a long, scuba-like scoop.

"My 'strength of personhood'?" she repeated.

"I overheard the queens of Atlantis talking. You must feel capable deep in your heart."

"But you don't have to do that."

"No. I had to learn to walk on the surface. It was frustrating, and I took many falls before I gained the strength to—"

She flexed.

Her feet shot out into fins.

"Oh!"

"—master standing upright..."

"That was easy!" Sheer joy bubbled in her chest. She kicked her new flippers and almost rammed into the coral wall. She skimmed it, twisted, and flew back.

A funny expression fixed Faier's face. "This is your first time?"

"My first." She gripped his shoulders. "This is amazing! Like falling except flying! It's not hard at all."

"I have never seen a woman master fins in one flex."

"Oh, sure. Someone must have."

"Queen Elyssa took a very long time. Queen Aya longer. Queen Lucy still has difficulty transforming. And Queen Zara—"

"No, no. You're just being nice."

"I assure you, I am—"

"If anyone had a problem, it would be me. I'm the opposite of athletic."

"Yet—"

"I took almost two years to walk. *Everyone* said I was developmentally delayed. My mom refused to take me to the doctor. She was in denial. And poor. And also afraid they might be right." Harmony looped and twirled as she talked, diving like a fighter jet at an air show. "Gosh, that's cool."

Faier lazily kicked alongside her. "You have a natural talent. Almost like a mer."

"And to think the first time I ever went swimming was just a...what, a day ago?" She cocked her head and slowed. "Long day."

He floated at her side. "Time passes differently here."

"I've been hungry all the time, and then sleep overwhelms me."

"That is because many, many surface days pass before your mer body must rest. And then many surface days pass while you are resting."

"Oh. That's weird and kind of a relief. And so are these fins." She twirled. "Now I can finally swim."

He shook his head again. "It is unfathomable a sacred bride should keep her daughter from the water."

"Actually, it makes sense. She was afraid of revealing she was a mermaid. Oh! Could she have fed me elixir? When I was a child?"

"Elixir is temporary. It wears off."

"Maybe she stole a Life Tree blossom...?"

"Life Tree blossoms die once they leave the hand of a warrior seeking his bride. Only in the presence of a future queen do they survive."

"Hmm. But your Life Tree blossom is alive in a fish tank in New York."

"Yes. I had intended to give my blossom to the first female I encountered. But that did not occur."

"Yeah, that was pretty optimistic."

"Optimistic? So far, I am the only mer who has not matched the first human female. King Kadir, First Lieutenants Soren and Elan, Warlord Torun, and Warriors Uvim, Dosan, and Xalu all matched females immediately after surfacing."

That was crazy.

Faier went on to list all the females who had not been his bride. Not the first female he'd met, not the dating site females. Nor any in the vast flood of souls he had observed from the city's tallest rooftops.

He had stored his blossom in the office's ornamental fish tank. As his hopes had dwindled and he'd left on rescue missions or interviews for longer and longer, he shared with Harmony how he'd expected it to die. But it never had. No matter how many days he'd been absent.

"One of the MerMatch staff members must be a future queen," he continued. "I have a guess. She denied it, but the fact remains that the blossom has lived on. Somehow, cut off from the Life Tree, it was receiving energy from a powerful female. And so, Harmony, for the nectar to work, your soul must resonate."

"I was really close to my mom."

"No." He rubbed his hands sadly. "Sacred brides often wish to protect their human children from drowning. But elixir is just water. Nectar also. A destined bride's soul must already resonate with her future husband when she consumes the nectar or she will never transform."

"Well, so, but I was 'destined' to be a sacred bride according to my great-grandmother..."

He shook his head firmly. "We have tested this across centuries. When sacred islands and mer cities teemed, other humans grew jealous. They requested nectar. Warriors hungry for human offerings broke off blossoms and injured their own Life Trees. But no human transformed from these stolen droplets. Without resonance of bride to husband, the human cannot survive. He or she will drown."

So Faier was sure.

Harmony flexed her fins, willing them to retract, and they did. She squeezed her toes. How funny it was so easy for her. "Now, when another fish attacks, I'm ready." She turned and bounced on the coral floor.

"Good. Any city that allows a beast to collapse a building will feel shame."

"King Kayo probably feels bad."

"Yes. And with such a first lieutenant, he has no need for a saboteur."

She laughed darkly. "We have a saying like that. It goes, 'With friends like these, who needs enemies?'"

He smiled. The aura around his body glowed.

Answering happiness filled her chest.

She stopped. "Actually, I wanted to talk to you about him."

"King Kayo?"

Her nerves twinged.

He turned to her.

They bobbed in the middle of a sparkling glen under the forest.

She forced the difficult words out. "What you did for me. Asking King Kayo to let me go. I can't tell you how much that means to me. Thank you."

"Do not thank me, Harmony. I failed."

"But you tried. And I hurt you when I refused to go."

His face filled with resignation. "He is your husband."

"About that... I do feel hopeful for King Kayo," she confirmed again. "I can help him. I know what he's going through. But I'm not his bride."

He lifted his head. Tentative hope glowed in his aura. "You are not?"

"I don't have those feelings for him."

"Your feelings can grow."

"No. They can't."

He swallowed. "Harmony. Do not crush your soul. Not for me."

"I'm not."

"I am selfish and dishonorable."

She strangled a laugh. "Also no."

"Mingling blood with multiple Life Trees was once a mark of great honor. Now, there are so few warriors, cities fear loss. Some call it betrayal."

He closed his eyes. His aura dimmed. He pressed his palm to his scarred chest.

"I am not truly accepted in any city." He opened his eyes. She saw the agony there. This pained him more than any physical injuries. "I have not melded with any Life Tree. I do not feel 'at home' in any castle. The only healing sap that has truly penetrated, that truly glows, is the remaining sap from my own dead city. Nerissa."

She floated closer. Ran her fingers up Faier's forearms to cup his biceps.

He struggled to complete his story. "You must honor your desires. You rule over King Kayo's house guardian—"

"She's mine, actually."

"—and Aiycaya is where you belong."

"I agree."

"You must unite with King Kayo."

"No way."

"Your souls resonate."

"No."

"When you communicate, you shine with the same colors."

"It is weird how comfortable I feel around him. He's like a virtual stranger."

"That is why you must unite. Only misery awaits you if you try to sever your souls."

"No," she said flatly. "And I'm very sorry about Nerissa, but your injuries are healing."

"They do not heal."

"Sure they do. Check out these thin white ones where the crocodile got you."

He studied the slender claw marks scraping across his chest. They'd thinned to white lines and almost disappeared into healthy skin.

"Even the older scars are looking better. Less red and inflamed. You're healing, Faier."

"Healer Hobin also said...but that is impossible..."

"But it's happening, so you must accept it." She poked him in the chest. "Anyway, I refuse to 'unite' with King Kayo. Saying it gives me the heebies."

"But you must unite with an Aiycaya warrior. Your destiny is the sea."

"Yeah." She snuggled closer. "But not King Kayo. I want to be the bride of another warrior."

"Another?" He frowned as her hands wiggled around his powerful chest and her hot breasts brushed his pectorals. "Luin? No. Second Lieutenant Xarin?"

"Why are you and King Kayo so obsessed with Xarin?"

"So, it is Xarin?"

"No, you kind, steady, honorable man." She nuzzled his nose. "I hope you're not pretending you don't know because you don't want it to be you. You can't guess?"

He shook his head.

"Of course it's you."

He shook his head again.

"Yes. The warrior I want, Faier, is you."

TWENTY-ONE

Harmony wanted him?

Faier's heart thudded hard in his chest. It was as if the Trench Jack had reappeared with its mouth gaping open and the current sucked him in. Her shock wave paralyzed him.

Harmony's soft, kind gaze and sweet, bright soul bathed him in gentle understanding.

Her confession was the most meaningful statement he had ever heard.

He couldn't form words. He couldn't.

No. He misunderstood. She misspoke.

Her brow smoothed. Her lips curved into a deeper, knowing smile. "I mean it."

She...she meant it?

No...

Harmony pressed her lips to his. Again. Like before.

Not like the after the crocodile attack when she had been so overwhelmed by the transition. Not like the prison just now where she had been distracted by the other warriors.

Like the first time, when she had caught him by surprise and ensnared his soul. She kissed him willingly, freely, whole-heartedly. She kissed him with abandon.

And then later she'd rejected him, screaming.

He jumped with electric-eel shock.

Her lashes fluttered. She pulled back. "Faier?"

Harmony's confession was too unbelievable, and he was too desperate. He prided himself on his control, but if she meant what she said, he couldn't speak or look at her.

Her chest thrummed with confusion. "I thought you wanted me."

"I..."

Her soul darkened.

He couldn't form words to explain. His cheek tightened—new scar from fighting Tibe, already healing against all odds—and he searched for the mystery-unraveling clues that turned Harmony's strange statements into sense.

If she really loved him, and he allowed himself to believe her, and then she took her love away...that would be as soul-destroying as his loss of Nerissa. He'd never recovered. He'd been so lighthearted, cocky, and, like King Kayo, self-assured of his place in the sea—and then had been swept away.

Captivating Harmony, enthralling her as his mate, and seducing her was what he wanted to do more than anything. And, at the same time, it was his worst fear.

She stroked his cheek. "I'm sorry."

He focused on her. "Sorry?"

"For all the ways I hurt you. You're a good person, and I shouldn't have doubted."

He shook his head. "You did not cause injury, Harmony."

She moved her hand and pressed her lips to his. *Again*, a kiss. He soaked in the feeling. Her. With him.

Warnings needled his heart.

The heat in his veins kindled yearnings only she could fulfill.

If he dared to ask her.

With their mouths mashed together and connecting, her chest vibrated. "Then, can I convince you I want you for my mate?"

His heart squeezed. *Warning*.

She continued. "You helped me even when I was horrible to you. And you believe in me. You still do. So much so, I'm also starting to believe in myself. You tell me the truth even when it's not what I want to hear."

"You trust I did not give you the elixir?"

"Yes. Because you said it and you don't lie. I believe you."

The tightness loosened. *She believes me.* He had done all he could to watch over, protect, and honor her. And she believed him.

"You were in my corner when I had no one. And you still are."

With her mouth pressed to his, she stroked her smooth index finger over his bicep. Tridents had cut a deep but healing scar into his arm.

"No one has been in my corner for a really long time."

He tried to comfort her. "It takes a monumental spirit to swim against a tide."

"You never lost faith in me."

"But I have lost my faith in me. Look at my lost honor."

"Lost honor?"

He gestured at the mauve honor-tattoos scraped off his skin in red, scarred ruts. Replacing them was impossible.

Like bonding to a Life Tree outside Nerissa. Like loving Harmony.

"Your injuries tell your story."

"What story do these tell but one of rejection and loss?"

"You sacrificed yourself, your past, your future for others. Selfishness surrounded me, and I couldn't see the opposite. Now, I see you." She teased the seam of his mouth. "You always tell me to believe in myself. So now it's my turn. Won't you believe in me and let me show you how I feel?"

———

FAIER OPENED his mouth to Harmony's kiss.

The trust shook her to her core.

She stroked his interior with her tongue. He touched her tentatively. She curled their tongues, reassuring and drawing him out.

His hesitation gave her pause. Didn't they share the same feelings? Was she wrong?

His chest expanded with a shudder, and he seated their mouths more firmly, deepening their connection. Hot arousal flushed through her veins. He returned her strokes, tangling tongues, giving and taking.

Fire kindled in her lower belly and between her thighs. Desire she had fought from the beginning bubbled up and spilled over.

Harmony had never been the one to ask for sex. Never the one to take. She was always the passive girlfriend, so grateful to have caught the eye of a nice man, she'd yielded to his demands and ignored her own.

She had given sex willingly but always knowing she would go at her partner's pace.

This was a new world for her. Faier would never force her to his pace. He would refuse her before he demanded.

And he thought she couldn't look past his scars. So she had to show him just how much she wanted the warrior within. She would not be refused.

Harmony looped her arms around his waist. Hard muscle flexed beneath her sensitive skin.

His fingers tightened on her shoulders, and the warm glow of his inner soul flickered to life, reaching her and resonating.

Desire to desire. Need to need. Hunger to hunger.

She stroked his flexing buttocks.

He moaned and broke free of her mouth to gaze into her eyes as if to question. *Are you sure? Do you really want this? Really want me?*

But she did really want this. Him. *Faier*. He made her ask. She couldn't passively receive. She had to know what she wanted and go hunt it.

Hunt him.

She hunted a male for the first time in her life. Faier was hers. She claimed him.

And she had never felt more alive.

Harmony rubbed her breasts over his chest. Her nipples tightened.

His features lifted. Arousal washed over him like a hot wave. His hard cock pressed into her hip.

She encircled his thick male member with eager fingers.

He closed his eyes and shuddered. When he opened them again, the mauve threads gleamed and his soul light burned hotter. "Harmony..."

She stroked from base to tip to base.

He shuddered.

Her pussy throbbed. She wanted him inside her, connecting their bodies as well as their hearts.

He caressed her buttocks, fitted his taut abdomen against the soft swell of her belly, and cupped her tight breasts reverently, stroking her aching nipples with his deliciously rough thumbs. He worshipped her as the queen he continued to call her.

Did he finally believe her?

Harmony wrapped her legs around his lean torso.

His cock nudged her waiting entrance.

Her nethers throbbed.

He pinioned her gaze with his mauve-threaded dark eyes, battered by his hunger but refusing to take until she offered.

She drew him in.

He yielded to her will, filling her channel with his cock slowly and completely until they were one. Faier shuddered. An earthquake shook his heart. It reverberated in her soul.

This was the man she wanted. Her male. She chose him.

They were both prisoners, and yet, in this exact moment, they were both free.

He eased out and thrust into her, filling her with sparkling heat, gilding her with liquid pleasure.

Yes. She wanted this dance. This transformation. With him.

He thrust again, and again, bobbing in and out of her channel, fulfilling her unspoken needs.

Harmony had given her body to doomed crushes and selfish lovers. Faier was neither. If she hurt him again, she would hate herself. And that made loving him the most dangerous act of all.

She clung on as her orgasm built. Fear crashed against hunger like two warring tides.

He drove into her pleasure spot, and the orgasm welled, pulling her on storm-driven currents that broke over her and tumbled them both out of control.

The pressure in her body released. She cried out.

A moment later, Faier thrust to his own completion and filled her with his essence.

Her veins tingled with blue sparkles like the ones she had seen in the twilit ocean on the surface, when her trust in Faier was new and for the first time since boarding Lifet's yacht, she'd thought maybe she would survive.

She felt that way again. Heavy and warm and safe. Everything would be okay. Together, they would find their way out of this prison on Aiycaya and survive.

Faier trembled.

She stroked his back. "Hey. You're okay."

His trembles grew to full shakes. He shivered as if an icy blizzard encased him while she, still hugging him and connected, rested in his arms toasty warm.

"Hey. Faier?"

His teeth chattered.

What? Had she hurt him? Harmony pushed back to look him in the eye. "Are you okay?"

He veered away from her gaze and nodded into her shoulder. "Yes."

"Are you sure?"

"Yes."

"Okay. Is there something I can do?"

He shook his trembling head. "I...do not regret..."

She pressed his dark head to her chest and teased her fingers through his hair, stroking his little ducktail, until the trembles soothed. She understood. The moment she'd realized he would always try to save her a hundred earthquakes had set off in her own heart.

They slept together in a tangle surrounded by the stillness of this undersea forest. An unknown time later, a distant echo of warriors shouted.

"...Harmony? Sacred bride! We are coming to rescue..."

Faier lifted his head. Dark knowledge dulled the mauve gleams in his eyes.

They could not hide here forever. And the last thing those warriors needed to see was her entwined with their supposed enemy.

She stretched and vibrated a sigh. "Oh, well. Someday we'll be together freely."

He seemed unsure but he agreed and released her.

They separated. Cold water rushed between their bodies. She shivered.

He rubbed her chilled arms and traced the small red dots on her chest from the mantis shrimp stings. Keeping her close and touching her sweetly, he eased the worry invading her heart.

She relaxed into his gentle grooming. "I can't believe I got those marks from just a couple of shrimp."

"Just?" His brows rose. "Mantis shrimp are formidable enemies. They drive off predators much larger than a Trench Jack. You have also presented a problem for the warriors. They cannot enter without significant danger."

"I supposed we can't leave either."

"They will tunnel another entrance elsewhere. What do you wish to do while we wait?"

"I don't know." She took both his hands. "I have to make King Kayo see you're not his enemy."

"I am a rebel, and his city is traditional. He must yield to the All-Council or risk plunging his entire city into war."

Faier stroked her cheek with his knuckle. "Besides, he will regard any warrior who takes 'his' sacred bride to be an enemy."

"So tell me what to do."

Faier floated with her. His support was a sun. He warmed her with his presence. "What do you want to do?"

He was encouraging her to decide. Even though her last ideas to fight the Aiycaya warriors had gone badly.

Lifet had taken her choices away and punished her for deciding on her own. These warriors hadn't helped by brushing away her wishes and trying to force their demands.

Faier encouraged her to try again. He healed her by believing in her. Now she had to learn to believe in herself.

Believe.

"If I can reach King Kayo," she continued, telling herself more than him, "and I will get him to see that First Lieutenant Tibe and Elder Bawa are colluding against him. I'm sure wherever Warlord Sao was taking me, Elder Bawa was at the bottom of it. And it's suspicious that Tibe has tried to kill you so many times, and then the short time we're left alone together, a big fish targets our prison."

"You would unbalance the whole city."

"Rebalance." She tried to smile. "I guess that's crazy, isn't it? Lifet was once a nicer man. He got led down a dark path. And I'm afraid the only way to get King Kayo to pardon you is to lead him away from the darkness into the sunlight."

"If you can accomplish this you will do the city and all the ocean a great favor." He frowned. "I must protect you."

"They'll imprison you if they see you leave here."

"Then they will not see me." He squeezed her hands. "Let us search again for another exit."

They explored the small sleeve of coral.

There was no other way out.

They returned to the meadow. Faier looked defeated and worried.

"We have no choice," Harmony said. But instead of that phrase marking the end of her resistance, for the first time it marked the beginning. "We have to wait here until the warriors break through and then we have to fight them."

"In close quarters," he agreed, reviewing the space like a fighter envisioning an arena, "while I heal my injury, and bare-handed."

Again.

She swallowed as a new, terrifying idea began to take hold. "I could...maybe I could approach King Kayo again."

"They will attack me as soon as we pass the mantis shrimp."

"You, yes. Not me."

"Harmony. Do not sacrifice yourself—"

"I'm not," she assured him in a rush. "Not like before. I'll convince King Kayo to pardon you. He'll keep me safe from Tibe and Bawa. We're getting out of here together. I promise you."

Faier set his jaw.

Nerves assaulted her. She tangled her fingers. "You don't think I can do it?"

He calmed and entwined her fingers. "You are a queen. The power to rule is within you."

"But not without you or King Kayo."

"Even alone without us."

"I know I can't really do anything on my own."

He nipped the tips, focusing her attention on him. "From the moment my leg cramped and the warriors surrounded me on the surface, my life was forfeit. But I am still alive. You have saved me, Harmony. Not once or twice. Many times. Although I greatly prefer to risk my life rescuing you I would be a fool to ignore that I am injured and in danger. I owe my life to you. You are more than capable of accomplishing a great many feats."

The confession was ripped from this proud male's soul.

She treasured it and him.

He did not like being rescued. Being the knight was in his blood. He had to rescue others. And she was perfectly happy to let a white knight carry her away to safety.

But due to his injury, it was time this fair lady—or, in her case, tan-beige lady—picked up his sword.

"Do you really think I can do it?" she asked.

"You have experienced this dark path before," he said. "Tell the king what you see. Your experience can save him. If he will be saved."

Worry wrinkled his steady gaze but he nodded as if he believed her.

Nerves crunched in her belly.

Faier trusted her.

She would just have to trust herself.

TWENTY-TWO

"The problem is leaving. Me. Leaving." Harmony twirled, her long fins and bright soul a powerful sign she was ready to claim her queen powers, even though she feared them and looked to him for reassurance. "Me leaving you."

He did not argue.

Aloud.

"Because if I can get out, what's stopping the warriors from using my escape to— Oh! Hello."

The king's house guardian jetted into her arms.

She cupped the bright creature, laughing with joy. "How did you get in? Did we miss an entrance?"

Faier's belly twinged.

Harmony belonged here. In Aiycaya.

But she had claimed Faier. Of Atlantis.

He pushed aside his deep discomfort. Harmony had proved a hundred times that she chose him. He needed to believe her.

But that was easier said than done.

"A house guardian may pass through any hole large enough to fit its beak."

Harmony tickled her. "You are such a good helper. How did you know I needed your help? And you're so modest too. You're such a lady."

The house guardian puffed up her funnel and preened.

"She likes that compliment," he noted.

"She's a lady? Oh, I see what you mean. You *are* a Lady. No Tramps around here, though. Just me and Faier." She grinned at him, and her chest was so light, it made his throat tighten. "That was one of my mom's favorite movies. *Lady and the Tramp*. Lady got unjustly punished, but she saved everyone." Her smile faded as she released the house guardian. "It seems appropriate."

They lingered in the meadow beneath the mantis shrimp.

The shrimp buzzed in the tunnel. Her house guardian, Lady, darted beneath the cloud, plucked stray mantis shrimp, and ate them with a crunch. The mantis shrimp clicked and swarmed Lady. She flew down a side tunnel, leading the swarm on a merry chase.

"Perhaps the warriors above can draw off the mantis shrimp."

"Good idea." She locked eyes on Faier as she drifted backward toward the buzzing shrimp. "I'll call out."

His heart stopped. "Harmony—"

She rotated upright beneath the hole and vibrated hard. "King Kayo!"

He kicked to rescue her.

But a strange thing happened.

The remaining mantis shrimp did *not* swarm her for disturbing them.

"King Kayo?"

They gathered beneath her fins and then boiled over, buzzing straight for him.

He kicked hard, flying away.

They stopped once he was halfway across the meadow. He floated at a safe distance, watching her call a third and fourth time.

"Sacred Bride Harmony?" a different warrior replied to her from a far distance. "You are alive?"

"Warrior Poro! Yes. Where's the king?"

"He is coming, Sacred Bride Harmony."

"Great. You can, uh, just call me Harmony."

"I cannot call you that, Sacred Bride Harmony. I must not speak to you."

"Oh. Right." She glanced down, and her vibrations returned to normal. "Faier? What are you doing over there?"

He approached cautiously. "Harmony..."

The mantis shrimp oriented on him. *Click click click.*

She saw them. Instead of fear, her first reaction was to turn thunderous. "Just a minute."

Click click click click.

"I said *wait*."

The mantis shrimp buzzed more furiously, but the warning noises ceased.

"Sorry. What were you saying?"

His chest heaved. Realization washed over him. He had known the truth. Facing it again hurt double the second time. "You can order them."

"I can order who? Warrior Poro? Oh. You mean the mantis shrimp." She frowned. "I did, didn't I? It just popped out. Sorry, guys. Or gals. My bad."

"You are very good. They think—they know—you are Aiycaya's queen."

Aiycaya. Not Atlantis.

She didn't understand him.

"You are linked to the Aiycaya Life Tree," he explained. "Its sap flows in your veins. These mantis shrimp—and all creatures of this forest—rely on the Aiycaya Life Tree for life."

King Kayo shouted from a great distance, "Bride Harmony! I am here. Warrior Luin will battle the mantis shrimp so we can rescue you."

The mantis shrimp disappeared up the tunnel. Distant clicks grated on his teeth.

She frowned and asked Faier, "Won't that be dangerous to Warrior Luin?"

"Deadly."

She vibrated hard to reach the king. "Wait! Okay? I don't want anyone to get hurt."

"—knows there is no other way. He will perish for your safe return."

"Perish? Stop! There has to be another way."

"—for death with honor," the king continued, droning over her as though repeating answers someone else had drilled into him. "Warrior Luin had the responsibility for watching over you, and he failed. He will perform this last act as penance."

"Listen! Will you listen?"

"Go, Warrior Luin."

"This was not Warrior Luin's fault. Just listen for one second."

"Bride Harmony, Warrior Luin is coming."

"STOP."

"Do not fear, Bride Harmony."

"I'm not afraid. I am PISSED OFF." She waved her fists.

The mantis shrimp buzzed, echoing her exasperation.

"Hurry!" Warriors shouted from above. "They are swarming. Go forth, Warrior Luin!"

The warriors screamed. Excited buzzing drowned out the sounds.

Harmony ground her fists into her forehead. "Argh. What can I say to make them understand?"

"The warriors understand," Faier replied cynically. "They prefer not to hear."

"Welcome to my life!" She laughed. Her soul light flickered. "This happens to me all the time. No one listens. No one." She glanced at him. "Except you."

"You must make them listen."

She closed her eyes. "I don't have it in me."

"It is in you. These mantis shrimp feel it. I feel it also. You can take control of the city, Harmony. You can do anything."

"Why? How come you feel this ability, this 'power' to issue orders, and the other warriors clearly don't?"

"Because they do not wish to. But you are my mate. Our souls resonate. Of course I would sense your power. Sense it and celebrate."

She listened intently.

"Be strong," he encouraged. "You have already ordered them. You rested with me in prison. You refused to marry King Kayo. You will save Warrior Luin also. Despite their wishes."

"Despite their wishes..." Harmony stared up at the tunnel and then back at Faier with new determination. "I always give up too soon. You make me want to fight. Be better. Take on more. Because of you I think I will change my destiny."

His chest warmed. "You will."

She smiled and evaluated her situation with careful eyes. "How come the mantis shrimp don't obey King Kayo? He's tied into the Life Tree too."

"You are a queen. You have powers he does not."

"I'm not getting stung, so you must be right." She lifted a palm, scooping up the mantis shrimp, and looked at the small creatures. "Let's be friends."

The handful buzzed cheerfully.

"Will you let Faier come with me?"

Click click click.

"No," he translated, keeping his distance.

"Right. I, uh, order you. Please?"

Click click.

"Still no. Are you sure I can boss the shrimp around?"

"Feel confident."

"Confident. Okay. Well, we are communicating. That's a start." She opened her palm wider and the mantis shrimp flew off in a multicolor, shimmering rainbow.

Her soul brightened, and her smile widened.

"You are growing confident."

"I have an idea." She squared her shoulders, scooped up a handful of mantis shrimp, and spoke to the small buzzing shrimp. "I need your help on this, okay? Back off. Let them get close enough I can talk again."

Click click click.

"Yes, I know you don't want to, but if they act out, you can just sting them."

The mantis shrimp flew off her hand. The swirling concentrated around her.

"Harmony?" King Kayo called. "Are you all right?"

"Barely." She made fists again. "Send no one else near me."

"We are sending in Warrior Luin."

"Do. Not."

"He survived the first attack, so he will once again—"

"You'll kill me." A mantis shrimp crawled across her knuckles. "I know Tibe wants me to die, but I thought you cared."

"My... Harmony, First Lieutenant Tibe wishes you no harm. Why do you accuse him of such a wish?"

"Because you're wrong and I'm hungry!"

"Hungry! Again?"

"Yes, again. I lost my food when that giant fish attacked."

Faier's heart squeezed. He had failed to provide for his mate. "I will hunt for you, Harmony."

She hushed him and rocked her head, then vibrated loudly to converse with the king. "And how long until you tunnel to free me?"

"Tunnel! That will take...that will require a long time."

"So bring me food! Enough to last 'a long time.'"

"We are... No, we are not tunneling. We are sending in Warrior Luin to—"

"To do what? Die? How will that help?"

"His sacrifice will empty the tunnel for you to escape."

"What?" Harmony screwed up her face. "Are you idiots? Whose idea was this?"

"This was Tibe's idea," King Kayo replied confidently. "Yes, we are idiots. Perhaps. What are 'idiots'?"

She blinked and shook herself. "Seriously, King Kayo, Tibe is actively trying to kill me."

"No warrior would dare to—"

"There are enough mantis shrimp to cover Warrior Luin and kill him with plenty left over to get mad and *kill me.*"

"Sacred Bride Harmony—"

"And then when that doesn't work, I'm guessing 'tunneling' will be the best choice, except that I'll *already be dead*."

"—it is not Tibe's intention to—"

"Furthermore, Warrior Luin is my guard, so his death leaves me vulnerable during the next fish attack, increasing the chances that a fish *will kill me*."

"Sacred Bride." Tibe's sharp voice pierced the sea. "You need no guard. After I free you, someone will escort you back to the king's castle where you belong, and you will not leave for the duration of—"

"And obviously Tibe was intending me to die in the prison, because he ordered Xarin to go away after you told him to stay."

King Kayo's vibration shortened. "I have punished Xarin for abandoning his post."

"Punished for obeying Tibe's orders to leave so the giant fish could *kill me*?"

There was silence.

"Bring me food," she snapped at them through the tunnel. "And a, uh, trident too!"

"She is hysterical." Tibe's cold voice took over. "Sacred Bride. Is the prisoner with you?"

She grinned at Faier.

"Sacred Bride? Sacred Bride, answer me at once."

She cooed to the mantis shrimp on her knuckle. "You are so pretty. Sting nobody except maybe Tibe, okay?"

It hummed.

"Sacred Bride!" Tibe growled with anger.

"Harmony?" King Kayo sounded worried. "Are you still there?"

"Yes," she answered. "Are my food and trident ready?"

"You did not answer First Lieutenant Tibe."

"Sacred brides only talk to their husbands."

"Yes, but you speak with many males you should not."

"Tibe is the only one who yelled at me for doing so. I just can't make him happy." She made a pleased thumbs-up gesture at Faier.

"Yelled? He did not—"

"In the prison, when you asked him to leave because he frightened me, he shouted, 'Anyone who disobeys me should be frightened!'"

There was another long silence.

The king's voice sounded more strained. "Is the rebel beside you now?"

"Nope." She waved at Faier across the meadow. "Not right now."

"But he is there with you?"

"I will not swim around looking when I'm *this hungry*."

Silence again except for the buzzing of the mantis shrimp.

"Harmony," Faier whispered, and she tilted her head his way. "You are a skilled negotiator."

Her chest brightened. "Thanks! I was just thinking about Lifet. And things I wished I could've said. Anyway, it's a lot easier to yell insults with a nest of killer bees between us."

Time passed.

Unease chilled his veins. The Aiycaya warriors would not bring Harmony food or a trident. They had found another way in and would burst around a corner, capturing him and dragging her away against her will.

The question in her eyes and the flickering in her soul said she harbored the same fears.

"Sacred Bride Harmony!" Warrior Poro's voice sounded nearer, making them both jolt. "Your food is here."

Boxes weighted with rocks dropped through the tunnel. She kicked backward to make room. A rusty old trident lanced between her long fins and buried itself in the coral up to the handle.

"And your trident!"

She put a calming hand on her chest. "Um, thank you! Warrior Poro."

"You are welcome, Sacred Bride Harmony."

She yanked on the trident, dragged it out of the mantis shrimp zone, and swam it and the food over to Faier. "This is for you to heal. And in case my plan fails. I'll do my best to get you pardoned. Buf if I can't..."

His heart shrank. "I will come for you."

"Yeah." She swallowed. "If that's okay."

Every nerve screamed, *No.* He could not protect her. The warriors had threatened her. *She must not leave.*

But she was a queen. She had the power to protect herself, challenge the king, and change the city. *If only she believed.* He must let her go. If he interfered with her awakening power and took away her confidence, then he would imprison her in doubts and crush dark her soul.

Like the others who had bruised her. Faier never would.

He rested his palms atop the boxes. "If they hurt you, I will pull up the Aiycaya Life Tree and poison its roots."

A relieved smile flashed over her face, and her soul brightened. "Okay. Don't raze the city."

"I will do this. You have my vow."

"Then I have to make sure I don't get harmed." She hefted the rusty trident. It rotated over her wrist and nearly smacked her nose. "Whoah."

He took it from her grasp and controlled it. "Thank you, Harmony. You are providing well for me."

"Well, you took care of me on the surface." She glowed.

"I've been living off others' kindness for so long. And it's my fault you're in this predicament."

"No."

"Yes." Her soul brightened, and her eyes reddened. "I just... I want to help you. In case..."

Yes. He understood. Even though he hated being unable to protect her, they both knew he was the one at greater risk. "Be safe."

"You too. Oh, come here!" She dove into his arms.

Faier closed around her protectively. She nestled against him. The fit was right. Pressed against him was where she belonged.

Someday he would draw her into his arms and she would remain there. Forever.

He tried to imprint every beat of her heart, every flash of her soul, every texture of hair and skin and softness into his memory. Like looking upon Nerissa the final time. What had been his final view? During his desperate escape, ash had obscured the city. So, when? He had not known it would be his last, or he would have looked for much, much longer.

She wiggled.

He released her.

"I'm ready for this," she said, but her soul light flickered. The words were for herself, not for him.

"You are strong."

She brightened. "Yes. Strong. I bet you wouldn't even recognize me from the first day."

"You have changed."

"Good, I hope."

Lady jetted around them with excitement.

Harmony held out her hand, and the house guardian entangled it.

"Stay with Faier," she told the small house guardian. "Keep him safe."

The house guardian made a throaty declaration of discontent.

"She should go with you," he said. "She is a formidable warrior."

"But I'm the untouchable sacred bride."

"Harmony—"

"I, uh, order her to keep you safe while you heal." She kicked to the mantis-shrimp-lined tunnel entrance, ending the argument. Her fins propelled her swiftly. Expertly.

She was such a natural. As if the surface world was foreign to her, and she'd always been meant to live under the water like him.

"Harmony."

She paused just under the entrance. "Yes?"

"Sacred brides do not make fins."

Her soul light flickered.

"Save them for an element of surprise."

She nodded jerkily, retracted her fins to ordinary human feet, and inched through the tunnel buzzing with danger.

TWENTY-THREE

Harmony ascended into a much quieter sea than the one she'd escaped.

Loosely above floated a small group of warriors: Xarin, Luin, Poro, and Kusi. They watched the progress of warriors tapping coral as if they were testing the thickness of ice on a lake. No one saw her exit.

Warrior Luin's fins were ragged on the edges and punctured, but pink with healing.

She squeezed up through the hole.

Lady yowled, melancholy, beneath her.

Harmony left the rainbow mantis shrimp behind and floated level with the group. "Where is King Kayo?"

The warriors startled and wheeled, tridents raised, jittery with shock. Kusi, closest to her, even slashed his trident at her.

She hugged her head. "Eek!"

Kusi raised his trident to slash again.

Clang.

Xarin's trident blocked Kusi's. "Stop."

Kusi didn't hear. He slashed. *Clang.*

"Stop!"

Clang.

Warriors Luin and Poro recovered and pushed her behind them, forming a thick wall of male and metal between her and the rampaging warrior.

Xarin parried Kusi's next blow and locked his trident so he could no longer move. "Stop. Calm. Think."

Kusi's nostrils flared and his face reddened. "She startled me."

"Blindly striking risks lives. Single-minded focus is only strength after you consider your actions. Understand?"

"Yes. Sir."

"Call the warriors." He jerked his chin at the group tapping the coral.

Kusi backed away, refused eye contact with any of them, and flew headlong at the other group.

The warriors in front of her parted.

Xarin fixed her with a dark, measuring gaze as though she had popped out to frighten them on purpose. "Sacred Bride Harmony. You found an exit."

"Er, yeah. Where's King Kayo?"

"At the Life Tree." Xarin studied the hole, his trident still gripped at the ready in his hands. "Tibe captured the exile that drove the Trench Jack into the prison. Where did you exit?"

"The mantis shrimp tunnel. It turns out that as a human, I'm kind of immune to..."

All three warriors were staring at her feet.

She also looked down.

Her fins! And after Faier had just warned her to keep them a secret. They must have come out when she'd ducked away from Kusi. She snapped them back to human.

The warriors stared at her wide-eyed.

You can order them. Faier's words echoed back to her. Could she really? But this was an emergency. She had to try. "Don't. Tell. Anyone."

Xarin's jaw clenched. "I must report to the first lieutenant."

"No!"

"The first lieutenant enforces the will of the king."

"You know it wasn't King Kayo's will to send you away from the prison."

His hard gaze snapped to her for an explanation.

Huh? Had he thought King Kayo had changed his mind?

"Tibe's controlling everything," she hissed. "With Elder Bawa, they're trying to get rid of me. And Faier. That's not the will of the king."

Xarin's eyes narrowed. "Your thoughts are treason."

"Didn't you hear how Warlord Sao tried to kidnap me?"

"No warrior would dare to cross mer law."

"He tried. On Elder Bawa's orders. Not King Kayo's."

"Elder Bawa continues on without reprimand. So his orders *are* the will of the king."

At her side, Warrior Poro reassured her, "Do not fear First Lieutenant Tibe, Sacred Bride Harmony. He sounds dangerous, but he is very skilled."

"Stop speaking to a sacred bride," Warrior Luin told Poro.

"Oh yes. Sorry, Sacred Bride Harmony."

Warrior Luin's aura flared in exasperation, and his chest vibrated to protest again.

Harmony turned away from them and lowered her vibrations to beg Xarin. "Please."

"I must report." Xarin's blue-green irises dulled with regret and duty.

The second party flew to Xarin. They carried long poles for plumbing the depths. No one had seen her fins.

She had only moments.

Make them believe you.

"Xarin. I know you want to reassure the king that you're not trying to take over Aiycaya. But blindly obeying Tibe is not the way."

He sharpened on her with a jolt. "How? You—"

"That's why you do everything he asks no matter how dangerous or unreasonable. That's why you obey First Lieutenant Tibe even when you know his orders go against the king. You want King Kayo to know you respect him. Someday, he'll recognize you. But only if I can reach him. Please, help me get him to that day."

He stared at her with a mix of distrust, horror, and awe. She had seen something in him no one else had.

"I watched you," she explained. "I listened to you. The king fears you because he thinks you are worthier to lead than he is."

His chin wrinkled. He shook his head. "King Kayo is the heart of Aiycaya."

"I agree. And once I convince him, he'll let go of his fears and see you not as 'worthier' or 'the warrior who might have been King' but as you. Xarin. Loyal second lieutenant who wishes him well."

He rubbed his chin, smoothing the wrinkles. The rims of his eyes reddened, and he swallowed. Hard.

The other group had nearly reached them. Her time was over.

Make them believe you.

"I'm not asking you to lie. Just stick to the facts." She changed tactics and raised her vibration. "Sacred brides can't make fins. That would be crazy. No one would believe you."

"That is true," Warrior Poro agreed.

"Do not speak to her!"

"I am not speaking to her. I am agreeing. It is a known fact that sacred brides cannot make fins. Eh, Xarin?"

The other group clustered around. Tattooed males unknown to her, seemingly relieved that she had escaped the mantis shrimp without harm.

New determination shone in Xarin's eyes. "Right. You are right. Sacred brides cannot do this."

"Great. So, there's no need to bother anyone with crazy talk."

"That is why we report to First Lieutenant Tibe," Warrior Poro said as if he'd not heard anything she'd just said. "Because the king is always busy. First Lieutenant Tibe will tell us the king's will."

Harmony wheeled on him. "Do *not* tell Tibe."

"Why not?"

"Because he doesn't need to know about me." She hugged herself. "He doesn't care. He already yelled at me, remember?"

"The king said it was a misunderstanding."

"Tibe's misunderstandings are likely to get me killed."

"No, Sacred—"

Xarin snapped to attention. "Warrior Luin. Warrior Poro."

Both straightened.

"Sir," Warrior Luin said. Poro echoed it an instant later.

"Quiet." Xarin turned to the other warriors. "The rebel Faier is still beneath the coral. Resume your work. Summon me once you have broken through."

The warriors in the second party returned to the distant coral.

Kusi lingered.

"You also," Xarin ordered.

The teal-and-white warrior eyed her with anger and rebellion in his eyes. But in silence, he flipped on his fins and flew back to the coral-testing group.

Xarin ordered the two warriors, "You are not to speak of fins to anyone. Understood?"

Their eyes widened, but both nodded curtly.

"And you will not leave Sacred Bride Harmony alone with First Lieutenant Tibe."

Warrior Poro frowned. "But, eh, sir, if he orders us to leave him, we have no choice."

Xarin's jaw flexed. He regarded Harmony. "Aiycaya is a traditional city. We obey our elders and superiors."

"Sir," Warrior Poro snapped his acknowledgment.

So if First Lieutenant Tibe got her away from King Kayo, then no one would intervene.

It was still better. "Thank you, Second Lieutenant Xarin."

The warrior glanced at her sharply. His aura plunged to a darker shade. He worried for her.

Well, Harmony worried for herself too. She'd have to be more careful.

"Convey Sacred Bride Harmony to the king right away." Xarin gestured to the two warriors.

She kicked her human feet.

They began their long ascent.

Xarin joined the coral testers. Breaking through would take a long time. Long enough for Faier to heal. She hoped.

Long enough for her to break through to the king.

She must convince King Kayo that Elder Bawa and Tibe were plotting against him before they overthrew him.

"Perhaps you could let slip those fins you do not have," Warrior Poro commented as they inched upward at her super-slow pace.

"Warrior Poro," Warrior Luin snapped.

"Just thinking we could give the king the good news much faster."

"We cannot. And stop speaking to Sacred Bride Harmony."

"You are conscientious since 'the incident,' are you not, Warrior Luin?"

Warrior Luin dropped silent. He crossed his arms over his chest. His aura diminished.

"Incident?" Harmony repeated.

"Ever since First Lieutenant Tibe passed him over for his personal guard, he has been the worst enforcer of nitpicky—"

"Poro."

"I am explaining why—"

"Poro!"

"You got passed over?" Harmony asked. "Promotions aren't based on succession?"

"Only the king is chosen by succession," Warrior Poro explained while Warrior Luin hugged his chest, finally defeated. "The other positions can groom a successor. First Lieutenant Bawa planned for Warlord Xarin to succeed him after he became the Aiycaya representative to the All-Council. But instead, King Kayo chose Tibe, a warrior barely older than he was. He said if a king can rule with youth and inexperience, then our first lieutenant can also."

"Poro..."

"I am not speaking with anyone. Just speaking aloud, Warrior Luin."

"You do not need to speak aloud this ancient history."

"Hmph. Should I instead remember how you acted with honor over First Lieutenant Tibe's orders? That is why you were punished."

"I would like to know," she said.

The two warriors glared at each other.

Make them listen.

She sighed. "Isn't it ruder to ignore a sacred bride than to answer politely?"

Warrior Luin grimaced.

"He does not know," Warrior Poro commented. "He has not seen a sacred bride since he was a young fry. Even I barely remember. That is why, when the rebel city Atlantis was founded, many of our warriors left to join. Some were dragooned into a war. Those who returned and begged for mercy were instead exiled as traitors."

Warrior Luin's aura darkened even further. "I knew and yet..."

"And yet, when an old friend begged for food and a trident to defend himself from the predators in the open ocean, our Warrior Luin showed him kindness."

"You gave him charity?"

"I said I had lost my trident over a vent," he said, clipped. "Which is true. That is where I released the trident and food."

"For the other warrior to pick up," Warrior Poro said.

"First Lieutenant Tibe saw the lie and turned the king against me." Warrior Luin's shoulders dropped with remembered defeat. "Now, I patrol the innermost circle of the Life Tree."

She loved the beautiful glow of the Life Tree. Its dais

loomed overhead, filling her with strength. She paddled toward it hard. "That should be a reward."

"They reserve such an easy patrol for trainees and young fry."

So it was an insult. "But you don't have trainees or young fry, right? And it's obviously necessary, because look at the Trench Jack that destroyed the prison."

"That was an act of war by another exile," Warrior Poro corrected. "While the competent warriors hunted, this traitor cut a large fish from the school and drove it to the prison."

"Why?"

Warrior Poro shrugged. "He wanted to sabotage Aiycaya before the All-Council. Kill the prisoner before the judgment."

That didn't fit with her theory that Tibe and Elder Bawa arranged the whole attack. "How did the exile know you had a prisoner? You guys aren't supposed to talk, right?"

The warriors both looked at each other.

"Perhaps he watched?" Warrior Luin suggested. "During the wedding ceremony, they reduced the patrols..."

The confusion made an itch in her brain. "But no one knew Faier was a rebel until after the wedding ceremony. So nobody knew the All-Council would be called to judge him until *after*. And how would an exile have found out without talking to an Aiycaya warrior?"

"The exile might have overheard Elder Bawa's message at the Echo Point," Warrior Poro mused.

"And then waited until you went out on a hunt and drove a fish into the prison?"

"It is a little strange," Warrior Luin admitted. "The giant fish should have been stopped well outside the city.

First Lieutenant Tibe will discipline any warriors who abandoned their patrols."

"Unless he was the one who ordered them to abandon their patrols."

Both warriors shook their heads firmly.

"First Lieutenant Tibe is loyal to the king," Warrior Luin told her. "The king approves everything he does. He knows the king's heart even better than the king himself does."

"First Lieutenant Tibe's coldness frightened you after the accident," Warrior Poro agreed. "He is a serious warrior, and perhaps he is not ready to soothe his own sacred bride, but harsher warriors have softened after entangling their souls. You will see."

She was afraid she wouldn't.

And their insistence, like Xarin's, frightened her much more than Tibe's coldness. If she didn't wake King Kayo up to the danger, Tibe would bend him around until he was as cruel and unstable as Lifet.

And all the warriors of the city would enter the darkness with him.

TWENTY-FOUR

Harmony, flanked by Warriors Luin and Poro, reached the lip of the gleaming Life Tree dais. The Life Tree rose magnificently over the city. Beneath its boughs floated a group of warriors, including King Kayo and Tibe, hovering over...something. She paddled forever to cross the ledge, and then she could see.

King Kayo floated over a blood-saturated corpse. His aura exuded darkness. Sadness fought with bitter anger.

This was a dangerous time for him.

Tibe argued confidently. "Do not linger on this exile. You waste precious time honoring him."

One of the waiting warriors, Warlord Sao, eyed her. He was still icy blue, including his eyes.

She shivered and continued paddling, approaching the cluster of warriors with determination.

"I only showed you the body to prove it was Mawa," Tibe argued. "Now, the warriors will destroy it."

King Kayo pinched the bridge of his nose. His eyes were red and his aura dim with tragedy.

Tibe waved at Warlord Sao to remove the body.

"Wait." King Kayo lowered his hand. "Wait, Tibe. I must...confirm."

"Confirm what? His identity is obvious. His scarring is not as disfiguring as the rebel's. And—"

"A moment, Tibe."

"This display is not proper, my king. Mawa turned his back on the city. He betrayed us."

King Kayo said nothing. His gaze fixed bleakly on the lifeless body.

"Elder Bawa awaits your aid. He prepares for the All-Council."

Silence.

"My king, I assure you—"

"You assure me you will wait," the king snapped, pulling away from the mango warrior. "I am king. You are first lieutenant. Be silent."

Tibe frowned harshly. "My king, I dislike this attitude."

King Kayo groaned. "Can you not be silent for a single moment?"

"You never disagreed with me before the rebel. He has poisoned your brain. And your sacred bride interferes. You must put her in your castle where she belongs."

She flushed.

The Life Tree tinkled as its resin gems clinked.

She was a queen. Be strong. Confident.

Harmony dropped so her toes bounced on the giant white pearls. "Uh. Hey. You, uh, just can't obey the king's orders, can you?"

Both the king and Tibe looked up.

The king warmed, his aura glowing. "Harmony. You are free."

Tibe cooled. "Where is the rebel?"

Behind her, Warrior Luin answered. "The coral still traps him."

"You just can't quiet down and give him a minute's peace," she continued. "And these warriors assured me you always do what the king wants. But, uh, I don't see it."

"You accuse me of ignoring tradition?" His teeth gleamed white in a facsimile of a smile. "That is a strange insult coming from a mainland-dwelling, *modern* bride."

The ocean shimmered with danger.

King Kayo had told Tibe her secret.

He had told Tibe.

All the warriors looked at Harmony with new eyes.

She wasn't a traditional sacred bride. That meant she was dangerous to them. They had to get rid of her. The All-Council would be angry.

Harmony heard those thoughts cross their minds with no one speaking.

Her hands opened and closed. Just as when Warlord Sao had cornered her with a harness, a crowd surrounded her and she couldn't see any allies. Not even the one male she had trusted.

King Kayo avoided her gaze. His aura darkened while his cheeks heated. "I asked you not to speak of this, Tibe."

"And I warned you of the dangers in allowing a bride, any bride, to roam beyond your castle." The sharp mango warrior tilted his chin at King Kayo, superior. "This mainland female's roaming endangers Aiycaya."

"She must be happy." King Kayo fixed Tibe with hard, bitter anger. "Her young fry is our only hope."

"Her visible presence hurts Elder Bawa's petition."

"He petitions for us to claim our sacred brides from *her* tribe. She would be the very next female we—"

"A mainland female would not have been the next sacred bride. You control her. Or I will."

Tibe turned toward Harmony with a dark, satisfied smile.

She braced, her feet half-flexed. Whatever he planned, she would not go quietly.

The king flew in front of him. A growl thrummed in his chest, and his protective aura glowed brighter than even the Life Tree. "She is mine."

Tibe stopped smiling.

"You *will not* threaten her."

Tibe floated back, confused and surprised. "My king. What are you saying?"

"Touch her, and I will end you, Tibe." His vibration echoed like that of a true king. The Life Tree made a bright tinkling noise.

Protectiveness flowed in the water and wrapped Harmony up safely.

Tibe looked stunned. "But I...I do not understand. You have never doubted me before."

"You did not threaten my bride before."

"She is just a female, my king." Dark lines creased Tibe's brow as he realized King Kayo would defend her before he would allow Tibe his way. "I have always been faithful. Always. I championed you. I defended you. And now you revile me?"

King Kayo's protective stance wilted. "You *have* always championed me. That is why you are my first lieutenant. I do trust and respect you."

"And this is how you show it? By throwing my loyalty away?"

King Kayo didn't answer. Shame shackled him.

A sneer returned to Tibe's face. He looked satisfied that

he still had ultimate control over the king. "I took your side, my king. Do not forget. Elder Bawa would send her to the surface without me to support you."

Harmony's heart beat loud and hot.

"Yes," King Kayo said, but it was weaker. "I understand. Leave us, Tibe."

"Remember who is your most loyal commander." Tibe squared his shoulders and waved forward his warriors. "Remove that corpse. Leave the king to his reflections. He will soon shut away his bride where she belongs."

King Kayo's shoulders slumped. He rubbed the bridge of his nose.

Warlord Sao and another warrior she didn't know approached the body.

Her blood pumped louder and hotter. The words popped out of her chest fast and angry. "You just don't listen to the king, do you?"

Tibe's warriors hefted the dead body. Old blood clouded the water.

"Oh, sure," she said. "You wanted to talk. Now, when I'm speaking the truth, you ignore me."

His glare stabbed like daggers. "Do not speak, Sacred Bride. You only irritate me."

"Because the king told *you* to be silent. And you weren't. Not for a single moment. And he told you to leave the body. But you're picking it up again. Can you follow any direction?"

"Harmony..." King Kayo sounded small and defeated. Like an ordinary, law-abiding citizen being mugged by a Haitian gangster.

Harmony could never stand up to the gangsters. But now she was the only person who could stand up to Tibe.

So she did.

"It's like, why are you even his first lieutenant? Since you can't do anything he tells you. I'd do a better job than you."

Tibe rounded on her. His vibrations dropped a register to shock. "Do you...? Do you *dare* insult me? Aiycaya's first lieutenant?"

"Tibe." King Kayo swam between them. "She does not know—"

"If me pointing out you do the opposite of whatever the king tells you is an insult, then I guess I do."

Tibe's nostrils flared. "You do not know who you insult."

"Harmony, do not..."

"But I call it 'stating the obvious.' Your behavior is what's insulting."

Tibe sneered. "You will regret the day you tricked King Kayo into bringing you here. A lying mainland female would be better off—"

"Um, am I the only one who remembers you convinced him to kidnap me?"

Tibe broke off. "What?"

"I was swimming on the surface, minding my own business, and the next thing I know, you're swimming around me with tridents, screaming at—and stabbing —Faier."

He frowned. "He was an exile who kidnapped you."

"First of all, he's a rebel."

"That is—"

"And second of all, he was saving me."

"But you—"

"And third of all, I had no desire to go with you. You forced me. Pretty brutally, threatening my savior."

"Because—"

"Pardoning Faier for saving my life and the king's is the least King Kayo can do," she said blithely.

King Kayo glanced at her sharply.

That was a fight she had yet to win.

She refocused on Tibe. "And now you say I will regret the day I had no control over myself. Am I the only one who remembers you having this warrior code that says, 'No warrior will ever hurt a female' and now you're threatening to hurt me?"

His frown deepened. "Hurt...a female...?"

"And there are six 'honorable' warriors around, but *nobody* except the king is doing *anything* to protect me?"

The warriors floated in total confusion.

"Tibe will not hurt you, Harmony," King Kayo ground out, speaking awkwardly for his frozen warriors.

She choked. "So Tibe issues empty threats? I should just ignore it? When he says, 'You will regret the day...' he's being friendly?"

"Tibe..." King Kayo opened and closed his fists. "He will not hurt you."

"He's just yelling to scare me. So, scaring sacred brides is okay? Now I see why you never have to touch them. Verbal abuse is fine."

"Abuse!"

"How about mental and emotional abuse? You can't see those scars."

"He does not intend to injure," King Kayo repeated doggedly.

"Oh. So, 'you will regret the day you tricked King Kayo' shouldn't strike fear into my heart. This is another 'misunderstanding.' Thanks for explaining."

She put her hands on her hips and glared at a confused, worked-up Tibe.

"King Kayo says I don't have to be afraid of you because you won't hurt me. So I can say you're the most disrespectful warrior I've ever seen. You're a jerk, entitled, cruel, and way overstepping."

Tibe's nostrils flared again, and his lips pulled back from his teeth. "Do not insult Aiycaya's first lieutenant!"

"Or what?" She tilted her head. "Are you going to stab me in the abdomen or unleash a giant fish on me when I fall asleep?"

His hands clenched on his trident. "I will—"

"Tibe?"

King Kayo's chest vibrated in warning. The other warriors stared.

Tibe unclenched his fingers and snapped at King Kayo, "Control your female."

She scoffed. "Or else what?"

"Or...else..."

"Tibe." King Kayo jerked his chin. "Leave."

"Discipline her."

"Tibe."

His gaze lingered on her in dark promise. He finally turned away and gestured at his warriors. They lifted the corpse.

King Kayo's jaw flexed.

"Hey. King Kayo. Tibe's stealing the body again."

The king closed his eyes, braced himself for a fight, and opened them again. "Unhand Mawa."

Tibe ignored him. "Dump it in the vent."

Warlord Sao's icy-blue eyes flicked to King Kayo...and then to her.

Okay. Fine.

She elbowed King Kayo. "Does the word 'loyal' have a different meaning under the water? Because on the surface, it means you actually do what your leader tells you."

"You have passed the proper time!" Tibe snarled at King Kayo, who floated like a broad shield in front of Harmony. "You wrongly honor the exile."

King Kayo squared his shoulders. He clearly wanted to argue. But he didn't.

So Harmony did for him. "Um, how long is 'the proper time'? Are you using a stopwatch? Or—"

"King Kayo."

"Is deciding how long someone can honor the dead the job of the first lieutenant? Because the king should—"

"King Kayo!"

"Tibe." King Kayo gestured for him to leave the body. "Now."

Tibe's face fell. "My king? What are you doing?"

King Kayo rested a hand on Tibe's bicep. "I will explain. Drop the body."

The warriors left the deceased on the pearls at the king's orders.

Tibe shook his head, confusion yielding to anger. "No, my king. I am the one you trust."

"I will call for you when I am ready."

"She must stay in your castle."

"I will talk to her."

"Talk? Why are you so weak before this female? She is a stranger. She knows nothing. I am your faithful first lieutenant."

"Just go, Tibe."

"Perhaps she must go to the surface after all."

King Kayo eyed him hard.

Harmony sniped at him, "When you 'speak for the king,' exactly how much is what he wanted you to say?"

"Everything." Tibe straightened and lifted his noble chin. "I am a faithful warrior of Aiycaya. I will guard it with my last heartbeat. No one will stand against what is right."

"Tibe. Go."

Tibe narrowed his eyes on King Kayo. "No one."

King Kayo hunched his shoulders, enduring his barb.

Tibe veered away. The other warrior left with him. Warlord Sao eyed her for a long moment before swimming after the first lieutenant.

King Kayo slumped and rubbed his nose, exhausted.

She vibrated urgently. "Stand up to him. Or else he will rule the city, not you."

He eyed her from the side. "You are a stranger to our ways."

"Coups are universal."

"Tibe would never disrupt the hierarchy." A cynical smile flashed across the king's face. "That is one law he would not break. My position is safe."

She wasn't so sure.

TWENTY-FIVE

Harmony hoped King Kayo's position was safe from Tibe.

But her entire plan for coming to speak with him now depended on her convincing King Kayo that Tibe was unsafe so he would get rid of Tibe and release Faier.

King Kayo bounced across the pearls to the body.

She followed. "I'm sorry for your loss. He was a friend?"

King Kayo gazed on the fallen warrior. "Mawa drove that Trench Jack into the prison to kill you."

She looked down.

But it was a mistake. Someone had slashed the dull, waterlogged body, and it seethed with lice. The head hung by a thin strip of skin. A bloody mess mutilated him between the legs.

Her stomach rolled. She looked away. "Why?"

"He approached us on our search for a sacred bride. I thought he wished to return to the city." Bitter hurt seethed in his chest vibrations. "Not destroy us."

"You *were* friends."

"He was my first trainer. I looked up to him very much.

He should have had a young fry long ago. But our sacred brides..." King Kayo looked into the white branches of the Life Tree as though staring into the past. "When Mawa left for Atlantis, I took it as a great betrayal. A challenge to my kingship. Mawa returned a different male. I wish I had not sent him away."

"So you caught him and had to, uh, execute him."

"Tibe caught him."

"Oh. Right."

"I wished to ask why. Why did he turn on us? Was there no way to reconcile? Now, I will never know." His nose wrinkled in anger at the corpse. "And Tibe is right. Delaying his destruction only conveys an honor he does not deserve."

"You never will know," she pointed out. "Tibe stole that from you."

His lips twisted in denial.

"Maybe it was an accident. Maybe Mawa got tricked. Maybe your first lieutenant is plotting against you."

"Harmony."

"The point is, maybe Mawa deserves your honors. So take the time. Honor him. You're the king. Stop letting your first lieutenant rule for you."

His aura glowed with the same anger that flashed in his eyes. He turned his shoulder on her and stared at Mawa hard, honoring the fallen warrior with his attention until his muddy aura cleared.

Then he knelt, arranged the body, and ululated a short song. She didn't know the words but it seemed like he conveyed sadness, confusion, and a sense of loss too soon.

Finally, he rose again and vibrated with calm. "Warrior Luin. Tell Warlord Sao he may take the body away. In the trench, the same jacks Mawa herded to attack our city may eat him."

The warriors returned and hauled the body from the Life Tree dais. The water cleared of its metallic tang.

"Feel better?" she asked.

"Yes. Thank you, Harmony. So." King Kayo turned to her. "We sent that food. I trust you are not hungry?"

"Er...actually..."

"Come." He hooked her arm with his.

"Oh. Can we eat by the Life Tree?"

His eyebrows furrowed. "You will be safe. I will eat with you."

"The Life Tree is more calming." Plus she'd be disobeying Tibe. "Is there a problem?"

"No. Kings often ruled from the Life Tree." He ordered Warrior Poro to the castle, and the warrior returned with a spread of legumes and meats.

While they shared a meal, Elder Bawa flew to the Life Tree. He harrumphed importantly. "My king, you must prepare for the All-Council."

He stopped midbite and packed up. "Patrols have sighted them?"

"No, my king, but you must prepare." He eyed Harmony and curled his lip. "Return your female to your castle."

King Kayo closed up his box.

She crunched a legume extra-hard. "Huh. That's funny. I thought you said *you* were preparing for their arrival."

"A king has many duties you do not understand, female."

"Yeah, but at the prison, you said he should go hunting, and now he can't eat a sandwich in peace. I guess you aren't that capable."

Elder Bawa drew up, stiff. "I am exceedingly capable. He can eat the 'sandwich.' I have prepared everything!"

"So then what's King Kayo supposed to prepare?"

Elder Bawa's mouth twisted, but no words vibrated in his chest.

King Kayo stopped. "Elder Bawa?"

The elder gestured angrily at the castle. "My king, she should not be in public viewing! Sacred brides belong in castles. Not in prisons, not in forests, and not at the Life Tree like an honored warrior!"

King Kayo lowered to the dais once more and reopened his food box. "Thank you for your advice, Elder Bawa. Inform me when you sight the All-Council at our borders."

"My king!"

"What is your and Tibe's obsession with getting me into the king's castle?" she asked. "Seriously. It's a little scary. It's like, what are you plotting?"

"It is tradition!" he almost shrieked.

King Kayo fixed him with a long look. "Elder Bawa. I expect you to focus on our petition. Not my sacred bride. If you cannot do this, I will ask another elder to take your place. Understand?"

The elder stiffened. "My king."

"Go."

The elder turned and kicked away. Harmony and King Kayo continued their peaceful picnic.

"You have no problem ordering him around," she noted.

He grimaced and selected another piece of meat. "He has more tattoos on one arm than I have on my whole body."

"That can change."

"Hmm. You have reminded me..."

King Kayo finished his food, flew to the Life Tree's

biggest roots, and removed a curved dagger. He pruned a small twig, notched an end, and embedded a metal shard at the tip like a pencil.

Returning to his seat, he pressed the tip to a big tattoo swirling across his bicep in a Caribbean pattern.

"What did I remind you?"

"I must record my recent deeds." He scratched a swirling line in sync with the existing tattoos, adding dots and lightning bolt crashes. A thatched pattern.

"So, the designs have a meaning?"

"This is the meeting of myself and my sacred bride. These lines mean we fought a great battle and defeated our foe."

"Yours look so unique."

"The markings may be unique, but we all record major events in our lives."

That made sense for a warrior culture that didn't have books, cameras, or archives to record their history. Her years in Haiti had blended together, and she had no documentation. Tattoos would have helped her to remember how skeptical Fab had been that she would last a week in the slums, how they had grown to be friends, and how cute Evens had been as a little boy. How he was just growing into a skinny, responsible, serious young man when Lifet's gang took him.

And if she didn't free him, he would die too young. She would cry over him like King Kayo cried over Mawa, a senseless victim of inexplicable violence.

Or Faier...

No. She needed to convince King Kayo to pardon Faier. If she could find commonalities with the king, she could reach him.

King Kayo was ambidextrous. He touched up older tattoos where the scar tissue had erased little bits.

"You are repairing them," she noted.

"I cannot lose my memories."

Faier had so many scars. He must have lost many memories.

"That is one reason an exile has such a difficult time," King Kayo said as if he were reading her mind. "His Life Tree no longer heals ordinary injuries, and scars erode his tattoos."

And others didn't see a kind, honest, capable warrior. They saw only the monster she had seen the first time she'd looked at him.

She had been so cruel.

"Can I use that tool?" she asked.

"Sacred brides do not use it."

"But could I?"

"The adamantium shard will not mark human skin."

"Well, how does that work?"

He held up the tool. "This rare metal cauterizes the Life Tree so cuts on it do not allow in the ocean water, which is poison. It also keeps the sap liquid. As I score my skin, a tiny drop of Life Tree sap enters my scratch."

"That's how human tattoos work too," she insisted. "We inject ink instead of tree sap."

"The Life Tree sap is not ink. It is colorless."

"Your tattoos are hot pink."

"The sap activates the existing color of mer skin. That is why you cannot mark a sacred bride. Do you think you are the first to ask for such a memento? Coloration passes from father to son. You are, despite your transformation, still a human."

Oh. He had thought she meant to use it on herself. "Can you tattoo another mer?"

"Yes. Look here." He showed her a swirly tattoo on his

calf that had a distinctive style different from the rest on his body. "This is when I succeeded my father. A rampaging spearnose flounder stabbed through his heart. I was too distraught from grief. Elder Wida inked this tattoo."

"I'm so sorry."

"You also... Many were sorry I succeeded."

"No! I'm sorry your father was killed so suddenly. And you still go hunting?"

"He was unwell." King Kayo neatened one line. "A strange headache had dulled his senses. Healer Hobin requested he stay behind. But my father had been a hunter before he was king. He always supported his hunters."

"That is so sad."

"Yes. I miss his counsel." He looked up at the Life Tree. "There are many things I should have asked."

"I know what you mean." She chewed a creamy legume. "I'd give anything to hear my mother scold me one more time. 'Get your head out of the clouds, Harmony. The earth is fine.' She always said things like that."

"You knew your mother?"

"She raised me."

"No mer has memories with his mother." He rested his tattoo pen across his knee. "My father was a good, strong male. I envy humans for knowing both parents."

"Oh, I didn't know my father."

"Surface dwellers do not know both parents?"

"Most people know their fathers, but single-parent households are super common."

He mulled that.

"And my mother died in an accident too."

"A hunting accident?"

"No." She laughed shortly. "No, she was in a car accident and got a nasty concussion. She was in the hospital for a few days with a bad headache. They were waiting for the swelling to go down when she had a heart attack."

One moment her mother had been commenting on the blue Jell-O for the third time—repeating herself was a problem due to the fuzzy thinking of the concussion—and the next, she had gasped and clutched at her chest.

"That is an interesting coincidence," he murmured. "My father and your mother both suffered head pain and then heart trauma."

It was an odd link, but probably that kind of coincidence happened all the time.

"The panic of being alone almost numbed me to the sadness," she said.

He commiserated. "I also was not ready to be alone in this world."

"You too," she said with feeling. "And then a few months later, my citizenship got challenged. The certificate I'd always used went missing and apparently my birth was never registered or it went into the system wrong. Nobody could find me. It was like a nightmare. You called Faier the exile, but I'm the one without a home. It was horrible."

He returned the tattoo stick to the base of the Life Tree.

Warrior Zaka flew to the edge of the dais. His face burned so redly that his tattoos almost melted. He shouted, "King Kayo! Return your f-female to the c-castle at once or I will lose all respect for you as a king!"

King Kayo rotated, hand reaching for the dagger at his bicep, aura darkening. "What did you say?"

Warrior Zaka's chest shook. "K-King Kayo! Return your female—"

"Did Elder Bawa tell you to say that?" Harmony munched the last crunchy strip of beans. "Or was it Tibe?"

Warrior Zaka sagged with relief. "Elder Bawa, Sacred Bride Harmony."

"Okay, thanks. Can you get me more of these bean things? They're delicious."

He bowed deeply to both, whirled on his fins, and flew to the castle as if an entire school of Trench Jacks chased him.

Harmony packed up her food.

King Kayo turned to her, a question on his face. "How did you know...? That Warrior Zaka—"

"That the shyest warrior in Aiycaya wasn't insulting you to your face?" She tilted her head at him. "Really?"

He stared after the warrior. "It was a surprise. But if even Warrior Zaka shared Tibe's and Elder Bawa's feelings, then perhaps I must reconsider."

"He doesn't. He's just obeying."

"How do you know?"

"Because Warrior Zaka worries more about how to fit your hunted meat into your pantry than he does about me. Anyway, he used the same intonation both times. He clearly rehearsed."

"He might have rehearsed his true feelings."

"Then he'd wait for a private moment."

King Kayo frowned at her. "You are preparing to visit the prisoner."

She rested her hands on her neatly stacked boxes. "You know that he didn't mean to trespass. He was saving me. He shouldn't be punished for non-crimes."

"I have no choice." His frown deepened. "Go to my castle."

"No."

"I forbid you from disobeying me."

"Then you will be very sad when I visit him anyway."

He rubbed his forehead. "Why do you disobey me?"

"Because you let Tibe disobey you all the time."

King Kayo dropped his hand, glared at her, and stared up into the boughs of the Life Tree. "I have no choice but to accept Tibe's... I am trapped. Understand?"

"You're the king."

"Yes, I am the king, but I am more imprisoned than your rebel. He, at least, knows respect from two cities. Whereas I cannot rule. No warriors will follow my leadership. Tibe keeps the warriors and elders in line."

She bounced to her feet. "He keeps them in line by lying about your orders."

"Because they obey. If not for him, Xarin would be king and I would be an exile."

"Xarin obeys you."

He wheeled on her with sharp fury. "So, you like Xarin and wish he were king also?"

"This again?" She tutted her tongue, making a clicking noise. "When they want to kill the dog, they say it's crazy."

He blinked. "Dog? What?"

"My cousin Fab used to say that. People will lie about a faithful companion when they want to get rid of him. You hate Xarin no matter how loyal he is to you."

"He is not loyal." King Kayo hugged his elbows. "He calls me a milk-fry."

"Milk-fry?"

"A male who cannot make wise decisions. He cannot see because he holds his face to his mother's breast." King Kayo darkened as he gazed at the dais. "In my case, it is more true. I was born too small. My mother remained a long time. Many extra human months. And even after she left, I was too small to compete with the other warriors."

"That's not a problem now."

"I worked hard. Now I am a great hunter." He raised his fist. "Strong and fearless like my father. Xarin sees only the weak trainee."

"I think he regrets what he said."

King Kayo shook his head, dropping his fist. "He often tells me what I am doing wrong."

"But he obeys you explicitly. Give him another chance."

"He has all the chances. He is my second lieutenant. What more to do you want?"

"Make him your first lieutenant."

"No."

"King Kayo—"

"I will never make him obey me. Only Tibe controls the warriors. They respect him."

"You doubt yourself, but even I can see how much the warriors like and trust you. Xarin included."

"You are an outsider to our ways."

"So I see more clearly. You are king. You're more capable than you know. Demote Tibe. Issue the order."

"It is not so easy. Like pardoning your rebel. I could not pardon him now when the All-Council representative is due. Not even if he saved my life a hundred times."

She was so close. "What is easy is not always what is right."

"Or left."

"Huh?"

"Or up or down. The easiest path is always with the current, and currents flow in every direction."

"Oh. Er, I meant honorable. The honorable action is not always easy."

"Hmm."

Elder Bawa scuttled across the city looking, to her outsider eyes, suspicious.

King Kayo noticed too. He straightened. "Where are you hurrying to, Elder Bawa?"

"My king." Elder Bawa jolted. "Your bride is not in your castle. Still."

"And?"

"I fear for her. For you both." A worried smile split his thin face. "The stress of exposure will make her ill. You, of all warriors, should not risk her health. Or the health of your future young fry."

King Kayo wavered.

She rose also. "Elder Bawa, I'll feel less stressed after you stop hiding All-Council business from King Kayo."

He grimaced and barked in his language. She didn't understand the words, but she felt intuitively he called her untrustworthy, hysterical, dangerous.

King Kayo held up a palm. "Speak so she may understand."

Elder Bawa flashed hot anger. "My king—"

"It's okay." She stretched, careful not to let her fins pop out, and collected the tattoo wand. She paddled to Warriors Luin and Poro. "This 'dangerous, hysterical, untrustworthy' female is going to check on Faier."

Elder Bawa watched her with narrowed eyes. He muttered something to the king about needing to treat her differently or else there would be trouble when the All-Council arrived.

She stopped and whirled to face him. "I'm not in any danger from them, am I?"

The king and Elder Bawa both turned and stared at her. Struck, as though they suddenly realized they could not keep secrets.

"No," King Kayo said, in English. "Of course you are

not in danger from the All-Council, Sacred Bride Harmony."

"Good. I'm so used to being in fear of my life on the surface. I'm glad I don't have to worry down here too."

Elder Bawa narrowed his eyes. "*She is not like other sacred brides.*"

Harmony flipped again. "Are you sure? How do you know? It's been an awful long time since you've seen a sacred bride. Maybe you don't remember."

Elder Bawa's lips thinned with anger. "I remember."

"Did you even have a sacred bride?"

"Of course. One does not become an elder without contributing a young fry."

"How did your sacred bride enjoy staring at your interior walls the whole time?"

"She did not stare at walls," he spat, suddenly looking like he might cry. "She stared at me. Our time was short. We treasured every moment. As should you." He drew himself up and firmly addressed the king. "A traditional sacred bride should know this."

Harmony raised her brows at King Kayo. "Would you like to tell him, or should I?"

Elder Bawa rubbed his nose. "Tell me?"

"Since you told Tibe."

King Kayo gritted his teeth. "That was a mistake. I thought he would understand."

"Tell me what?"

She flipped forward and paddled toward her warriors. They would escort her to the depths once again.

"What is she doing with that tattoo stick?" Elder Bawa demanded.

"I do not wish to ask," King Kayo said.

"My king, you must keep her under tighter control. She must respect your authority."

"Apparently, she is not the only one. Explain the All-Council business."

"Er...my king, I must go—"

"Elder Bawa." His tone sharpened. Finally, he was taking Harmony's advice. "You *will* explain. Now."

TWENTY-SIX

Faier passed the time sharpening his trident.

Harmony had ingeniously asked for a weapon. The Aiycaya warriors had equally wisely given her a damaged trainee trident. Dull, bent, and useless.

But it was still a weapon.

He'd found a polishing stone and scraped the growth off with long, even strokes.

Harmony's house guardian, Lady, gallivanted through the meadow. She twirled around him and batted a dead fish—an arm-length black gill—in front of him before settling on one of the coral perches and ripping out tasty chunks.

He noted the width of its body. "They enlarged the new tunnel."

Lady's plus-sign-shaped eyes rotated around her body in assent.

He lifted his trident to examine the blade. The handle was smooth and the blade sharp. Now he polished the aesthetic pieces.

An ugly trident could still kill. But a well-tended trident

might make his opponents pause long enough to save their lives.

He would soon test his work.

"Faier?" Harmony's vibration called.

His chest spasmed. *Harmony.* He flew to the meadow.

Mantis shrimp buzzed a warning.

He pulled up, mindful of their clicks. His blood raced. Anticipation throbbed under his skin. Her body and her soul addicted him. Missing her made him sick.

Had she missed him?

Harmony emerged from the rainbow-iridescent tunnel and oriented on him. Her soul brightened like the sun. "Faier!"

"Harmony." He opened his arms.

Her fins unfurled, and she barreled into him, laughing. "Oh, god, it's been an hour, and I already missed you so much."

He held her tight against him. "It has been longer than an hour."

"Okay." She pulled back. "I can't wait until we're both safe and we can be together all the time."

He wished for that future too.

She sobered. "You're looking better."

"A little."

"Only a little?" She studied him for a long moment, dropped his hands, and wheeled behind her for the box she had dropped. "I brought you more food."

He accepted her box. "This is welcome."

"Great." Her smile crinkled, and the warmth of her soul nearly overpowered him. "And I brought this."

She held up a long, tapered stick embedded with a cool, white shard of opalescent resin.

A tattooing implement?

Harmony waited eagerly for his reaction.

"There it is," he commented.

"I will fix you," she said, suddenly fierce, "so when you swim out of here a free merman no one will confuse you for an exile ever again."

His heart squeezed. She cared for him so much. Her kindness warmed his soul. "Thank you, Harmony."

"Hmm." She squeezed his biceps. "Your skin is smoother."

"Forced rest is healing."

"Look here." She traced three fingers diagonal across his belly from nipple to hip. "The lines where the crocodile scratched you are almost gone."

Her familiar touch was easy and intimate. She'd claimed his body as hers and now reaffirmed it.

His cock pulsed.

She noted his swelling hardness. Her own awareness brightened her cheeks, her eyes, and her soul. She lifted her gaze, and her lips parted, revealing her pink tongue. "Did you miss me?"

He drew her into his arms. "Very much."

Her lashes fluttered closed, and her chin tilted up to invite his kiss.

He accepted her invitation. Delving into her mouth, he supped on her heated moans. Her breasts rubbed his chest. He cupped her smooth globes. His fingers kneaded her dark teats.

She wrapped her legs around his waist and impaled her wet heat on his throbbing hard cock.

Mine.

A hard shudder racked his body.

Like the first time she had claimed him, his soul warred

with his heart. He pumped her full of pleasure while probing his feelings deep inside. He hadn't realized how many barriers he had wrapped around himself. How many layers screened him from feeling her love as anything more than a need?

Her hungry moan as she nibbled on his jaw tore down another screen. "Faier. Yes."

He shuddered.

Her channel squeezed his cock. "Mmm. There."

His soul reached out of his body and tangled with hers. Uniting them. Centering him.

Enslaving him.

Her passion broke his control into pieces. He couldn't breathe. Couldn't escape. Couldn't think.

"You are...everything I want..." she murmured.

Shudder.

She cried out and then rested on his shoulder.

Crashing waves of pleasure from her release swept him away. He shattered and filled her with his white-hot seed. She was his mate. His soul. His.

For one brief instant, his last view of Nerissa—golden, sparkling grounds, shimmering Life Tree—filled him with peace.

But this peace could not last. Harmony, like his beloved first home, could be ripped away at any time.

His soul plunged into chilly blackness.

"Mmph!" Harmony shivered and flailed, separating them and brushing herself as though she'd been swarmed with mantis shrimp. "Oh, I must have fallen asleep. A little nightmare. Hahhh."

He stroked her back. "Rest."

"Not yet. There's too much going on. Especially since— well, anyway." She shook herself and grabbed the tattoo implement. "I'll fix your tattoos, and then I'll never worry about a stranger attacking you for being an exile again."

He offered his arm.

She pressed the flat tip to his bicep and stroked like a human painting brush.

He gripped her fist, oriented the tool perpendicular, and pressed firmly to score the skin.

The bite of adamantium and the sting of Life Tree sap was so familiar, it put his teeth on edge. *Concentrate on now. Not the past.* Faier closed his eyes. He was grateful to share this time with Harmony and feel her presence, her love, while they could still be together.

Before the Aiycaya warriors broke in and he had to fight his way to freedom, leaving her behind.

"You did not convince the king," he guessed.

"I'm close." She bit her lower lip. "I think he would have agreed already if the All-Council weren't coming."

He surveyed the meadow. When the warriors broke through they would come from the other side. How much time did he have?

"You should know I'm a semi-famous artist." She connected his sleeve to curls around his wrist. "I used to sew rag dolls for kids at the hospital after my mom died. I used their parents' clothes and sewed in a pressure module. It made a 'thud-thud' sound, so when the kids were alone at night, they could hug these dolls and hear heartbeats."

He concentrated on her heartbeat filling the ocean. "That sounds comforting."

"It was. They got a little popular, and my ex at the time —he was a law student—set up a company. He felt bad about breaking up with me during the 'turbulent era.' I would sell these to pay my way through college. And it kind of worked. They got featured on the local news, and I made a semester's worth of profits. Then I got approached by a toy company about trademarking the dolls."

She followed the inner lines up his sensitive elbow and across his chest. Her heartbeat increased. The water tensed even though her tonal vibrations remained calm.

"The company rep was super nice. He took me out to pancakes. I thought he would buy the rights or offer me a job or something. I told him how rough it had been because my mom wasn't a natural-born citizen. After the dinner, he called up my ex and demanded the trademark or else he'd get me deported. My ex thought he was crazy. The next thing I knew, I was in an interrogation room guessing—wrongly—where my dead mom had lost my birth certificate. Ow!"

She stuffed her thumb in her mouth. Her eyes reddened.

He rested a palm on her leg. "This pains you."

"Oh, it's fine." Her chest vibrated dismissively as she sucked on her thumb. "I jabbed my thumb with the tool."

"Your memories. They pain you."

"Only because I wish I could go back in time and yell at myself. 'It's a trap!' or 'He's not a father. He's a crocodile in human clothing!' I was so naïve."

She released her thumb with a pop. A vee-shaped chevron bled from the tip of her thumb. She tutted at her clumsiness, then leaned over his chest again and examined where she had left off.

"I would have given him the trademark. Like, just have it. Don't ruin my life. But I just waited for my ex to deal with it."

"He did not wish to lose this trademark."

"Right, he thought the guy had no case. After I got deported, he felt terrible and promised to bring me back.

But," she dismissed the past with a shrug, "he studied intellectual property law, not immigration. He got depressed, took drugs, and years passed. And I am now an exile."

She pressed the tip into his skin and connected the star compass over his heart.

"It's sad." She concentrated on a squiggly curve. "But the real moral of the story is that I've waited my whole life for someone else to save me. You, Lifet, Fab, my ex. Monsieur Joseph. Evens. My great-grandmother. I should have just stood up and solved my own problems."

"Would that have found your birth certificate?" he asked.

She shrugged a shoulder. "Maybe I would have taken more responsibility and never lost it to begin with."

The surface world was complicated. He knew. He had lived there.

"My scars are visible on the outside," he pointed out. "Yours are carried within. Do not let their invisibility make you forget. An injury is an injury even if no one can see your pain."

She softened. "Your scars are healing. Does that mean mine are too?"

Deep hope welled in him. He wished to heal her. From his first touch he had wished it.

She rested her forehead gently against his for a moment of silent support. "If you're well enough to leave soon, I think we have to escape. I don't want another fight because I'm almost through to King Kayo. But I can't risk your life on 'almost.'"

He considered an alternative, even though it tore at his soul to say it aloud. "You can remain if you think you can change the city."

"What? No." She tapped his forehead with hers reprovingly. "We're together. Okay? Stay or go. I'm not ever leaving without you."

His throat closed. He couldn't look her in the eye.

Harmony obligingly looked away. She followed a swoop low around his torso to his backside and exclaimed, "Your legs are as scarred as your hands. It's like you've been dancing with weed whackers. Why didn't you ever try to repair your tattoos?"

He cleared his throat even though he spoke with vibrations in his chest. "I could not tattoo across angry scar tissue."

"It's not angry now."

She was correct. His skin had healed.

He swallowed again hard. "Your invitation to treat me in Council Bluffs touched me deeply."

"I meant it." She traced the half-seen lines diligently. "I can't wait to show you my home. Why do you look surprised?"

"I am a citizen of two cities and yet I have never truly belonged. Even now."

"Faier." She lifted her head and nailed him with a gaze. "You belong. The Coast Guard asked you to help them how many times?"

"They use my skills. I am not one of them. And citizenship can be stricken away. In my case it has already happened twice. It is devastating to lose your home. Everything is gone."

"Friends," she agreed, dropping her head back to her task. "Job. Past. Hope."

"You understand. It is the same under water. And, if a warrior does not find sanctuary with another city, he will sicken and die like his fallen Life Tree."

"That would suck."

"It is visceral devastation." He swallowed, feeling the constant scratch, reawakening his dormant skin like scraping off the growths of the unused trident. "The first was the worst."

He found that as he described the fall of Nerissa, the words poured out, as uncontrollable as the lava that had swept it away.

"I was so young. The city was ancient. I thought such a thing could not happen. But my father had sent me away once to another city. Rusalka. When he forced me to escape the undersea volcano, I sought refuge there."

The oldest, injured warriors had perished during their long flight. No one could give them proper funerals. They had reached the city of Rusalka, and only Faier had been strong enough to accept sanctuary.

The others had been too happy by then to die. Slip into the eternal darkness of the Blacknight Sea.

"One warlord whose own son had died took me in. I worked hard to be recognized, repay his kindness, and honor the elders and king. I even earned the right to claim a sacred bride. This angered the 'true' sons of the city. They abandoned me during a raid. I fought my way free, and you see the result."

"That's awful. What wretched jerks. People like that don't deserve a bride."

"Jealousy twists many honorable souls," Faier agreed. "The elders declared me unfit to seek a bride after my injuries. So I betrayed them and joined rebel Atlantis."

"And Dragao Azul." She filled in the details, both with the tattoo implement and with her words. "You've been through so much. And you still don't feel like you belong?"

He shook his head.

She set aside the tattoo implement and clasped his

hand. "That's on you. Because you belong. I know you belong."

He nodded because that was the correct response. Of course she was right. Intellectually he knew this. In his soul, though, he was still confused.

"And if you don't belong to any city then make your home me."

His heart tripped.

"Make my home *with* you?" he repeated.

"That's what I said." She held his hand in both of hers and pressed his palm to her chest. "Home is right here. Wherever we go it's together. You and me."

A lump choked his throat.

He swallowed hard and stroked her peaceful cheek. "Then I will not leave it. You."

Her soul burned even brighter. "That's right. Together."

Lady swooshed through in a panic, stirring the mantis shrimp to a *click click click* warning.

"Lady?" Harmony rose. Her fins extended. "What's wrong?"

The house guardian flew around her with arms extended as though ready to beat on an enemy.

Danger.

"Retract your fins," he ordered, and Harmony did so. He'd thought they had more time. Where was his trident? There, across the meadow—

The teal-and-white warrior, Kusi, darted into the clearing and cut Faier off. His trident slashed.

Faier reversed course.

Kusi followed, slashing aggressively. Other warriors poured into the clearing. Chiba and Kusi together smashed him into the coral. They manacled Faier, yanked his limbs back, and bound him so he could barely breathe.

"Stop!" Harmony shrieked.

The mantis shrimp swarmed in alarm. Lady circled Harmony, arms out.

"Leave him alone. Or else!"

Tibe entered behind Harmony. "Do not listen to your female, rebel. Come at us. Fight."

She jerked away from him. "Tibe? Get away from me."

"You should have obeyed King Kayo." Tibe floated too close to Harmony. "Now you will watch your male die in front of you."

"No!" She lifted her hand to the mantis shrimp. The shrimp swirled around her open palm. She turned to unleash them on Tibe.

"You are immune?" Tibe watched her movements with shock and then fury. "No." He dropped his trident and popped the dull handle into her belly.

She folded over with an oof. The mantis shrimp dissipated harmlessly.

Lady attacked.

Tibe swept the house guardian aside with the trident base and jabbed her with the sharp blade.

"No," Harmony croaked. "Lady."

The green house guardian evaded and puffed dangerously around Harmony, yowling in warning.

The warriors binding Faier had not noticed Tibe's attack on Harmony.

Rage colored Faier's gaze to deadly. "Do not injure a sacred bride!"

"Come at me." Tibe lifted the point of his trident near Harmony's neck. "Give me a reason to slip. Slash you all."

The warriors brought Faier to Tibe. A knowing smile filled his sharp features, just like those "true sons" of Rusalka, who'd known they would not face any consequences. He gripped Faier's index finger. "How well do you fight without hands?"

"Stop it," Harmony begged weakly, shaking hard, her soul as black as when she had first screamed in fear and called him a monster.

Her fear and pain hurt him. "Harmony. Be str—argh!"

Tibe cracked his index finger past the breaking point.

Harmony cried. Her chest vibrated. "*Please.*"

"Speak again, and I will break the rest." Tibe kicked past Harmony, leaving her behind.

Faier's tortured fear eased.

The sharp mango warrior sneered at his relief. "Too bad you will not be alive to see, once your life is severed, how quickly she entwines her soul with my king."

The other warriors dragged Faier through the hole they had drilled and out into the open ocean.

Tibe grinned sharply. "Are you grateful to escape your imprisonment? You should not be. The All-Council has arrived to bestow its judgment!"

TWENTY-SEVEN

Harmony's stomach throbbed, hot and painful.

This was nothing. Lifet had kicked her harder. Tibe hadn't ruptured an internal organ. Probably.

She forced herself to unbend.

Faier's life was in danger. She should have guessed Elder Bawa was lurking because he'd sighted the All-Council judges. King Kayo had made him promise to tell when they were sighted, but he hadn't. She should've known to skip the sex and the tattooing and instead focus only on escape.

She should've known. But she hadn't. So now she needed to act.

Harmony scooped up the trident. It was heavy, awkward, and weirdly balanced. If she lifted it, she banged into walls, and if she didn't lift it, it dragged on the coral with a nerve-shredding shriek.

Lady curled her small tentacles around the heavy head and heaved, pulling Harmony through the twisting maze of coral.

"Thank you," she murmured.

Lady's free tentacles curled into fists.

Around them, mantis shrimp swarmed, mirroring the aggravation in Harmony's heart. Her fins unfurled.

The jagged new entry hole swirled with fearful fish.

Above, Faier writhed. They dragged him into the center of the city. Warriors crowded the space. Most were from Aiycaya, but some were not.

His struggle tore into her soul. Her heart flopped like a fish in her empty chest. Her strength drained out the hole.

In Port-au-Prince, she'd sat on the harbor wall and watched boat after boat leaving. Day after day. Each one she'd imagined was heading back to America. They had left her behind, powerless and alone, each time.

Now, despite her work to reach King Kayo and the other warriors, they were taking Faier away from her.

Make them listen.

Anger swelled in the place where there had been weakness.

She would not lose Faier. She would not walk onto a plane without a fight. She would not.

"There she is!" Warrior Poro kicked hard toward her; Warrior Luin flew right behind. They had been waiting at the other entrance. "Are you hurt? Sacred Bride Harmony!"

"Don't call me that," she snapped.

Warrior Poro's face fell.

"I told you," Warrior Luin sniped.

Warrior Poro slowed. "I apologize, Sacred Bride. I—"

"That. I told you before I'm not a sacred bride. I'm just Harmony."

They both protested.

"You will address me the way I ask."

They dropped silent.

Her anger swelled to a new rainbow color. Iridescent. Clicking.

She kicked out of the new hole. Her fins unfurled and Warrior Poro, still smarting from her shortness, pointed them out. "The fins you do not have are showing."

"Here." She hauled the trident around and shoved the sharp tip at him.

He kicked back, shocked. "Sacred Br—er, Harmony! Do not be angry."

"I'm not attacking you. Take the end."

He touched the honed edge. "Sharp."

"No, beneath the blades. I need to get up there," she pointed at where Faier had disappeared in the center of the city, "as fast as possible. So you take that end, and Warrior Luin take that end, and I'll grip the middle. Go fast."

Warrior Luin gripped the dull end. He jolted and lifted one hand. A mantis shrimp crawled across his knuckles. He bit back a scream.

"Grip it," she ordered, snapping him to attention. "Fly me to Faier. And don't argue."

Warrior Poro growled at him. "Luin."

Warrior Luin hardened, mastering his fears. Deadly mantis shrimp buzzed around in a cloud, and her octopus flew. She gripped the trident in the center and kicked. The two warriors kicked hard. As a trio, they flew up the stalk into the center of the city.

Warriors crowded around the open area before the Life Tree. In their center, Faier writhed, suspended between Kusi and Chiba. Tibe hung back, out of reach, a wary hand gripping his trident. Even though Faier was tied, Tibe considered him a threat.

An unfamiliar, distinguished older warrior judged Faier.

Behind the judge, dangerous-looking guards flanked him. The crowd of Aiycaya warriors made a respectful separation for a unit of the All-Council judge's warriors. They carried shiny, reflective daggers and large, imposing tridents.

Well back from the judgment, King Kayo argued with his elders. His words were muffled, but his passionate disagreement was obvious.

Harmony slowed her approach and floated in the back.

The warriors in front of her barely noticed her arrival. The strange All-Council representative and his personal guard of dangerous-looking warriors consumed their attention.

"—and, Representative Rikoy, with this presentation of the notorious rebel Faier, you must accept our petition to woo females living on other sacred islands," Elder Bawa was saying.

The distinguished Representative Rikoy threw back his haughty shoulders. "You have a sacred bride now."

"Yes." He harrumphed. "Now. But—"

"One sacred bride fulfills the ancient covenant. When her duty finishes, acquire another."

"Yes, of course, honorable Representative Rikoy. That is very logical. However, we have found only one bride in twenty-nine human years—"

"Search harder."

"—with King Kayo himself being our last young fry born of a sacred bride. His mother had told his father, then-Warlord Kamuy, that disaster had struck our sacred island, as I have explained in my petitions—"

"Mer must stay hidden."

"Yes, but we must seek brides at a new island. We must. Or King Kayo will be the last young fry of Aiycaya."

His words hit Harmony square between the eyes. She almost saw stars. "King Kayo was the last person born from a sacred bride?"

The nearest warriors looked back at her.

"Yes, Sacred—er, Harmony," Warrior Poro murmured. "It is common knowledge."

"But my mom was the last sacred bride."

"Oh? I see." But he didn't, actually.

"I can't be King Kayo's sacred bride," she pushed.

"Yes, you explained that you are no sacred bride below." His aura dimmed with hurt again.

"But don't you understand why?"

He stared at her blankly. So did Warrior Luin and the warriors closest enough to have heard her speak.

"Have you ever heard of siblings?" she demanded.

"No," Warrior Poro said.

"Brothers? Sisters?"

"Ah. We have not had one in generations. Twin seeds. They are rare. Two young fries produced instead of one."

The heck? "No, like an older brother and a younger brother. You know. The same parents having multiple children?"

They stared like she was crazy.

"You, there!" Representative Rikoy called out to their group. "Silence, rude ones. Warriors who disrespect the All-Council will taste our blades."

His guard lofted their tridents and gave an intimidating shout.

Warlord Sao squinted in her direction as though noting who to discipline later. He saw her and blanked. He kicked forward and muttered to Tibe.

Tibe fixed on her with cold anger.

"Excuse me, Representative Rikoy." Elder Bawa harrumphed again. "Back to our petition. We—"

"Denied."

"But Representative Rikoy, we have captured this valuable rebel—"

"Useless." Representative Rikoy motioned for his guards. One swam forward. "Rebel Faier is no good to us alive. The rebels refuse to negotiate. They do not assign him any value. Execute him."

Her stomach dropped.

The guard aimed his gleaming trident for Faier's abdomen.

Faier writhed in his tight bonds.

Elder Bawa kicked forward in protest. "But our petition!"

King Kayo's voice cracked across the ocean, arresting everyone. "All-Council Representative Rikoy. You have forgotten your manners."

The distinguished warrior twirled and looked down his nose at the king. "You believe you, the youngest king of the ocean, can quote mer law to me?"

Her anger built. The buzzing in her ears and on her skin increased.

The Aiycaya warriors growled low.

Tension filled the city with dark unease.

"Yes, my improper guest." King Kayo kicked into the center between the All-Council guard and Faier. "I believe I, King *of Aiycaya*, captured this prisoner. We offered him to you as a courtesy. He is of no use to you? Then leave. He is of use to me."

Oh, thank goodness. King Kayo had heard her after all. He was saving Faier.

Representative Rikoy laughed a deep, disturbing belly

rumble. "Your youth is showing, small king. Do you truly believe you rule this city? No. The ancient covenant rules. Tradition rules. And I am the highest, most traditional representative. *I rule.*"

King Kayo showed his teeth. But his aura changed color. He did not trust the others would support his decisions. That was why he relied on Tibe. He was just like her.

Just. Like. Her.

Well, of course he was.

They were family.

King Kayo tried to recover. "You think to unseat a king inside his own city? With what army?"

"My army is a human day away."

"But now, my army surrounds you." King Kayo forced his cocky authority. "We will report your death to the All-Council. Perhaps they will accept our petition."

"It would be tragic if Aiycaya's king died without a successor. Again." The representative turned his shoulder to the king and studied the restless warriors. "But I will select an appropriate replacement."

His gaze slid across Xarin and lit on Tibe.

Elder Bawa kicked forward, hands shaking, chastised. "Representative Rikoy, do not be angry with King Kayo. He is young. We will teach him."

"Some warriors cannot be taught."

"Yes, but Representative Rikoy, please—"

"This city has been a colossal disappointment, Elder Bawa. There is no need for me to waste any more courtesy."

"Representative Rikoy!"

The representative flicked his fingers at his guard. "Execute the rebel."

His guard lowered his trident once more.

King Kayo snarled and kicked forward, his trident out, to stop the execution. But he was too far away.

No one would save Faier.

She had to act.

Harmony screamed. "No!"

Shing!

The Life Tree made a shattering sound, as if all its arms cracked off and the pearls exploded. The Aiycaya warriors spasmed with pain, as if someone had stabbed them in the heart. A shock wave pushed the foreign warriors out a few lengths.

Representative Rikoy's guards surrounded him, tridents out, defending against their invisible attacker.

She yanked her trident from Poro's and Luin's lax hands and kicked through the twisting Aiycaya warriors.

Tibe recovered first. He floated between her and Faier. "Sacred Bride Harmony. I should have—"

"Fins!" a warrior exclaimed through a groan. "She has fins!"

Harmony kicked her fins. They were about to see a lot more.

"A queen!" Representative Rikoy scrambled away from her, shoving his guards before him. "Get her away from me! Guards!"

They formed a wall of tridents separating her from the representative.

"She is a queen?" Tibe eyed the representative with disgust. "Coward." He focused on Harmony again. "Her power is a mild irritation. The giant hagfish wields a more deadly shriek."

"Get out of my way," Harmony demanded.

"You have no place here. Go in King Kayo's castle and gestate his young fry."

"Ick. No." She clenched Faier's trident to keep it from slipping. The metal bobbed and wove in her untrained hands. "But since we're calling each other out, you're supposed to obey King Kayo's orders, not lie."

A vein stood out on the first lieutenant's forehead. "Do not embarrass King Kayo in front of his warriors."

"You're the embarrassment," she shot back. "He attacked while you watched. Are you going to sit around while a stranger replaces your king? Where's your loyalty?"

King Kayo held her gaze for a long moment. His aura fluctuated bright to dark. He wanted to thank her, protect her, and deny her.

Tibe's feelings were less complicated.

He growled. "Go on now, Sacred Bride, before I do something dangerous."

"Attack me, and you'll regret it."

The vein throbbed. But his tone was cool as he tightened his grip on his trident. "Perhaps I will surprise you."

"Perhaps *I'll* surprise *you*. All of you." She addressed the panicked All-Council representative. "I'm the last descendant of their sacred brides. Understand? You should approve Elder Bawa's petition. I can tell you where they've gone."

"Do not speak to me, queen scum," Representative Rikoy spat.

"She is no queen," Elder Bawa protested. "She is an impostor sent to sow confusion."

"Actually, Elder Bawa, my being here is your fault. You sent King Kayo to the surface. He found me. But I'm not King Kayo's sacred bride. We're not even married."

Shock ricocheted through the warriors. Mutterings and outcries followed. Accusations.

In the center of the storm, Faier's aura glowed calmly.

He stopped struggling and, through the bindings that immobilized every part of him, smiled. He was proud of her. He believed in her. He was in her corner.

He was the only one.

"Get rid of her." Representative Rikoy curled his lip. "She is a sea snake at your breast. Elder Bawa, you have turned Aiycaya into a rebel city."

The elder blanched. "No, representative. She does not know what she says."

"I know exactly what I'm saying."

"We are traditional," Elder Bawa insisted.

"Look at her rudeness. Her confidence. She is a rebel queen."

"The king indulges her. He will do so no longer." Elder Bawa motioned imperiously to King Kayo.

And King Kayo kicked toward her. "Go to the castle, Harmony."

"No."

"Harmony." He took her arm.

She yanked free. "Don't let them push you around. You're the king."

He flicked his gaze from side to side. The pressure of his warriors—who still did not support him—made his position awkward.

She leaned in and vibrated softly. "Now is the time to be honorable, King Kayo."

He lowered his vibrations to match hers, his gaze flying over the enemies and his own warriors. "I cannot protect you in a fight."

"Free Faier."

King Kayo grimaced. They had backed him into a corner. He glanced past her and increased his volume. "A sacred bride must not act this way."

Was she on her own?

Fine.

"Well, good news, because I'm not your sacred bride." She threw her hand at Faier. "He's my soul mate."

The warriors grumbled.

Tibe brightened. "I told you we should kill him. Then her soul will disentangle from his and entwine with yours."

"That will never happen." New strength filled her with purpose. "Because our souls are entwined too. King Kayo, I'm not your bride. I'm your sister."

The rest of the warriors reacted as if she'd spoken a new language.

King Kayo gave voice to their confusion. "What do you mean you are my 'sister'? What is this meaning?"

Seriously? "What part confuses you? I don't have to explain basic biology, do I?"

"I understand the biology of young fries. I do not understand why you believe it links us."

"Your mother was Aiycaya's last sacred bride. *My* mother was Aiycaya's last sacred bride. We have the same mother."

"Ah." King Kayo smiled.

Everyone calmed, relaxing with smiles. They were relieved. Even the All-Council representative peeked out from behind his warriors as if the fact that she was related to the king explained her outburst—and it was no big deal.

"Yes, I see the resemblance now," Elder Bawa said quickly, changing his position. "Their souls are both young and impetuous. Of course she would refuse to be his mate."

"No wonder he cannot order her," Elder Wida boomed. "They share the same mother."

King Kayo's shoulders dropped in relief. "Then, because you cannot be my sacred bride, you will become the sacred bride of...hmmm...only the most honorable warrior..."

She gripped her hair. "No way. No way!"

As she grabbed her hair, a flash of color caught her eye. On the tip of her outstretched thumb, a bright pink mark gleamed, as if she'd dipped her finger in iridescent paint.

Total realization filtered in.

She knew what it was. Deep down, she knew. She'd always known.

"I will choose the most honorable warrior for my half sister," King Kayo said, grateful that he did not have to choose between his city and her.

"I'm not your half sister."

"You just said we share the same mother."

She held up her hand. High, so everyone could see the lines of neon pink on her thumb.

His brows lifted as he realized their colors matched. His tattoos and hers. Blood carried through the mer line.

"And also the same father."

He kicked back a pace. "Impossible."

"I scratched my thumb with the tattoo rod. And now I have this."

She put her thumb right next to his tattooed wrists. It looked as if the tattoo moved from his skin to hers.

They were the same colors.

The same.

She was, and always had been, a full-blooded mer.

TWENTY-EIGHT

The city of Aiycaya rocked with Harmony's revelation.

Even Faier reeled.

"What is the female saying?" Representative Rikoy leaned over his guards' tridents to peer at Harmony and King Kayo. "What is this mockery?"

"She is his sister," Elder Bawa repeated, slack-jawed with awe.

No females had been born to the mer since the Great Catastrophe a thousand years ago.

Until two years ago when Queen Lucy, a modern woman, gave birth to twins. Feisty, giggly, well-loved twins. One male. And one female.

But Harmony was much older.

Her transformation made sense considering Harmony's naturalness under the water and how she easily accomplished the things surface women had struggled with. Only her fears had held her back. Now her soul light shone with the beauty of the Life Tree. She was at home in Aiycaya not because her soul entwined with

King Kayo's but because she *was* home. Aiycaya was her home.

She was a natural-born mer.

But the explanation did not enlighten the other warriors.

King Kayo's soul fluctuated dark to light to dark again. He struggled to accept her truth.

"Do not believe these lies," Tibe argued, rejecting her outright.

Whispers and mutterings once more filled the ocean with tumult. "How is this possible? A female—"

"A true mer—"

"Is she King Kayo's equal? But she was raised on the surface..."

Tibe shoved King Kayo's shoulder. "Do not be misled. That is paint."

She whirled on him. "It's not paint."

"You have collaborated with the prisoner to frighten us. That is a false coloration." He bumped the king again to jolt a reaction. "Lies."

"It's real. I swear."

"Real? Then why did you not tell us before?" Tibe's lips curled in a snarl. "You lie."

King Kayo blinked and lifted his head. His brows darkened like his soul. "Yes, Harmony. Why did you let me believe you would become my sacred bride if you knew we had a family relationship?"

"Because... But I didn't realize it until just now."

"All her words were lies."

King Kayo puffed out his chest. "Tibe is right. You lied to me."

"Are you kidding?"

"Explain yourself."

"Yeah, right." Harmony's soul burned twice as bright. "Even if I had known from the beginning—and I didn't—there would have been no point in telling you."

"And why is that?"

"Because you still don't listen."

He frowned at her hard.

Tibe tsked. "My king, what a ridiculous claim."

King Kayo held up his hand. "I am listening now."

"My king—"

"Tibe." King Kayo's voice sharpened with unusual authority. "I am listening."

Harmony laid out her facts. "My mother never let me go swimming. Water terrified her. Yes, she was a sacred bride. But she didn't keep me out of the water to avoid revealing the truth about herself. She avoided revealing the truth *about me*."

"That proves nothing," Tibe sniped.

She focused on King Kayo. "You were born too early. Our mother stayed under the sea longer than usual to nurse you back to health. She stayed so long, other warriors grew jealous. Long enough that she became pregnant with me."

"Lies, my king."

"Our father never knew. Nobody knew. She didn't even know. Not until he had left her on the shore."

"She never contacted us," King Kayo said stiffly.

"How could she contact you? You don't have cell phones."

"Sell-fones?"

"Look. She would not cross the ocean alone with a child. She'd already lost all her children, and she knew how dangerous the ocean could be. So she kept me. Maybe she was going to tell me someday. Or maybe she had a different idea of how my life should be."

"Yet you are here."

"Exactly! We're not orphans any longer. I'm here."

He shook his head.

"You're not alone," she insisted. "I can help you."

"Help? We cannot agree on anything."

"That's good! We argue like brother and sister. I don't know the rules, and you insist on following a crazy code of honor. But we're on the same side. We both want to protect the city. Aiycaya is your home, and it's also mine." She linked hands with King Kayo, their tattoos matching, souls the same bright color. "We'll do this. Together."

He looked down at her fingers wrapped around his hand. King Kayo's soul light brightened. Her impassioned words were reaching him.

Faier understood. He had struggled alone, long believing he would never find his soul mate. Harmony had changed him. Now she gave King Kayo strength.

"Together," King Kayo repeated. His fingers curled around hers.

She beamed.

"Anathema." Representative Rikoy's dark judgment shot fear into Faier's heart. "A surface female has no place in a traditional city."

Darkness clouded the city.

"She is no surface female." King Kayo pulled Harmony behind him, placing himself before the warrior's wrath. "You are wrong."

"Her existence damns you."

"She is a miracle!"

"She is a mistake. Your father's sins must be eradicated."

King Kayo tightened his grip on his trident. "What are you saying?"

"Your father broke the ancient covenant. Her existence

is a violation." Representative Rikoy raged at them from behind his guards. "The only way to save our traditional standing is to end her."

King Kayo growled. "She will rule beside me."

Representative Rikoy sneered. "Then I will take pleasure in razing your Life Tree."

King Kayo released her and flew to the representative. "Die!" He slashed.

Representative Rikoy's guards parried his first blow with a loud *clang*.

No one else moved. The king fought the guards alone.

Representative Rikoy shouted over the commotion at Elder Bawa, "I deny your petition and rescind your traditional status!"

"Representative!" Elder Bawa wailed. "Give me another chance. We did not know!"

"You failed. Broke the ancient covenant."

"We never—in twenty-nine human years, not once did we ever break—"

"You have broken the ancient covenant. Get rid of her. And him." He pointed his long trident at Faier.

Elder Bawa turned in confusion. "Who?"

"Tibe." King Kayo slashed again and again. "Help me repel the intruders. Tibe!"

Tibe floated with a lax trident. "My king. *I* am to rule beside you."

"Release the rebel! Tibe! It is my order!"

"Rebel?" Tibe swiveled to watch the king fight. "But what about me?"

His warriors milled in confusion. They did not join their king. They waited for a sign from another warrior— any leader—for what to do.

"Tibe!"

The personal guard swirled around Representative Rikoy, tridents out and bristling. The guard expertly parried King Kayo's thrusts without bothering to return the blows.

Xarin flew behind Faier. With a *shink*, his trident sliced through the bonds around Faier's wrist. The knots fell away.

Faier grabbed his trident from Harmony. His pumping heart drowned out the shriek of his dislocated finger. He pulled it back into place with a sharp, painful snap and forced it to curl around the trident. But he could not rely on it alone.

Armed again, he was much better. He pressed Harmony to his protected side. "You saved me."

"For the moment. Tell me what to do," she demanded tightly.

"You are queen. Take control of the city."

"How?"

She asked a good question. The city was in chaos.

Xarin continued flying. He raised his trident and shouted, "To the king!"

Warriors rallied to him, raising tridents and shouting.

The representative and his guard retreated, flying between castles to escape the angry army.

"No!" Elder Bawa grabbed his head. "Tibe, stop the representative. He must take back his judgment."

Tibe gripped his trident. "Warlord Sao! First phalanx! To me!"

Over half the warriors peeled away from the main force and wheeled to Tibe. They chased the All-Council representative, swarming him like the mantis shrimp. Tibe fought side by side between Xarin and King Kayo. No one watching him would ever doubt his dedication to Aiycaya or its young king.

But the personal guards were braver, stronger, and far more experienced. They feinted and drew the warriors away from their intended escape route, and Representative Rikoy darted through the gap they had cleared.

Representative Rikoy and his guards escaped.

King Kayo shouted at Xarin. "Go after him! He will not threaten a king in his own city. Bring back his head!"

Xarin hesitated. His gaze leveled on Faier. Harmony would be on her own. He whirled and led his smaller group of warriors after the fleeing All-Council representative.

Warlord Sao's army hemmed in Faier and Harmony.

Tibe approached. His eyes glowed with cold intention. "You have poisoned our city for the final time."

"Tibe." King Kayo rubbed a bleeding cut on his bicep. He looked older and exhausted. "Faier has done nothing wrong. Stand down."

Tibe regarded the king coldly. "Since when do you side with a rebel over me?"

"Since you turned your blade on my sister."

Tibe jerked upright. "Traitor."

King Kayo eyed Tibe. "Are you calling me a traitor? A king of his own city, a traitor?"

"Yes." Tibe doubled his accusation. "You betray your father. A great king."

"According to Representative Rikoy, he was the true traitor." King Kayo frowned. "Back away from Harmony."

Warlord Sao obeyed, giving them a little more room.

Faier kept a tight grip on his trident.

Tibe followed King Kayo, more upset. "You betray your own honor. Ever since the female came, you do not listen. And why? She is a liar who disobeys."

King Kayo growled, "Careful."

"But—"

"My king," Elder Bawa interrupted. "Tibe. The situation of our city is dire. Of course you do not wish harm against a sacred bride. But we must show the All-Council evidence we are a traditional city."

"Evidence such as?"

"The remains of...or, the eradication of...er, the dead rebel and the disappearance of your anathema bride."

"She is my sister," he growled.

"Not to the All-Council. They will come, King Kayo. Xarin can hold them only so long. You must prepare for war."

"So we prepare." He turned to Warlord Sao. "Secure our borders."

Warlord Sao's gaze flicked to Tibe.

Tibe twisted his trident, increasingly upset, but said nothing to countermand the king.

Warlord Sao led a group of warriors out of the city.

"We will help you, my king," Elder Yane said, and the other elders with him nodded sagely. "Do not panic. We will guide you."

"Give up the rebel," Elder Bawa pushed. "We do not have to touch your female. The All-Council will escort her to the surface."

Harmony nudged Faier. "Really?"

"No. They kill queens."

"Injuring a female violates mer law," Elder Bawa retorted, without looking at Faier.

"The All-Council says queens are not true females, Elder Bawa, as you should well know."

He frowned. "Sacred Bride Harmony is female. No one would mistake her for a male."

"Do not trust the All-Council to agree."

Elder Bawa fidgeted. "You must trust us."

King Kayo listened to their interaction, then shook his head. "I cannot."

"Tibe will—"

"No, Elder Bawa." The thread of steel returned. "I will not bow to those disrespectful so-called warriors. Representative Rikoy *would* break the first law of the mer. No one hurts my sister."

Elder Bawa's shoulders sagged. "Then we make an enemy of the All-Council."

"No!" Tibe kicked for them.

"Tibe?" King Kayo jerked up. "What are you doing?"

"Your weakness will not destroy our city." He thrust his trident at Harmony's heart.

She shrieked in surprise.

Faier wheeled around the thrust, securing Harmony and parrying Tibe's blow.

Tibe twisted and slashed at Faier's chest.

Faier parried him again.

"Tibe! Stop!"

"If you do not do it...I will." He slashed.

Faier repelled him. Strength flowed into his veins. He pushed the angry first lieutenant away from Harmony. "Even rebels obey their kings."

"I will slash your face with scars!"

"You are years too late." Faier parried another blow.

The first lieutenant's lips curled into a snarl. "I will end you."

"You are only ending yourself. Hear your king shouting for you to stop? How will he trust you after this? Your career as first lieutenant has ended. You will reside in my old prison before long."

Tibe's eyes darted behind him to King Kayo floating beside Harmony.

"Stop now, Tibe," King Kayo shouted. "Do not make me force you!"

Fury chased dark hurt in Tibe's soul. He flicked back to Faier, rage fueled by pain. "This is your fault."

They tangled, weaving and thrusting. Faier's side burned, but his muscle held.

Tibe tired, slowing his strikes. "Why do you not fail? Die already."

"I am used to fighting through pain." Faier parried his slash and rotated, locking the blade at Tibe's jaw. "How familiar are you?"

Tibe froze.

Faier pressed him. "Do you yield?"

His cheek muscles twitched with fury. He gripped Faier's trident.

King Kayo's shoulders lowered. "Finally. Tibe. You must prepare the city for siege."

"My king." His brows drew together in pain. "Why can you not see what these rebels are doing to you?"

"Tibe."

"No!" He lofted his own trident. "I serve you faithfully."

"Tibe—"

"I serve you!" He curled his hand around Faier's sharp trident blade, cutting his hand to the bone, and shoved Faier back. Into the open space, he hurled his own trident at Harmony.

King Kayo shouted, "Tibe!"

But the trident was not thrown spear-first. It tumbled so the flat middle hit Harmony's belly. "Chiba! Kusi! Take her!"

The two warriors grabbed each end of trident and used their own to interlock, scissoring her into a cage. They kicked hard.

"Faier!" she shrieked.

"Harmony!"

Tibe trapped Faier's trident, stopping Faier from chasing and forcing him to prove just how capable he was of fighting through pain. "Take her to the surface."

"No! Faier!" Harmony shrieked.

King Kayo shouted at his warriors. The elders watched the shenanigans, nonplussed, as though confused about why they were playing a childish game when the All-Council's threat of death clouded their city.

The warriors chased Harmony past the Life Tree while the king berated them. Harmony shrieked.

Faier shouted, "Use your queen powers!"

"What queen powers?"

Oh.

Curse it. She was so natural. Faier assumed she would already know how to use her powers.

She had already channeled the Life Tree once in this fight. Not to save her own life. To save his.

He screamed, "Help me, Harmony!"

She arrested and turned blindly. On cue, the Life Tree flashed. Tibe jolted.

Of course. Because she used her powers to help him. Not herself.

Her little house guardian flew into the city, arms akimbo, and bashed into Chiba. The warrior released her and hunched over his abdomen as if a ball of lead had struck him. Lady whirled and wrapped all her arms around Kusi's head, beak boring into the teal-and-white warrior's forehead. He released Harmony with a scream.

Faier jerked his trident free from Tibe and kicked away from the injured warrior.

"No." Tibe hugged his injured hand, pale and even more furious. "Warriors! She is the poison. Eject her!"

The warriors milled. At Tibe's command, they snapped to attention and turned on Harmony.

"No!" Elder Bawa raised both hands. "Stop! You will only injure yourselves. Save your strength for the All-Council!"

"Attack!" Tibe shouted.

Faier fought through them to reach Harmony first.

So long as she was in the city, her presence would divide the warriors.

Harmony turned to Faier and closed her eyes.

Click. Click click. Click click click.

Iridescent rainbow specks surrounded Harmony. She commanded the mantis shrimp. They landed on the stunned warriors.

She opened her eyes on Tibe. "I said you'd regret it."

Tibe's smile faltered. "You are immune. But not... What is this?"

BOOM.

Chaos erupted as the warriors scattered.

Faier's chest stung.

She flew to Faier. "Ow! I'm sorry."

Click click click.

"Harmony, we must go."

"I know."

Boom! Boom! Boom!

King Kayo watched them, one hand pressed to his heart, worry mixed with resignation, as if he knew he might never see his sister again.

Harmony held his gaze until the first round of castles cut them off.

Then, she fixed her eyes on the city as they escaped it. And long after.

"This will not be your final view of Aiycaya." Faier kicked hard, navigating currents and watching for smart predators. "We will get help and return."

"Get help from where?"

He would save her city. He would save *her*.

Because Faier was not an exile. He was a warrior. A citizen of two cities. Connected with friends.

"From Atlantis."

TWENTY-NINE

They crossed the ocean.

Harmony had failed. Once again, she'd lost her home. She'd tried so hard this time to keep it. And King Kayo had stopped fighting to watch her leave.

Yes, he really was like her.

Make them listen...

She jolted in Faier's arms. "Am I doing the right thing?"

He broke his steady stride. Below, spires of barren rock flew by as the fast current carried them to Atlantis. Her arms wrapped around his torso, over the trident he held tight to his side.

"What do you mean?"

"Running away."

"We are not running away from danger. We are running toward allies."

Yes. That too was weird. She'd felt alone for so long. Striking out with her true mate to return with a stronger force seemed crazy.

Was that the source of her unease?

Time passed differently under water. Which meant

several days had already passed. Had the All-Council representative returned and wiped out the Life Tree? She felt so anxious.

"You have a doubt," he noted. Always calm, that Faier.

"Yeah, I guess I do." Her heart thudded in her chest. She rubbed her skin, trying to soothe the nervous feeling. When she'd lifted off US soil for the last time, the runway had felt way too short and she'd felt every bump. "Atlantis is half the ocean away. What if we don't make it in time?"

"Then you will know."

"How will I know?"

"You will know," he repeated heavily. "Your heart will rip out its roots. Sour sickness will rise in your throat. Tight bands will constrict your chest. You will not eat. You will not breathe. And your colors will fade."

"My colors?" She lifted her hand off his comforting broad chest and examined her thumb. The small chevron was DayGlo pink. "This will fade to skin color?"

"It will darken and gray like a wilted plant."

"Yours weren't always dark mauve?"

"My tattoos were once a bright purple you call lavender."

She stroked the dark lines of his skin. Now they were a deep gray-tinted purple, or mauve, and they lacked iridescence. "Are they gone forever?"

"Perhaps, someday, my soul will heal enough to form new tattoos. My history will start again."

The lines she had traced to unite his tattoos glimmered stark red. His scars had healed. But his tattoos had not returned.

Because he had not accepted a Life Tree?

"You've accepted me," she blurted. "Haven't you?"

He kicked steadily. "Hmm?"

"Our souls united. Right?"

"Yes, Harmony."

"But you still haven't fully healed?"

His aura dimmed.

He was hiding something from her.

Faier? Hiding?

"What is it?" she demanded.

"No. I do not know. It is nothing."

She shoved back, putting distance between them in the current so she could look him in eye. "I'm a mer. So my tattoos are shiny because of the Aiycaya Life Tree. And we're together. So I should heal you."

His troubled gaze held hers. He rubbed his red-scratched skin. "I am healed. More now than ever before."

"So what's the holdup? Your skin is healed."

"My body is healed," he confirmed.

"So what is it? Your heart?"

"Warriors do not speak of hearts, Harmony. But please understand that any part of my body belongs to you."

"Then, what?" The answer smacked her even as the words left her vibrating chest. "Your soul. Mermen are all about souls. Ours are entwined. Everybody said so. You haven't fully committed your soul?"

"I have committed everything I can commit."

Her stomach dropped. "What kind of answer is that?"

He avoided her gaze. "Losing Nerissa was very difficult."

"And what am I?"

"You are...the female I wish to be my mate."

"You wish? *You wish?* We should be long past the wishing stage. Why aren't we long past that stage?"

He had no answer for her. "I have been an exile for a long time."

"You're not an exile any longer. I'm your home."

But this was a huge problem. No wonder she felt so anxious. Faier promised allies in Atlantis, a foreign city she knew nothing about, and he hadn't even fully committed to her as his mate.

"Do you even love me?" she demanded.

His gaze flashed. He drew her into his arms. "Yes."

She felt the power of his love wrapping around her, heating the water, forming an impenetrable layer of safety. He *loved* her. Loving her wasn't the problem.

"I cannot lose you." His chest vibrated roughly. Ragged with his love and his fear. "If I lose you as I lost Nerissa, then I will die."

That was a very reasonable fear.

She squeezed him. "I'm not going anywhere."

"You also have doubts. You do not have control of your queen powers. Why can you not drive off an army and protect the city?"

"That's why the slimy representative was freaking out?"

"Yes. For you, it must be easy. Every step has come more easily to you."

"Did those other queens have total commitment from their partners?"

He set his jaw. "Yes."

And she didn't have his total commitment yet. So the logical thing was to continue on to Atlantis, gather Faier's friends into an army, and invade her city to protect it.

Not much in her life had gone according to logic.

"I want to go back to Aiycaya." As soon as she vibrated it, transmitting the thought through the water into reality, she felt calm. Certain. Strong. "Let's go."

"Harmony. You have not yet mastered your powers."

"You said all I had to do was believe."

"And you do not."

"I have a plan. Please, Faier. This is right. Going back is what I have to do."

He kicked out of the fast current, swam through the open water, and sought a current to return them to Aiycaya. She studied the barren land, the deep trenches, and the strange yet familiar creatures veering away from them at these brilliant depths. Giant millipedes, shiny eels with spots instead of eyes, and tiny hydras that floated like the blown bits of a dandelion casting wishes upon the deep.

Faier entered the swift current flowing in the opposite direction. Relief filled her as they flew back toward Aiycaya.

He kicked. "What is your plan?"

"Develop my powers on the way." She nuzzled him and kissed his earlobe. "And convince you to fall completely in love with me."

His cock hardened against her thigh.

Encouraging.

She sucked on the lobe and licked the sensitive skin beneath.

He shuddered. "I do love you. Never doubt I love you."

"Convince me." She encircled his hard cock. "I can see your aura, you know. You've always had an honest aura."

"Soul light."

"Is that what the mer call it?" She placed soft kisses along his jaw. "Yours is beautiful."

He groaned. "Harmony."

She tangled her legs with his, entwining with him in the huge, open tent of the ocean.

His cock entered her, and their bodies joined into one.

She loved him. She trusted him. She needed him.

And when the orgasm took her, she closed her eyes.

On the insides of her lids, she saw stars.

Faier made her strong. He took the strength she already possessed and showed her she could grow even stronger

All her life, people had denied her strength. Hidden it. Tried to capture and twist it for their own ends.

Her mother had hidden her strength out of love. Lifet had tried to exploit it out of greed. The warriors of Aiycaya had out of ignorance and then fear.

With Faier's help, she broke free.

Harmony was capable of more than she had ever dreamed. Now, she needed to find her wellspring. The heart fed by Aiycaya's Life Tree.

Before it was too late.

They made love again on the return trip. Then they reached the outside edge of city territory. Familiar spires appeared, and coral grew from barren rock.

The distant glow of Aiycaya's Life Tree warmed her soul. It lived on. She was not yet too late.

An army surrounded the city.

She tensed.

"Prepare yourself," Faier warned. "We may have to fight."

A fearful lump settled in the pit of her stomach. "O-okay."

He barreled out of the current.

A war party of strange, dangerous warriors surrounded them. "Yield, strangers! Or die."

Her heart thundered in her chest. This was the time to show her strength. Show amazing powers. Even though she didn't know how.

She would fight.

THIRTY

Faier felt Harmony keying up in his arms. Tensing. Preparing.

He untucked his trident from his side.

This would become a very messy fight very quickly.

"Yield, warriors." A confident warrior in pepper orange grinned at them. "This city is under siege by order of King Kadir and Queen Elyssa of Atlantis."

Harmony's fire went out. "Atlantis?"

"Yep." He jerked an angular, previously broken thumb over his shoulder. "They have our buddy Faier in there, and—"

"Gailen?" Faier released Harmony, separating from her so that the young male could see him. "What are you doing here?"

"Faier!" Gailen's jaw dropped. He rubbed his forehead and laughed. "You are on the wrong side of the siege! Or, I guess, you are on the right side. But how?"

"Is the city okay?" Harmony asked. "Is King Kayo all right?"

Gailen's friendliness cooled. "You are?"

"This is Harmony." Faier squared his shoulders. "My soul mate."

"Mate!" Gailen's smile returned full force. "Welcome."

Harmony interrupted. "And also Aiycaya's queen."

"Ah. Okay. I think some people are desperate to speak with you. Come on."

He indicated for his second-in-command, a warrior Faier did not know, to close the patrol around them. The warriors formed up neatly. A well-ordered patrol from a well-ordered city.

"But what are you doing here?" Faier asked as they swam, hands linked with Harmony, after the peppery warrior.

"You may not know this, but I am from Aiycaya." Gailen pointed at a flat rock jutting above the verdant coral. "That is where the fish-excrement first lieutenant Tibe broke my thumbs to keep me from escaping."

Harmony's soul flared. "I've met him. He is fish excrement."

"And I escaped anyway." Gailen flew sideways, rolling over his former territory. "More warriors joined our army than we intended. Queen Elyssa would turn no one away."

Away? He still hadn't answered Faier's question. "Gailen, why is an Atlantis army besieging Aiycaya?"

"To free you, of course." He wove to the central knot of strategists around the king and queen. "Look, everyone! Faier is free!"

A wild celebration surrounded them. Warriors patted, hugged, and rejoiced over his safe return.

King Kadir gripped his arm. His silver-streaked eyes gleamed. "It is very good to see you, Faier."

He swallowed the sudden lump in his throat. "Sir."

"Yes, you look wonderful!" Queen Elyssa threw her arms around him and squeezed him in a soft hug.

The lump grew.

He tried to swallow it. His chest vibrated awkwardly. "Where is young Prince Kael?"

"At home. Lucy and Torun are holding down the fort." Queen Elyssa released Faier with a friendly pat and then entwined herself with King Kadir. "We're past weaning, and he's guarded by so many beloved uncles. There's nothing like a little siege to enjoy couple time." She squeezed King Kadir.

King Kadir smiled at her indulgently.

"But why..." The lump cut off his words.

"We overheard your capture in a message from Aiycaya to the All-Council," King Kadir said. "I asked for volunteers to free you. You see the result."

"It took longer to organize because so many warriors volunteered," Queen Elyssa said. "It warmed my heart but was kind of stressful. I hoped we weren't too late."

"But..."

King Kadir raised a brow. "But?"

Faier gestured at his chest. "Why?"

The king and queen looked at each other like they didn't understand his question. Then something seemed to dawn on Queen Elyssa. "You mean, why did we set off with an army to cross the ocean and come to your rescue?"

He nodded.

Queen Elyssa's smile softened. "Maybe you don't remember, but my husband has spent time in prison. The experience sucks."

"It is not pleasant," King Kadir agreed.

"But also, you're you." She pressed a gentle hand on Faier's forearm. "You defended our city and saved our lives a dozen times. You welcomed me to Atlantis when I was new and terrified of making a mistake. You're like a symbol of the rebellion."

"You have represented us honorably to our enemies and to our friends," Kadir said.

"If I could do anything to help you, I'd be there. In an instant."

Around her, everyone nodded.

His chest shuddered.

"So here we are." She smiled, her human eyes red, and she swallowed hard. "You're one of us, Faier. You've risked your life for us so many times. We'll always come to your rescue."

He shook his head. Silently asking, yet again, why?

The representative had told Elder Bawa the rebels didn't value him. It had been too easy to believe. In comparison, the idea that his fellow rebels valued him so much was impossible to believe.

King Kadir chuckled and gripped his arm. "If you must ask again, you do not know your worth. Listen to my queen. She will explain until you understand. She has such patience."

"I need to hear the important words more than once myself," Queen Elyssa agreed cheerfully. "But if you're free, we can save it for the return trip. Let's pack up."

Gailen interrupted. "And this is Faier's mate, Queen of Aiycaya, Harmony."

Everyone swung to Harmony, who had been pushed out of the inner circle by the sheer joy of his fellow citizens. Surprise and welcome filled the water.

"Welcome, human female," someone said.

"Human? No." She held up a palm, stopping Queen Elyssa mid-hug. "Check my tattoo. I'm a mer."

New amazement shook his friends. "Mer? A female mer? Secret, in Aiycaya, all along?"

He kicked to Harmony's side, desperate to ease her transition to the warriors who had become his family. "Queen Elyssa is from Miami, Harmony."

"I was born near there but I was raised in Iowa."

"Nice to meet you." Queen Elyssa's soul burned eagerly, but she clasped her hands in front of her to respect Harmony's reserved nature. "Have you been queen of Aiycaya long?"

"My whole life, it turns out, but I only found out about it a few...what? Days ago?"

"That must have been surprising."

"Oh, you have no idea. One day, I'm shipwrecked, and the next, I'm a queen."

Queen Elyssa's eyes widened. "Of course! You dismantled a Haitian drug-smuggling operation and got thrown overboard."

Harmony's soul brightened. "You know what happened?"

"We got more details because the Coast Guard had to explain what happened to Faier. The teacher who helped you got hurt, and your cousin was kidnapped."

"And? What happened to Evens and Monsieur Joseph?"

"The teacher was hospitalized. Your young cousin Evens was freed and reunited with his mother, Fabi...Fabia? Fab."

"Oh, thank goodness." Harmony's shoulders slumped, and she rubbed her face. "You have no idea how grateful I am to know that. It's been tearing me apart for...I don't even know how long. So under the sea, how's my brother? King Kayo?"

"We have not seen him," King Kadir answered. "Only his elders have negotiated with us."

Her soul darkened with worry. "That's weird."

"Is it? Some kings would insult an army by refusing to speak with them."

"He's not like that," she insisted. "He'd prefer to meet with you."

"Different cities have different traditions."

"Something's wrong. Nobody's seen him?"

King Kadir called in his scouts.

Lone-wolf Lotar, the gray-eyed, gray-tattooed warrior, confirmed. "I have not penetrated the inner circle of castles."

Harmony twisted her fingers together. "Then he might be at the Life Tree."

"Or within a castle."

King Kadir frowned. "Your elders speak as though King Kayo rules."

"Tibe issues the orders." Gailen's normally cheery face chilled to cold calculation. "He is capable of anything."

"Would this Tibe cut down his own Life Tree?" King Kadir asked Gailen.

"I would not put it past him."

Everyone looked at Harmony.

As a mer, her blood was tied to the Life Tree. Any injury to the Life Tree injured her.

"We must storm the city." King Kadir studied the distant castles. "We must not hurt your Life Tree."

"But won't the defenders fight?" Queen Elyssa worried. "I don't want to cause any needless deaths. I'm against storming if we can avoid it."

"Gailen. Is there a secret entrance to the city? Could we enter from beneath?"

"Not secret, my king, but they do use old fish pens for prison holding cells. Lotar saw them on his last, er, patrol. One collapsed, but others might mask a small patrol's approach."

His Atlantis friends plotted how to return Harmony to King Kayo with the least damage to them or to Aiycaya.

Harmony's soul light dimmed. She knotted her fingers with Faier's. "I also don't want to storm the city. I don't want to sneak in at all."

"What do you want?" he asked her quietly.

"I just want to walk in, declare myself ruler, and make everyone listen."

"That sounds reasonable."

She blinked. "It does?"

"Better than sneaking in. And you may not hurt anyone."

"Really?"

"Yes."

Her chin dropped. "You really think I can just walk in?"

"Better to swim."

"Ha ha."

"But why not? You are Aiycaya's queen."

She blinked rapidly. "Yeah. You're right. I *am* Aiycaya's queen." Then her soul darkened again. "Um, how do I tell your friends I don't want their help?"

He drew her into his arms, rested his chin against her head, and savored her soft curves against his hard planes. "You tell them exactly like that."

"Faier? Why are you hugging me?"

"Because I am so thrilled to have the support of thoughtful friends and the love of a beautiful, strong, indomitable female who tells me her desires."

Her soul steadied. "You think I'm indomitable?"

"You stayed with me in prison. No one visits a mer prisoner. Yes, you can accomplish anything."

"On the surface, nobody listens."

"You are under the ocean now. And you are mer. This is your home."

Her soul light flared.

His own soul tingled. The red lines on his arms itched. Scabs had formed.

Harmony eased free of his arms, cleared her throat—even though she was speaking by vibrations in her chest—and called out. "Um, hi. Excuse me. Yoo hoo! Hello?... LISTEN TO ME."

Everyone stopped. Silence reigned. They listened to her.

She hesitated.

Faier teased one finger along her spine.

She leaned into his arms, soaking up his support, and addressed the crowd. "Thanks so much for trying to help me sneak into the city. If it's okay with you, I'm just going to swim right up and demand they let me in. I think if I tell them firmly, then they will. We can forget the other plans. If that's okay right now."

King Kadir consulted his chief ground intelligence officers, Lotar and Gailen, and both shrugged.

"It's fine with me," Queen Elyssa said.

"Whatever you would like to do," King Kadir agreed, and the rest fell behind her, opening the way for her to swim first.

She linked fingers with Faier. "I want you to come too."

"Of course, my queen." Faier gripped his trident in his other hand, enjoying how her soul brightened with strength. "I will follow you."

THIRTY-ONE

A knot of Aiycaya warriors guarded the official entrance to the city.

Harmony hesitated outside. "Faier, tell me what I have to do."

Her warlord regarded her with steady faith as though she should already know the answer. "Be the queen you know you are. I will be right beside you."

His answer filled her with calm.

Of course.

"Thank you." Harmony kicked her fins.

Faier flew at her side. "You believe me."

"Yes, because it's you."

He glowed.

Behind them spread the weight and breadth of the Atlantis army. So many warriors dwarfed the population. The army breathed like an animal.

A hunched, waiting animal.

The Aiycaya guards braced. She recognized Elder Bawa, Chiba, and other warriors who had never been introduced.

She flew straight over them. Her intention was to fly into Aiycaya as if she belonged there. Because she did.

The guards realized her intention at the last moment.

Elder Bawa kicked hard to intercept her. "You, there. You! So, you are back, leading a foreign army to attack."

"Why would I do that?" She waved as she flew over him.

"Huh? No! Stop, there. Where are you going?"

"I'm going to my Life Tree."

"Wait. Halt!"

Elder Bawa scrambled his guards. They blocked her entry at the outermost ring of castles.

He drew himself up importantly. "I will die before I allow a foreign army to pass."

"That's noble of you." She dove beneath them. "Well, don't mind me. Carry on."

He raced in front of her again. "But—but you must not lead an army in here."

"Good news. I'm not leading anyone."

Elder Bawa pulled up. "Your army has not come to destroy us?"

"They came to rescue Faier. And he's rescued. So, they're waiting outside. As for me, this is my city. I don't need an army to take over my home. It's already mine."

"This is King Kayo's city."

"And I'm his sister." She kicked.

He surged to meet her. "Anathema."

Faier slashed his trident. Elder Bawa jerked back. The other warriors ranged around Faier, tensed, to engage.

But she felt pity. "Really, Elder Bawa? Is that how you treat all the relatives of your kings? Or just the females?"

He flinched. "You should not exist."

"And yet here I am."

He lowered his trident to engage her.

She tutted. "Look, Elder Bawa, I don't need your permission to enter my own city. You can either swim with me, or you can get out of my way."

"Or?"

"There is no third option. But I will tell you it's my idea to talk to King Kayo alone. If anything happens to me, then there's plan B." She jerked her thumb over her shoulder.

He gazed beyond her. "So you are leading the army."

"Only if you make me."

He grimaced. "Chiba. Go tell King Kayo that his...that Harmony has returned."

The pineapple-yellow warrior turned and flew.

Harmony let go of Faier's hand and kicked. Her fins unfurled. She darted past the guards and caught up to Chiba. "We'll go together."

He jolted in surprise and dove away from her.

"Stop!" Elder Bawa cried, far behind.

She torpedoed after Chiba's fins, kicking for all she was worth. The water slipped around her like silk. Darting behind the warrior felt like winning a race. Not running it. *Winning it.* She wove between the castles, soaring and diving, to keep Chiba in her sight. The clash of metal behind her said Faier guarded against retaliation.

Chiba flew through the innermost ring of castles.

The Life Tree gleamed, pale and beautiful. A ring of warriors guarded the dais. She picked out Kusi, Zaka, Poro, and Luin. Elder Yane led them.

A figure slumped against the trunk of the mighty tree. King Kayo. The small, green form of Lady was curled in his lap.

Her stomach dropped.

The unease returned times a hundred, and a consistent thought banged inside her brain. *I'm too late.*

"Warrior Chiba!" Elder Yane broke from the ring of dais guards. "Are we invaded?"

"Yes!"

"Not yet." Harmony flew past Chiba's fin tips. "What happened to King Kayo?"

"Happened?" Elder Yane relaxed. He had never seen her as a threat. Not even after the mantis shrimp incident when she'd left. "Nothing has happened. He is sleeping."

Her stomach twinged. "That's crazy."

"The threats of the All-Council and of Atlantis were too stressful. The young king could not handle it."

"He's not a child."

"But he is." Elder Yane used the long handle of his trident to bar her from passing. "He needs his rest."

"He's not resting," she insisted.

Elder Yane frowned. "What do you mean?"

She shoved Elder Yane's trident aside. The shy warrior beside him—Zaka—allowed her to pass. "Where's the doctor? What's his name?"

"Healer Hobin," Faier supplied, arriving at the dais's edge.

"Why do you need the healer?" Elder Yane demanded.

"Something's not right." She retracted her fins and bounced across the cascade of pure, holy pearls. They tinkled with warning.

Lady watched her with her big plus-sign-shaped eyes.

It felt like the day she'd awoken to an empty house and police knocking on the door to inform her that her mom had never come home from her late shift because there'd been an accident. Or the walk from the parking lot into the federal building to meet with the interviewers about a question of citizenship.

Dread rose in her throat until it choked her.

"King Kayo?" She spoke gently just in case. Please, let her instincts be mistaken. "Are you awake? Kayo? It's me. Harmony."

His chin bobbed on his unmoving chest. His legs splayed and his arms hung loose, palms open.

Wrong. Something was wrong.

She knelt at his knees. "King Kayo?"

His aura was dark. So dark. And his tattoos were duller than she remembered. Salmon pink instead of iridescent neon.

"Kayo?" She brushed dark hair off his forehead.

His aura glimmered. He sensed her presence. Her touch. But he could not awaken. Something prevented him.

She trailed her hand over his chest to the new dot tattoo on his heart.

No.

That small dot was no tattoo. It was hard. Like the end of the tattoo stick. The long, slender rod was tipped with a shard of adamantium. Metal that could impale a body and penetrate the Life Tree.

A puff of blood leaked around the circle of hard wood.

"No. No! NO!"

"Harmony!" Faier flew over the tangled warriors and grabbed her shoulders. "What has happened?"

"Someone stabbed him. Through the heart. To the Life Tree!"

"Stabbed?" The guards crowded them. "Our king? He is hurt?"

"Give him air," she ordered. "I mean, water! Get back."

The warriors moved back, craning to see the truth for

themselves, horrified someone had mortally wounded their king while they were guarding him.

"Where's Healer Hobin?" Harmony grabbed the stunned Elder Yane's immobile trident and shook it. "Answer me!"

"H-healer? He, ah, he is…"

"He is at the Echo Point," Chiba said, actually helpful for once.

"Yes! The Echo Point. Go, Chiba."

"Kusi is fastest."

But Kusi stared, stunned.

Elder Yane waved at Chiba. "As fast as you can. I will fly right behind you."

Chiba flew out of the city at an upward angle. Elder Yane sent warriors to other positions—first phalanx, second phalanx, rear guard—and then flew after Chiba.

Five guards remained, including ragged-finned Warrior Luin and shy Warrior Zaka.

"Are there any other healers?" she cried. "Anyone?"

The remaining warriors shook their heads.

Faier gripped her. "I will get Queen Elyssa. She brought King Kadir back from death. More than once."

Harmony hesitated.

His aura dimmed. "Believe in me."

"I do." She shook herself. "I was just worried about managing without you."

He checked. "I will remain. Another warrior can go."

"Are you sure?"

"Harmony. You are my queen. I will obey you." But something else lingered beneath his tone.

She stopped.

Yes, she worried about managing on her own. But that

was just the nerves of a new monarch. She had no doubt she could rule.

Faier was worried about something else. What was it?

"I will not leave you," he said.

"You're not." She touched his repaired compass rose. "I'm here with you. And you're here with me. No matter where we are we're together. And we're home."

He straightened. New belief filled him. "I will not disappoint you."

"Of course you won't." She nuzzled him. "You're the greatest hero who's ever lived. You rescue everyone no matter what. An entire army came to repay you. And you have my total faith and love."

He nodded sharply and glared at the five guards. Everyone heard his silent threat. If anything happened to Harmony, he would exact vengeance. He kicked away.

Her hope flew with him.

She knelt again beside King Kayo. "Please. King Kayo. Come back. You never listen, but now you have to listen."

His lashes fluttered. Or was it a slight current? She pressed her forehead to his. *Please. Of all the prayers in my life, let this one come true.*

"Don't leave me alone," she whispered.

"Is King Kayo dead?" Kusi asked. He'd crossed the dais and stood behind her.

She rocked back on her heels and looked at the warrior.

He gripped his trident with both hands, locking it to his chest as though defending himself from a hidden attack.

"He's not dead yet." She pointed to the ring of blood around the tattoo stick. "His tattoos are dulled but there's still color."

"But someone stabbed him all the way through?"

"Yes. That's why he's upright. They pinned him to the Life Tree."

He wrinkled his nose as though he was suppressing a terrible sneeze.

"How long has he been like this?" she demanded.

Kusi didn't respond.

She looked at the other warriors. They shuffled, jostling the pearls. No one had any idea.

"How long has he been 'sleeping'?"

Warrior Zaka answered, "Right after you left, he went to sleep."

"Did you see that?"

No. No one had seen that.

"Did anyone else speak with him? Anyone?"

"First Lieutenant Tibe said not to bother him while he was resting."

Her heart cracked into two. She drew his name out into an epithet. "Tibe."

"They argued over the All-Council." Kusi still looked like he needed to sneeze.

"What happened?"

"Elder Bawa thinks the army from Atlantis scared off the All-Council," Warrior Luin answered for Kusi. "They must have expected rebels to destroy Aiycaya. But then Atlantis never attacked."

"Where is Xarin?"

"He chased after the All-Council representative and never returned," Warrior Luin said.

It made sense. A horrible sort of sense. She glared at her brother. "I'm gone for days and look what happens."

King Kayo's aura—no, Faier called it a soul light—glimmered as though he'd heard her complaint somewhere deep within and reacted with amusement.

Her heart squeezed.

Kayo wasn't here to decide. Neither was Faier. She had to.

"Kusi. I need you to find Xarin."

The warrior's face twisted into fury. "You do not rule me."

"Don't do it for me. Do it for Aiycaya. We need Xarin."

"I cannot leave him."

"Kusi. Think."

He squeezed his eyes shut and scrubbed his face. "Never was too good with thinking."

"Well, now's the time to start. Do you want your king to die? Do *you* want to be the reason?"

No. He did not want to hurt the king. Worry and fear showed on his face and in his terrified soul light. In the way he twisted his fists around his trident.

"You can help him, Kusi. We need allies who are loyal."

The teal-and-white warrior whirled and kicked hard, flying for the ocean floor beneath the city. She followed to the edge of the dais and watched him go. He was single-minded in his purpose.

And that was why when he passed Tibe—and Tibe called out to him—Warrior Kusi did not reply. He flew as though the life of his king rested in his hands.

He flew for all of them.

Tibe watched him leave. Then he looked up and locked eyes with Harmony.

Cold filled her belly.

Tibe was deadlier, angrier, and more assured than when she'd fled. His warriors—the bulk of Aiycaya's army— ranged behind him with ready tridents.

"Sacred Bride Harmony." Tibe kicked upward. "You look as though you have seen a dead king."

"You stabbed him," she accused.

"You left me no choice."

"You did this?" Warrior Zaka's chest vibrations broke. Red-faced from speaking over his shyness, he floated behind Harmony. His tiny honor guard stood between the new warriors and the unconscious King Kayo. "You attacked our king?"

"She left me no choice," Tibe repeated. He rotated his trident while studying Harmony as though considering where to stab her first. "Aiycaya is a traditional city. She lost our good standing. I could not allow the proud legacy of our noble kings to die with weak King Kayo."

"So you stabbed him." Harmony drove home that point. "He trusted you."

"Not at the end."

"Because you betrayed him!"

"He betrayed me first," Tibe snarled. "He betrayed all of us. King Kayo was a decent ruler until you arrived. I made him enforce the rules. He would give traitors a second chance to betray us."

"You mean he believed in forgiveness."

"Weakness."

"No, he was never cruel and violent like you."

"He could have been a great king. I guided him. You made him question. Doubt his purpose."

"I stopped him from letting you rule, you mean."

He smirked. "Do you think I acted alone?"

"First Lieutenant Tibe." Elder Bawa floated to the dais perpendicular to the two forces. He had left the other guards at the city entrance. "The rebel says King Kayo has been mortally stabbed. You knew. Is that true?"

Harmony's heart leaped. Of course the Aiycaya guards led by Elder Bawa had tried to capture Faier while he left the city to get Queen Elyssa. Somehow he must have convinced them of the truth.

Elder Bawa was on the same side as Tibe. But he seemed confused, which meant he must not have been in on Tibe's plan to murder her brother.

"Tibe stabbed him," Harmony accused.

Elder Bawa frowned. "No. You have not committed such a crime."

The warriors held their positions, taut with silence, and the truth slowly dawned on Elder Bawa. His aura darkened and his expression slid beyond shock. He shook his head roughly. His vibrations trembled. "How dare you?"

"Come now, Elder Bawa. You prefer my assistance." Tibe's lips curled. "I distracted King Kayo while you slipped All-Council orders through."

"King Kayo always agreed with you."

"Yes, after I explained. But that does not matter now. You support me. I support you."

"No." Elder Bawa drew his trident. "A male who murders his king deserves death. First Lieutenant Tibe, by the highest tradition of Aiycaya and the All-Council, I challenge you."

"First lieutenant? Ah." Tibe twirled his trident. His warriors formed a tight unit behind him. "That is King Tibe to you."

Elder Bawa straightened, clearly aware he fought a murderer who controlled Aiycaya's army. "You dare to assume the throne? When the king dies, and there is no blood heir to rule, the *elders* decide who next will rule."

"I have ruled since long before King Kayo's death. Yield, Elder Bawa, and I will deign to give you back your position as our representative to the All-Council."

"I will die before I follow you."

Harmony piped up, "And anyway, King Kayo's 'blood heir' is right here."

Everyone stopped and stared at her in confusion.

"Did you forget?" She tapped her chest. "Me."

Warrior Zaka looked horrified. He and the other warriors shuffled in front of her to form a tight guard. Although they were outnumbered, vastly, they would not let her die.

Tibe laughed. "You bow to a queen now?" He threw back his head and howled. "How 'traditional,' Elder Bawa. This surface-raised anathema is your improvement over a most loyal first lieutenant?"

Elder Bawa gritted his teeth, not thankful for her chiming in.

Tibe's amusement subsided. "Perhaps I must spill more of old King Kamuy's blood to safeguard our traditional city." He smoothed his cheeks as though to erase the momentary, unfamiliar smile lines, and gestured with his trident. "Destroy them."

Warlord Sao waved his trident behind Tibe. His army spread out, encircling the warriors.

A small, iridescent mantis shrimp landed on the back of Harmony's hand. It snapped its claws. *Click. Click.*

She did not need it now.

Harmony rose above the warriors striving to protect her, drawing all eyes. The brilliance of the Life Tree flooded their small argument.

Boys. Yes. Argument.

"No, Tibe." Her chest vibrated so calmly that the mantis shrimp on her hand did not even ruffle. "You are not the future of Aiycaya. Yes, you tried to kill our hope. You stabbed the last 'young fry' born in this city through the heart."

"And I killed him," Tibe growled, while the others squinted in the Life Tree's brilliance.

"You failed. Kayo is not dead."

Tibe blanched but recovered. "Lies. Always with you surface dwellers are lies."

"His tattoos are still light."

The guard parted to show the slumped king. He was, at this moment, alive.

Tibe gritted his teeth. "Give him time."

"In time, I will save him."

He snorted. "You will try."

"I will save all of you. The dark future where you kill my brother and assume control will not happen. King Kayo will live. He will find his soul mate and have a child. Everyone here," she cast her arms over the warriors on both sides, "will find their soul mates, and this city will overflow with life."

"Your fantasies are impossible."

"My existence is impossible. Yet here I—"

"Sickly Kayo should have died. Your mother should never have birthed him or you. Xawey should have succeeded King Aka, not Kamuy. I will correct all the mistakes of the old kings."

"But it's not a mistake, don't you see? It's the reason your old king chose Kayo's dad to succeed him."

They did not see.

"The old king chose hope. He chose the future. King Kayo, like his father before him, is honorable. He values mercy. Kindness. Strengthening connections to thrive."

The mantis shrimp buzzed off, seeking a new perch.

She floated in front of the guard and faced Tibe. "And so do I."

Tibe pressed the trident tip to her chest and sneered. "You intend to stop me? You and what army?"

"My army." She did not hunch away from his weapon. She let it scratch her skin without flinching. "The army of Aiycaya."

He tilted his head. A flash of doubt undermined his usual certainty.

"They're listening to me right now," she explained, feeling the souls of her warriors strengthening the same way she felt the purity of her sacred Life Tree. "Listening to your future and to mine. You've ruled too long, Tibe. We know what future you promise. You silenced King Kayo by pretending your voice was right. Now, it's time for King Kayo's true voice to ring out."

"Ridiculous." Tibe vibrated louder. "Warriors, destroy the anathema and her guard. Retake our Life Tree."

Her guard tensed.

Elder Bawa gripped his trident. He remained by Warrior Zaka's side.

Behind Tibe, no warrior moved.

His cocky smile dropped. "Warlord Sao. Engage the threat." He finally turned. "Warlord Sao?"

Warlord Sao's eyes reflected chips of ice. "We obey our king."

"What? No!" Tibe slammed his fist into his chest. "I am the true king. It was always me! King Kayo is nothing. Nobody obeys him. I made his rule, and now I have destroyed it."

"Our king lives."

"She showed us a trick. Kayo did not survive. No one could live through such an injury. Where is Healer Hobin? I am the rightful king."

"The rightful king is King Kayo."

"She will never rule. This insanity cannot remain. Her words poison you!" He wheeled and raised his trident to Harmony's chest. "You will never defeat me!"

Warrior Zaka whooped and flew forward. Elder Bawa planted his hand on Harmony's chest and shoved her behind him, out of danger, while he thrust his own older body in front of the trident.

Tibe froze mid-swing.

Warlord Sao's sharp blade rested against Tibe's Adam's apple. Tibe's sense of self-preservation stopped him from slicing his own throat open.

The rest of the warriors rushed in. A hundred tridents pressed against Tibe.

The warriors of Aiycaya had listened and chosen the future of their city.

They chose King Kayo.

And Harmony.

Now, where was Faier? He had to save King Kayo!

THIRTY-TWO

Faier flew away from Aiycaya, his recent escape from the guards on his mind, and crossed the sea floor toward the waiting army.

Elder Bawa hadn't wanted to believe that King Kayo was injured. He hadn't wanted to let Faier pass, but Faier had convinced him to investigate himself. The death of a king threw any city into chaos. Faier had to bring Queen Elyssa to save King Kayo and stabilize the city before it descended into anarchy.

A warrior flew below him. Teal and white. Kusi? The warrior trailed his shadow.

Behind him flew gray Lotar. He'd seen Kusi and now followed the suspicious warrior. On the opposite side, Gailen's patrol broke off from the main army and dipped to surround Kusi. Kusi's behavior was strange.

Kusi plowed through them, raising shouts of surprise. He veered up and attacked Faier.

Faier slashed the water. "Back!"

Kusi kicked hard, rolling with Faier's attack, and knocked him sideways. He wrapped his arms around Faier's neck in a choke hold.

Faier grappled with him.

The warrior resisted his attack. He was strong. Faier elbowed him in the chin. He let go. Faier rolled free and lifted his trident. Kusi shouldered off the attack and dug out a blade. He shoved the pommel into Faier's lower back.

Pain burned. Faier grunted. "Disloyal traitor."

Kusi ground in the blade harder. "I need you."

"You? Need me?"

"I cannot think. You think. Come now."

Gailen's patrol surrounded them. "Release him!"

"I need him," Kusi snarled.

"He does not return your feelings," Gailen said.

Faier eyed Gailen.

The pepper-orange warrior grinned. He'd always picked up the phrases and emotions of surface humans easily, despite spending all his time at the bottom of the sea.

Gailen rested his trident, gripping it with his palms to compensate for his broken thumbs. "Let him go."

"Wait," Faier choked. "Explain, Warrior Kusi."

The warrior shoved his weapon harder into Faier's back. "She ordered me to free him, but I cannot free him!"

"Who?"

"Xarin!"

Faier grunted again. "You need my help freeing Xarin. I will give it. First, let me bring Queen Elyssa into the city to heal—"

"No. She will kill him."

"What? Queen Elyssa will not—"

"Yes! Because he is held by Rikoy!"

"The All-Council representative captured Second Lieutenant Xarin?"

"We did," Kusi said. "First lieutenant's orders. We surrounded him and gave him to Rikoy. He is a prisoner."

Okay. A glimmer of sense emerged from the warrior's confused babbling. Faier pursued it. "Why will Queen Elyssa's entrance to the city risk Xarin?"

"Rikoy waits for Atlantis to destroy Aiycaya. Xarin is his trophy to execute in front of the All-Council. If Aiycaya rebels, he will execute Xarin now."

So if Queen Elyssa entered Aiycaya on friendly terms to heal King Kayo, Rikoy would know they had changed allegiance and quickly murder Xarin.

"She wants Xarin alive," Kusi finished, obviously referring to Harmony.

But she also wanted King Kayo alive.

And she trusted his judgment.

He pressed his hand over his heart. She was with him. *She* was home. He was no exile. Never again.

Faier looked at Gailen. The pepper warrior waited for Faier's orders. He had control of the patrol. They would obey Faier's wishes.

Xarin was at serious risk. Rikoy must be nervous the armies hadn't attacked each other. Had he seen Harmony and Faier enter the city without repercussion? King Kayo had lived for days pinned to his Life Tree but any moment Rikoy might end Xarin.

"How far?" Faier asked Kusi.

"Close. His scouts are closer. I spy for them."

"Lead us."

Kusi released him and dove for the seabed.

Faier led Gailen's patrol after Kusi. They fanned out. Lotar, without being asked, flew far ahead. Even while Faier watched, the ghostly warrior disappeared into the rock, swallowed by his own stealth.

Kusi flew over a small rise and barreled into an unwary scout. The scout cried out. Kusi slashed him, cutting off the sound with a strangled hiss. The scout curled over and died. Kusi flew on, tireless.

They crossed the rich ocean floor demarcating the territory of Aiycaya.

At the edge of the territory, they sighted the army camp. Lotar stopped them from disturbing a hidden patrol. The small unit crept to the last outcropping that shielded them from their enemy.

"They hold Xarin there." Lotar pointed to the center of the camp.

The blue-green warrior hunched over his knees. He was bound head to toe and staked to the sea floor. He looked emaciated and exhausted.

The All-Council recruited the strongest, most talented warriors. Hundreds of powerful, well-fed, rested All-Council warriors relaxed around Xarin.

Meanwhile, Faier commanded Gailen's patrol of ten average warriors.

"What can we do?" Gailen studied Faier. "Return with the Atlantis army?"

"No. They support Harmony." And they would be impossible to hide. Faier needed to finish this fast. Now.

Faier evaluated their options with the Atlantis patrol. Lotar was quick and stealthy, but stealing an injured warrior from the center of an army was impossible no matter which route they contemplated.

Kusi wrinkled his nose as if he needed to sneeze. "I will attack Representative Rikoy."

The Atlantis warriors stopped talking.

"Where is he?" Gailen asked.

Kusi pointed. The All-Council representative was

lounging over a rack of Trench Jack meat at the edge of the army.

"Suicide," Lotar murmured.

"Fine by me." Kusi rubbed his face. "I do not think well. But I never wanted to betray my king. I watched the first lieutenant argue with King Kayo. I should have known he was not sleeping."

Faier suspected many warriors shared Kusi's regret.

Forgiveness started now.

"Your plan is not bad," Faier said. "Lotar, you will steal Xarin while Kusi and I capture Representative Rikoy."

Kusi shook his head. "Alive? Stop me in time."

"I will make a very slight effort to stop you from killing him," he agreed cynically.

The All-Council representatives had terrorized the ocean long enough. If Representative Rikoy did not survive the attack, no one would cry.

They got into position. Everyone looked to Faier. Even Kusi.

This was the leadership he might have assumed in Nerissa. The respect he might have received in Rusalka. Nobody stared at his scars or wondered about his weakness. Warriors from different cities were united by his battle cry.

He signaled to Kusi.

The warrior put his head down and rocketed for his prey.

Faier kicked after him, trident out.

The All-Council army roused. They were complacent. Relaxed.

Faier shouted. "Representative Rikoy!"

The representative jolted and stared up at Faier. "You!"

"Prepare to die!"

He pointed his trident at Faier. "Warriors, attack the —oof!"

Kusi plowed headfirst into his abdomen. The representative folded in half, releasing his trident in shock. Kusi flew him across his own stunned army.

The army shook off its stupor. Warriors attacked Kusi.

Faier parried their slashes. He safeguarded Kusi while the single-minded warrior flew Representative Rikoy clear.

A second cry arose. The army caught Lotar half-finished freeing Xarin.

The battle began in earnest.

Faier shook Kusi free and held his trident to the representative's throat. "Release Xarin or die in pieces."

"You will die, you disgusting rebel," Representative Rikoy spat.

"Kusi, cut off his hand."

The representative blanched and held up both hands. "No! Wait!"

Kusi slashed. The blade severed his wrist.

The representative screamed. "Stop!"

His warriors surrounded them.

"Tell your army to back away."

"Back away," Representative Rikoy squealed clutching his stump. "Back away!"

His warriors reluctantly moved back.

"Release Xarin and let us go."

"Do it. Do whatever the rebel says! We obey. We obey!"

His warriors backed off from Gailen and his beseiged patrol. Lotar finished freeing Xarin. On Faier's orders, Kusi dragged the injured Representative Rikoy across the ocean. He left his army with orders to stay.

"If your army keeps their distance, we will release you before we reach Aiycaya," Faier told Representative Rikoy.

"I do not know which Atlantean may wish vengeance on you, but Aiycaya warriors may well blame you for King Kayo's injury."

"King Kayo is injured?" Xarin raised his exhausted, battered head from Lotar's shoulder.

Representative Rikoy spat at Faier. "You will die, you pitiful, scarred, damaged rebel. You may have tricked me today, but no warrior will follow you. Your reputation is well-known to the All-Council. We regard you with pity. You belong to two cities because neither will have you! Not even a rebel respects a warrior so scarred he looks like an exile."

"Scars? Exile?" Gailen glanced back at the representative and then at Faier. He quirked a freshly cut eyebrow. "What does he mean, Faier?"

"I may have lost a hand, but it will grow back," Representative Rikoy snarled. "Whereas you, disgusting rebel, have turned stomachs for years from your unhealing..."

He trailed off.

Faier's scabs had peeled off in the fight. New skin underneath glowed iridescent lavender.

Bright. Light. Full of color.

"What is this madness?" Representative Rikoy muttered. "How do you heal after all these years?"

"I found my soul mate and was accepted by her Life Tree."

"Her?" The representative turned red and then paled so white, he was green. "No. No! Impossible."

But it had happened.

Harmony had given Faier the words he'd needed in his heart.

Nerissa was gone. Forever.

But Faier was here. Alive. Right now.

With Harmony.

He flexed his arms. His tattoos gleamed. He was whole. A true warrior of Aiycaya now, in addition to Dragao Azul and Atlantis.

A warrior of the sea.

"Release the representative," he ordered Kusi.

The teal-and-white warrior let go.

Representative Rikoy kicked away, hugging his wrist to his chest. "You will regret this day, Faier! I will raze your Life Tree! All of your Life Trees! You will never recover!"

"We will stop you," he replied calmly. "Me, the warriors of Aiycaya, and our queen. Harmony."

He shrieked and flew away. His personal guard surrounded him. They glared at Faier and the other warriors but departed.

Faier led the return to Aiycaya.

He had rescued Xarin. Lotar carried the exhausted second lieutenant toward the Atlantis army. Faier aimed for Queen Elyssa. His Harmony was counting on him.

She must heal King Kayo in time.

THIRTY-THREE

The warriors of Aiycaya surrounded Tibe with tridents poking his skin. They affirmed Harmony as their queen.

She prayed Faier would return soon and Aiycaya would also reclaim its king.

"Destroy the traitor," Elder Bawa growled.

Tibe sneered. "You will not trium—erk."

Warlord Sao silenced his vibration with a powerful arm around his chest. "Yes, Elder Bawa."

His warriors bound Tibe into silent immobility.

"Execute him," Warlord Sao ordered.

"Wait." Harmony forced her guards' tridents down, flew over Elder Bawa, and met Warlord Sao eye to eye. "Where are you taking him?"

The icy warrior answered, "He must face justice for his crimes."

"Like Mawa?"

Warlord Sao nodded.

"Did Tibe trick Mawa? King Kayo thought he wanted to rejoin the city again."

"Tibe told the exile he must regain the king's trust by destroying the prison. At their later meeting spot, Tibe executed him."

Warlord Sao reported the incidents in short, emotionless phrases.

She shuddered at the coldness. "Didn't that upset you?"

He studied her for a long, hard moment.

The male frowned slightly as if he knew that he should feel upset, but he'd pushed away such feelings long ago. This particular injustice hadn't upset him. He'd seen much, much worse.

"I obey my king," he said finally.

She accepted that.

Warlord Sao had witnessed Tibe's brand of "justice" for over a decade. Yes, Tibe had ruled with fear and cruelty, but the city had gone along. Some obeyed blindly, like Kusi. Others because they got a benefit, like Elder Bawa. Even King Kayo had acted cruelly in ways he'd regretted.

Here was a second chance. For all of them.

"Don't kill him," she ordered.

Warlord Sao's eyes narrowed. "You have a misplaced sense of mercy."

"It's not for me. King Kayo wanted to question Mawa but never had the chance. Tibe was a close friend. He'll want to say goodbye."

Warlord Sao nodded once. "Until the king regains his health, Tibe will not die."

"Thank you."

A clash of weapons grew louder, and a small army spilled into the square. Atlantis warriors parried the city guards' attacks, letting them exhaust themselves without ever landing a single blow.

Inside the small army, Faier led an altogether cheery Queen Elyssa. Gray-eyed Lotar carried an injured Xarin.

Warlord Sao and his army turned to engage the new threat with warlike shouts.

"Stop!" Harmony raced in front of them and held up her hands. "Queen Elyssa's a healer. Let her through. Stop that fighting!"

"Warriors of Aiycaya!" Elder Bawa took up Harmony's shout. "Retreat and *stand down*!"

The confused, exhausted guards pulled back.

"You did not return," one commented plaintively at Elder Bawa.

He harrumphed. "I had to defend our king from First Lieutenant Tibe."

"Excuse us." Queen Elyssa kicked forward, her long fins trailing like a pretty dress. "We didn't mean to be rude and enter without an invitation, but Faier said it was an emergency."

"He's here. My brother." Harmony led her through the warriors to slumped King Kayo.

Lady curled an arm around King Kayo's knee, yowling softly.

"Oh. Wow." Queen Elyssa rested before him. "He looks... Should we remove the spear? Or is he... Huh. Ow."

Desperation gave way to panic. "Faier said you were a healer."

"Healing is my queen power." Elyssa rubbed her hands together, sounding a lot less like mystical mer royalty and a lot more like a woman from Miami. "Lucy got the 'shelter loved ones' power and Aya's got the 'push enemies away with a sonic boom' type. But I'm not a doctor. Not even on TV. You know?"

"So you don't know what you're doing?"

"No, but that's never stopped me." Queen Elyssa pressed her hands to Kayo's slumped temples and closed her eyes. "Oh. He's still in here. But we have little time. His strength is almost gone."

Harmony bounced from toe to toe on the tinkling pearls while Elyssa moved her hands, closed her eyes, and made a trancelike "Ommm" sound. Could she bring Kayo back to life?

Behind Harmony, the warriors held a strange reunion.

"Gailen," Zaka cried in surprise. "You came back."

"Just for a visit. I have my castle in Atlantis."

"And a sacred bride?"

"Not yet, but we already have five queens."

"Five! I had heard three."

"We might have even more now. Every warrior who surfaces finds his bride. Except for Faier. But now he's found Queen Harmony. And once we complete the tower, my bride will swim down." The cheery warrior continued his greetings. "Hello, Warlord Wida."

"That is Elder Wida to you now."

"Uh-huh. Warlord Sao."

The de facto leader of the Aiycaya army regarded Gailen with forced casualness, but at any moment, either side could spring into bloodthirsty combat. "Thumbs healed?"

"Healed!" He blew a raspberry. "What warrior needs thumbs? Come on now."

"That idiot attitude caused more of your punishments than your behavior."

"My 'idiot attitude' is the only reason I float before you now." He grinned. "Who but an idiot crosses an ocean unarmed, bleeding, alone, and without thumbs? I ask you."

An unwilling smile cracked Warlord Sao's hard face. This Gailen had the ability to lighten the tense mood.

Queen Elyssa leaned back on her heels, a frown creasing her usual hopeful expression. "He's gone."

Harmony's stomach dropped. She rushed to his side and gripped Kayo's flopped head. "No!"

"Oops! He's back."

"What do you mean, back?"

"Hmm. It's hard to tell."

"What's hard to tell?"

"Mmm."

Harmony's heart thudded. Did she need to kiss Queen Elyssa or strangle her? "*What?*"

"I can't heal him." Queen Elyssa rested her palms on her knees.

"But I thought healing was your queen power!"

"It is. I don't have the juice."

"Juice?"

"I mean, his heart merged with the wood, and I'm not connecting to this Life Tree." She rose on her fins, floated back, and gestured at the elder warrior hovering behind them. "You try."

The coral-tattooed elder swam forward.

"Healer Hobin!"

Chiba, Elder Yane, and the other warriors who had swum to fetch him hovered in the back.

Faier rushed to Harmony's side. He was bleeding again from fresh cuts and slashes, and he held her tight, comforting her. "You have done it. You rule them."

"Yes." She took strength from being in his arms. "I'm so glad you're here."

"I had to rescue Xarin. It delayed my return with Queen Elyssa."

"Okay." She hugged him tightly. "I know you did the right thing."

He glowed.

Xarin hovered with the other warriors. He was gravely injured but didn't call for the healer. All watched Healer Hobin examine the king.

Worried tuts emerged as Healer Hobin poked and prodded, lifted lids, pinched toes. He backed away and shook his head. "It is a conundrum."

"Should we take out the spike?" Harmony asked.

"Not until he regains his strength. No, I would not pull that out until he tells me to do so with his own words."

"So he'll improve on his own?"

"Normally, pressed so close to the Life Tree, his healing would be assured. This proximity is the reason he survived. But because the spike pierces his heart, his life force drains with every heartbeat."

The answer dulled her. "We have to remove the spike so he can heal, but we can't remove the spike because he needs to heal."

"Yes, that is the conundrum." Healer Hobin kicked away, looking small and helpless. "I do not have an answer. This healing is out of my hands."

He passed her and scanned Faier. "You are injured again, rebel warrior."

"We fought the All-Council army." Faier pointed to Xarin. "He is more injured than I."

Hobin kicked to Xarin.

So...there was nothing more to do. Kayo would die.

Harmony's heart cracked, and her last hope leaked out. Her brother was right in front of her, slowly losing the fight for his life.

Faier held her, filling her with silent love.

She had been alone too long. Losing Kayo just when she'd found him wasn't fair. It wasn't right.

"Perhaps healing is your queen power," Faier said softly, reading her mind.

"My queen power is summoning mantis shrimp and other ocean animals, like a Disney princess."

"Oh! I could totally see you as a Disney princess," Elyssa piped up. "The actress who played Tiana. Or wait! You could be Moana."

"I haven't seen a movie in ten years," she said flatly.

"After this, you must surface with us! I'm showing Kadir the entire catalog."

Faier centered her. "Power over your surroundings is one boon of your connection to the Life Tree. But that is a small boon. There is more greatness within you."

Okay. There was even more greatness within her than fending off a coup and overseeing a revolution.

"What if healing's not my power?" she whimpered. "Isn't there anyone else?"

Again, Faier came to her rescue. He called over to the remaining Atlantis contingent. "Where is Healer Balim?"

Queen Elyssa froze. King Kadir grimaced.

Faier frowned. "Ah. Is Balim still on the surface? Leading medical research on the healing power of Sea Opals?"

"No," King Kadir said, stilted. "He is not."

"They exiled him," Gailen said.

Faier's aura—no, soul light—dipped. "Exiled!"

"He brought poison into Atlantis and killed—"

"Gailen." King Kadir quelled him with a look.

The pepper-orange warrior lowered his head. "Sir. His treason is common knowledge, sir."

"In Atlantis." King Kadir eyed the Aiycaya warriors as

though one might be a spy. "We will stop the Sons of Hercules. Balim will pay for betraying us."

"Sir."

That name was familiar. *Sons of Hercules*. An organization Jean-Baptiste had consulted with to determine whether the mer were a scam. The organization had given him tips on how to lure, maim, and kill any warrior who surfaced.

Faier dimmed. "Balim. I cannot believe it. He was always skeptical of false hopes and promises. How could he be misled? He warned me not to give in to depression because I had not found my bride."

"You found your bride. You found me."

"Yes." He hugged her. "I have faith in you. Whatever you do."

Her heart throbbed. "If healing isn't my true power, I could make Kayo worse."

"I have faith," he affirmed and released her.

She knelt in front of her brother. Was it her imagination or had his tattoos paled? Harmony swallowed hard. No more delay. Her indecision was killing him.

Harmony brushed back his hair once more from his forehead.

His soul light remained dark.

She was already too late.

No!

Harmony gripped his cheeks. She closed her eyes.

Heal. Heal. Heal.

Deep inside, her words echoed, as if she was in a big empty room. They had kept the interrogation warehouse in Iowa uncomfortably cold. Just like her mother's hospital waiting room.

You have to heal. We're waiting for you.

...took you...long enough...

Harmony focused on that accusation.

Were her own doubts echoing in her brain? King Kayo's soul was draining out his heart into the Life Tree. She visualized gathering that bright pure energy from the Life Tree's roots and reversing it. Pulling it up the plant, through the tattoo tool, and radiating it back into Kayo's own body.

Her palms warmed.

She refused to crack her lids. What if it was all in her mind?

Heal.

...took you long enough...

Kayo needed to come back. He needed to tell her the rules of Aiycaya so she'd know which ones she was breaking when she promoted Xarin to first lieutenant.

Not Xarin. He was supposed to be king.

Xarin would do great. He had showed his loyalty a hundred times over.

You cannot promote Xarin. Only the king can do this.

"So get back here right now, or else I will," she said aloud.

King Kayo's skin glowed. And his tattoos brightened. His chest rose and fell.

But he did not open his eyes.

"I will win this argument." Her chest warbled with feeling.

You...cannot win...against a man who is asleep.

He moaned.

Lady popped out of his lap and twirled in excitement.

Harmony clapped her knees. "Well then, wake up!"

King Kayo winced, lifted one hand to his chest, and groaned. "Why...?"

"Hobin!" she shrieked. "Healer Hobin. Healer Hobin!"

The healer flew to the king. He checked Kayo over and

motioned for Warrior Zaka. Xarin arrived first. He helped pull the wincing, groaning, struggling king off the slender spear and laid him flat on the healing stones.

The tattoo tool remained embedded in the trunk as a bloody tombstone.

"He sounds terrible." Harmony clutched at Faier for strength. "He's going to die."

"Yes. The pain is excruciating." Healer Hobin straightened, stretched, and yawned. "He will survive."

Kayo groaned. "Prop me...against...the Life Tree."

"Already? Are you sure?"

He nodded.

Faier and Xarin rested him next to the spear, so close he could place his elbow on it, while Harmony arranged his feet. He looked uncomfortable but his pale color was strengthening.

Lady curled in his lap once more.

"Now," Kayo said. "Now..."

Of course. Now they were ruling.

She whirled to Xarin. "Will you be our first lieutenant?"

Xarin cupped his bruised, scarred shoulder. "Our?"

Kayo explained. "I do not think...now that Harmony has spoken...I can rule...alone. It will be...quite challenging...to obey *both* our orders."

"Exactly," Harmony concurred. "What he said. So? Will you?"

Xarin swallowed several times. He had obeyed the king, tirelessly and without hope. His dedication was finally seen and valued. "Yes, my king. My queen. I will try."

"You're doing great already," she said encouragingly. "Go pump Gailen for information on how to thrive as rebels."

He nodded and pursued Hobin, who was tutting his way across the injuries of the field.

Harmony hugged Faier and then dropped in front of Kayo. "So, how are we going to handle the castle? Divide it down the middle? I get the half with the pantry."

"You...*would*...claim that."

"Of course I would. I've had a rough, hungry ride in the open ocean while you've been relaxing at the foot of the Life Tree."

"Heh. Ah. Do not make me laugh."

"Sorry."

"Yes. Here I must 'relax' a little longer." He nestled against the trunk, where the healing power was strongest. "You may...enjoy the king's castle...for now."

"Fine, then. Once you're well, I must claim the queen's castle."

"That...is?"

"Whichever castle is just as big and impressive as yours."

He smiled and winced. "I told you. Do not...make me...laugh."

"No problem. I'm not that funny."

"You will grow a castle...from sheer spite...that is twice the size...of mine."

"Good idea. Now I have something to aim for." She twined hands with Faier and rose, looking around the Life Tree. The city seemed well in order. Except for one thing. She tightened. "Your friends from Atlantis are leaving."

"Yes." Faier waved his free hand at them. "We will see them again."

"You want to go with them, don't you?"

"Why?" He gazed on her, lavender and mauve threads

gleaming, calm and sweet and male. "Aiycaya is your home."

Her heart squeezed. "But you couldn't accept my Life Tree."

"Look at my tattoos, Harmony."

Light lavender shimmered and entwined with the older mauve. And in his eyes too, the threads of mauve joined with bright lavender.

She gaped. "You healed. But how?"

"Sacred brides gain the power of their husband's Life Tree."

"But I never went to Atlantis. I didn't even see your Life Tree."

"You are mer." His amused smile deepened. Kindness twinkled in his eyes and brightened his soul. "So, it seems, I am your sacred bride."

"You? Are my sacred bride?" She burst out laughing. Joy filled with relief. "Will you marry me?"

"Of course." He brought her to the opposite side of the Life Tree from King Kayo, where it was quiet and private, and knelt at its base. "I, Faier of Atlantis and Dragao Azul, marry my queen Harmony. Shower your blessing and healing on our union so our joining will produce a healthy young fry."

She touched the warm wood. "It's not going to hurt my brother, is it?"

"It will heal him," Faier assured her, nuzzling her neck. "The Life Tree grows more powerful in response to joy."

"I, Harmony of Aiycaya, marry Faier. Shower your blessing and healing on our union so our joining will produce a healthy young fry. And heal King Kayo."

The Life Tree glowed and tinkled radiating holiness across the sea.

Faier was right.

And now he was her husband.

Harmony twined her arms around her husband's powerful shoulders. Once she'd been terrified to look at him. Now she couldn't look at him enough. Her heart filled with so much hope for the future. Today was a new beginning for all of them.

He twirled her in the circle of the Life Tree, away from her brother and the other warriors, in a close circle of their own. "Now we are married."

"Don't worry." She recovered her amusement. "We're not traditional in Aiycaya. I won't force you to stay shut up in my castle and 'gestate my young fry.'"

"This is good." Faier teased her lips with a sweet kiss. "Such duties might challenge me."

"I'd rescue you." She squeezed his fingers. "It's hard to believe only a short while ago, I was alone, but now I have you, and my brother, and a whole city of warriors on my side."

He rubbed her back while the magnitude of her blessings sprinkled over her like starlight.

But of course, things were not perfect. Her brother was still recovering. The city was still vulnerable.

And above the city—above the surface—she had things left to do.

"I am a citizen of three cities. The first in a thousand years." He sobered, reading her mind and matching her mood. "There will be difficulties."

"You do get around," she agreed. "A real citizen of the undersea world. I think we're going to benefit a lot from your experience."

"I suppose it is only fitting that the first mer to join three cities is united to the first female mer born in a thousand years."

"Yeah, we're both rare." But just acknowledging that allowed her to ask the questions she'd been wanting and dreading. "Okay. Tell me what to do now."

He teased her lips with another sweet kiss. "You tell me, my queen."

"Do you think I could get help? On the surface?"

He pulled back. "What kind of help?"

"Lifet and Jean-Baptiste are in jail now. And Evens is free, thank goodness. I still want to help them. Evens should come to America so he can study oceanography. Monsieur Joseph needs the best medical attention for his knees. And I'm worried about Fab's job. My birth certificate's still lost. And my tribe is counting on me to reunite them with the warriors of Aiycaya."

"Anything else?"

"I know it's a lot to ask."

"You now have 'a lot' of resources." His soul and his dark eyes twinkled. He kicked to twirl them again. "Queen Aya knows many intimidating people you call lawyers. You possess the wealth of Aiycaya's Sea Opals. And you may order your warriors to seek brides at any sacred island—or mainland—you choose."

The plethora of resources buoyed her to new hopes. Imagine a team of lawyers on her side. Money to invest. Three whole mer cities full of warriors dedicated to helping. And one gorgeous, steady, healed warrior who had her back from her darkest hour to now, stepping together into a new dawn.

What couldn't they achieve together?

"Yes," he agreed, as though he heard her silent words. "We can achieve many, many things together."

"I always wanted to help." She rested her forehead against his as they twirled. "One person trying to change things is like screaming at a wall. Like my brother attacking the All-Council representative on his own. But your faith made me carry on. And now the whole world has changed."

"You are my mate. My soul. My wife." He nuzzled her. "I will always believe in you."

Sweet arousal filled her. She was his wife, and he was her husband. They'd been through an incredible journey. And it had been a hundred years since she'd last slept. Time dilation or not, she was tired.

But before she fell asleep, she had things to do. With Faier. In private.

Naked things.

She tugged him toward her temporary castle. "Will you follow me in?"

"Yes, Harmony. You are my home." Faier linked their hands. "Wherever you go and whatever you do, I will always follow you."

———

Dear Reader,

Thanks so much for reading.

The next book in the series is *Spellbound by the Sea Lord* starring Balim and new heroine Bella.

Would you like more mer shifter goodness? Join my newsletter and receive super secret bonus epilogues full of yummy mer warriors + the women who tame them. It's like the happy ending to the happy ending.

For example, Harmony longs to return to her beloved Council Bluffs, Iowa. But returning home isn't always possible — and Faier will have an all-new chance to shine as

Harmony's hero in "Faier Keeps His Promise," an exclusive for newsletter subscribers!

Subscribe here: http://smarturl.it/StarlaNewsletter

See you next time!

Sincerely,

Starla

ABOUT THE AUTHOR

USA Today bestselling author Starla Night was born on a hot July at midnight. She hikes, scuba dives, and swims naked in the ocean. She writes about smokin' hot dragons and tattooed mermen at StarlaNight.com.

starlanight.com

9 781943 110278